ACCLAIM FOR CAROLINE GEORGE

CURSES AND OTHER BURIED THINGS

"Pulses with Southern Gothic mystery and atmosphere like the hum of summer-night cicadas, and glows with hope and love like the fireflies that illuminate the sultry dark. The only thing that will slow your page-turning is pausing every other line to read a perfect sentence a few more times."

—Jeff Zentner, Morris Award-winning author of _The Serpent King_

"Caroline George spins an immersive, beautifully crafted tale about overcoming the life-defining words we've always heard about ourselves and finding the courage to live in freedom. Unforgettable."

—Laura Taylor Namey, _New York Times_ bestselling author of _A Cuban Girl's Guide to Tea and Tomorrow_

"Caroline George creates an authentic sense of place for her deep south small town—it feels like sitting in someone's living room listening to local gossip."

—Isaac Marion, _New York Times_ bestselling author of the Warm Bodies series

"Past and present are richly intertwined in this gorgeously written, atmospheric novel."

—Lygia Day Peñaflor, author of _Creep: A Love Story_

"Caroline George weaves an intricate, soul-stirring story that wonderfully illustrates the power of our words—both spoken and unspoken—and the authority we grant them over our lives. Brimming with poetic and lyrical language, Caroline breathes vibrant life into her characters and into the hearts of everyone who reads them."

—Ellen Everett, author of _I Saw You as a Flower_ and _If Hearts Had Training Wheels_

"Full of mystery and an eerie resonance, *Curses and Other Buried Things* explores the bonds, the beauty and the bitterness of family inheritances against a southern gothic setting that seeps into the reader like swamp water."

—Autumn Krause, author of *Before the Devil Knows You're Here* and *A Dress for the Wicked*

DEAREST JOSEPHINE

"*Dearest Josephine* is an epistolary novel about grief and coming of age, disguised as a paranormal gothic romance. It is a sweet, clever, beautiful book, and I adored it . . . This book transported me to the Yorkshire moors; it made me laugh, and it made me gasp, and it kept me up way past my bedtime. I loved it."

—Catherine Heloise, *Smart Bitches, Trashy Books*

"Caroline George infuses an epistolary love story with a romance and charm that crosses centuries. Touching and inventive, it bursts with wit, warmth, and a blending of classic and contemporary that goes together like scones and clotted cream. *Dearest Josephine* is a delight."

—Emily Bain Murphy, author of *The Disappearances*

"*Dearest Josephine* is more than an immersive read. It is a book lover's dream experience. Josie's residence in a gothic English manor and her deeply romantic connection to Elias, who lived years in the past, is as chillingly atmospheric as Rochester calling across the moors. This story is George's treatise on the power of books and character to creep across centuries, to pull us close and invite us to live in a fantasy where we find love—literally—in the kinship of ink and binding. But it also acknowledges the dangers of letting ourselves fall too deeply when sometimes an equally powerful connection is waiting next door. This love letter to books, and the readers who exist in and for them, is a wondrously singular escape."

—Rachel McMillan, author of *The London Restoration* and *The Mozart Code*

CURSES AND OTHER BURIED THINGS

ALSO BY CAROLINE GEORGE

Dearest Josephine
The Summer We Forgot

CURSES AND OTHER BURIED THINGS

CAROLINE GEORGE

THOMAS NELSON
Since 1798

Published in Nashville, Tennessee, by Thomas Nelson. Thomas Nelson is a registered trademark of HarperCollins Christian Publishing, Inc.

Published in association with Cyle Young of C.Y.L.E (Cyle Young Literary Elite, LLC), a literary agency.

Thomas Nelson titles may be purchased in bulk for educational, business, fundraising, or sales promotional use. For information, please email SpecialMarkets@ThomasNelson.com.

Library of Congress Cataloging-in-Publication Data

CIP data is available upon request.

Printed in the United States of America

23 24 25 26 27 LBC 5 4 3 2 1

For Susana Godwin (1793–1897)
And the women who gave me their grit

AUTHOR'S NOTE

All of this is true except for the parts made up.

The story you're about to read was inspired by my family's history and folklore. Since childhood, I've heard tales about my great-great-great-grandmother Susana Godwin. She was Creek and lived in the Okefenokee Swamp of South Georgia, where she ran a commissary. People in the area called her a witch, either because of her ancestry or the mystical encounters recorded in Robert Latimer Hurst's historical text *This Magic Wilderness*.

Of the many books I've written, this is by far the most personal. I wanted to celebrate my Southern heritage by returning to my roots and decided to use familiar names, events, and settings to give the story a richer authenticity.

Although I spent months researching, I acknowledge the experiences portrayed in this book are not inclusive of everyone and may prove triggering. I did my best to handle sensitive topics with grace, choosing subject matter well-known to me.

The journey to bringing this story from conception to the page required a year of honest reflection and forced me to confront my generational trauma. I realized, like protagonist Susana Prather, I had curses of my own and needed to reckon with things passed down.

My sincere hope is that you'll leave this book freer than you came.

—Caroline George

PROLOGUE

The swamp will not take her.

Nor will the monsters that idle within caves of cypress roots. They watch from the shoreline, their eyes blood-red coals burning the South Georgia night. Some rustle and writhe from leaves to ripples. A splash here, the flick of scales there. Teeth bared and ready to devour.

But neither alligator nor snapping turtle nor fanged snake will dare maul the girl approaching the bank. She is the cursed and the curser.

The cursed, the curser.

From her grandparents' farmhouse she drifts, past the propane tank, past quilts pinned to a clothesline. Her eyelids flutter. She doesn't see. She won't remember. Sleep claims her limbs and propels her forward. Inch by inch. Toward water darker than ebony and pitch.

She isn't the first to complete this pilgrimage, and she likely won't be the last, for history prefers continuation. It clings to blood and bone and generations. She is marked by those who walked this walk before her. She carries a collection of oral traditions and secrets left to rot in graves. Her secrets may weasel their way into similar holes.

With each of the girl's nearing steps, the swamp becomes more agitated. Its insects buzz, gators hiss. Cicadas and crickets harmonize an age-old hymn, or perhaps they recite a spell. Muttering louder and louder until all goes silent.

The girl freezes. Her toes sink into mud. The hem of her night-dress sweeps across water, slurping inky pigment up its skirt.

Stillness, forlorn and insidious, breathes across the landscape. It pauses the rocking chair on the back porch. It adds scents of soil and decay to the greasy after-smell of chicken livers and gravy. Primordial and familiar. Loving and wicked.

Desperate for her.

She must sense the lure. Her right foot lifts from trembling earth and guides her into the quagmire. Another step washes her ankles with liquid the color of sweet tea. Water stained and made acidic by the Okefenokee's cypresses.

Within the farmhouse hums the fuzzy voices of *Andy Griffith* re-runs. Papa must've fallen asleep in his recliner with a basket of strung beans on his lap. If he awoke and peered between curtains, he'd see his granddaughter in a frightful state, wading to waist-deep, clothed in nothing more than a hand-me-down nightgown.

He will not wake for hours; neither will she.

The girl cuts a path through lilies blooming white in the tannic darkness. She lowers into depths softer than silk as alligators sail toward her in a V formation. Their snouts glisten. They swim circles around her, their rough hides grazing her legs.

Water up to her chest, then her neck. Swamp devouring her as it eats the bank, chewing grass into ribbons limp and squirming.

Down she goes into the murk.

Until she vanishes beneath a single ripple.

CHAPTER 1

SUSANA PRATHER

JULY 4TH

B *lood holds all kinds of curses.*

I've heard those words since I was in diapers. A saying of sorts, like "get while the getting's good" and "cain't never could." I figured all families cautioned their young to remember their ancestry. To mind their inclinations. I assumed I wasn't the only person in Berryville, Georgia, whose great-great-great-great-grandma cursed her bloodline.

Around here, there's no shortage of ghost stories, but hexes aren't so common, especially ones like mine. Going back generations, every firstborn daughter, from Suzannah Owens to Mama, lost her mind and met a tragic end.

The curse remained dormant until their eighteenth birthdays.

Nanny won't admit she believes the folklore. She thinks superstition isn't Christian and claims stories are stories and curses are the consequences of sin. Whenever someone mentions the hex, Nanny rolls her eyes and calls it hooey. Even Papa says the family curse is nothing more than a scapegoat, what people blame when life isn't fair.

But my grandparents nail horseshoes above doorways to bring luck to all who enter. They never leave a rocking chair rocking to prevent haints from taking a seat.

Occasionally the words leave their mouths.

Blood holds all kinds of curses. Mine holds more than most.

My grandparents deny belief in the unnatural, but I sense their dread. They won't look me in the eyes and confess what we all know.

They're waiting for the curse to take me too.

Even now, as they huddle with everyone around the dining room table, counting candles for my birthday cake, I feel their unease like the breeze from the box fan.

Nanny impales the sour cream pound cake with eighteen candles.

I crush an embroidered napkin in my fist. I pick at its stitched flowers as everybody lowers their forks and swivels in their seats to watch me blow in another year.

My grandparents divided the party between two tables. My friends sit at a foldout. JC Owens, Cleo Shealy, Daisy Ruger, Stokes Burrell, and Holler Sloan. My family occupy the main table. Nanny; Papa; Aunt Missouri Jane; her boyfriend, Randall; Uncle Ronnie; his wife, Kaye, and my eight-year-old cousin, Charlie.

Nanny wouldn't risk the bad luck of seating thirteen people at her dinner table.

Papa shimmies a disposable camera from his pocket. "Smile big for me." He glances through the viewfinder. "Oops. Hold on. Forgot to wind it."

I maintain a smile until his camera clicks.

Missouri Jane fumbles with a lighter. She holds the flame above wicks, quivering as she lights candles one to eighteen. "Make a wish,

Susana." She squeezes my shoulder before lowering into the chair next to me. Her powder-blue uniform reeks of burnt sage and incense.

She's never been one to camouflage her superstition.

I lean over the spread of Southern cooking. Cheese pie, chicken livers, purple hull peas, tomatoes sliced and seasoned. I extinguish the candles with two breaths.

I wish for cooler weather. I've tried wishing for other things, but Mama hasn't emerged from the swamp, and the curse hasn't become any less of a threat.

Smoke wisps toward the chandelier, through a canopy of streamers and balloons. Never in my life has Nanny purchased decorations. The summer heat must've gone to her head.

Or maybe she worries this is the last party I'll have.

Dread churns my stomach like butter. I avert my gaze from the cake to keep from getting sick. Dread, the nameless kind for a nameless curse. It does have a name, I suppose.

Suzanna Yawn.

Her portrait hangs next to the grandfather clock along with photos of Mama and Great-Aunt Susie. In keeping with tradition, firstborn daughters are named after Suzanna. We all bear a striking resemblance to her. Nobody has been able to explain the oddity.

Same name. Same face. Perhaps it's all meant to remind us of the fate breathing down our necks. Of the curse we're rumored to share. If I survive long enough to have a daughter, I won't name her after the person who supposedly doomed us.

Charlie blows a kazoo. I flinch at the sound, my heart leaping to my throat. I accept a slab of cake from Missouri Jane, who squeezes my shoulder again. Her focus goes to the pictures on the wall and the clock with its hands reaching toward eight thirty.

I was born at 11:05 p.m.

"Open your gifts, Susana!" Charlie bounces in his seat.

Papa tacks him down with a hand to his head. "Hold your horses."

As if on cue, my friends rise from the foldout and beset me with presents. A Dairy Queen gift card from Stokes and Holler. A butterfly necklace from Cleo and Daisy.

"Happy birthday, Susana." JC inches forward, dressed in his Okefenokee Swamp Park uniform and a ball cap that never leaves his scalp. He swings a key chain from his thumb. At the end of its chain dangles an alligator claw shriveled into a fist.

"Is that for me?" I motion to the mummified appendage.

Last year, JC took me into his family's laundry room and showed me the mason jars above the washing machine. Each housed a serpent preserved in formaldehyde.

He told me to choose one for my birthday gift.

"You might like this better." He offers a paper bag from Floyd's Gas Mart.

I reach into the bag and unearth a poetry book. Its binding has decayed into thread and glue. I leaf through its pages, each fragile piece of parchment decorated with old handwriting.

JC cracks a smile. "Figured you'd appreciate that more than a snake."

"A bit." I rise from my chair and collide with his chest. I embrace him a second too long, maybe because he smells like childhood. Netting fireflies and playing in antlion burrows.

Maybe because he gives me safe feelings.

"Okay, leave room for Jesus." Cleo prods my arm with her acrylic nails, remnants from last weekend's pageant. Her doe eyes flash a warning. She acts like this when JC gives me attention. Ever since they started dating, she's only tolerated cordial exchanges between us.

The fact he's my fifth cousin doesn't matter. He took me to junior prom, so Cleo is convinced we're secretly in love.

My friends return to their table and talk about football and who's pregnant at Berryville High. The six of us grew up together. I met

JC and Stokes in kindergarten and Cleo, Daisy, and Holler in first grade. We were joined at the hip throughout elementary and middle school.

Now we share a handful of classes.

I think we might've parted ways years ago if our town was a little bigger, if we thought we could make new friends at school. History and proximity keep us tethered.

No matter how intolerable Cleo becomes, how much we all change, the excuse of *You've been together forever* echoes through my head whenever I get the urge to cut ties.

Missouri shovels cake into her mouth, still gazing at the clock. "What'd you wish for?" she asks me. Her hand shakes. The cake sloughs off her fork and lands in her lap.

"I'm not supposed to tell."

Missouri swears under her breath and rushes to clean the frosting from her skirt. "Sorry. My nerves are shot." She conjures a smile. "I'm being silly is all."

She found Mama's cardigan floating among lily pads.

Mama vanished into the Okefenokee, and no one heard from her again.

"Just another day," I whisper and hope my aunt believes I believe it. The clock will tick past 11:05 p.m. Curse or no curse, I won't perish in the night.

The swamp won't take me like it took Mama.

I want to believe I believe it.

Ronnie and Kaye hand me thirty dollars as they begin their farewells. The process takes an hour. They migrate from the dining room to the hallway, where they chat about the upcoming school year. Then, they wander to the foyer and exchange hugs.

Papa takes Charlie out back to show him a possum trap, which delays the ritual.

Eventually my relatives wave goodbye and pile into their Buick.

As much as they come around, I should be closer to them, but they're the sort of people who can talk for hours without getting personal. I know more about the guys in Papa's bluegrass group.

My friends leave with Randall in tow. Once their vehicles reverse down the driveway, Missouri Jane reveals a thermos of Green Frog coffee, superior to the Folgers Nanny keeps on hand. We relocate to the kitchen's laminate table for a second round of cake.

Papa leans back in his chair. "Tell that man of yours to set a date," he says to Missouri. "Before I pull my shotgun on him."

"Daddy, you've been threatening to pull a gun on Randall for the past eight years." Missouri downs her coffee, then nudges an empty mug to the table's center.

She and Randall moved in together after their engagement. Eight years later, there's no wedding in sight. Nanny and Papa disapprove, as do the folks at Hard-Shell Baptist.

Randall isn't a bad man. He doesn't beat Missouri, and he co-owns an automobile repair shop with Willy Burrell. An entrepreneur, Missouri calls him. I consider that a stretch.

He spends too much time on the couch, and he keeps the liquor store in business. Whenever I visit their trailer, I find bins of empty beer cans out back.

Missouri won't leave Randall. She doesn't think she deserves better. After her first man cheated, all she wanted was a guy who'd stick around. She got her wish.

"And I've meant it every time. Ain't right of him to give you that ring and not marry you." Papa dusts cake crumbs from his mustache.

"Seaborn, there's no talking sense into her," Nanny says with a sigh. She tunnels fingers through her short, gray-blonde hair. No matter how often she does so, the strands always return to their styled places. Even they know not to test her patience.

"Into *me*?" Missouri scoffs, propping her elbows on the table-top. "You've made your feelings clear, Mama. Everybody from Kettle

Creek to Berryville knows the pious Agnes Prather frowns on her daughter's love life."

"Shacking up with that man . . . it isn't God's way." Nanny takes a long sip from her mug. "Perhaps if you'd gone to community college like I told you, you wouldn't be stuck waitressing and taking care of your deadbeat fiancé—"

Missouri groans at the ceiling. "Do you see what I have to deal with, Susana?"

I grab her hand and lace our fingers.

Nanny and Missouri go together like oil and water, or perhaps fire and gasoline. The problem is, they don't understand each other. Missouri hates farming and long sermons. She goes to the nail salon every two weeks and buys her clothes new.

She turned out different from the rest of us. I'm glad. Without her, family gatherings would consist of Ronnie's jabber and Kaye's latest multilevel marketing scheme.

I do think Nanny and Papa are too hard on Missouri. They tell her, "Life is what you make it." As if she could become a millionaire out in Beverly Hills. *Life is what you make it.* But not everybody receives the same material.

I finish my coffee and rise from the table. "I better head on to bed."

The microwave blinks 9:59 into 10:00.

The grandfather clock echoes its music through the farmhouse.

Another hour closer to the dreaded hour.

Missouri Jane stiffens and glances from Nanny to Papa to the back door. Beyond its screen, the swamp glistens blacker than onyx, smoother than beeswax.

I force air into my lungs. "Thanks for the party." I kiss Nanny's temple and hug Papa's neck, then meander down the hallway.

"Susana," Nanny calls after me. Her voice wavers as though deciding whether to continue. "Good night, sweet pea. Happy birthday."

I've had nightmares about this day and what'll happen after it. Other people dream about their futures. I dream about the curses in my blood.

Before I knew about Suzanna Yawn and the hex, I sensed the countdown. I imagined my life until eighteen, but my mind refused to go further. Teachers asked what I wanted to be when I grew up. I couldn't answer them. All I knew was I didn't want to end up like Mama.

The expiration date has followed me all these years. I'd like to believe it's folklore and superstition and the side effect of losing a parent too early.

I want to imagine a future beyond eighteen.

Flipping a light switch, I enter my bedroom and toss my dirty sneakers into a basket. Not much has changed since Mama and Missouri Jane occupied the room. It still has floral wallpaper, lace curtains, and paintings by Great-Grandpa Clyde.

Heirlooms make up most of the furniture. I sleep on the white iron twin-sized bed, which Nanny brought from her childhood home. Quilts and embroidered pillows layer the mattress, all handmade and passed down from one generation to another.

Missouri once slept on the trundle.

Little of the room belongs to me. I claim the baby's breath on the nightstand. Papa buys a fresh bouquet for me whenever he shops at Penny Pinchers.

I own the books shoved under the bed, all decades older than Nanny and Papa. They're inscribed with notations from strangers long since laid to rest. I wouldn't call myself a reader, because I haven't read most of the works in my collection.

The fascination began years ago when Papa took me to an estate sale. He bought a crate of old novels, saying he'd exhausted Berryville Library's supply.

Our town is so rural, its library goes months without receiving new books.

I leafed through the novels' pages and spotted names written on their end sheets and notes in their margins. The texts belonged to people before me.

I liked holding a fragment of their history.

With a bated sigh, I shut the bedroom door. Its hinges squeak. The floorboards creak. And if I'm not mistaken, beyond the window, the swamp takes a breath.

Mama watches me from a picture frame. We look the same. Same hair the color of pecan bitters. Same figure, the Southern kind, sturdy and feminine. Same hazel eyes and symmetrical features. A serious face. Pretty like a cypress, not a flower.

I do not live in Mama's shadow. I am her shadow, one she cast and left behind.

I am all that remains of her in this house.

My heart racing, I go to the bed and push it straight against the wall. I tiptoe around the dusty footprints stamped on the floor, careful not to disturb them. It's bad luck to sweep after sundown. It's bad luck to expose all sides of the bed to the dark.

I lower onto the mattress's edge and draw my knees to my chest. Bullfrogs and cicadas perform outside while, inside, clocks tick and my grandparents whisper down the hall. I wonder what they talk about when I'm not around, if they admit they're scared of the curse.

They are frightened, maybe not of folklore but of what Mama left in this house. I think grief is a stranger kind of haunting. It stays closer than a ghost.

Susan Prather was a good girl, or so goes the bedtime story. Everyone believed she'd amount to much until she succumbed to her temptations and found herself in the family way.

I've heard the account so many times, it doesn't sound true anymore.

After the baby was born, Susan celebrated her eighteenth birthday. She battled insomnia and neurosis, which doctors believed were linked to postpartum depression. She fell asleep at the wheel of her car, nearly killing herself and her child.

The insomnia worsened over months. Susan was seized with regular fits of hysterics, and then one day she walked into the swamp.

Over the years, people have tried to figure out what happened to Mama. One explanation trumps the others. Susan Prather was cursed by Suzanna Yawn.

I crawl under quilts and wait for the clock to strike my birthday. Maybe I haven't been able to imagine beyond this day because the curse—or the idea of it—has filled in the blanks for me. It says what I'll become. A woman on the wall trapped in a picture frame.

Teen pregnancy followed by derangement.

An empty grave in the Hard-Shell Baptist cemetery.

No matter what my grandparents say, I know I'm the result of the curse in Mama's blood. No matter what I tell myself, I can't shake the feeling it's only a matter of time until I follow in her footsteps and the swamp takes me too.

1855

She wished for death as one did for sleep.

To resign herself to where her mother and brothers rested would be a solace.

Suzanna Yawn recalled their faces as she waded from stable ground. She felt inclined to perish, if not from the water rising along her calves, then from the violent grief racking her chest.

Such misery had plagued her for months. She could bear it no longer, especially now that blame rested upon her shoulders. It was her blood that had prompted the tragic loss, or so the people of Kettle Creek believed. They swore her family had been cursed by its forefathers, a consequence of the sin in their veins, and thus were destined for terrible fates.

No wicked deed could go unpunished, and even God's pardon did not seem to relieve the Yawn family's torment. If their ancestors had indeed committed atrocities, what suffering would satisfy justice? What amount of pain would pay their debts?

Too much had already been given.

With fear heavy on her breath, Suzanna trudged forward, dressed in her Sunday best, her skirt laden with muck. Already the swamp tugged at her as though eager to devour.

Nature seemed an equalizer, for it offered everyone the same brutality. And so Suzanna roused hope for an ending as swift as her mother's.

The Okefenokee had mangled the woman and discarded her pieces among lilies for trappers to find and gather. Despite an extensive search, no one had located her right leg or left thumb, both of which were thought to reside in the bellies of beasts.

Now her executioners sunned on the bank, their slit eyes rotating within sockets.

Suzanna paused her descent to absorb the wetland's breadth, its Spanish moss and trees contorted into tortured angles, a labyrinth of vines and briars and thickets. She wished not to be discovered by fishermen or trappers, rather for reptiles to swallow her fragments. This seemed preferable to limbs pale and bloated, tangled in greenery.

With a splash, alligators launched into the black water. They paddled toward Suzanna, their ribbed tails carving lines through spatterdocks.

She muttered a prayer and wept her way forward. Swamp gulped her waist, then her bodice. It clawed at her neckline and lapped her chin, rolling across her lips, thick like tar.

Until it consumed her with darkness.

The cursed, the curser.

Suzanna Yawn sank deeper, her dress blooming into a shroud.

She extended her arms as if they were wings, hands lifted, fingernails stained with dirt.

Graceful as the grave, she gave herself to the water and its monsters.

But the swamp would not take her.

CHAPTER 2
SUSANA PRATHER

JULY, PRESENT DAY

I awake to the sound of dripping.

My head rolls to one side, expecting to greet a threadbare pillowcase. Instead, my cheek lands on wet hair, wet cloth, a shock of cold and strange.

I jolt to an upright position and blink my bedroom into focus.

A box fan whirls in the window. Quilts encase my legs in a patchwork of greens, shades darker than I recall. They're no longer mint and olive, rather the color of the ivy that grows around Papa's toolshed.

Liquid dribbles from the blankets onto the floor.

I touch my nightgown. It's sopping and molded to my form like decoupage. I glide my hands across the mattress. Water oozes from the foam topper.

Something within me says to run, so I kick off the quilts and lurch from bed. My heels slide when they hit floorboards. I grab the nightstand to steady myself.

A vase drops and shatters, baby's breath exploding like a confetti bomb. The white blossoms float onto puddles. Not puddles. Footprints.

The marks trail across my room and out the door.

Shivering, I amble down the hallway. I reach the back door, where the footprints go dry. In their place are cypress leaves strewn across the welcome mat.

Chills snake through my body, followed by a familiar dread. I sense what happened, the event a stranger watching me from my peripheral. I don't want to look it in the eyes or acknowledge what it did, but its actions are blocked across the floor.

Puddles to mud to an open door.

The panel is swung back on its hinges, the screen ajar. As if whoever brought the water came from outside. Or they left and returned and crawled under my sheets.

I swallow hard and pull the door harder. Its latch clicks into place. Papa must've gone outside to check on the chickens. Or perhaps Nanny forgot to lock up after the party.

Neither scenario explains the footprints or my wet clothes.

I clutch my mouth, wheezing against my palms.

The backyard falls in a gradual slope to the Okefenokee Swamp. From where I stand, I can make out a break in the shore's foliage, where cattails shrink to waterlilies and sable water.

I used to beg Nanny to let me swim. One summer afternoon—I must've been eight—I waded to waist-deep and let fish nibble on my toes. Nanny spotted me from the garden. She screeched and rushed to the bank, terror on her face as she dragged me from the quag.

"Gators will get you," she said. "The swamp takes all kinds of people, and it doesn't give them back, you hear me? Remember what happened to your mama."

The coffee maker gurgles.

I snatch a blanket draped over a chair and drop to my knees. I soak up the footprints, wiping and scrubbing all evidence from the floor. If my grandparents see the puddles, they'll ask what caused them. They'll believe the curse has taken root in me.

Papa calls from the kitchen. "Is that you, Susana?"

"Yessir." I crawl down the hallway, pushing the blanket in front of me. Tears cascade over my cheeks and splash between my hands. Against the wood, they appear red.

When I was a kid, I cracked open my skull. I slipped on a boardwalk—its planks were slick with algae—and bashed my head against a rail. According to Papa, I wandered into the house as if nothing had happened, went to the kitchen, and fixed myself a sandwich.

Nanny followed the trail of blood from the back door to the fridge, down the hall, to my room. She found me sitting on my bed, eating a ham and cheese.

A nurse sealed the wound with staples, and Nanny scrubbed the floor until her knuckles were raw. She couldn't remove the stains. She told Papa she was worried, that what happened reminded her too much of Mama's episodes.

"You want some breakfast?" Papa asks.

"Give me ten minutes." I hurry to my room and strip the bed. If Nanny probes, I'll tell her I got my menses last night. That should prevent further questions.

Like the ladies at Hard-Shell Baptist, Nanny believes the workings of a woman's body are private business and unsuitable for conversation. Missouri once spent a church supper talking about mammograms to get a rise out of them.

I toss my wet clothes into a hamper and take a piping hot shower. Brown water pools around my feet before swirling down the drain.

Brown like swamp peat and swamp tannin.

An empty feeling nags at me as if I awoke from a nightmare without memory of it. Except I do remember. I dreamed about Suzanna Yawn. She walked into the swamp, hoping she would die. Inch by inch, she lowered beneath the surface.

My face gazed up at me from the black water.

Panting, I twist the valve and climb from the tub. I dry myself with a plush towel, then change into a sundress. Within a matter of minutes, I erase the night from my body.

Maybe the curse isn't to blame.

I join Nanny and Papa in the kitchen. They ask how I slept, and I lie because I don't want to scare them. Whatever occurred during my sleep was a fluke, nothing more.

"On second thought, I better skip breakfast. I have a lot of deliveries to make." I gather vegetables from the pantry and package them in plastic bags.

"You got enough time to eat a biscuit," Nanny says as she fixes herself a cup of coffee.

"I'm not hungry."

"You ain't hungry? What's that about?" Papa lowers his newspaper and furrows his brow into a bushy black dash. "You're all bones as it is."

"Hardly." I muster a smile, bolstering the produce against my chest. "Don't y'all worry. Missouri will give me a bite to eat at the Green Frog."

My grandparents appeased, I leave the farmhouse and stride past the carport to where my 1958 Cadillac Eldorado sits within a cluster of fig trees.

A stray cat—the one Papa named Barney Fife—sprawls on the

hood. At the sight of me, he jumps to the gravel and bolts across the front yard.

Nanny emerges from the house, cradling a mug in her work-worn hands. "Susana, tell Missouri Jane to stop by for birthday cake. We got plenty left over."

"I'll tell her." I unlock my car and place the delivery bags on the back seat.

"Well, I'll be. My grandbaby is eighteen years old," Nanny says with a sigh.

"Don't remind me." I slide behind the steering wheel.

There must be another explanation for what happened last night.

Nanny waves from the wraparound porch as I speed to the road. She and the gray-and-white house shrink into miniatures in my rearview mirror.

Papa inherited the property from his father. He and Nanny restored the home when they moved here in the eighties. According to an inscription on the chimney, it was built in 1910.

Four generations of cursed women have lived under its roof.

My Cadillac jounces over a pothole. The radio fizzles from static to a few notes of gospel music. Papa must've driven my car to Floyd's Gas Mart for his weekly bluegrass night.

I pound my fist against the dashboard until the Staple Singers croon into clarity. Eventually I'll take up Stokes on his offer to replace the sound system. At least one thing in this vehicle should work. The maroon paint is chipped and faded. The trunk is rusted out. I can't put groceries back there without dust from the tires staining food Georgia-clay red.

Papa bartered an old tractor in exchange for the Cadillac and tossed me the keys on my sixteenth birthday. I didn't have the heart to complain about the lack of air-conditioning, the shredded vinyl back seat, or the smell of cigarettes.

Wiping hair and sweat from my eyes, I veer onto Swamp Road. To my right, balers cut lines across a cotton field, reducing Southern snow to twigs and nubs. Soon all the crops will be harvested, and farmers will ready their land for spring planting.

I reach a stretch of timberland and hit the gas, a cloud of burnt-orange dust in my wake. Longleaf pines reel past, mile after mile, as far as the eye can see.

The drive from Kettle Creek to Berryville takes fifteen minutes. I've timed the route countless times, looked up mileage on Papa's Commodore PET.

Growing up I never believed my stopwatch. The trip seemed an eternal rerun of flat land, dirt roads, and cicadas hissing from trees. It still does after hundreds of drives.

I drape my arm over the windowsill. Heat gusts across my knuckles, and honeysuckle scents the air. I filter its perfume through my nostrils as the Cadillac dips and rattles.

My car seems to sigh with relief when I turn onto Jacksonville Highway.

The word *small* doesn't begin to describe Berryville, Georgia. An hour's drive from the nearest Target, the town appears preserved in a snow globe. Storefronts look the same as they did in the 1960s. Antebellum homes stand on every corner, their yards full of Spanish moss, live oaks, and hydrangeas, the pride and joy of Berryville's garden club.

Logging put the town on the map in the mid-1800s, and when the railroad laid tracks on the northwestern edge of the swamp, people came here in droves. They stuck around, had babies, and those babies had more babies. If not for reproduction and a general dislike of change, Berryville might've died out with the factories and tobacco warehouses.

Those born here never seem to leave.

And newcomers are about as common as unsweet tea.

I pass the high school and Shealy Pharmacy, then take a right at Strickland's Department Store. Evidence of yesterday's parade litters sidewalks. Hard candy and American flags. Divots in the grass from lawn chairs.

Nothing says *God bless America* like the varsity marching band performing "Seven Nation Army" while Freemasons zoom around on go-carts.

JC's mama waves at me when I park in the lot beside the Green Frog Restaurant. She rises from a bench and taps the ash from her half-smoked cigarette. "Susana, baby, did you have a nice birthday party?" She takes a drag, smoke curling from the sides of her mouth.

JC gave her nicotine patches, but they didn't help.

She spends more time on smoke breaks than waiting tables.

"You know Nanny. She doesn't do nothing halfway." I grab bags of produce from the back seat and haul them to the diner's entrance, where a wooden frog holds a chalkboard sign of today's specials. Country fried steak with gravy. Liver dumplings and butterbeans.

My grandparents have sold to local businesses for the past thirty years. The Green Frog buys our eggs, bacon, and any vegetable that can be creamed, casseroled, or stewed with ham.

I nudge open the front door and shuffle past the hostess podium. My sinuses tingle from the restaurant's fumes, a mix of grease and mothballs.

The place hasn't changed in decades. Tables still wear checkered vinyl from the fifties. Photographs decorate the paneled walls, all faded and caked with dust.

A taxidermy alligator perches in the dining room's center.

Lucinda refills a cup before waddling toward me. She resembles half the women in Berryville. Hair curled high with perm. A physique more breast than anything else.

"Where do you want these, Lucinda?" I struggle to grip the plastic bags.

"Set 'em behind the counter, hon." Lucinda snatches a pitcher of tea from the bar and beelines to the back porch. Beyond its screens glistens a pond blanketed with lily pads. Egrets wade along the shore, luminescent white against the ebony water.

I shiver at the sight.

Missouri Jane emerges from the kitchen. "Thought I heard your voice. What're you doing here? Daddy came by with deliveries yesterday." She rushes to my aid as I unload the produce.

"Lucinda left a message on the answering machine, said y'all were running low on tomatoes and okra." I peel the bag handles from my forearms. "Oh, Nanny told me to tell you—"

"This ought to be good."

"She wants you to come over and eat leftover birthday cake."

"I'm watching my figure."

"Since when?"

"Since whenever it'll save me from Mama. I'm tired of hearing about how I messed up my life," Missouri says, leaning against the bar.

"All right, I'll tell her to freeze the leftovers."

"Lord willing, she won't thaw it out until Thanksgiving. I've had my fill of pound cake for a while." Missouri signals for me to stay put. She goes into a back room and returns with a gift box. "Speaking of your birthday, I have something for you."

"You shouldn't be spending your money on me." I accept her present and lift its lid. Inside the box sits a bottle of perfume, the expensive kind Cleo wears at pageants.

"I would've given it to you at the party, but I figured Mama would get her panties in a wad. She was fit to be tied when I gave you that bikini last year." Missouri watches me spritz the fragrance onto my wrists. It softens the restaurant's musk with scents of peonies and champagne.

"This is too fancy—"

"Nonsense. I like spoiling my niece." She also knows Nanny refuses to buy frivolous things. Last Christmas, my grandparents gave me school supplies, a pair of thrifted Wrangler jeans, and two dresses Nanny sewed from a borrowed pattern.

Missouri Jane took me shopping in Waycross the next day.

She's always wanted the finer things. She might've gotten them if her first fiancé hadn't cheated on her all those years ago. He's now a doctor in Atlanta, and she's stuck in Berryville, waitressing and wishing life had been kinder.

Lucinda retrieves a platter of biscuits from the kitchen window. "Missouri Jane, we got June bugs all over the porch again," she says with a huff.

"I'll put out a jug of water and molasses." Missouri touches my arm. For a moment her blue eyes appear less sad and tired. "You'd tell me if you were in trouble, right?"

"Why do you ask?"

"You're eighteen now." Missouri holds my gaze as if to pass along a warning.

She was born ten months after Mama. They were so close in age, people joked they were twins but Missouri dragged her feet. Everything the sisters had, they shared.

Except for the curse.

"Do you believe it's real?" I whisper. My heart races, and my stomach knots. I've never asked the question point-blank. Its answer has been evident, the context underwriting my life.

Most of what I know about my family I learned from what *wasn't* said.

"Forget it. You'd be wise not to pay me a lick of attention." Missouri clears her throat and flashes a smile. "I love you is all."

"I love you too."

Lucinda calls from the back porch. "Quit your lollygagging."

"I'm coming, I'm coming." Missouri winks at me, then props a wash bin against her hip. She ambles into the dining room, exchanging small talk with customers along the way.

Out of all the Prather women, I think she's the most beautiful. Even now at thirty-four years old, she could beat any of our kin in a pageant.

She belongs somewhere far away from Berryville.

A group of blue hairs give side-eyes from their corner booth. They sip tea and motion to me, whispering against each other's earbobs.

"Spitting image of her. Same age too," one lady says. I recognize her as Keziah Douglas, the chairwoman of the food committee at my family's church.

The others nod in agreement, staring at me as if I'm doomed. That's the pitfall of living in a small town. Nothing stays a family matter.

I clutch the perfume bottle to my chest and flee outdoors.

Heat seizes all coolness from my clothes. I slide behind my Cadillac's wheel and tuck the perfume into the glove compartment, where Nanny won't find it. One glance at its label—the words *Allure Me*—and she'd blame Missouri for polluting my mind.

She'd remind me of how I came to be.

Blocking the thoughts, I finish my deliveries and head back to Kettle Creek. The drive takes nineteen minutes and twenty-one seconds thanks to an accident downtown.

I veer onto Swamp Road, passing Floyd's Gas Mart and Hard-Shell Baptist. I reach Kettle Creek seconds later, a heritage community nestled on the banks of the Okefenokee.

Almost every town in South Georgia has a Kettle Creek, like they have a Main Street. Ours was founded in 1838 when soldiers pitched tents near the water. They didn't have a kettle, but sure enough, when they reached the campsite, they found one there.

My family has worked this land for over a hundred years.

The road narrows into a single lane of red dirt. Oak trees line the embankment, their arms outstretched and draped with moss. Cotton fields lie beyond, most of them owned by Prathers or Godwins.

They're separated by trailers, farmhouses, and remnants of original homesteads.

I ease my foot off the gas as I near Gus Godwin's place.

His son carries boxes from a Chevy Silverado. He crosses the yard of dandelion weeds and climbs onto the front porch, which is more rot than wood.

Nanny and Papa told me he moved back to town. With Gus in court-ordered rehab, the property needs a caretaker. Who better to run the farm than August Godwin Junior himself.

The boy has his work cut out for him.

Gus left the farmhouse in a sorry state. The mailbox is lopsided, the roof needs replacing, and the exterior could use a pressure wash and fresh coat of paint.

There's no telling what Gus did to the inside.

Godwin flings open the screen door. He glances at my idling car before crossing the threshold. His gaze lingers a second too long, and my heart jumps to my throat.

He hasn't changed much over the past year. He still has dimples and angular features and wears his blond hair tucked under a ball cap. Except now his body is broader, wiry but roped with muscles. Stubble glistens across his cheeks.

His fair skin is burned a deep crimson, his cool eyes an even deeper blue.

For centuries, the Godwins have been known for their pale complexions. They were meant for gloomy places, yet they ended up in fields, laboring beneath a sun that hates them.

I don't think I've ever seen a Godwin without a burn.

My body tenses, buzzing with feelings I know I shouldn't feel. I wave at Godwin as if we didn't part ways on bad terms. He gives a nod, then vanishes into the house.

The screen door claps shut behind him.

August Godwin Junior. Nobody calls him that around here.

Besides the fact it doesn't suit him, the name has too many syllables, like calling a chinaberry by its genus.

He goes by Godwin, always has.

Last year he graduated from Berryville High and landed a scholarship to a big university. Out of seventy-five students, he was the only person to leave the state for college.

He must've dropped out to work the farm.

I return my attention to the road and the oaks that guard it.

Godwin and I grew up together. Like good neighbors, his daddy and Papa helped each other farm. They became friends, and eventually Godwin and I did too.

When I think of him, I think of potlucks and three-legged races, us rope-swinging into the Satilla River. I remember the smell of gardenias baking in the dog days of summer.

He and I were inseparable until we got older.

After he turned fifteen, he stopped treating me like a friend. He came over on Sunday nights, brought ice cream for us to share. He told me he wanted more than what we were.

That scared me.

Because I wanted him to want me.

My whole life, I've carried the fear that what happened to Mama will happen to me too. Everything I felt toward Godwin seemed proof of the curse living inside me. So, I stopped talking to him. I figured if I didn't welcome romance, I'd lessen my risks.

I was sixteen when I saw Godwin and Betty Ruger kissing on the roadside. They were pressed against a tree trunk splintered and charred by lightning. Her body was tucked into the grooves of his. Their lips fused while his fingers roamed the hem of her sundress.

I watched him touch her, and I wanted him to touch me.

Nanny had warned about that propensity, said I'd likely inherited it from Mama. I felt it then as I observed two people kissing themselves delirious.

Their junior and senior years, Betty wore Godwin's letterman jacket around school. I saw them exchange notes in the hallway and spotted Betty's Camaro parked in the field outside Godwin's house night after night. They had Mama's temptation; I was sure of it.

Betty and Godwin broke up after graduation. He left town in a hurry. She got engaged to JC's older brother. "Ring before spring," people call it.

Berryville girls who don't go to college tend to find husbands by their twentieth birthday.

For years, I thought about Betty and Godwin, their bodies latched together, kissing like the cursed, and how the sight of them gave me unnatural feelings.

I wondered how long I had until willpower wouldn't be enough.

A flutter stirs my belly, no gentler than a swarm of biting flies. I continue the drive, but my thoughts stay with Godwin, zigzagging between the memory of him now and our fight a year ago.

1855

Suzanna Yawn forgot her eighteenth birthday, as did the surviving members of her family.

They awoke that Sunday to brumal temperatures, for the night had brought a frost. Suzanna hastened to build fires, because the cold house—among other things—inflicted her daddy and siblings with poor health. They huddled beside the smoking hearth, wrapped in quilts, to escape the world's bite.

Only the Lord's mercy would spare them from winter, Suzanna realized. In hopes of being granted a miracle, she donned her best dress and bonnet and walked to Hard-Shell Baptist.

The morning was gloomier than most. Those in attendance brightened the church sanctuary with lanterns and pressed into pews as the preacher read Scripture from the pulpit.

Suzanna tightened a shawl around her shoulders. The air was damp and reeked of decay. Bats dangled from the rafters in cocoons of coal-black skin.

Even the creatures appeared frozen.

Hour after hour, the preacher driveled on about suffering and atonement, with which Suzanna was well acquainted. She'd lost nearly everything of value to her. Why and for what, she could not determine, although the inhabitants of Kettle Creek believed her to be cursed.

The service concluded without an epiphany. Suzanna retreated outside, where folks offered their condolences. The scene would linger in minds. Suzanna Yawn dressed for grieving. A crowd gathered in the churchyard under moss-draped trees.

History would note the foreboding tension, like the quiet before a tornado.

Martha Douglas pointed her finger at Suzanna. "I cannot bear the sight of her no more!" She withdrew the crape from her bonnet and clutched a handkerchief to her shriveled lips.

As a child, Martha witnessed a tribe attack her family's homestead. The massacre haunted her. She did not know whom to convict for the violence, so blame fell to the Yawns.

Because of their ancestry.

Because blood held all kinds of curses.

The churchgoers dispersed from their clusters, drawn to the imbroglio. Their attention went to Martha and her relations, then to Suzanna, who stood alone and unarmed.

"The devil walks with you," Martha hissed.

Suzanna clenched her jaw. Memories flared through her mind like smelted iron. Her brothers' violet faces and bruised throats. Her mama tormented by past wars and atrocities. If bygones were punishable, all persons would receive condemnation.

Generations left their stains.

"Don't pretend your kin never killed nobody." Suzanna approached the Douglases and lowered her voice to a whisper. "We've all lost in terrible ways."

Too many crimes had been committed in the name of vengeance. Suzanna did not wish the feud between her family and the Douglases to continue. Despite her rage, she was willing to offer clemency in exchange for a truce.

"My family were slaughtered in their beds," Martha wailed. "You got the sins of your forefathers in you. Your poor mama and siblings died 'cause of what—"

"I am not the mistakes of my blood!" Suzanna screamed.

"Misery follows you. Cursed is the ground you tread upon." Martha spat on the dirt.

She'd obsessed over the past until it poisoned her with delusions. Fact and fiction blurred into a narrative of her own creation. In it, the Yawns were to blame for all misfortunes.

Come hell or high water, she would ensure Suzanna followed the other Yawns in death.

"The Good Lord does not count the sins of His children, nor does He hold grudges like you. I pity your blindness, for you cannot see what you've passed down to your own kin." Suzanna beheld the Douglases, the youngins dickering with a tortoise shell, the staunch adults flanking Martha. They all believed the Yawns were responsible for their pains.

They held on to lies as they did their tithes.

"Do you think yourself above the law?" Suzanna fumed. "I know your secret. I know you killed them. Does the guilt steal your sleep?"

"Tell your papa you lot ain't welcome here!" Martha shouted.

Suzanna trembled with anger. She took a step toward the Douglases, and they stepped back. Indeed, they feared her, not for what she'd done—she was innocent—but because of what Martha believed. The woman claimed Suzanna had unholy powers.

"You are what you say I am." Suzanna addressed the congregation. "May the curse of my mama's spirit and mine be placed upon the people of this here land. Your kin shall walk in your footsteps. Generation after generation. Your voice will decide their days. Your deeds will stain their hands. Until you see the truth of what you are."

Without an option for peace, Suzanna wanted revenge for what the Douglases and the people of Kettle Creek had done to her. She knew the townsfolk were superstitious.

They would believe her hex.

Suzanna extended her arms. "Your kin will be what you say I am. Until they scrape and crawl from your silence and lies and say otherwise. With my blood I make what only my bones can break."

A gasp tore from Suzanna's body. Unable to breathe, she clawed at her bonnet's ribbons, choking like a pine enveloped by kudzu.

The churchgoers swapped murmurs and nervous glances.

Whatever force came upon Suzanna released her. She hunched forward, watching in horror as the flowers around her shoes died from yellow to rust.

She didn't expect her words to carry weight.

"No good shall befall you. Your only comfort will be in death," Martha yelled.

"I don't yearn for this life anymore," Suzanna said in a sepulchral tone. "I'd rather join my dead than spend another moment with you. Let me reunite with them in peace."

Folklore would give varying accounts of the curse. One story maintained that lightning veined across the sky in response to Suzanna.

Thunder clapped like a gavel approving her sentence.

Over time, the stories evolved into tall tales. Eyewitnesses swore the earth quivered as the Yawn girl marched from the churchyard. A Douglas spoke of the great wind that came at sundown and whistled four words: *The cursed, the curser.*

Whether truth or a myth, history would never learn. No amount of study could verify incantation. Even so, generations later, people reached the same conclusion.

From that day forward, the folks of Kettle Creek believed Suzanna Yawn to be a witch.

CHAPTER 3

SUSANA PRATHER

JULY, PRESENT DAY

The curse is real.

I sob into a wet pillow, shaking from what the night left on me. I peel blankets from my body and pine straw from my feet. I writhe like a worm exposed to the light, but no matter what I do, I can't get warm or ease the hollow ache in my chest.

It happened again. I sleepwalked into the swamp.

With a groan, I untangle myself from sheets and rise onto weak knees. I tear off my pajamas, strip the bed. I dry the floor and myself and everything else.

Until now, part of me wasn't convinced. I figured the curse was less a thing and more an anomaly, a tragic repetition in my bloodline. I didn't expect this. Who would?

Bile lurches up my throat. I swallow it, the sting and sour taste lingering. My terror melts into sinking devastation. Because the curse is real. I will end up like the women before me.

What if I sleepwalk into the swamp and don't come out?

I wiggle into jeans and a work shirt, then drag a towel down the hallway to the back door. A lily pad drapes the mat. I toss it outside before twisting locks and sliding deadbolts.

The Okefenokee Swamp looms at the edge of the yard, curtained with rose-lilac mist. An anhinga suns on a cypress knee with its wings outstretched. I've gazed at the scene countless times, but it looks alien now. I wish I knew what it wanted from me.

Eyes in picture frames watch me as I backtrack down the corridor. I try not to envision my photo alongside the similar faces. After I lose my mind and die, Nanny will hang my picture next to Mama's as a warning—

I rush to the bathroom and puke in the toilet. Great-Aunt Susie fell asleep at the wheel of her car and crashed into a tree. Mama battled insomnia until the imaginings drove her mad.

Imaginings—a softer word than *hallucinations*, which is softer still than *psychosis*.

They must've sleepwalked too.

Meat sizzles in the kitchen. On days when we get an early start, Papa likes to make sandwiches from leftover biscuits, country ham, and whatever preserves Nanny has in the fridge.

I wipe my mouth and flush my sick. Mustering what remains of my composure, I finish getting ready, then join my grandparents for breakfast.

"What's on the itinerary?" Nanny hovers over the sink, washing red Solo cups and Cool Whip containers. She hoards plasticware, reusing them until they crack.

Papa carries a plate of sandwiches to the table. "Susana is helping me rewire the hog pen," he says. A toothpick juts from the corner of his mouth. "We gotta get a jump on the day. Don't want us overheating like Pastor Walker."

"That man knew better than to mow his yard at high noon. Praise the Lord he didn't stroke." Nanny scrubs a pan with steel wool. She refuses to use the dishwasher for no reason other than she likes cleaning by hand.

I pour coffee into a mug, filling it to the brim.

"Rough night?" Papa asks me.

"What?" I give him a wide-eyed look. My heartbeat goes haywire. If he and Nanny learn about the sleepwalking, they'll realize their worst nightmare is coming true.

I don't want to admit they'll lose me.

Papa motions to my cup. "You're drinking more than usual."

"Yeah, I'm dragging this morning." I lower into a chair and gulp the caffeine. I refill my cup, but exhaustion nags at me. My eyelids dip lower and lower.

Did the firstborn daughters keep the sleepwalking a secret? If my grandparents knew about it, they would've told me. Or maybe not. They have their share of secrets.

I pick apart a biscuit and take small bites. Instead of buttery, the bread tastes like ash.

There must be a reason for the sleepwalking. My dreams have offered glimpses of the past, Suzanna Yawn wading into the swamp, the origin of her curse.

Suzanna hexed the people of Kettle Creek, but somehow it backfired on her. That day at the church, she gave the Douglases instructions for reversing the spell.

What if I can break the curse before it destroys me?

After breakfast, Papa and I load supplies into his truck and drive a quarter mile down the road to the hog pens and cotton fields. He feeds the Yorkshires—we have thirty-six of them now that the sows farrowed their piglets—and I uncoil new fencing for the enclosure.

Papa mucks out stalls. I crouch alongside the pen and use a hammer claw to rip nails from posts. Hogs squeal and snort, churn mud with their hooves. Most of them—the dry sows and young boars at slaughter weight—will meet the butcher soon.

They'll end up as parcels in the Green Frog's refrigerator.

I drown my anxiety with chores as the sun climbs the sky and Papa's friend Mark Shealy drives a picker across our fields. Sweat pours from me, drenching my clothes.

If the answer to breaking the curse lies with the past, I'll find it. Papa owns the best genealogy and history books in Ware County. Somewhere, hidden within the forgotten pages of his records, must exist a remedy for Suzanna's hex.

I startle as Godwin snatches an extra hammer from my toolbox. "Morning." He lifts a panel of wire mesh and secures it with the nail tucked behind his ear.

I sit back on my knees and use a bandana to wipe the sweat from my face.

Papa must've asked for Godwin's help. Around these parts, farmers barter their services. Not many folks can afford to hire workers, so the trade system compensates.

"Pass me that spool, would you?" Godwin motions to a roll of wire netting.

I nudge the material toward him. "What's the swap?"

"Your granddad said he'd fix my cotton stripper." Godwin removes his Yosemite ball cap and tunnels fingers through his hair, piles and piles of golden strands that become copper when the sun hits them just right. He returns the hat to his scalp.

Curls escape the brim and tumble into his eyes.

He doesn't match the boys Cleo and Daisy call *hot*, so I'm not sure the word suits him. He looks like himself, sharp and sunburnt, with a dimpled smile that defies his dour expression.

Every inch of me burns from his proximity. I'll blame the summer heat.

"You settled yet?" I peel my gaze from the ridges of his rib cage. He must've cut off his T-shirt's sleeves with a pocketknife.

Godwin holds a nail between his teeth as he measures and cuts wire. "I unpacked a few boxes and cleaned the dead squirrels out of the attic," he says from the corners of his mouth. "Once I get the AC working, I won't hate the place so much."

I uncap my water bottle and drink until the knot in my throat loosens.

Godwin hammers mesh onto the fence, each motion careful and considered. His hands, like mine, belong to the earth. They're scarred from fishhooks and hard work, calloused, with dirt under their fingernails. Gentle hands that can thread lines and gather bolls.

He touched me that night at the bar.

A fuzzy sensation washes through my body, followed by goose bumps on my forearms. I shouldn't allow these feelings. I know where they lead. But Godwin returning gives me hope. Maybe we can make amends for what was said a year ago.

"You'll be a senior at Berryville High, right?" Godwin asks.

"Don't pretend you forgot," I say with a huff.

"What if I did?"

"You didn't."

Godwin locks eyes with me. He must sense my hurt because he gives a nod in place of an apology. "What're your plans for after graduation?"

"I suppose I'll stick around here. Nanny and Papa need help with the farming."

Unless I break the curse, I don't think I'll live long enough to see graduation.

Godwin pries rusted wire from the hog pen. His arms flex with each pull. "You should leave town. The longer you stay here, the more likely you'll never leave."

"My family has farmed this land for over a hundred years—"

"If you decide *this land* is the only place worth being, come back." Godwin tosses wire mesh onto the ground. "You won't know who you are until you go and find it."

"Is that why you left?"

"I don't like the swamp."

"But you came back."

"Didn't have much of a choice," Godwin snaps. He wears anger on his face. His jaw is set in its ways, perhaps because he knew something good, and life confiscated it from him. "Once Dad finishes rehab, he'll work the farm, and I'll reenroll in school. Get out while you can, Susana. This place will suck the potential clean out of you."

He doesn't care where I plant my roots.

He fears his have already taken to the soil, and no amount of tugging will set them free.

I rise and confront him with hands on my hips. "Next time you decide to leave, do me a favor and say goodbye before you hightail it out of town. Papa was upset—"

"*He* was upset?" Godwin snorts.

"I know you think you're too good for Berryville."

"Why do you want to stay here, Susana?"

"This is my home."

"See, that's not a reason." Godwin fingers his gator-tooth necklace. "You don't like Berryville. You're just too scared to want something for yourself."

"I'm not you, Godwin."

"You're not your mama either."

A breath catches in my throat. I grit my teeth and drop my hammer into the toolbox, shaking with an emotion I can't name. "I'm done with this conversation."

"Fine, if you're so in love with this town, tell me why."

"I don't have to explain myself to you. I can do what I want."

"And what is it you want, Susana? Did you figure it out this past year?" Godwin sighs and shakes his head. For a moment, we're a year younger, standing across from each other in a smoky bar. Nothing has changed. "Yeah, I didn't think so."

"You don't know what it's like. The curse is all I think about."

"Don't give me that malarkey." Godwin steps closer. His voice softens to a whisper. "What, you're gonna let superstition rule your entire life?"

He's heard the stories like everyone else in Berryville.

"I'm tired of having this fight, Susana. I'd rather not hang around someone who thinks they're cursed." Godwin fits another nail between his teeth and busies his hands with rough work. "Come find me when you decide to think for yourself—"

"Knowing you, you'll be long gone."

"Yeah, I hope so." He looks at me without a trace of remorse. "Curse or no curse, believe something long enough, and it's bound to come true."

I yank the ball cap from his head and throw it into the hog pen.

Godwin scoffs. "Mark my words, Susana Prather. Next time I leave, I ain't never coming back. I want more than arguing with you next to pig crap."

"Careful with that bitterness of yours. Carry it around long enough, and nothing'll ever taste sweet again." I turn on my heels, creating distance between us.

The worst part is I think he's right about me. I'm too scared to want anything.

If I break the curse, maybe that will change.

1850

Swampers found three bodies dangling from Hangman's Oak at the old Trader's Hill.

The boys had been dead for well over a week. Their corpses were swollen. Birds had picked the flesh clean off their faces.

One look, and the swampers knew an unlawful lynching had occurred. They sent word to Kettle Creek for the Yawns to come retrieve their dead.

The bodies appeared of Muscogee descent.

News reached the Yawns' homestead in the dead of night. Thirteen-year-old Suzanna awoke to her daddy's hand on her spine and her mama sobbing nearby.

Mr. Yawn instructed Suzanna to fetch her shoes and coat and follow him outside. She obeyed, careful not to disturb her little brother, who slept beside her.

With a lantern as their only light, Mr. Yawn led Suzanna from their cabin to a pole boat camouflaged on the shoreline. He pushed the vessel into water, then signaled for Suzanna to climb aboard. In his possession were three quilts, three ropes, and a knife.

Suzanna inquired about their destination and the reason for the late hour. She studied her daddy's expression in hopes of learning his intentions, but his face was inscrutable.

She realized their brief spell of luck had ended.

Following the Indian Removal Act of 1830, the Yawn family had lived as border trotters, crossing from Florida to Georgia to Alabama to escape state laws. Their Muscogee blood restricted them from work, hunting, and fishing.

Certain death for a household with nine mouths to feed.

Suzanna, along with her siblings, did not know the comfort of four walls until they sought refuge in the Okefenokee. The Yawns retreated into the labyrinth of cypresses, to the haven Kettle Creek, where Muscogees deemed "friendlies" had gathered among Scottish farmers.

There, the Yawns settled and filled the pews of Hard-Shell Baptist. They never breathed a word of what was—not the War of 1812 or the Creek civil war, nor the atrocities committed against them. Kettle Creek was a good place, a safe place, or so Suzanna's daddy swore.

He called the "land of trembling earth" their home, but to Suzanna it seemed a secret, a stolen freedom, the *tick, tick, tick* of a clock soon to die.

Mr. Yawn propelled the boat across Skull Lake.

Suzanna huddled on the bow seat and beheld the dark, inhaled its miasma—the smell of earth dying and birthing in unison.

The swamp played parlor tricks on the senses. At first glance, it appeared simple, its essence contained to tupelos, pines, and tannic water. But dissect it, uproot and slice open a shoot, and the swamp became an enigma.

Suzanna understood it as well as she understood her daddy's silence.

Protection came with conditions. Those hidden in the swamp, behind curtains of vines and Spanish moss, were free to go about their lives if they assimilated, or until soldiers discovered Kettle Creek and dragged the Muscogees from their homes.

The Yawns wanted peace, so they cloaked the past in taciturnity. They committed themselves to the Good Lord and inhabited a cabin near Skull Lake, once a spiritual place for local tribes. Bones from cattle and other creatures still hung from trees like mute sentinels.

Rumors swapped among children suggested Muscogees or Seminoles had filled the lake with blood twice a year and bathed in its red water, believing the ritual would drive away evil spirits. Of course, no adult would confirm the hearsay, nor speak of their ancestry. History was reserved for headstones, nightmares, and glares from church pews.

Suzanna wished to learn what lurked beyond the secrecy. She had asked for stories from Creeks living in Old Nine, but they spoke only of loss and relocation.

The fear of the silent thing—whatever prompted her mama's

nightmares—haunted Suzanna. Her daddy called Kettle Creek a safe place, but Suzanna smelled the danger like blood in the water. Anything could become a monster, she'd learned.

There was no telling when a smile would sprout fangs.

Mr. Yawn nudged Suzanna with the toe of his boot. She lurched awake, covered in dew. Around them, dawn brightened the landscape with a blue haze.

"Where're we headed?" Suzanna asked again. She rubbed the sleep from her eyes and studied the shoreline. They must've traveled six or seven miles south.

The channel had widened into a creeping river.

Mr. Yawn guided the boat into a cypress grove. He lowered his pole and gathered the quilts, tucking the knife into his pocket. "I can't have you crying. Understand?"

"Yessir." Suzanna balled her fists to still their tremors. She climbed from the boat, sinking into peat, and followed her daddy upriver.

They reached a campsite where two swampers loitered around a smoking fire. One man had teeth so rotten, he wore dentures made from wood and animal bones.

"We're here for 'em," Mr. Yawn told the men.

The swamper with bad teeth motioned to Suzanna. "Best to leave the girl here. Sight ain't a pretty one. The smell might burn the hair from her nose."

"She goes," Mr. Yawn insisted.

The swamper tipped his felt hat at Suzanna, perhaps in sympathy. He abandoned the campfire and headed into a stretch of prairie. Mr. Yawn and Suzanna trailed behind him, wading through grass that reached their waists.

Eventually they reached an oak tree larger than any Suzanna had seen. It towered like a monolith, its nodose branches contorted into elegant shapes.

Three bodies hung from the lower boughs. They swung from

nooses, clothed in nothing but underwear. Their faces were so mutilated, bone peeked through gaps of skin.

Organs spilled from gashes in their abdomens.

Suzanna froze, unable to pry her gaze from the horror. She clutched her mouth to cage a scream, the stench of death so noxious, she vomited onto her shoes.

The corpses belonged to her brothers.

"All these yours?" the swamper asked Mr. Yawn.

"I'm their pa." Mr. Yawn unsheathed his knife and cut down the bodies. He arranged them in a row from eldest to youngest, then bound them in quilts.

He ran his fingers through each of their raven hair before covering them.

"Who did it?" Suzanna gasped, resisting a swell of tears. She would abide by her daddy's request. With the three brothers gone, she was the eldest child.

She wanted to prove herself fit for the role.

"There's no telling," the swamper said. "Mister, I hope you don't mind me saying so, but these parts aren't safe for the likes of you."

Mr. Yawn pulled two bodies away from the tree and told Suzanna to drag the third. His face was stone and steel, unbent, unbroken.

The belief in safe places began as a fairy tale, yet over time it grew into a religion for the Yawn family. Suzanna had watched her daddy convert into a devout believer. He'd kept the faith, preached belonging as though his words could make it so.

He needed to believe to lessen the hold of what he'd endured.

After the Creek civil war, the government stole his parents' land and redistributed it to white settlers in a lottery. Mr. Yawn didn't remember the land, but its theft gnawed at him.

He took his family on the run when soldiers rounded up Muscogees to move them west. Eventually he found Kettle Creek and endeavored to reclaim a meager portion of what had been stolen. He deserted his Muscogee heritage and became like the Scotch.

He was baptized in the Okefenokee.

His hell-bent wish for survival or acceptance—to Suzanna the two seemed intertwined—led him to strike a deal with half-Creek landowner Willard Ruger.

Since the law banned Muscogees from trapping, Mr. Yawn worried he would face arrest—or worse, the gallows. To avoid lynching and starvation, he registered himself as a slave to work as a sharecropper on Ruger's property. In return, Ruger promised a fair wage—paid with the utmost discretion—and a plot of land for the Yawns to homestead.

Mr. Yawn claimed he'd never been a free man. At least as a slave, he could farm and provide a safe home for his children.

Safety. The word took residence within the Yawns' home, spoken as a prayer or bedtime story. A sacred precaution like painting sheep's blood over a doorway.

"Why were your boys out here?" the swamper asked.

"Tempting death, I reckon." Mr. Yawn backtracked toward the river, pulling two of his sons behind him. He glanced at Suzanna, and she followed suit.

Using every bit of her strength, Suzanna dragged her brother across the prairie, fighting brush and sloshing through water. She focused on her daddy's back to distract from her fatigue.

She breathed through her mouth to avoid the stink of rot.

Her brothers had fallen victim to the promise of safety. Over the years, they'd gone swamping with Scotch boys and sold pelts in Old Nine, ignoring the laws against them. They'd accepted work from loggers in secret and rafted yellow longleaf pines to sawmills on the coast.

Someone must've intercepted the boys and taken the law into their own hands.

"We will not speak of today," Mr. Yawn said once he and Suzanna reached the boat.

They lifted the bodies on board, stacking them like feed sacks.

"Look at me." Mr. Yawn crouched in front of Suzanna and cupped her face in his leathery palms. "I should've kept the boys at home—"

"Why'd you bring me here?" Suzanna blinked, but the images remained. The oak tree and its gruesome ornaments. The swamper's dentures, each beastly tooth filed into a point.

"I wanted you to see what happens to people like us," Mr. Yawn whispered. "I was wrong, Suzanna. We're not safe."

"Let's go someplace else." She bit her lip to keep from weeping. Blood oozed into her mouth.

"Pain will follow us. It's better you learn that now." Mr. Yawn hoisted Suzanna into his arms, then placed her gingerly in the boat. He tapped his thumb against her bloody lip.

Suzanna never told a soul about Hangman's Oak.

Her brothers were buried in a hand-dug grave four days later. Mourners gathered in the Hard-Shell Baptist cemetery to pay their respects. One by one, they tossed dirt into the hole as a farewell handshake, a Muscogee custom that had not been forsaken.

Mrs. Yawn wailed for her dead sons. She cradled a babe to her breast and a toddler to her hip. She grieved so violently that Mr. Yawn removed the children from her grasp.

Suzanna participated in the bereavement from a cautious distance. She stood among women from Kettle Creek who swapped theories as to what had befallen the Yawn boys.

Martha Douglas joined the gossip. "Serves them right for breaking the law."

In the wake of such a vile crime, Suzanna didn't understand why her daddy had sworn her to silence. Withholding the truth seemed unjust.

"My brothers were murdered," Suzanna muttered. She squirmed as the memories resurfaced from their silent, secret places.

"Your brothers were criminals," Martha said, fingering her hummingbird brooch.

"They didn't hurt nobody."

"Lose all hope in fairness, child." Martha leaned close to Suzanna as though to offer consolation. Instead, she whispered, "Hell will follow you all the days of your life."

A chill washed through Suzanna's body.

"You'll attract disaster like a moth to a flame. Know why?" Martha flashed a cruel smile. "Because you're cursed. Every wicked deed your ancestors committed is on your family. That's why your brothers died. To atone for old sins."

The Douglases clung to grudges with white knuckles. They blamed anyone with Muscogee blood for the 1838 massacre, when a raiding party attacked their Scotch settlement.

"We're not cursed," Suzanna said.

"How else do you explain that?" Martha pointed at the grave. "Either the Lord despises you, or you're being punished. Which feels truer?"

A tear escaped Suzanna's left eye and cut a line down her cheek.

"You will suffer for the past," Martha said with a nod. "Peace and happiness will be strangers to you as they have been to me."

From that day on, Suzanna Yawn wondered if Martha Douglas was right.

CHAPTER 4

SUSANA PRATHER

JULY, PRESENT DAY

My fingertips wear the night.

Each is shriveled and ribbed like muscadines left to dry in the heat. I've never understood how, on skin, too much water resembles not enough.

I tack sheets to a line, pinning the damp linens with wooden clothespins.

Nanny will notice the laundry.

Eventually she'll emerge from her bedroom, dressed for church, and brew her ersatz coffee. She'll pour its dregs into a tumbler and part the curtains above the kitchen sink.

She'll ask why I stripped my mattress for the third day in a row. I won't know how to tell her the truth, that I woke up again, soaked through, and all signs point to sleepwalking down the embankment, past the propane tank and toolshed, into gator-infested water.

That's what happened. I could use words like *might've* to give myself a shred of hopeful doubt. But to exist, doubt needs space for options. No other scenario explains the mud on my nightdress, the taste of tannin in my mouth, or the spatterdock I found glued to my chest.

If I don't find a way to keep myself inside, I'll wake up tomorrow in a swampy bed.

Locks don't help. I unlatch them in my slumber. Chairs against knobs are easy to remove unless I ask Papa to barricade my door from the hallway.

That would require me to explain my situation, and I'm not sure how to put what's happening into words, especially words that won't cause my grandparents to panic.

I hang the final sheet and stumble back a step.

A breeze disrupts the treetops. Spanish moss wags from branches, and the first breaths of daybreak awaken the Okefenokee from its stagnant sleep.

How do I not drown?

Rather than ruminate on the question, I power walk to the house, away from the clothesline and blankets dripping swamp water.

Papa once told me, *"You can't run from something when that something is you."* I try to prove him wrong. I step over the salt I poured across the threshold.

It should ward off bad luck.

AC greets my skin like the cool side of a pillow. I rush to the bathroom. My reflection has dark circles under her eyes. She looks haggard, like she hasn't slept in weeks.

She looks like Mama.

I rummage through the vanity and remove a bag of expired makeup that belonged to Missouri Jane. I uncap tubes of concealer and foundation and smear the paste under my eyes.

How long until the curse won't let me hide it?

Once the skunky smell of Nanny's coffee floods the house, I slip into my bedroom and finish getting ready for church. I wiggle on a new-to-me cerulean-blue dress. Its polyester fabric cascades over my hips and lands at my calves.

The garment is outdated by decades, with shoulder pads and an elastic waistband.

Nanny purchases my clothes from consignment stores. She picks dresses with long skirts and high necklines. I wear them before washing them, which might seem weird, but I like the smell of other people's clothes. A perfume of someone else, somewhere else.

The blue dress smells of gardenias and mothballs. I pair it with my sneakers, now a reddish-orange color, and Mama's butterfly earrings.

Nanny calls from the kitchen, so I grab the largest Bible from my collection and hurry to join her. The leather cover is embossed and latched with a gold clasp.

JC gave the book to me. He found it buried in his uncle's attic, its original inscription made out to a Civil War soldier by the name of Henry Obediah Owens.

My great-great-great-great-grandfather, Suzanna Yawn's husband.

Bibles are my favorite to collect. They chart births and deaths, list family members and prayer requests. They smuggle records through the ages in an unassuming way, like carved names in the back sides of school desks. Sometimes, when Pastor Walker gets long-winded, I flip through whichever Bible I escorted to church and search for annotations.

Henry Obediah Owens enjoyed the Gospel of John. He spent a lot of time in Psalms, his underlines exclusive to passages about grief. I think he mourned a great deal of loss.

A goat bleats from a nearby pasture as my grandparents and I cross the front yard. We cram into the work truck. I sit on the bench, sandwiched between Nanny and Papa.

My nostrils prick from the vehicle's fumes, gasoline mixed with the faint scent of honeysuckle. I squeeze my Bible tighter. I try not to think about how my skin feels taut with swamp water, like a face after a hard cry.

Papa keys the ignition, and I bounce my heels against the muddy floorboard. He grabs my left knee. His mustache hints at a smile. "What got you in a tizzy?"

"Bout of the jitters is all." I tap on the radio and relax into a gospel melody. Pickers and crooners harmonize "Are You Washed in the Blood?"

Nanny cradles a plate of biscuits in her lap. She baked them for Pastor Walker as consolation for his heatstroke.

Cattle huddle together in one of the Godwins' fields. They cluster near a dilapidated schoolhouse and eye the clouds as if they sense a thunderstorm.

"Cows are lying in a bunch," Nanny says. "Rain must be coming."

Or perhaps they're as superstitious as my family.

The drive to Hard-Shell Baptist should take five minutes and thirteen seconds. I watch the clock while Papa fiddles with the radio and Nanny removes a pair of clippers from her purse. She trims her nails into triangles, cutting so close to their beds, the quick of her pinky bleeds.

"Did you do the washing?" Nanny broaches the subject without glancing from her fingernails. She asks the question so nonchalantly I forget how I planned to respond.

"I spilled tea on my blankets last night."

"Back door was unlocked when I got up this morning. Know why?"

My heart leaps to my throat. "I went outside to hang up my sheets."

"The door was unlocked before then," Nanny says, returning the clippers to her purse. "Your mama had trouble sleeping after her eighteenth birthday."

"Did she . . . do anything strange?" I ask.

Papa chuckles. "She took a piss in the pantry, thought the onion box was a toilet."

"Seaborn, mind your language," Nanny huffs.

"We tried all sorts of home remedies. Nothing could get that girl to sleep, bless her heart." Papa drapes his arm over my shoulders and hugs me to his side.

"If you're having trouble sleeping, Susana, you need to tell us," Nanny says. "Your mama nearly killed herself because she fell asleep at the wheel—"

"Everything's fine." I must break the curse before Nanny learns otherwise.

"Maybe a haint unlocked the back door." Papa winks at me. "Just last week Floyd saw a spook light over near the train depot. Scared him half to death."

Nanny looks at me with concern etched across her face.

"Don't y'all worry. I'll bolt the doors before I hit the hay," Papa says as he flips his turn signal and veers into the Hard-Shell Baptist parking lot. He brakes under a live oak.

Relief courses through me.

I won't be able to reach the barrel bolt in my sleep. If Papa follows through, I shouldn't wander into the swamp anymore, not unless I sleep-climb through a window.

Nanny pulls me aside the moment I exit the truck. Her Bible and biscuits press into my rib cage like a gun. "You're not sneaking out, are you?"

Her tone asks a different question. It adds a tremor to her voice and makes her blue eyes water. An exhausted, nothing-left-to-give blue, like the horizon after a downpour.

"Of course not." I imagine a home video projected onto Nanny's face. It flickers a story about a daughter whose curse led to pregnancy, and a mother who blamed herself for the fallout.

Nanny's question isn't whether I sleepwalked. It's more complex, dyed with fear, trauma, and her love for me. She wants to know if I fell into temptation.

If I snuck out to meet a boy.

"Of course not," I say again with as much resolve as I can muster. "I'm not *her*."

"You're right." Nanny gives my cheek a sensible peck. She adjusts her cap-sleeve cardigan, then strides toward Hard-Shell Baptist.

Her kitten heel shoes chomp gravel.

Papa joins my trek to the church doors. He jokes about Deacon Overstreet's new motorcycle, and I laugh so he won't notice I'm scared out of my wits.

A steeple doesn't make a building holy. I've been to holy places. The front porch at dusk, when the sky hazes into peach preserves and Nanny reads Scripture aloud.

Long dirt roads during a thunderstorm.

Fishing in desolate channels with JC and Stokes.

Hard-Shell isn't a holy place. Whenever I cross its threshold, I don't feel the Spirit, only dust. Layers and layers of dead skin cells, some older than Kettle Creek.

I feel the need to tug my skirt over my knees.

A single AC unit thrums within a corner window, pumping sticky air into the stale auditorium. Elderly women attempt to cool themselves with paper fans from last year's Berryville Family Reunion. Their permed curls still go flat.

I proceed down the aisle and filter into what Uncle Ronnie calls the Prather Pew, a bench located three rows from stage left. Our kin have burdened it for generations.

Unlike other churches, Hard-Shell doesn't offer much to the eyes. United Methodist has stained glass. First Baptist has chandeliers and sconces to count. Here, I can't tilt back my head and determine who'd die if a gilded fixture popped off its chain.

The sanctuary consists of pews and wooden floorboards with a ceiling to match. Its worship hall begins at the double doors, where Mr. Capers hands Tootsie Rolls to kids, and stretches to the pulpit, occupied by a podium the Presbyterians donated after the original rotted.

Ronnie and Kaye step into our row, tugging Charlie behind them. They occupy the farthest end of the pew as they do every Sunday. I wouldn't call them religious, not in a God-fearing kind of way. They like routine. Before service, they eat breakfast at Dairy Queen. Kaye wears the same pearl jewelry set week after week. Ronnie insists on an aisle seat to give Charlie an easy exit when he goes outside after hymns.

Hard-Shell began a Sunday school class for children. Nanny claims the decision was made to entice younger families to join the church.

I suspect parents got tired of their kids drawing on offering envelopes during the sermons.

Now the youngins roughhouse outside, fueled by stale vanilla wafers and watered-down apple juice. I don't think Charlie has left church without a bruise in weeks.

Randall and Missouri Jane scuttle down the aisle. They squeeze into our row, careful not to step on toes, and fill the space between Kaye and me.

They come to church once a month to appease Nanny.

Missouri wears her yellow sundress. Out of everything in her closet, it's the only garment suitable for Hard-Shell. At least, she's said as much, give or take a few expletives.

"Scoot your buns, Susana." Missouri nestles against my side. She hands me a stick of Juicy Fruit, then unwraps her own and places the gum on her tongue. She'll make origami with its wrapper during Pastor Walker's sermon. "You got that hog pen rewired?"

I bend the stick around my thumb. "Sure did."

Keziah Douglas enters the sanctuary from a side door. She takes a seat on the front row, which is always vacant, and glances over her shoulder.

She looks identical to Martha Douglas.

Missouri stretches her arm behind me. "Did you hear about Godwin moving back?" With a yelp, she retracts her arm and massages a red splotch on her wrist. She leans forward, glaring at Nanny. "Gracious, Mama, you nearly took my skin off."

"Shush. You're in the Lord's house." Nanny lifts her pen to attention. She must've delivered the biscuits. Her lap now holds a notebook and the family Bible.

"I'm fellowshipping," Missouri says. "God likes fellowship, ain't that right, Mama?"

The congregation stands for worship, and we follow suit.

"Less jabber, more singing," Nanny hisses. She plucks the gum stick from my hands—I think to spite Missouri more than me—and feeds it to her purse.

Missouri shakes her head. "I've read the Bible cover to cover. Take it from me, Susana. Jesus ain't stuffy like this lot."

Deacon Overstreet belts a song. His baritone voice echoes in the rafters.

People join one by one until the melody becomes a jumble of notes.

I place Henry Owens's Bible on the pew and grab a hymnal from the cap rail. I rub my palm against its faux leather cover, then flip it open to "Blessed Assurance."

Worship concludes with Pastor Walker shuffling to the podium. Papa takes his seat before everyone else. He sinks into the pew, supporting his head against the backrest. He'll nod off once the preaching starts. If Nanny fusses, he'll say he was praying.

To my uncle, God is an appointment that follows his pancake platter and drive from town. To my aunt, God is disappointed, because her mama wags fingers and calls her a sinner, and because she thinks life reflects what she deserves.

My grandma knows her Bible like she knows her kitchen. To her, God is rules and discipline and hard work paired with soft hospitality. Then there's Papa, who prays most Sundays while the preacher obsesses over hell like he has a timeshare down there.

Papa believes God wants to forgive everybody. He gives money to those who need it, offers kindness the way Nanny does her biscuits.

I like Papa's God the most.

Because when I think of Jesus and salvation, I think of Papa singing gospel music at sunrise while he feeds the hogs. I remember the way he cradles me in his lap after a long day, his insistence that I'll never outgrow him, and his whispered *"I love you"* as we watch reruns.

I'm not sure what I think of God, but I know what I think about Papa.

If Papa says Jesus makes his soul well, I want to know Jesus too.

Pastor Walker leans against the podium, I suppose to lessen the weight on his bad knee. He looks as he often does, dressed in slacks and a white button-up.

He wears his remaining auburn hair slicked to one side.

As Missouri folds her gum paper into shapes, I return my hymnal to the cap rail and balance the Good Book on my thighs. I unlatch its clasp, flipping to the dedication page.

Henry Obediah Owens.

Near the back of the sanctuary a man hacks into a handkerchief. He coughs at least once during every service. His croaks are followed by the crinkle of lozenge wrappers.

"G' morning," Pastor Walker booms. He dabs his forehead with the tip of his necktie.

He sweats more than a person should.

Pastor Walker bows his head and waits for us to do the same. He calls for repentance, asks God to help us deny ourselves.

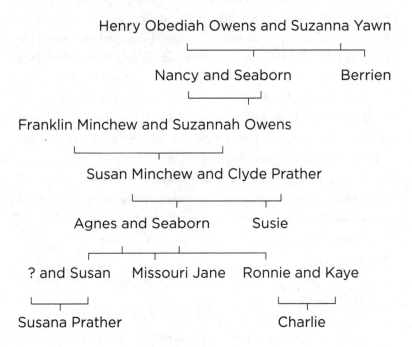

Henry Obediah Owens and Suzanna Yawn

Nancy and Seaborn   Berrien

Franklin Minchew and Suzannah Owens

Susan Minchew and Clyde Prather

Agnes and Seaborn   Susie

? and Susan   Missouri Jane   Ronnie and Kaye

Susana Prather   Charlie

His prayer finishes with a resounding amen.

I riffle through the Bible, stopping at a family tree diagramed in umber ink. The chart begins with Suzanna Yawn and Henry Owens, then branches into Seaborn and Berrien Owens and their offspring. Berrien didn't have a daughter. His sons had more sons.

From Seaborn's line came Suzannah Owens, Susan Minchew, Susie Prather, and my mama, Susan. I need to pinpoint how long it took for each woman to lose her mind and die.

"It is because of our iniquity," Pastor Walker shouts while shaking his Bible, "and the iniquities of our forefathers! We shall rot away like them."

Papa snores. His mustache twitches.

I wipe my hairline and let my head loll side to side. The way Pastor Walker speaks, it's as if I must atone for sins committed so long ago even the stars forgot what they were.

Keziah Douglas turns in her seat and looks at me. She wears the hummingbird brooch from my dream pinned to the lapel of her church suit.

There are too many similarities between the past and present to be coincidences.

Pastor Walker pounds his fists on the podium, causing most of the congregation to jump.

Papa awakes with a snort, then relaxes back into his nap.

I shut the Bible and wedge it between Nanny and me. Until my expiration date, I will do everything possible to absolve myself of the curse.

A hummingbird slams against the nearest window, colliding with glass as if trying to break through. One final blow and it falls limp to the sill.

My skin crawls. The air is molasses inside my lungs.

With an amen, the service concludes. Papa jerks awake, and

Missouri leaps to her feet. She yanks up Randall beside her, nagging Ronnie and Kaye until they drain into the aisle.

I follow them from our row.

"We're gonna make a run for it." Missouri Jane motions to Randall, who loiters near the coatrack in obvious want of a cigarette. He squirms, dressed in the only suit he owns. Its sleeves are so short no matter how much he tugs, the cuffs won't reach his wrists.

"See you tomorrow." I give Missouri a hug and wave as she and Randall scuttle out the front doors. I'll deliver produce to the Green Frog bright and early so I can drink coffee with Missouri before her shift. Lucinda keeps a pot brewed for us.

Keziah Douglas appears out of nowhere and clamps her gnarled hand onto my arm. "You look more like Susan every day," she croaks. The oxygen tube slips from her nose.

Town gossip says her health declined after her son mysteriously dropped dead.

"Prather genes run strong," I say with a forced laugh. Keziah stares at me as if she sees a spook light on my face, and goose bumps rise across my forearms.

She's always given me special attention, maybe because of what happened to Mama.

When I was in middle school, the church hosted a picnic. I helped Keziah organize the buffet tables. She told me to fix myself a plate before everyone else, asked if I wanted to visit her house and look through the toys in her attic.

I'll never forget the look on her face when Nanny and Papa approached. Suddenly, Keziah regarded me with disgust, like I was damaged goods. She piled a foam plate with food, wrapped it in foil, then retreated to a willow grove to eat alone.

Since then, she's only stared at me from across rooms.

"I've known two other Prather girls, both of them dead now."

Keziah pulls me close, her outfit reeking of spearmint and the sweet decay of pine. "You're doomed too."

My stomach flips.

"Leave this place," she tells me. "Before you curse everyone in it."

"What do you mean?" I peel her bony fingers from my bicep.

Keziah glances around, perhaps to make sure Nanny and Papa aren't in range. She leans to my ear and whispers, "Cursed people curse other people."

With that, she rolls her oxygen tank out the front doors.

Cold returns to my bones, that hollow chill I felt this morning. I should follow in Godwin's shoes and leave town for a while. Perhaps distance from the swamp will dull the curse.

Ever since the conversation at the hog pen, I've thought about my reasons for staying in Kettle Creek. I love Nanny and Papa and the farm, but if I'm being honest with myself, I want to stay because I don't think I'm allowed anything else.

Mama never left the state of Georgia.

While Nanny fellowships, I meander around Hard-Shell's ingress. Framed photographs decorate the walls, displaying the church's history.

I follow the images down the timeline, from colored to sepia.

The oldest picture is from the 1800s. It shows a congregation posed in front of Hard-Shell Baptist, clothed in antebellum fashion. Their grim faces stare from behind aged glass. Men with mustaches and broad-brimmed hats. Ladies wearing stiff dresses that cinch their waists.

Suzanna Yawn stands among them.

Papa fills the space to my right. "The resemblance is uncanny."

"If I had darker features, I'd be her doppelganger."

"Every firstborn daughter resembled Suzanna. Startled people at first, I think, because I heard a story about a preacher who visited Franklin and Suzannah Minchew. He laid hands on their daughter, Susan, your great-grandma, said he'd break the curse on her. Everybody blames the curse around here. Don't matter what goes on, the darn curse must be to blame."

"Nanny believes in it."

"She believes in a different kind," Papa says, twisting the end of his mustache. "We're the best and worst of those who came before us, and we'll be the best and worst of whoever comes next. Key ain't to blot out all the bad. Nobody's perfect. I think all we can do is work to ensure whatever bad we pass down won't leave an irreparable wound."

"Do you think I'm cursed, Papa?"

He ignores the question. "Interesting woman, that Suzanna Yawn. I've read about her in our family books. You got her grit, her bones. Blood gets diluted over time, but not bones. What made her up—I reckon the same material holds you together."

"Yeah, that's what scares me."

"Folks around here called her a witch."

"Was she?"

Papa chuckles and shrugs. "Plenty of women have been condemned for doing impossible things. *Possible* is too small a cage to live inside." He steers me away from the picture. "Suzanna is buried in the cemetery out back. You did a rubbing of her headstone."

When I was a kid we frequented the Hard-Shell graveyard. Papa gave me crayons and printer paper, and for hours we meandered among the plots, talking about genealogy while we gathered impressions of names and dates carved into stone.

"There's a lesson to be learned here, Susana. Live a life so impossible that when you die and people tell your story, listeners will question whether you're a tall tale. Stories turn even the most ordinary of persons into myths."

We leave the ingress and move across the churchyard. My head swims from what Keziah and Papa said. If Suzanna was a witch, what does that mean for me?

She might've passed down more than her curse.

1854

Suzanna Yawn kept two effects on her person: her daddy's rifle worn close to her spine and a gold coin stitched into her corset. Despite never seeing war, she lived in the shadows of its horrors.

Violence scarred everything and everyone, visible as charred homesteads and Old Man Jacobs's missing leg. The injuries, mostly unseen, infected like a viral wound, passed down from father to son to son to son.

From mother to daughter.

Suzanna woke each night at its deadest hour to her mama's screams from dreams tainted with memories nobody would mention. It was this—the impenetrable silence—that possessed Suzanna to pack a knapsack and keep it at the ready, stored under the bed she shared with her two younger sisters. She could not shake her fear, so she armed herself against it with the rifle and coin that would secure her passage from Kettle Creek to an island deep in the swamp.

Should the need arise.

With her brothers laid to rest in the Hard-Shell Baptist cemetery, Suzanna picked cotton in their stead, halving her summer days between rows of crops and household chores. She appreciated the routine, for it distracted from the fear that stuck to her thoughts like burs to her skirt. The harder she worked, the more exhausted she became.

And the less likely she was to wake from her mama's night terrors.

Suzanna didn't let herself want, not extra sleep nor food on her plate. Her brothers had made that mistake, and it led to their demise. No, Suzanna chose to accept what life—all seventeen years of it—had given her and guard herself against its brutal nature. She found peace in the breeze and stroke of plants against her fingers.

She mourned through each shove of the plow.

Grief exorcised *safe* from the Yawns' vocabulary. They held each other tighter, wary of everyone in town, and shrank their world to Ruger's land and their homestead.

Mrs. Yawn swore her boys haunted the log cabin. She filled cups with water and placed them outside. She'd heard that souls taken by violence to the neck would not find peace until they quenched their thirsts. Night after night she enacted the rite until one day she rose from bed, clear-eyed and lucid, and said their spirits had passed on.

Over time she became obsessed with the supernatural—omens and harbingers, the spook light that appeared near Ruger's barn. She panicked at the sound of a whippoorwill, believing its song meant a death in the family. She wouldn't allow cats inside the house, for felines could bring about death by sucking the breath of a sleeping person.

News of her aberrant behavior spread through Kettle Creek, rampant after she tied a frog around Gertrude Burrell's neck and said it would help the child teethe. A home remedy, she called it, like putting a spiderweb on a fresh wound to stop its bleed. Her explanation did not appease the townsfolk, so she confined herself to the land near Skull Lake.

Suzanna considered their neighbors' ill remarks a travesty of fairness. She knew Willard Ruger dabbled in superstitious practices. She once discovered four persimmon limbs, nine inches in length, buried on each corner of his property. Talismans to ensure a plentiful harvest.

Everything owed to the Yawns would come when the swamp iced over, Suzanna thought. Such a day seemed inconceivable in a place so far south.

A stranger came to Kettle Creek in late August.

As she did most mornings, Suzanna guided her boat across Skull Lake to a stretch of sand bordering Ruger's land. She lowered her pole into murk and pickerel weeds.

Slit eyes watched from among purple flowers as she propelled her vessel onto a bank.

Across the water, under a canopy of epiphytes, floated an old copper moonshine still. It sat upon a raft, submerged and half filled. Swampers had once pulled the raft behind their boats to relocate it whenever revenue men got hot on their trail. They'd go where nobody would follow and make what they called "block and tackle." If a man could drink a pint and walk a block without passing out cold, he could tackle anything in the Okefenokee, or so the story went.

Now the still remained as a landmark.

Suzanna dragged her boat through yellow-eyed grass and propped it against a stump. She hurried to firmer ground, past herons wading in shallows and an alligator nest made of twigs.

Her daddy had given instructions for navigating the wetland: walk fast, think light, and never step in the tracks of the fella ahead of you. Because the Okefenokee did not contain soil but peat deposits, its earth trembled, always threatening to give way.

Suzanna followed a narrow footpath to Ruger's property. Her skirt dusted pine needles side to side. A red-coated woodpecker hammered treetops, and the air smelled of moss and decay. Suzanna found both torment and comfort in the details. They knitted unease within her and yet soothed the ache in her chest.

The swamp had such an effect on people. No other place possessed the same degree of life and desolation. It appeared forbidden, a garden of Eden with its gates barred.

Suzanna reached the fields, where laborers picked crops and loaded baskets into wagons.

Beyond the stretch of cotton stood Hard-Shell Baptist, a white church with a modest steeple. Folks from Kettle Creek swarmed its doors on the first Saturday and Sunday of each month. They packed into pews and remained there for six to seven hours, long enough for preachers to conclude their sermons and for Louisa to fall asleep on Suzanna's lap.

The next service would continue until dusk, Suzanna predicted.

Missionaries known as circuit riders had come to town and intended a revival for the people of Kettle Creek.

With picking underway, Ruger's harvest scheduled for an early September auction, Suzanna joined a group of women near the road. They sorted through baskets, removing leaves and other debris from the fibers and seeds.

Midday brought a vengeful heat. The ladies slowed their work. Mrs. Minchew hummed songs while the Capers girls battled sweat and flies with fans woven from grass.

Suzanna arched her spine and shivered.

"You know the superstition, don't you?" Mrs. Minchew asked Suzanna. "If you shiver without cause, somebody is walking over the ground where your grave will be."

"Where your death will be," the youngest Capers girl added.

"I ain't scared of dying. I've already seen my grave," Suzanna said. "It's next to my brothers, a plot of land over yonder. I've walked that ground, and I've walked this ground. I know good and well the dirt that'll take me."

After four years of grieving her brothers, Suzanna believed the words spoken at their funeral. Her family was cursed, if not by God, then by an unmentionable past. Life only confirmed what Martha Douglas had said, that the Yawns would suffer.

Peace and happiness would be strangers to them.

Suzanna thought of death as a boon companion, for it promised to rescue her from the anguish. She did not have faith in a future without tragedy, so she waited for the grave to claim her, prayerful the Lord would forgive the old sins for which she was atoning.

The curse was a noose around Suzanna's neck. It grew tauter each day.

Afternoon found her walking toward Kettle Creek behind a wagon loaded with cotton. She intended to purchase turpentine for her daddy and, despite invitations from Ruger's son, declined a ride to town. She thought wheeled contraptions too wobbly, her legs far more stable.

Mrs. Minchew joked the swamp would ice over before Suzanna Yawn rode in a buggy.

Douglases passed Suzanna without offering a glance or a nod. They refused to acknowledge anyone with Muscogee blood, for their memories contained only slaughter, though Muscogees helped settlers retreat to Fort Bainbridge during the Creek War of 1836.

They hated because they wanted to hate.

Suzanna maintained an insouciant expression, grateful for the lack of attention. The Douglas men had a habit of calling out to her when they were drunk and lonely. They issued threats, grinning like coyotes, until Suzanna cocked and aimed her rifle.

Even now, she grabbed the rifle's strap and pulled it tight over her chest. If someone from Ware County spotted her with the weapon, they would confiscate it.

Laws prohibited Muscogees from owning firearms.

With shoes laden and stained red with ochre, Suzanna and the cotton wagon entered a stretch of timberland, where loggers tore apart pines like beasts to bodies. There, she came upon a boy with the coloring of a ghost traveling in the opposite direction. He rode a buckskin gelding and looked fresh from the swamp.

The wilderness had drained his weight. Trousers draped his slender frame, anchored by suspenders. His cheeks appeared sunken and starved by the slow hunger of the backcountry.

Nobody could depart the Okefenokee without paying a toll. Suzanna had realized this when her brothers returned from their first hunt. They'd gone straight to the cupboard, smothered bread with lard and butter, and feasted until their empty stomachs no longer pained them.

The ghostlike boy locked eyes with Suzanna and tipped his felt hat. He trotted his animal in the opposite direction. Beaver and otter pelts swung from his saddle.

He must've passed through Kettle Creek on his route to Old Nine, Suzanna decided. Trappers often refreshed themselves in the settlement before heading north to sell their furs.

Suzanna quickened her stride to keep pace with the wagon as the *click-clack* of horseshoes faded to a distant ictus. The landscape resumed its symphony of mule hooves, wagon wheels, and the splitting groan of axes to wood. She expected the *click-clack* to go silent. Instead, it grew louder, from a patter to crescendo, until the gelding caught up with her.

The boy tugged his reins to slow the horse to match her gait. He offered Suzanna a brittle smile. "Howdy, ma'am. You be needing a ride?"

"I'm nigh onto town."

"It'd be no trouble."

"Much obliged, but I got legs that work fine."

Another horse approached them, a paint mare Suzanna helped birth two years prior. She'd clutched the foal by its hooves and pulled it into the world, Obediah quick to rub the newborn with a quilt. Now he sat tall upon the mare's back and looked at Suzanna as he had then, with independence and devotion, like the moon beholding the sun as they shared skies.

"Hard as nails, that Suzanna Yawn," he declared to the man on the gelding. Obediah turned his horse to walk abreast.

Every young woman in Kettle Creek thought him handsome. He was taller than most boys, with dark and rugged features. Elizabeth Ruger described him as *"Adam fresh from the dirt,"* a compliment that might've garnered attention from Obediah, had he read his Bible.

Suzanna fought a smile. "I thought you were out in the swamp."

"Nah, I traded my pelts, reckoned I'd stick around these parts for a while." Obediah propped his elbows on the horn of his saddle. His gaze for her was always so intimate, and regardless of his banter, everything he spoke sounded of poetry. He had sworn that she'd bewitched him. Since his fifteenth birthday, he'd chaffed her about casting a spell on him.

His love for her was a tall tale. It grew with each repeat, budding and blossoming into a story too lush for belief. He cared for her—that Suzanna knew for certain—but so much of his life was cloaked in myth, his truth got lost in the legend that was Obediah Owens.

The timber trade brought his family to Kettle Creek when he was six years old. He grew up a mile from the Yawn homestead and became a swamper at age seventeen. He didn't belong in civilized places, nor did he wish to spend his life taming the earth, so he ventured into the Okefenokee to hunt and trap. Within a year, he managed to build a reputation for himself.

Folks told stories about Obediah clubbing a bear to death in unarmed combat. They marveled at his height and claimed he was related to the Okefenokee's first inhabitants, an explanation devised by Old Man Jacobs.

In the 1500s, when Spaniards came to the swamp in search of gold, they discovered burial mounds of unknown origin, each containing skeletons well over six feet tall.

Everything about Obediah seemed larger than life. Suzanna didn't know which stories to believe. Whenever she asked for his accounts, he maintained his mystery. For that reason, she understood they could never become what his eyes wanted. Besides, they were solitary creatures, and two people who were happiest alone could not find peace together.

Obediah gestured to the other rider. "Suzanna, this is my friend August Godwin."

The boy gave a nod.

"What brings you to Kettle Creek, Mr. Godwin?" Suzanna asked.

August rubbed his cheeks, where bristles glistened like cobwebs. His face appeared young, but something about him seemed older than the oak trees that bordered the road. "I got four hundred acres in a land lottery, moved here from the coast."

"He'll work for the Rugers until he gets settled," Obediah said. "We're headed there now for supper. Join us. You know Willard always welcomes the company."

"Mama's expecting me."

Obediah huffed and clutched his chest as though Suzanna had broken his heart. He'd learned early in their relationship what made her smile. Few things did, but he always could.

Since he couldn't kiss her, he used jokes to stay close to her mouth.

"I ain't been to a proper supper in months. How am I supposed to act civil and the like without you around to domesticate me?"

"You forget your audience, Obediah." Suzanna halted and spun toward him. "Ask one of Willard's daughters to tame you. His youngest seems mighty keen."

"Nobody keeps me on the straight and narrow like you. I need—"

"You need a miracle, and I ain't the Good Lord."

August laughed, exposing rows of good teeth.

Obediah patted his torso and hissed a curse. "I forgot my darn vest at the campsite. Wouldn't be right to show up for supper without it."

"You best go on, then," Suzanna told him.

He jerked his reins to one side, then swiftly leaned back in his saddle. "Hold up."

He dropped to the ground, drew a cross in the soil with his left boot, and spit on the mark for good luck.

"You ain't one for old wives' tales," Suzanna said. Superstition dictated that if something was forgotten, before a person could turn back for it, he needed to complete a rite to avoid misfortune.

"Think of it as insurance." Obediah returned to his saddle. "I'll call on you tomorrow morn if that's all right."

"Mama will be pleased to see you. I reckon she'll whip up a batch of those biscuits you fancy." Suzanna veered her focus to August. "Mr. Godwin."

"Miss Yawn." He spoke her name with care as though it deserved reverence. His mouth lifted into a smile so brief, so faint, Suzanna wondered if she'd imagined it.

"There'll be plenty of biscuits to go around," she told him.

"If that's an offer, I'll take you up on it."

"Please. Any friend of Obediah is a friend of mine."

"Yes, ma'am." August tipped his hat. "I'd like very much to call on you."

Suzanna held a breath captive.

No man gave her bouts of the vapors. She was far too sensible. Even so, her heart lost control, racing from a terse feeling she couldn't name.

She blamed the reaction on piqued curiosity, not August's strong jaw, clear eyes, nor the aroma wafting from his threadbare clothes. A tonic of woodsmoke and leather.

Nor the laugh that sprung from his melancholy disposition.

He was quite young, not handsome enough to tempt her emotions, yet she couldn't ignore the pull she felt. It wasn't lust, rather a current that drew her to him. She'd felt the same while wading through rushes. The swamp had towed her deeper and deeper as though it wanted her. It was intended for her. She was as much a part of it as it was of her.

August motioned to the cotton wagon, now far down the road. "Why're you walking?"

"I suppose I don't trust anything not attached to me." Suzanna warmed at the confession. A flutter like bird wings flailed within her belly. Because of how August looked at her.

Obediah beheld her in the same gentle way.

The notice took Suzanna by surprise, for such looks seemed reserved for ladies who spent their days indoors, perfecting their porcelain cheeks with a poultice of buttermilk and meal.

Suzanna had no use for lace and soft graces. She was of the earth, meant for fields and hoes. She wore clothes the color of grief, her hair parted down the center and fastened into a tight knot.

Whatever beauty she possessed she buried under calluses and dirty petticoats to prevent men like the Douglases from badgering her. August Godwin was different. He studied her as though she was a morning glory, elegant and tender, exposing herself for gasps of sunshine but wilting at the mere brush of a finger, closing herself captive at the threat of shadows.

"You can trust us," August said.

His eyes brimmed with hope. Suzanna couldn't help but feel their overflow. A thought rooted within her, that perhaps she could have more than curses.

"Mister, I don't know you."

August flashed a smile. "I'll prove it, then."

With a kick of their heels, the boys galloped toward Kettle Creek.

Suzanna tensed with another shiver as their silhouettes vanished into a fog of copper dust. She rolled back her shoulders, rubbed the bumps from her forearms.

Mrs. Minchew said a shiver in the heat meant someone had walked over the ground where your grave would be. Suzanna knew other wives' tales to say it meant you were falling in love. As if death and devotion bore equal curses.

But such was a thing of folklore.

CHAPTER 5
SUSANA PRATHER

JC prods me with his Timberland boots.

"Susana, are we boring you?" He casts his line across the channel into a field of lily pads. Already he's added three pickerels to his cooler.

The aluminum jon boat drifts toward Billy's Lake. Turtles lift their heads from the mirrored water. Storks perch among tupelos, and gators coast through patches of duckweed.

The air carries its usual weight, stagnant and sweltering.

As if the Okefenokee holds its breath.

"What do you know about Muscogee legends?" I close a history book and cradle it in my lap. A yellow fly lands on my arm. I smack it too late.

Pain shoots across my bicep.

Stokes leans against the bow and pierces a night crawler onto his hook. He purchases worms only from Floyd's Gas Mart, convinced they catch the largest bowfins. So far nobody has proven him wrong. "I heard about Tie-Snakes."

"Do your grannies believe any old superstitions?" I spit into my hand and coat the fly bite with saliva. It won't prevent swelling, but it should minimize symptoms.

"Mine has a mirror on her front porch to keep the devil away. Says he's so vain, he'll look at his reflection and won't come inside," JC says with a laugh. He grips the tiller and steers us beneath a canopy of epiphytes.

Banana spiders, some larger than my fist, web the treetops.

"Nothing about curses, then?"

JC reels in his lure and recasts. He nods at my backpack. Its pocket is unzipped, exposing a genealogy book Papa self-published years ago. It documents our family tree to the 1500s. "What's going on? School don't start for weeks."

"I'm researching family history is all."

He isn't a reader. Once, I dragged him to the Berryville Library, and he wandered around with his hat on backward, pockets filled with minnow plugs. He grabbed a novel and said, *"Folks spend hours staring at pieces of trees, but few know what it's like to live among 'em. Whole lotta world out there, and people choose* paper *over* trees."

Stokes digs a cigarette from his pocket and fits it in the corner of his mouth. "Boring stuff, my family history. Bunch of drunks and crackheads." He rolls a flame from his lighter.

"Give me that." I snatch the cigarette from his lips and wave it at him. "You wanna end up like your pawpaw? Tobacco will rot your insides, mark my words."

"Yeah, well, my insides are shot." Stokes groans when I drop the cigarette and grind it beneath my shoe. He tunnels fingers through his curls, sweeping them away from his angular face. Without his mane, he'd resemble a skeleton. His body is all bones and strappy muscles.

He's been called "beanpole," "scrawny," and "meth baby" his entire life.

I prop my feet on his bench seat. He squeezes my ankle, a miniature hug, then casts his bait and wedges his rod in the holder he made from PVC pipe.

William Burrell. I've never called him by his real name. He goes by Stokes, always has. Where he got the sobriquet, I'm not sure. Holler takes credit for it, but I remember Stokes being Stokes before our friend group expanded. He might've created the name to distinguish himself from his father, Willy, who shows more kindness to cars and pills than his own kid.

"What happened to that canoe of yours?" I ask JC.

"I put it in storage. Gators are friendlier than they used to be." He guides us past old tram roads. Tracks sat upon them years ago when flat cars hauled logs out of the Okefenokee.

"Yeah, we were paddling along last Saturday, and the entire back side of the canoe rose out of the water. I turned around, and no lie—biggest gator I'd ever seen. He was trying to tip us." Stokes reaches into the picnic basket I brought and removes a Cool Whip container. He uncaps it, scooping a handful of jumbo marshmallows.

Nanny keeps them in her candy drawer with her Mary Janes and circus peanuts.

"Maybe they'd leave you be if you stopped feeding them," I say as he chunks the marshmallows at a cluster of cypress knees.

Alligators lurch from hidden places and devour the confections in a splashing frenzy.

"We ought to stop." JC swipes a marshmallow from the container and hurls it.

I punch his arm. He fakes a wince. For years he and Stokes have used marshmallows to decoy gators away from the boat. Reptiles mistake them for eggs, their favorite snack.

"You see that platform over there? It used to be a commissary for swampers." JC points at a structure enveloped by greenery. Its rotten planks sag into quagmire.

The building squats on the edge of an island, where the channel widens into flat prairie. At one time the debris must've resembled a cabin with a dock extending from its porch.

Now all that remains are posts reaching from pitch-black water.

"What've you learned?" JC asks me.

"I researched our great-great-great-great-grandma Suzanna Yawn." I flick through the genealogy book, lingering on notations Papa added to the margins.

He finds the dead more interesting than the living.

Stokes wipes night crawler guts onto his white tank. The smear joins a collection of engine oil and mud. "I keep forgetting y'all are cousins."

"We're barely related," JC says, recasting his line. "I bet my bottom dollar all three of us share blood with most of Berryville."

Stokes laughs. "That explains the deformities around here."

JC throws marshmallows at Stokes's head.

"You've seen Mark Shealy's janky finger, haven't you?" Stokes bats the marshmallows into the water. "The man doesn't have joints in his pinkies. Inbreeding, I tell you."

"Fifth cousins wouldn't be inbreeding."

"What are you saying, JC?" Stokes raises his eyebrows, grinning from ear to ear.

"Nothing. I just . . . don't think it'd be unnatural." JC turns beet red. He avoids looking at me as if I don't already know the truth about us.

"Y'all ain't right," Stokes says with a snort. He scratches his arms. They're dotted with mosquito and no-see-um bites. For some reason, his blood attracts insects like sugar water.

"Anyway, I spent yesterday afternoon in Papa's shed, reading his books on local history and folklore. I gathered every scrap of information about Suzanna Yawn. She had twin sons with Henry Obediah Owens. People called her a witch because—"

"I'm related to an outlaw," Stokes says. "Son of a gun hammered nails into the soles of his boots so his footprints would leave a cross pattern. Supposed to ward off evil or something."

"What else?" JC asks me.

Suzannah Owens was born in the year 1912. The oldest of five children, Suzannah grew up on a farm outside of Berryville. Her dad, Seaborn, worked for the railroad.

At seventeen years old, Suzannah married Franklin Minchew, an accountant for the furniture manufacturing plant. He was ten years her senior and eager to start a family.

By the time she turned eighteen, Suzannah was pregnant with her twins, Robert and Susan. The curse took hold before she gave birth. She began sleepwalking, an oddity doctors blamed on the pregnancy. They insisted Suzannah be confined to her home.

Records say the families kept the sleepwalking hush-hush. They locked Suzannah within her room, believing she'd contracted hysteria. Not long after delivering her children, Suzannah escaped the house. She wandered onto the train tracks and was struck dead by a steam engine.

She was nineteen years old when she died.

She lost her mind four months into her eighteenth year.

"Let's just say my family is the reason ghost stories exist." I shut the book and stow it in my backpack. If the hex on me follows the same timeline, I have four months until I go insane.

I have four months to break the curse.

Papa secured the barrel bolt last night, but it didn't stop me from sleepwalking. The back door was unlocked when I woke up. Someone—I assume *me*—dragged a chair from the kitchen table to use as a ladder, disabled the barrel bolt, and opened the door.

I found the chair abandoned next to wet footprints.

The dreams seem to be laying a groundwork for something. There are too many similarities between my life and the past. Keziah looks like Martha Douglas. JC is a spitting image of Obediah Owens. And what about the appearance of August Godwin?

I can't decide if the flashbacks are true reflections of the past or if my mind alters them. Regardless, I think they're meant to help me understand the curse.

JC touches my shoulder. "What you're worried about—it's not real, Susana."

He must be a mind reader.

"Yeah, I know." I fake a smile and shove the backpack under my seat. I doubt JC would believe me if I told him about the sleepwalking. I'm scared he would.

"Those stories are nothing but tall tales," JC says.

Maybe I should be more afraid of sleepwalking. At this point, it seems the lesser evil. I haven't drowned or been eaten. My only loss has been a nightgown and some quilts.

I need better sleep if I'm going to break the curse. I'm so tired, I could burst into tears. Since doors won't keep me inside, I must consider other options.

Rain crashes from a clear sky. It falls in torrents, pelting the metal boat like gunfire.

Stokes bares himself to the rain and sunlight. "You know that saying about sun showers," he yells over the patter. "Devil's beating his wife."

"He sure beats her an awful lot." JC places his ball cap on my head to block the deluge. He continues fishing, unbothered by the weather or the steam that follows. If the wilderness was a personality type, an Enneagram number, a star sign, it would be his.

I wring my shirt once the rain subsides.

Stokes unpacks my picnic basket and distributes a lunch of goobers, fried apple pies, and egg salad sandwiches. He sinks his teeth into slices of cheap white bread.

"How are things at the shop?" I ask him.

"Dad has me working overtime," Stokes says between chews. "I'm tore slap up."

"Is he treating you well?"

"He hasn't hit me recently if that's what you're asking." Stokes forces another sandwich into my hands. "Let's talk about easy stuff, leave all the hard back home."

He makes faces at me until I relent and eat my lunch.

Our bond is different from what I have with JC. Neither of us knew our mamas. His disappeared not long after his birth, and rumors blame a meth addiction.

People in town call Stokes a screw-up because of his upbringing. Even my family thinks he'll either end up dead or behind bars. That's hard for me. Really hard. Because I see him trying to build a life for himself. He does his homework. He plays church league basketball on the Presbyterian team. He respects people, doesn't judge. Nobody I know has a nicer heart than his.

But people's opinions get too loud sometimes. Stokes believes them and lives as if he's a heartbreak waiting to happen. Nanny describes Stokes as a walking disaster, which isn't far from the truth. Misfortune finds him. That, or Stokes welcomes it because he doesn't think he deserves better. "*Trouble likes trouble,*" he says whenever he comes to school with bruises and bloodshot eyes.

In many ways, I think he understands why I've been afraid of curses all these years.

We both live in our parents' long shadows.

Stokes takes another bite and motions to JC. "Your boy picked up extra shifts."

"At Floyd's or the park?" I ask.

"Both. My truck needs a new transmission." JC cuts the motor and reels his line.

He works more than anybody I know, either to replace something broken or to save up for his escape from Berryville. On weekdays he guides tours at the Okefenokee Swamp Park. Evenings and weekends, he mans the register at Floyd's Gas Mart.

"Cleo must like that, huh?"

JC shrugs. "I haven't seen her in a while."

"We come out here whenever we get a spare minute," Stokes says, perhaps as a defense for why JC hasn't spent time with his girlfriend.

The boys have used the swamp as a clubhouse since they were kids. They fish and frog, piss on trees, and make themselves sick off hot dogs and cold beans. Cheaper than therapy, they tell anyone who asks why they boat and camp on their free days.

"Do you realize what'll happen when Cleo learns I went fishing with you? She'll get all passive-aggressive."

I do a one-eighty on my bench seat. My knees rest against JC's knees.

He crinkles the side of his face. "Cleo is busy too, you know, getting ready for a pageant. And it's not like she wants to hang out with us."

"Yeah, that would mean she'd have to sweat." Stokes bloats his cheeks to hide a smile. He and I betted against Holler that JC and Cleo would break up after graduation. If before, Holler wins thirty dollars and a meal from the Green Frog.

Cleo must sense their fate. She's become clingy and possessive, more than usual. She expects JC to follow her to the University of Georgia and move back to Berryville, where they'll get married and live downtown. If she understood JC, she'd realize how bizarre that sounds.

Nanny told me there are two types of critters—those meant for inside, and those intended for the outdoors. I think the same principle applies to people.

"Busy or not, Cleo will flip a lid if she finds out about this. She already thinks we're secretly in love." I nudge JC, and he nudges me back.

"There's no reason for her to be jealous." JC gives an expression reserved for me. I didn't understand what it was, that softness in his eyes, until Papa teased him about being sweet.

He stares as if we're seconds away from a kiss.

I get why Cleo resents me.

Stokes finishes his lunch with a sigh. "Susana, thank your grandma for me." He digs through his tackle bag, unclips a metal cup from its carabiner, and dips it into the swamp.

"Water has oil and gasoline in it," JC says when Stokes guzzles the murky liquid. Although tannic acid purifies the water, nobody recommends drinking from popular channels.

Stokes dries his mouth. "Tastes fine to me."

"That ain't saying much," JC scoffs.

"You and Holler eat my cooking all the time, no complaints."

"The deer meat."

"All right, so I made one little mistake."

"How can anyone mistake Coffee Mate for flour?" JC yells.

"I put 'em in similar containers. If I recall correctly, you ate a good bit."

JC yanks the pull start, and the motor purrs to life. "It didn't thrill me none."

In eighth grade, JC considered hopping a train. We practiced running alongside the tracks after school. He dreamed about the life we'd find in some far-off place, and I dreamed about the life we had here. One afternoon we climbed onto a stationary car and decided if God wanted us to leave Berryville, the train would lurch into motion, and we'd be on our way. It never did, and we never left. JC held on to hope, blind in so many ways. His hope was the wild, a place without money or walls, where he could be anyone, and anything could grow.

He'll leave town after graduation, likely move across the country. He assures me if he goes, he'll take me with him. We both know that's a lie. He wants a scholarship to a prestigious university. I have no doubt he'll get it. For someone who dislikes reading, he's smart as a whip.

Stokes calls him a hillbilly genius.

My eyes sting with tears. I don't want to think about what'll happen in four months or if I'll live to see JC go to college. That's my biggest fear, bigger than sleepwalking and insanity.

I don't want to leave pain in my wake.

"We almost stepped on a snake earlier, a big ole cottonmouth," Stokes tells me.

"You sure it wasn't an earthworm with a thyroid problem?" JC asks.

"Want me telling everybody you squealed at a worm?"

"I did nothing of the sort. Your line's pulling." JC nods at the rod bent to a curve. Its thread yanks toward a patch of golden clubs.

Stokes frees the pole, whooping as he reels a bowfin the length of my thigh. He grabs the fish by its lip and tail and raises it over his head. "Magic bait, I tell you."

JC and Stokes were my first real friends. Our group started as the three of us. I have a feeling it'll end that way too, with us fishing in some backwater channel.

Scales like coals slither among bladderworts.

Razored fangs grin from below, embedded in pink gums.

I lean over starboard. The boat rocks, and the water ripples before steadying into a mirror. Its surface, darker than black, reflects my face.

The Okefenokee relaxes into an eerie stillness. Then, as if on cue, nature erupts in a symphony of frequencies. Cicadas hiss from treetops. Animals rustle in the wire grass.

I must have imagined it. I blink and rub my eyes.

Around JC's boat, lily pads feather into bloom, unfolding into magenta-white blossoms.

"You guys . . ." Stokes curses. His hazel eyes widen into saucers.

Alligators sail toward us in formation, dozens of them organized into rows. Reptiles dive from the embankment. Splash after splash after splash. They circle the boat in a vortex.

I open my mouth, but air won't enter my lungs.

Stokes drops his fish onto the floor. He dumps my Cool Whip container and pelts marshmallows at the beasts, shouting and swearing. Fear bleaches his face.

JC points at the bowfin. "Give it back!"

"No." Stokes trips on my foot and face-plants. The boat dips sideways. Blood trickles from his bottom lip. He coughs and waves at JC. "Get us out of here!"

JC hits the accelerator. Jerking the tiller, he steers us from the swarm.

1854

A scream pried Suzanna from her sleep.

She awoke with a start. Her eyes filtered the room's darkness, the moonlight smoking through cracks in the shutters, the lantern dead on the side table. She reached for her rifle.

Louisa touched her hand instead.

All three sisters lay beneath quilts, the youngest, Vicy Ann, whimpering into her pillow. They knew the shriek belonged to their mama, for the woman battled terrors whenever she entered slumber, and rarely did she emerge victorious.

Suzanna folded back the blankets and lowered her feet to the cold floor.

Another cry pierced the night, followed by the fizz of a struck match. Firelight sizzled bronze in the room beyond. Her little brother, John, must've descended from the loft to assist their father.

Clatters and wails grew to a clamor.

The shouts were disrupted by the dong of pots against wood and the splinter of furniture.

Mrs. Yawn staggered past the doorway. She sobbed and clawed at empty air, howling like an animal caught in a snare. Her ink-black hair was wild, her eyes glazed with nightmare.

"Mama!" Suzanna yelled as she inched into the cabin's main room with her sisters following close behind. She reached for the woman now thrashing near the hearth.

Mr. Yawn wrestled his wife from the fire. "Keep the girls back," he commanded Suzanna while John attempted to restrain the sleepwalker with a bearskin.

Tripping on her shift, Mrs. Yawn broke free.

She rushed to the door and sprinted outside. Suzanna raced after her, across the porch and down a step, into dark so thick Suzanna could hardly make out the white of her mama's gown.

"Wake up, Mama. You're dreaming." Suzanna grasped a handful of the sleepwalker's hair and tackled her to pine needles. She gathered the woman's frail body into her arms.

Mrs. Yawn screamed at the stars.

Her face wore a horror too severe for Suzanna to understand. It rippled beneath her flesh, veiny and tormented, and poured from her mouth.

Mr. Yawn approached, out of breath. "Go back inside, Suzanna." He pried his wife from the ground and cradled her, lifting.

"Why does this happen to her?" Suzanna rose gingerly and dried her hands on her skirt. Liquid coated her fingers, mud or blood or her mama's urine.

"I'll fetch the doctor in the morning." Mr. Yawn carried his wife toward the house. He called to John, who hurried from the porch with a lantern.

"Daddy, why won't you tell me?" Suzanna yelled.

Her mama pleaded in a language Suzanna was not allowed to

speak and raked fingernails against her chest as though to dissever what ailed her. The cause of her mania, no Yawn dared to speculate aloud. Suzanna believed its roots stemmed from *before*. Before her older brothers found their deaths. Before the Yawns settled near Skull Lake.

A gap of time clouded by war and secrecy.

"The past only lives on if we let it," Mr. Yawn said.

"It's living in her, don't you see?" Suzanna screamed.

History was not so easily buried. It made itself known in whispers from townsfolk who claimed Mrs. Yawn had the devil inside her. It tempted Suzanna's sisters to hoard food beneath floorboards. History sank its claws and held tight, whispering the word Suzanna despised. *Cursed*. And without an explanation, the word seemed more and more true.

They retraced their steps onto the porch and into the cabin.

"Lock the door," Mr. Yawn instructed. His gaze challenged Suzanna, his expression an additional latch clicking into place. He would go to his grave without talking of bygone days.

As Vicy Ann and Louisa watched from a doorway, Mr. Yawn carried Mrs. Yawn into their bedroom. The world became silent once more.

A reticent place where nobody would give words to the night.

Its terrors diminished by dawn.

CHAPTER 6

SUSANA PRATHER

JULY, PRESENT DAY

A whippoorwill ends the dream with a call that snaps back my eyelids.

I don't bother to wipe the swamp from my face. Instead, I lay cloaked in darkness as crickets hum beyond the screen of my cracked window.

The clock on my nightstand ticks past three.

Dripping, I peel back a sheet trimmed with eyelet lace and rise from the mattress. I slough off my pajamas, replacing them with dry clothes.

My body aches from exhaustion. I shuffle to my desk, flip on the lamp, and take a seat.

The bedroom's floral wallpaper seems to writhe, growing up the walls, across the ceiling. Scions climb into vines into blush roses with thorns and papery leaves. They smell of citrus and honey and mourning, like a funeral wreath left to rot in a parlor.

My tired mind is playing tricks on me.

"Jesus," I whisper as a precaution, to ward off demons or haints. I open the desk drawer and exhume a bundle of sage Missouri gave me. I ignite the stalks with a match, waving their smoke until my anxiety dims and the wallpaper goes still.

The sleepwalking must've passed down from Mrs. Yawn.

When Suzanna issued her curse, she mentioned her mama's spirit. Maybe the flashback was meant to show me the origin of the sleepwalking and madness.

I sort through Papa's records, organizing my notes on Suzannah Owens. I grab a blank sheet of paper and jot down information about Suzannah's daughter, Susan Minchew.

Born in 1930, Susan and her twin brother were raised by their father. They lived in downtown Berryville, often staying with their relatives on the family farm. Throughout her teenage years, Susan became embroiled in scandals involving married men. At one point, she was sent to live with an aunt in North Carolina to prevent further relations.

Susan married Clyde Prather—a well-to-do lawyer from Waycross—when she was eighteen years old. Her son Donald was born seven months later.

A written account from her uncle Berry suggests she married Clyde to escape her father. Frank Minchew was a known drunk and rumored to have mistreated his children.

Papa added his own account to the records. As the fourth-born son of Susan and Clyde, he mentions the family's secrecy, how no one talked about his mama's insomnia. He remembers his parents slept in separate rooms. Clyde locked Susan in her bedroom each night.

According to Papa, the family pretended not to notice.

Susan birthed five children. After her youngest, Susie, was born, she battled severe paranoia and took to the bottle. She refused to leave her home. Eventually her family placed her in a mental hospital, where she died at the age of forty-five.

I lower my pen.

Maybe I have more than four months.

Susan managed to delay the inevitable for years, I assume because Clyde locked her away at night. If I stop myself from sleepwalking, I might prolong the curse and have more time to break it.

Clyde must've known about the sleepwalking. Why did he keep it a secret?

I open Papa's genealogy book and flip to the chapter on Suzanna Yawn. I study the curse she uttered until dawn paints golden lines across my room.

A moth flits from nowhere and lands on my knuckles. It bats its orange wings, twitches its antennae. I dust it onto my notebook, wheezing as it crawls toward me.

"Go away!" I clutch my face, then my ears, but I can't block the doddering rasp from somewhere and everywhere that says the swamp wants me, it won't rest until it has me.

The incident with Stokes and JC was proof.

I count my breaths until they steady.

Once the smell of buttered grits drifts from the kitchen, I shut the text and strip my bed. Mama watches from her picture frame as I dry my puddles.

I get the sense of déjà vu.

The Green Frog requested a later delivery, so I spend the morning canning with Nanny. We fill dozens of mason jars with okra, peas, and pickled squash.

We labor in a sort of dance, slicing and boiling.

The thermostat reaches ninety degrees around noon. Nanny and I move our work close to the window unit. Our house has two: one in the kitchen, another in the den.

Papa returns from the farm and pours himself a glass of iced tea.

He pecks Nanny's cheek, snickering when she complains about his itchy mustache. "I'm gonna write a letter," he says as he shuffles to the bathroom with a box of matches.

Yesterday it was, "*I gotta go read the paper.*"

I stow jars in the pantry, and Nanny starts on lunch. She reaches under the sink and removes a bin of flour. Within minutes, she has chicken and dumplings simmering on the stove.

Normal doesn't feel normal anymore.

It's only the space between last night and tonight.

Kaye drops off Charlie at two thirty. Nanny and Papa take him to feed the cows, and I load produce into my Cadillac. I pass Gus's house on my drive to town.

Godwin crouches on the roof, hammering shingles to a naked piece of plywood. He wears a red ball cap, work boots, and his jeans cut into shorts.

A radio sits on the hood of his truck, blasting country rock. He drinks from a Floyd's Gas Mart cup and nods along with the music. As I near his mailbox, he looks my way.

I floor the gas.

Neither of us waves.

1854

The Yawns were accused of manslaughter after an accident brought about a death.

Such was a stroke of poor luck, or perhaps divine appointment. If any other persons had been involved, the people of Kettle Creek would've considered the loss a mishap, nothing more.

Mr. Yawn had been tasked with driving Ruger's wagon to town. With him were Joseph Owens and Whitey Burrell. During the journey, a back wheel broke off its axle, throwing Whitey from the wagon box. His neck snapped on impact.

Nobody could explain the malfunction. Ruger examined the wagon and found not decay nor evidence of tampering. Thus Mr. Yawn believed the whispers calling his family cursed.

Townsfolk grew warier of the Yawns.

Suzanna clutched her rifle ever so tight when she ventured from her family's homestead. She felt her neighbors' animosity like a blade to her throat. If they further honed their hatred, Suzanna worried they'd lynch her parents and younger siblings as they had her brothers.

Memories of Hangman's Oak prevented her rest. She feared who might visit in the night, so she kept watch, stroking her sister Louisa's temple as the child greeted slumber.

Her mama spun the spinning wheel until witching hour, then latched shutters over glassless windows and sank under a quilt. She, too, denied sleep.

Following the wagon incident, a swamper drowned in Skull Lake a stone's throw from the Yawns' cabin. The Douglas boys found the dead man and swore he'd fallen victim to witchcraft. They spread rumors of the Tie-Snake, a Creek legend said to drag people underwater.

They claimed the Yawns had summoned it.

Suzanna despised the Douglases for refusing to grant her family peace. She loathed their insistence that her blood was cursed and herself for allowing their words to be of consequence. Not a thing could disprove them. On the contrary, the circumstances in which the Yawns found themselves only confirmed the Douglases' sinister allegations.

Late one afternoon, Suzanna discovered the Douglas menfolk behind Ruger's barn, sullying their senses with moonshine. She overheard them speak of her brothers.

They said the boys cried before they died.

What possessed Suzanna was more than suspicion. She knew the truth like she knew her own name. The Douglases were responsible for her brothers' hanging.

The hypocrisy flooded Suzanna with rage. For years, the Douglases had condemned the Yawns for the sins of past generations, all while committing murder with their own hands.

Suzanna buried her fury and kept her rifle blameless. She bided her time. If she was damned by the past, the Douglases were too.

They would pay their debts with blood.

A visit to the mercantile presented Suzanna with an opportunity. There, perusing bolts of fabric, was Martha Douglas, too occupied with silk to pay anyone notice.

Suzanna approached the woman. "I heard talk not long ago."

Martha glanced up from her shopping. She wore a plaid day dress and a bonnet trimmed with frills, both new by the looks of them.

"From your kin." Suzanna clutched the strap of her rifle. "They were imbibing, you see. A habit of which I know you disapprove."

"You're mistaken," Martha said, lifting a bolt.

"The liquor got their tongues wagging." Suzanna knocked the jade silk from Martha's hands. "They spoke of stringing up my brothers."

"You're lying."

"We both know I'm not." Suzanna leaned closer, seething at the woman's contempt. Around them, people milled about the store, purchasing striped candies and sacks of meal.

"Nobody will believe you," Martha whispered.

"That don't matter." Suzanna clenched her jaw to steady her voice. "I don't need to drag your name through the dirt. You've already put it there. You've dug your own grave."

"Is that a threat?" Martha stiffened, growing an inch taller. Abhorrence contorted her face until she no longer resembled herself.

"It's a promise. I see you for what you are." Suzanna gripped

Martha's wrist and peeled back the woman's fisted fingers, exposing her palm. "The blood on your hands won't wash off. It'll stain you and the generations after you. On my honor, you will grieve what I have grieved."

The words left a bitter taste in Suzanna's mouth.

CHAPTER 7

SUSANA PRATHER

JULY, PRESENT DAY

Cleo answers her front door and greets me with a squeal.

She rushes forward. Her wholesome brown eyes and trophy-winning smile blur into one shade of beauty queen. When she hugs my neck, I catch a whiff of JC's house.

He must've invited her over to compensate for the fishing trip.

"Thanks for letting me crash here," I say into her thick hair.

Asking to spend the night was a last resort. No matter what I do, I can't stop myself from sleepwalking. Yesterday, I used a belt to anchor my wrist to a bedpost. I woke up drenched in swamp water, with bruises the color of grape jelly.

Distance from the swamp might help. Cleo lives in downtown Berryville, miles from the Okefenokee. Hence why I asked my sort-of-friend for a slumber party. I figured I could play the role of childhood bestie in exchange for rest.

"Are you kidding? I've been wanting a sleepover, like, all summer." Cleo withdraws and motions for me to follow her inside. She wears a gingham minidress that makes her look sweet and Southern, the kind of girl mamas want for their sons.

Too bad Mrs. Owens cares more about nicotine than who dates her children.

As moths ping-pong in the sconces, I step into the foyer and kick off my sneakers.

The Shealys live in a historic home across from town hall. Their ancestor built the showplace a century ago, when he moved his furniture manufacturing plant to Berryville.

"Daisy's upstairs." Cleo leads me past the living room, where her mother exercises on an elliptical machine to the beat of the cooking channel.

"Susana, darling, it's good to see you." Mrs. Shealy waves and pants. For as long as I've known her, she's used the living room as a makeshift gym.

Her workouts consist of Tracy Anderson DVDs and hot-pink dumbbells.

"Hi, Mrs. Shealy." I stall in the threshold.

The room, like most of the house, is decorated with heirlooms and stuff bought from Facebook Marketplace. Placards cover the walls in tacky slogans.

I crouch near an ottoman and pet Cleo's elderly terrier.

Mrs. Shealy pumps her legs, huffing and puffing. She works at Shealy Pharmacy with her family, but her fitness regimen suggests another profession, maybe film star or first lady. She never goes to the store without a full face of makeup.

According to her, Berryville is a stage, and everybody watches the show.

She took Cleo and me grocery shopping years ago. Before we left the car, she flipped down her visor mirror, applied lipstick, and said,

"Wanna be famous? Don't leave your small town. No red carpet will give you more attention than Walmart on a Saturday night."

The Shealys are the definition of hometown celebrities.

Once I finish petting the dog, Cleo and I head upstairs.

"This feels like old times, huh?" Cleo says, I suppose to guilt me for hanging out with JC and Stokes more than her. She toys with her necklace, a purple stone the shade of foxglove.

"Yeah, it feels like a couple weeks ago," I say, which isn't mature. I shouldn't fight petty with petty, but I'm exhausted. The lack of restful sleep is messing with me.

"I made Oreo chocolate-chip cookies. Felt like splurging, you know? I can hate myself tomorrow." Cleo pats her flat belly. She cuts calories and portion-controls in the name of pageant season, but pageant season turns into bikini season.

She obsesses about weight loss year-round.

The floor vibrates with *Call of Duty* gunfire as we pass her brothers' room. Cleo goes to a doorway and swipes aside its curtain of plastic lavender beads.

Daisy lies across Cleo's bed with her cellphone held so close to her face, her pupils glow white-blue. "Holler left me on read—" She twists onto her stomach and flashes a smile. "Susana! Okay, honest opinion. Would it be wrong to snap the whole football team?"

"Snap what?" I toss my backpack into a corner.

"Like, a hot selfie or something." Daisy lowers her arm over the mattress's edge and feels around for her McDonald's cup. She guzzles at least a gallon of sweet tea per day.

I collapse into a swivel chair. "What's going on with Holler?"

"He's an idiot," Daisy says, rolling her eyes. "We're taking a break." She drinks from a bendy straw and flips her golden hair. Somehow, despite her sugar addiction and family history of obesity, she's built like a swimsuit model.

"Ignore him," Cleo says. "That's what I do. Works like a charm."

"On JC, really?" Daisy types a text. Her acrylic nails rap against the phone screen. She wears Holler's letterman jacket. After their fourth breakup, she stopped taking it off.

"Quickest way to get a response out of him." Cleo plops onto the carpet and crisscrosses her legs. "Don't you think, Susana?" Her voice has an edge as if she wants it to cut me.

"I wouldn't know. I've never had a reason to ignore him."

"Yeah, well, y'all haven't dated." Cleo leans back on her palms and holds my gaze.

The shelves behind her are lined with trophies, sashes, and crowns. She's won Miss Berryville Teen four years in a row. She competes in pageants across the state and models for local boutiques. Her social media following outnumbers everyone in Ware County. If she wanted to prove herself, she did so years ago.

But the pageant never ends. She's in constant competition with the universe and everyone who loves her. If she isn't the best, she isn't winning, and if she isn't winning, she's no longer worthy. How exhausting it must be to live as though love is something to earn.

Daisy sits up with a start. Hair floats around her in a static halo. "Holler texted. He said, 'I'm not playing this game with you. You stared the—'"

"Started," Cleo autocorrects.

A blush pinkens Daisy's cheeks. She continues to read. "'I'm sick of your aptitude.'"

"Attitude."

"Enough," Daisy snaps. "I suck at reading, okay? I don't need you to remind me." With a bounce, she falls onto her side and curls into the fetal position.

She has dyslexia. Anywhere else, she'd do well in school, but Berryville High is outdated and underfunded. Students with learning disabilities receive extra time for tests, that's all.

Cleo must feel threatened by Daisy. She holds the reigning title of beauty queen, but she isn't Berryville's only it-girl. Daisy Ruger dominates the high school scene. She's cheer captain and dates star quarterback Holler Sloan—that is, if *dating* is the appropriate word. They've broken up so many times I've lost count. Their relationship follows a pattern: fight, break up, make up, with intermissions of Daisy rebounding with other football players.

"Did you catch anything?" Cleo asks me. "When you went fishing with JC and Stokes?"

"I didn't take a rod."

"You're such an outdoorsy girl. No wonder you and JC are close." Cleo stands and wanders to her vanity. "We both know he'll always be in some kind of love with you."

My jaw drops. "Cleo, we've talked about this."

"Y'all being related doesn't seem to bother him."

"It bothers me, okay? I don't think of JC like *that*, cross my heart."

My friendship with Cleo used to be sincere. I remember a time before she won her first Ultimate Grand Supreme, before Daisy sent pictures of herself to half of Berryville. I remember us, young and giggly, feeding catfish at the boat ramp while swallows performed in a sunset sky.

The birds spiraled and dipped, feasting on mosquitos, and we beheld them in wonder, locking our arms like pinkies in a promise.

We haven't broken it yet. After graduation, all bets are off. Cleo will go to the University of Georgia for nursing. Daisy will attend the local cosmetology school.

As months pass, we'll drift apart. Our relationship will become exclusive to Instagram likes and the occasional meme sent to our group chat. We'll collect new experiences and interests, shed our skins like reptiles until we are freshly printed versions of who we used to be. We won't recognize each other, nor will we care enough to reintroduce.

That'll be the end of us.

At this point, I think we're holding on to each other because some bridges deserve the respect of slowly burning. Some ties should be loosened only with gentle tugs.

Daisy glances up from her phone. "Did y'all know Godwin moved back?"

My stomach wrenches at the mention of his name.

"Yeah, he's working the family farm while Gus is in rehab," Cleo says.

"Have you talked to him, Susana?"

"A little. He and Papa help each other."

"Betty is gonna blow a gasket." Daisy lifts her legs and points her toes at the ceiling. "They broke up because he said he'd never move back here."

"Isn't your sister engaged?" I ask.

"Yeah, but she was heartbroken after Godwin. She didn't get out of bed for days."

"Karma got to him." Cleo folds her arms, bracing her weight against the vanity. "Some people are small town, and they can't do nothing about it."

"You don't think he'll leave again?"

"All I'm saying is everyone talks big about going places."

"I was surprised when Godwin left," Daisy says while scrolling through his Instagram profile. "He's a country boy through and through."

"Didn't he compete in the rodeo?" Cleo asks.

"Bull riding, yeah." Daisy clicks a photo and zooms in on Godwin's face. "He acted different his senior year. That should've been a clue. He has this look in his eyes, like he's watching his house burn, and he can't do anything to save it."

Cleo does a running jump onto her bed, tackling Daisy in a cacophony of squeaky springs. "You should *definitely* snap the football team." She laughs, Daisy laughs, and they motion for me to join their pile as if we're still kids oblivious to our incompatibility.

We honor tradition with movies and delivered pizza. I pretend not to feel out of place while Cleo and Daisy chat about boyfriends and prom and take turns painting each other's nails.

Once midnight rolls around, I zip myself into a sleeping bag.

The curse won't reach me here. I meditate on those words, chant them like a spell. I sink into warmth, slippery nylon, and the lingering scent of woodsmoke.

Godwin appears in my darkness. I will away the memory of him, but he glues himself to my thoughts. His eyes glimmer with the fiery grief Daisy mentioned.

A nail tucked between his teeth.

Cleo and Daisy tossing bread to catfish.

Quilts dangling from a clothesline. The buttery scent of peach cobbler.

"Susana, wake up. Please wake up."

Hands clamp onto my shoulders and shake.

"Wake up, Susana!"

My head jerks to the left. I blink as a sting widens across my right cheek.

Cleo and Daisy stand in front of me, wearing pajamas and terrified expressions. Daisy's car idles across the street. Its headlights illuminate the highway.

Jacksonville Highway.

The stretch of pastureland between the drive-in movie theater and Swamp Road.

Two miles from Cleo's home.

"You sleepwalked," Cleo pants. Tears stream her face. "I woke up, and you were gone. We drove for, like, thirty minutes. You could've died."

I clutch my mouth and wheeze, drawing the muggy night air through my nostrils. The dreams must only come when I enter the water.

An eighteen-wheeler zooms past. I lower to the asphalt, collapsing where gravel merges with grass. The swamp and the sleepwalking must be connected. Perhaps that's how Susan Minchew delayed her fate. By keeping herself from the water, she prevented the flashbacks, which in turn postponed her expiration date.

"Where were you going, Susana?" Daisy asks.

"Home." I can't run or hide. The curse will always find me. Unless . . .

CHAPTER 8
SUSANA PRATHER

JULY, PRESENT DAY

I must run far enough.

Hugging my backpack, I burst from the Shealys' house and make a beeline across the dew-soaked lawn. Cleo and Daisy shout at me to come back and eat breakfast. I don't want to explain what happened, so I unlock my car and slide behind the steering wheel.

An orange moth perches on the dashboard, flexing its wings.

The swamp will continue to grab at me unless I move beyond its reach. I need to leave town for a while, maybe visit Great-Aunt Leona near the coast. From there, even if I sleepwalk all night, I won't get to the Okefenokee by daybreak.

I toss my backpack onto the passenger seat and key the ignition. Flooring the accelerator, I speed down the street, heading toward county lines.

Leona won't mind an impromptu visit. Every Christmas, she talks about her spare bedroom, says I'm always welcome. I'll phone Nanny and Papa once I arrive.

They'll understand when I tell them I'm scared of the curse.

Shaking, I leave Berryville's city limits. Historic neighborhoods reel into pine forests and cotton fields. The green sign marking county lines appears in the distance.

I drive faster.

Until I find a remedy for the curse, I need to conserve my time. Escaping town is the right decision. Every mile between the swamp and me slows the clock—

My eyelids flutter.

I lift my head, squirming as pain shoots up my spine.

The car sits in a ditch, still and smoking.

"No, please." I unbuckle my seat belt and climb from the vehicle. At the sight of the Ware County sign, I crumble into a fit of sobs.

I passed out before I reached Brantley County.

The curse won't let me leave.

Dropping to my knees, I scream at the ground. Mama and Great-Aunt Susie fell asleep at the wheels of their cars. Mama nearly killed herself and me. Great-Aunt Susie crashed into a tree.

I think the women tried to leave Berryville.

And the curse said no.

CHAPTER 9

SUSANA PRATHER

JULY, PRESENT DAY

A bell chimes when I enter Floyd's Gas Mart.

JC stands at the register, organizing a bin of lures. His eyes light up like fireworks. "Well, I'll be—Susana Prather, what're you doing here? I figured you'd spend the day with Cleo."

"Would you do me a favor?" I hurry to the checkout counter, past a slushie machine and rack of plastic cowboy hats. Outside, Godwin's truck rolls to a stop next to a gas pump.

"Stokes and I knew you wouldn't last more than twelve hours with the girls," JC says with a laugh. "Let me guess. You bailed when Cleo offered to do your makeup."

"I need you to drive me to Woodbine."

"For any particular reason?"

"To visit my great-aunt Leona." I prop my elbows on the counter and gasp for breath. My body vibrates with adrenaline, but the rush doesn't ease the soreness from the accident.

"Are you having car trouble?" JC tips back the brim of his ball cap and peers out the window. He points at the Cadillac. "I can take a look at her if you want."

"Please, JC. I can't explain right now. I just need you to drive me."

He must detect the crack in my voice. His smile fades. "Yeah, okay. Whatever you need. I'll call Floyd and see if he can get someone to cover my shift."

"Thank you." I fight back tears.

If JC drives me across county lines, maybe I stand a chance.

He moves from behind the counter and pulls me into an embrace. His arms bind my shoulders, and his hands cup the back of my head, as if to guard me from the world.

I relax against his chest. Warmth leaps from his clothes onto me. For as long as I can remember, he's been my bonfire, where I go to escape my cold.

"Wait here." JC hurries to the back office. He glances at me with a familiar softness, then vanishes through a doorway. Perhaps I shouldn't take advantage.

We don't come out and say it, so neither of us addresses what we both know, what he tells me in subtle, overlookable ways.

JC returns a few minutes later. He flips the Open sign to Closed and signals for me to follow him outside. "We can go. Floyd said he'd cover my shift."

I leave the gas station, enveloped in heat so thick, walking feels like wading through water. JC locks the door and strides toward his truck.

Godwin waves. "Hey, I need my receipt!"

"Sorry. There's been an emergency," JC says, pocketing his keys.

"Anything I can do?" Godwin crosses the parking lot, passing my Cadillac and the ice machines. "Susana, what happened?"

"Nobody is dead or dying," I tell him.

He stops in his tracks. "Is this how it's gonna be?"

His expression adds the words *between us*.

"Yes." I grit my teeth as memories lift their heads from the black water of my mind. The conversation at the hog pen. That night Godwin dragged me to a bar. His hand on my thigh, the electricity beneath my skin. We're better off cutting ties.

Like him, I'm tired of having the same fights.

"All right, so be it." Godwin extends his arms in surrender.

With him watching, I slide into JC's truck and buckle my seat belt. Sweat rolls down my cheek, or maybe it's a tear. I swipe it with my finger.

"What's the address?" JC asks once he starts the engine.

"I'll direct you. For now, go east."

He leans forward and studies the dusty sky, its streaks of cirrus clouds. "As fun as playing Lewis and Clark sounds, how about we stick with *left* and *right*?"

"Right."

JC gears the truck into Drive and pulls onto Swamp Road. He drums his fingers on the steering wheel. "Can you give me a hint as to what all this is about?"

His shriveled gator claw dangles from his rearview mirror, swinging as we jounce over potholes. Its talons curl into a palm of obsidian scales.

"I don't want to lie to you," I whisper. "Would you trust me?"

JC reaches for my hand and laces our fingers. With a nod, he signals to the crossroad up ahead. "Just tell me what to do. Left or right?"

We near Brantley County eight minutes later. I bounce my heels to keep myself alert. Even if I fall asleep, the curse won't stop JC from driving me out of Berryville.

"Why don't we head south?" JC offers a weak smile. "I figured we'd go somewhere interesting the day we *finally* skipped town."

He means it as a joke, but it rings with truth.

Berryville has always felt like a cage to him. One of five kids, he grew up duct-taping his hand-me-down sneakers and rationing his breakfast cereal. Now he buys groceries for his family. He gives his parents two hundred dollars a month to help with rent.

I think he's spent the past decade waiting for a chance to drive—

JC's voice brings everything into focus. "Susana!" His fingers curl around my shoulder, his thumb pressing my collarbone. He shakes me hard, then harder.

I snap to attention and survey the landscape spooling past, the pines and farmland and antebellum homes. My heart drops when the Welcome to Berryville sign comes into view.

The dashboard's clock reads ten thirty.

I was asleep for over an hour.

"Why'd we turn back?" I whip to face JC. My body tenses, racked with panic and something more visceral than fear. I must get out of town. I'll jerk the wheel if need be.

"You wouldn't wake up," JC gasps. "I'm taking you to the hospital."

I revived the moment we crossed into Ware County.

"No, JC. I'm fine." I force a smile but immediately burst into tears. If I leave Berryville again, history will repeat itself. I'll fall asleep, and I won't wake up until I return.

There's no escape.

"What in the Sam Hill is going on?" JC yells.

"Take me back to Floyd's." I fish a crumpled napkin from a cupholder and dry my face. Without the option to run, I must find another way to keep myself from entering the swamp.

"Please tell me, Susana."

"I need you to forget this happened."

JC slams the brakes, halting next to First Baptist of Berryville. He pivots in his seat and looks at me. "I don't want to lose you." His nose reddens, and my chest aches.

Because of the words neither of us will say.

"I don't want to lose you either." I lean over the middle console and hug JC's neck. "Soon, you'll leave Berryville and move to who-knows-where, and you'll forget all about me because you'll have an incredible new life—"

"Bull crap, Susana." He rubs circles on my spine. His breaths slow, and his heart rate steadies. Maybe this moment will replace my scare in his mind, mask it with a nicer memory.

Our friendship changed when we were fifteen years old.

Hard-Shell Baptist hosted a youth sleepover. JC and Stokes insisted on coming with me and snickered as chaperones patrolled the sanctuary.

We sprawled near the pulpit, zipped into sleeping bags. Once Stokes fell asleep, JC wiggled close to me and rested his cheek on the edge of my pillow. He told me I was his best friend and said, "If soul mates exist, I think soul friends do too, like God reached into a bucket of whatever souls are made of, took a handful, and formed it into the two of us."

I laughed at him for being sentimental.

He waited until the chaperones bedded down, then swore me to secrecy. He leaned his mouth to my ear and whispered, "I have a crush on you. Don't worry. I'll get over it."

A smile blazed across my face. "Wait, you *like* me?" I rolled onto my side, and he groaned into the pillow. "Joseph Chaldran Owens—"

"It's nothing, okay?"

"You think I'm pretty?"

A huff escaped him as if the answer was obvious. "Some girls need everybody to notice their beauty. I ain't saying that's bad. I just find other girls more interesting. It's like going out into the wilderness, where trees and swamp don't care who sees them. The woods aren't beautiful for any reason other than they are." His gaze lingered on my lips. "Once you see her, you realize nothing else could ever be beautiful again."

That was the only time he talked about his feelings.

We understood our care for each other was best in friendship. Besides the fact we're distant cousins, I think we decided we're too alike, or maybe JC realized I didn't feel what he felt. No matter the reason, JC won't admit he's in love with me.

And I pretend not to notice.

He should focus on his relationship with Cleo. I know I've worsened the situation. We have something between us—it's undeniable—but something isn't always enough.

I believe everyone loves a person who they realize won't end up with them.

Squeezing JC tighter, I make a promise. "You won't lose me."

1854

Mrs. Yawn rushed from the cabin with blood on her hands.

"Obediah, you be looking skinny as a rail," she called to the rider guiding his mare toward the homestead. No matter the day or the night before, her manner became lucid whenever Obediah Owens came to call, as though his charm lured her mind from its cobwebbed corners and reminded her of the world's sunshine.

Suzanna placed a basket of string beans at her side. She perched on the porch steps, the wood in a constant damp state and slick with mildew. She reserved her emotions, for she knew an expression of joy would fuel Obediah's sentiments.

He took pride in her affection for him. Further encouragement would only stretch his ego, Suzanna thought. His head already seemed too large for his hat.

Obediah dismounted near the well and left his horse to graze. "I can't stay long."

Mrs. Yawn wiped the gore from a gutted rooster onto her apron. She'd done away with the animal minutes prior. "Have you got anything clean to eat with?" she asked Obediah.

"I washed my knife a couple days back."

"Ain't nothing on him been washed in a fortnight." Suzanna motioned to his filthy clothes. "I doubt he owns a bar of soap." Unable to avoid his gaze any longer, she locked eyes with him. A smile swept undammed across her face.

He kept parts of her soft despite life's desire for calluses.

Obediah removed his hat as though stepping foot in church. He sank to the porch steps, took a bean from Suzanna's basket, and fitted it between his teeth.

Mrs. Yawn wagged her bloodstained finger. "You better not run off on me, Obediah." She'd fix a plate of whatever nourishment she had on hand, likely bread and cured meat, and force Obediah to consume every crumb.

"No, ma'am. I wouldn't dare," Obediah said with a laugh. Once she disappeared inside, he turned his attention to Suzanna. "Is your mama well?"

Concern tainted his voice. It knifed through Suzanna. He loved her mother, perhaps more than his own. Mrs. Yawn had always nurtured him. After her eldest sons died, she beheld Obediah as her own kin. She believed he and Suzanna would one day wed.

The hope burned in Mrs. Yawn as it did in Obediah. They kept the faith regardless of Suzanna's protests, their conviction too bright to stifle. Obediah Owens would make a fine son-in-law, Mrs. Yawn swore. Suzanna agreed. He would. But they were too familiar, two bodies cut from one cloth. He was as much a part of her as she was of him.

Obediah gnawed his bean to a pulp while Suzanna cracked and strung. He watched her, perhaps to glean an answer from her movements.

"Mama don't get much rest," she muttered.

A somber expression tensed his face. He lolled against the top step, gliding his knuckles across Suzanna's wrist. "I ain't going nowhere, not for a while. If you need me—"

"I don't want you to stick around on my behalf." Suzanna fitted her hand with his, lacing fingers and holding tight. "Come back. That's all I ask."

"On my grave."

"Your grave's what got me worried."

"Now, that ain't gonna happen."

"Why not?"

"I'm too lucky." Obediah flashed a grin, one fueled by tall tales swapped around campfires. He thought himself invincible. After hearing stories about the larger-than-life swamper who roamed flat prairies and wrangled gators, he became the folklore.

"Your clover don't exactly run deep." Suzanna feared his recklessness would end in death. The Okefenokee was not a forgiving place, nor were its monsters.

"Got these here rabbit feet and a talisman a woman in Old Nine traded for a coon pelt." Obediah patted his belt, which housed various trinkets.

Growing up, he wasn't superstitious, but the swamp altered him. Whenever he returned from a hunt, he claimed to have encountered Muscogee spirits in the channels.

Suzanna assumed he'd forgotten his roots, or perhaps he chose to ignore them.

Obediah hadn't come from lavish circumstances. One of seven children, he matured poor and forgotten, dreaming of money the way Suzanna did of peace. His father and brothers made their livings from lumber. He chose the Okefenokee, believing it might provide a life beyond Kettle Creek. He still dreamed of money, talked about everything he wished to do and never did.

He wanted more. Suzanna couldn't fault him for that, but she sensed a curse on him, one set in motion by his father's cruel mouth and lack of food on his plate. Even now, years after he left home, he refused to share his past, asserting that men shouldn't talk about what pains them.

"I doubt rabbit feet will do you a lick of good." Suzanna resumed cracking and stringing. "I suppose I worry that my curse will rub off on you."

"You ain't cursed. Don't pay those Douglases any mind."

"Everything I love is taken from me."

Obediah pried the beans from Suzanna's hands. "You ain't cursed. I'll prove it to you. What is it you want, Suzanna? What do you dream about?"

"Food on my plate and a pillow under my head. I dare not want more."

"Try," Obediah said with a nod. "In the meantime, I'll dream for the both of us."

"Until you're taken from me too."

"Listen here." Obediah crouched in front of Suzanna and clutched her hand to his chest. "As God is my witness, it'll take more than death to pry me away from you."

Whether imposed by heaven, fate, or sheer force of will, Obediah would keep his promise to Suzanna. Lore claimed his life so intricately woven to hers, he refused to exist anywhere she was not present. History narrated a different story, but one thing remained the same.

No tale of either could be told without the other.

CHAPTER 10

SUSANA PRATHER

JULY, PRESENT DAY

I nail shut my bedroom window.

Then, I build a wall using my book collection and a trunk so heavy, I need felt sliders to push it. I stack the items, books on trunk, nightstand on books. The barricade rises to the ceiling and blocks the door. If I knock it down in sleep, the noise should wake me and everyone else in the house.

If my cursed body tries to disassemble it, the process should waste the night.

Research doesn't answer my questions. I memorize Papa's records and chart my family history. Susie Prather died in a car wreck three months after turning eighteen. Mama died five months after her birthday, when the swamp didn't give her back.

I must have anywhere between four months and a couple of years, depending on if I can keep myself out of the water. What matters now is time. Before I can focus on breaking the curse, I need to delay my expiration date.

My wall remains intact. I wake up dry as a bone.

A week passes without dreams, then another. July eases into August, and I settle into a normal rhythm. Each morning I deconstruct the barrier. I help Papa with the cotton harvest. I sell cucumbers at the farmers' market.

Peace is an hourglass dripping toward empty.

By trapping myself inside at night, I postpone the inevitable, but I don't get much sleep. My thoughts race from the curse to Suzanna Yawn to the what-ifs.

The Okefenokee creeps nearer as though vexed by my plan. I find real dandelions sprouting from my bedroom's floorboards. I peel real briars off the windowsill.

One day I awake to the whoosh of fluttering wings.

Moths blanket the ceiling, vibrating as they dust the plaster with their rust-colored scales. I kill them with a book and scrub their residue. I do everything in my power to bat away the swamp's fingers. It won't take me—I won't let it.

Fatigue comes with a vengeance, and no amount of rest or melatonin pacifies it. I think exhaustion might be a greater threat. It purples the circles around my eyes and dulls my senses.

I can't read without dozing off.

Although my dreams stop with the sleepwalking, I have peculiar nightmares, their contents sensory and jumbled. Skin against weeds, supple and milky white. A kiss in the dark as limbs tangle like vines. Ashes to ashes. Dust to dust.

I discover moonflowers blooming from an air vent, saturating my bedroom with a dark floral scent. Whatever happens in my head must be linked to reality, or vice versa.

Or maybe I'm losing my mind altogether.

Papa takes me to the fishing hole near Shiloh Cemetery. We net minnows to use as bait, then cast our lines at cypress knees. The normality grounds me, as does Papa's gentle conversation. He talks about tractors and what he read in the newspaper.

He mentions the swamp's black water, how it's filled with monsters.

Folks live around the Okefenokee and maraud its resources. Nobody swims in the channels. They fear the reptiles that lurk within shallows.

I suppose the swamp is a metaphor for the past. We all live in proximity to our histories, but many of us choose not to wade too deep, afraid of what might bite.

Everyone has monsters that go unseen.

Another week passes. I repaint the porch's lattice, coating it with fresh white. Nanny works alongside me. She repots her lantana while Papa rocks in his rocker, nursing a sweet tea.

"You should've gotten a look at it, Agnes," Papa says, tousling his silver hair. "Godwin has the fattest hog I ever did see."

"Quit being ugly." Nanny wipes her palms on her skirt. She never wears pants, not even when she gardens. It's a quirk on par with her laundry habits.

She washes clothes twice a month, but she rinses her pantyhose and underwear in the sink each night. Her bathroom is decorated with knee-highs on shower rods.

"That's a compliment, I'm telling you. Creature's a hoot and a half," Papa says.

JC's truck rolls down the driveway. I perk at the sight of it and drop my brush into a paint can. I haven't spoken to JC since the county border incident.

He parks next to the carport, waving as he climbs from his vehicle.

My stomach does cartwheels. I abandon the porch and sprint across the front yard. If he talks with my grandparents, he might bring up the sleep scare.

I block his path. "JC, what are you doing here?"

He stares at me for a moment, his silence inhabited by the hiss of cicadas. "I've been thinking about what happened a couple weeks ago."

"Nothing happened." I still can't bring myself to explain the curse.

"Don't gaslight me!" JC shouts. He must sense my confusion because he sighs and shakes his head. "I read an article online."

"Look, I'm sorry for dragging you into my drama. It was unfair of me."

"Why the secrecy? We used to tell each other stuff." JC grabs my shoulders and looks me dead in the eyes. "You can trust me, Susana."

"I'm not your girlfriend."

"No, you're not. You're my best friend," JC scoffs, grinding his teeth. He steps back and pockets his hands. "Is this about the curse?"

Something like guilt chews through me. I squint as sunlight pours between the pecan trees, golden for the late hour. "I'm scared of it, JC."

The world is most alive in its dying light.

"You're not your mama," he says.

I cross our divide and give him a brief hug. "I do trust you."

Just not enough to tell him about my impending fate. He doesn't need another worry. Besides, how could I burden him with the truth?

Years ago, we went hunting for spook lights. JC took me to Shiloh Cemetery, to a mausoleum stained green with moss. He pried apart its iron gates and shone a flashlight inside.

Near an empty crevice, scraped into stone, were claw marks.

As if someone had been trapped within the crypt and tried to escape.

I'll never forget what JC told me. His words repeat in my thoughts, a reminder that no matter how long I avoid the curse, my wall can't hold it forever.

JC leaned to my ear and whispered, *"Some dead things don't like to be buried."*

1854

Suzanna carried a feed sack to Ruger's barn.

Traversing a grove of oak trees, she neared the log outbuilding. Hens milled about in the entrance, scratching the hoof-trodden dirt for provision. Suzanna shooed them from her path and hastened to a trough. She emptied the grain into the manger, her senses overwhelmed with the sweet musk of hay and animal hides. A loving scent, Suzanna thought.

She'd always felt most nurtured around nonhuman creatures.

Wandering farther into the barn, Suzanna came upon a group of men—five by her count—tarrying between stalls. Willard Ruger was among them, propped against a stall door.

"Pardon my intrusion," Suzanna said.

"Nonsense. We're merely having ourselves a repose." Ruger signaled to a man seated upon a wooden crate. "August, you've met Miz Yawn, have you not?"

Sunshine poured through the barn's entrance, illuminating the man in a burst of gold. He turned his head, and his face was light, a remarkable display of sunburn and blue eyes.

At the sight of him, Suzanna drew a sharp breath.

"We've met." She maintained a cool disposition, for she believed her reaction to him, foolish as it was, did not merit attention, not even from herself.

August had not called on her, nor had he proven himself worthy of her trust. Following their abrupt introduction, he'd vanished into the ether. Suzanna had not beheld him since.

"You'd do well to learn from her," Ruger told August. "Farmers don't come any better."

"I follow orders is all." Suzanna warmed at the sentiment, burning when August smiled and bowed his head. She liked the arrangement of his teeth. A trivial detail to notice, perhaps.

She appreciated the slope of his nose and his dimpled cheeks.

He reminded her of a gelding, his demeanor mild, with undeniable humility. He appeared at peace with his environment, optimistic even, as though the world had not yet broken his spirit. Of course, Suzanna could only assume his character.

"Good day." Suzanna turned on her heels and departed the barn.

"Miss Yawn . . ." August chased after her. "I owe you an apology."

"You don't owe me nothing."

"I meant to call on you."

Suzanna paused midstride. She confronted August, her heart racing unbridled. "By no means did you inconvenience me. Obediah ate enough biscuits for the both of you."

August removed his felt hat. "Will you allow me to redeem myself?"

"If a man wants something, he doesn't neglect an opportunity to get it," Suzanna said with a shrug. "He doesn't require a second chance."

"Then I'll await the next opportunity." August returned the hat to his scalp and tipped its wide brim. "I won't make the same mistake."

"For biscuits?"

"I like biscuits," he said. "I also like pretty girls."

If people could bloom, Suzanna would've done so in that moment. She fought a smile, but it appeared victoriously. How vain to feel elation from a compliment, she thought, but kind words were few and far between. And *pretty*? The word hardly belonged in her vocabulary.

Suzanna hurried to the road, blushing when August bade her farewell.

Obediah had encouraged her to want.

And so, she did.

CHAPTER 11
SUSANA PRATHER

Nanny herds Missouri and me through Strickland's Department Store.

The shop hasn't changed in decades. Speakers older than my car broadcast fizzy music from the local radio station. AC blasts air so cold the tip of my nose goes numb.

I doubt anyone would patron this place if it wasn't the only clothing store in town, besides a Tractor Supply and a boutique that caters to sizes zero to four. I wouldn't shop here if Missouri hadn't convinced Nanny to buy me new school clothes. Not thrift-store new. Real new. Clothes without mystery stains and pleats that went out of style in 1989.

"What about this?" Missouri holds a pair of cutoff shorts against my body.

"And have people think Susana is white trash?" Nanny scoffs. "Why don't you give her beer and cigarettes while you're at it?"

Missouri clenches her jaw. "I own a pair of these shorts."

"Yes, well, I meant what I said." Nanny pulls me to a rack of cardigans and arranges her selections on my arms. The hangers cut into my skin.

Last time Nanny and Missouri went shopping, I gave them my measurements and stayed home to help Papa pressure wash the front porch. Unfortunately for me, Papa woke up this morning with a cold. We left him slumped over a pot of boiling water. Every fifteen minutes, he deserted his makeshift humidifier and stuck his face in the freezer.

Right now, he's probably watching *Bonanza* reruns and eating vegetable soup with riblies, a term Nanny coined for her pea-sized dumplings.

"We gotta figure out your style," Missouri tells me. She holds up a floral-print dress with puffed sleeves. "How do you feel about this one?"

I feign interest and say I like it. This is good for me. Being here with Nanny and Missouri is good. I need a day in town, away from the farm and what happened last night.

I sleepwalked again.

Same as before, I woke up drenched with swamp water. My barricade was intact, but the window was raised. Mud and cypress leaves webbed its lace curtains.

The nails I'd hammered into the pane were strewn across the floor.

Vines dangled over the windowsill, reaching from outside. During the night, the greenery veined into my bedroom as if to liberate me.

Barricades won't stop the curse. I'm not sure anything will. If the other women in my bloodline couldn't break the cycle, what makes me think I'll be able to do so?

Perhaps I should give up and enjoy the time I have left.

"What about a denim jacket?" Missouri asks.

"Mama had one of those."

My nose prickles with the sour musk of mothballs and mildewed carpet. Almost everyone in Berryville carries the stench, what Stokes refers to as the old-folk stink. It won't wash out of clothes. I've tried lemon juice, white vinegar, and baking soda.

Holler waves from the men's department. He stands frozen while his mama flits around him. She drapes his shoulders with coats and shirts, maybe to outfit him for his signing day.

Recruiters came from around the country to scout him.

It wasn't a surprise the star quarterback of Berryville High landed a football scholarship. Everyone thinks he's destined for the NFL. Even Dairy Queen has his photo on their bulletin board with the headline Proud to serve Bufford Holler Sloan.

He'll play for the University of Georgia next fall.

I wave back and make a face as Nanny examines a dress the color of Pepto-Bismol. Holler grins, flashing perfect teeth framed by dark skin. He's what Missouri calls "hometown hot." That's when there's a small pool of boys, and the girls collectively curve the grade.

Around here, Holler is a perfect score.

Nanny and Missouri argue over which clothes to buy me. After an hour or so, they decide on a pair of jeans, two skirts, and a handful of blouses. We check out, then walk toward Shealy Pharmacy, where Nanny parked the car.

"Lord love you," Missouri whispers into my ear as Nanny rambles about school supplies and how in her day a teacher needed only a chalkboard, not laptops and fancy books.

I pat Missouri's shoulder and offer a smile.

We pass the hardware store. I pause to pet the Labrador—Mr. Frick's dog—waiting out front. Missouri and Nanny stride ahead, bickering about where to eat for supper.

A poster decorates the store window with information about this year's Berryville Family Reunion. The event has taken place every November since the 1950s. It includes a parade downtown and festivities at the fairground, everything from a pageant to carnival rides.

I've seen the parade so many times I've memorized its order.

Holler Sloan will ride on a float while Berryville High's marching band performs, and Freemasons will zoom around on their go-carts. Mayor Jackson will cruise down Main Street, chucking butterscotch candies from the back seat of his vintage Mercedes.

Godwin emerges from the hardware store with a paint can and bag of fertilizer. Toothpick jutting from the corner of his mouth, he goes to his old Chevy and places the items on the truck bed. He wears his baseball cap backward, its color matching his burnt skin.

"I'll be over your way tomorrow." Godwin turns, and I realize he's talking to me. "Seeing as your grandpa is under the weather."

"A cold won't keep Papa from work."

"He asked if I'd help around the farm, said he'd lend me his tractor."

"You have a tractor."

"Not like your grandpa's." Godwin smiles, gnawing his toothpick. He opens the truck's side door and tosses a half-drunk Gatorade onto the bench seat. "Means less chores for you."

"I like chores."

"Well, then, I'll think of something for you to do."

"Pass." I give the Labrador's head a final stroke, then make after Nanny and Missouri.

"You dropped something," Godwin yells.

"What?" I spin around.

Godwin leans against the hood of his truck and grins. "Your smile."

I continue walking.

"Hey, lighten up." He chases after me and blocks my path. Like he did when we were kids, he wears dirty Nikes and his bootcut jeans rolled.

His resemblance to the first August Godwin is uncanny.

"That emergency a few weeks ago—did everything work out?" Godwin asks.

"What are you doing right now?"

"Being neighborly, I guess."

"Let's not pretend, Godwin."

He reaches for my arm but hesitates. His palm hovers above my skin, his wrists layered with handmade bracelets, maybe souvenirs from girls he's dated. "Look, I'm not sorry for what I said at the hog pen. I'm sorry it made you sore, but you *should* leave town. You should know how it feels to start over, to be a stranger somewhere."

"Susana!" Nanny waves from Shealy Pharmacy.

"Come on"—Godwin follows me down the sidewalk—"you can't tell me you've never thought about, I don't know, seeing the Grand Canyon or El Capitan."

"Plenty of rocks here."

"Stretch yourself a little. Everything you see, everything you do makes your world bigger, makes *you* bigger. Small towns aren't just small because of their size."

"What gives you the right to decide what's best for me?" I shout. "Admit it. You look at me and see yourself from a year ago, a kid from some Podunk town. You think if you save me from this place, it'll compensate for the fact you came back."

He grinds his teeth. "Tell your grandpa I'll drive over around seven o'clock."

With that, he turns and moves toward his truck.

"You don't get it, do you?" I ask his back. "Just because someone isn't like you doesn't mean they're wrong. My world is plenty big, and I don't need you to approve of it."

He slides behind the wheel and keys the ignition. Nirvana blasts from the stereo.

Papa once told me we judge from our own empty places; criticism says more about us than it does others. If that's true, Godwin doesn't only have empty places, he's a drained vat.

I storm to the driver's-side window. "And for the record, you said you didn't want to spend time with me. You made the choice. I expect you to hold to it."

"No, I said I didn't want to hang around someone who believes they're cursed."

"This is who I am!"

"Dagnabbit, Susana. Don't you remember anything?" Godwin looks at me as if I forgot our history. He nods, his cheeks mantling with emotion. "I know you."

"That was a long time ago." I swallow the lump in my throat. Whatever simmered between Godwin and me doesn't matter. It *can't* matter.

My chest aching, I back away from the truck. "I'm tired of fighting too."

"Sure, walk away. That's what you do best."

"At least I don't run."

"You can't stand the thought of anyone getting close to you," he scoffs.

"That's not true."

"Fine, it's me." Godwin shrugs and props his elbow on the windowsill. His face doesn't wear anger, only pain. "You've never wanted *me* to get close."

"We're too different," I say even though I'm not sure it's true.

"Keep telling yourself that." Godwin leans out the window. "I'm not an idiot, Susana. I know you pushed me away because of that darn curse."

"We were kids, Godwin."

"I'm talking about last year." His expression rewinds the clock to a bygone June.

"You were dating Betty." I won't let my thoughts wade into the memories. All that matters is Godwin claimed to love his girlfriend.

His love was muddy water masquerading as sweet tea.

I cross my arms. "We're not friends."

"One less goodbye, then." Godwin tips his ball cap's brim. The gesture floods me with the feeling of déjà vu.

Suzanna Yawn married Obediah Owens, but she had a connection with the first August Godwin. My dreams made a point of showing her and August's interactions, either to highlight their importance or to prove irony. Maybe this is history repeating itself.

I prefer August Godwin over his namesake.

Without another word, Godwin reverses onto Depot Street.

Soot puffs from the muffler as he drives away.

Baggage is called baggage for a reason. If a person doesn't unpack and deal with their problems, they'll carry the problems from place to place. And if they can't find happiness where they are, how can they expect to find it where they go next?

Godwin fled Berryville a year ago. He left behind the farm, his daddy's addiction, and sought a better life elsewhere. He must've forgotten . . .

Hometowns are like the dead. Part on bad terms, and they'll always haunt you.

1854

Soldiers clad in navy passed through Kettle Creek on the first of September.

The men rode across Ruger's property around noon, en route to Florida. A response to the Seminole conflict, Mr. Yawn reported. He often scavenged for newspapers when he ventured to Old Nine.

The military's presence, although brief, sparked unease within the community. Suzanna kept her rifle loaded and busied herself to distract from worry. She labored in the fields alongside her father and only surviving brother as the summer harvest neared completion.

On the final day of picking, shouts drifted across the farmstead. Suzanna recognized the voices. She dropped her basket and surveyed the land.

Sure enough, boys gathered near the barn, cheering up a storm.

The Douglases hadn't come to start trouble. Suzanna knew who to blame for the ruckus and who she'd find throwing punches for sport.

She untethered the rifle from her back and marched to the barn.

Her brother, John, fled a hay bale, sprinting in the opposite direction. His felt hat whipped from his head. He didn't risk turning back for it.

Suzanna went to a corral where men surrounded a tangle of sweaty limbs. They hollered and wagered as competitors tussled across the enclosure.

Willard Ruger had broken up the matches so many times he'd ceased trying.

The fighters grappled, their brawl fogging the air with dust. One tackled the other and pulled him into a headlock.

Applause erupted from the crowd. Bets exchanged hands.

Suzanna fired a shot at the clouds. Everyone ducked and went silent, one of the Burrell boys so intoxicated he fell over, spilling what appeared to be moonshine.

"Obediah, you fool!" Suzanna hiked her skirt and scaled the corral's fence. She elbowed a path to the competitors and clamped her palm onto a bare shoulder. Her heart skipped. The shoulder did not belong to Obediah. Its skin was alabaster, its muscles hewn into ribbed edges.

August Godwin turned his head.

Suzanna withdrew her fingers, but the feeling of him lingered.

Released from a choke hold, Obediah rose to his feet and smeared dirt, now a paste, from his abdomen. He considered wrestling a pastime, a lucrative one at that. Whenever he visited Kettle Creek, he fought opponents for a portion of the wagers. Menfolk wanted to see if they could defeat the fabled swamper, and if not conquer him, then make coin from his triumphs.

"I better not catch you back here," Suzanna yelled.

"We ain't doing any harm, are we?" Obediah snatched his shirt from the ground and wiggled it over his head.

"Unless you intend to work, I suggest you make yourselves scarce." Suzanna waved the barrel of her rifle. "I won't be having you set a poor example for my brother."

August stood, uncurling into a chiseled pillar. Suzanna let her gaze roam his torso, the sunlines across his biceps from rolled sleeves.

"Why do you bother yourself with the likes of us?" he asked. The question posed others. It peered into Suzanna, at her days spent tending Ruger's fields.

She lowered the rifle. "My daddy says I ain't so good at being a girl."

August rubbed his mouth, perhaps to hide a smile. It appeared just the same, dimpling his cheeks and wrinkling the corners of his eyes. "Ma'am, I don't believe that one bit. I reckon you're more woman than this town has ever seen."

Warmth rushed to Suzanna's cheeks.

Her feelings were soft and lacy, and she'd only known herself as coarse.

Farmhands chuckling, Suzanna stepped toward August, so near to him, sweat from his hair dripped onto her skirt. "Sweet talker, huh?"

"No, ma'am." His voice reminded her of melted butter.

"Take your roughhousing elsewhere," she told Obediah. Her

skin tingled from August's proximity. The sensation came as a shock, for her emotions had seemed plaited and pinned like her tresses, as stiff and starchy as her petticoats.

Obediah retrieved clothes from a fencepost and shoved them against August's chest. He breezed past Suzanna, his audience following in an exodus from the corral.

August whistled. "Well, I'll be darned. You got these boys under a spell or something?"

"You best go and wash up." Suzanna turned to leave.

"Miss Yawn, I ain't one for superstition," he called, "but if magic exists in this world, I'm convinced she looks like you."

CHAPTER 12

SUSANA PRATHER

AUGUST, PRESENT DAY

Sleep has a particular smell.

Like that of Strickland's Department Store, both sweet and stale, reminiscent of rotted figs or pond water green with algae. It is the smell of skin and spit and sweat. It is a pillow drawn from its case and exposed naked to the light, with brown stains ringing across its fabric.

My sleep reeks of earth. I manage to wake without its metallic perfume by resealing my window. I hammer three-inch nails into the pane, then build a wall over my door. At this point I'm unsure whether my efforts are meant to keep me inside or to keep things out.

Vines branch into a curtain over my window.

I oversleep because their leaves block the sun.

Before anyone notices, I hack their tendrils with a machete. I cut them to the ground. There, hopping and slithering in the grass, are dozens of toads and snakes.

CAROLINE GEORGE

They creep from the swamp in an organized horde.

Nails and barricades don't prevent my sleepwalking for more than a couple of nights. I can drag my feet all I like, but I'm still headed toward my end. I feel it beneath my muscles and bones, festering as my exhaustion grows. An instability, something wild and unhinged. It sinks its roots deeper. It appears on my face as blue veins and a sallow complexion.

No matter how much I research, the question of what to do next remains unanswered. I dissect Suzanna's curse and rearrange its words.

Until you see the truth of what you are.

I study my family tree and write an analysis of each firstborn daughter.

Until they say otherwise.

I mutter over and over that I'm not cursed.

With my blood I make what only my bones can break.

Careful not to set off the smoke detector, I burn herbs in the center of my room. I line the baseboards with salt, whisper prayers, and hang a wooden cross over my bed.

I go about my days as if the curse isn't slowly eating me alive.

Godwin comes around. He works the fields and does odd jobs even after Papa recovers. They fix the irrigation pump. They load hogs into a trailer and drive them to the butcher.

Nanny wants to expand the vegetable garden, so Godwin accepts the task of clearing land in exchange for Papa replacing his AC unit. Day after day, Godwin chops and burns.

His woodsmoke fogs the house.

I avoid him, or at least I try, by delivering produce to the Green Frog. Whenever I return from errands, he stands in the yard, shirtless, dressed in brown overalls and boots.

He digs up stumps with a hoe. "I could use some help if you're done piddlin' around."

"Eat dirt." I hurry past him. A ball of mud explodes across my

126

back. I arch my spine as the soil oozes down my neck, between my shoulder blades.

"You first, darlin'," Godwin says with a laugh.

I can't say I hate him. What I feel is more like repulsion, as if we're forces so opposed, we cannot exist together. Even his nearness destabilizes me.

I find Godwin in the carport a couple of days later. He crouches next to the riding lawn mower, tinkering with its control panel.

"What're you doing?" I ask him.

He fits a jumper wire to the ignition switch. "Hot-wiring the mower," he says without glancing from his work. "Your grandpa couldn't find the key."

"That's the most redneck thing I've ever heard."

"Girl, I used to race these things." Godwin hops into the seat and presses the tip of his test light against the ignition switch. The engine rumbles awake. "Yee-haw!" Shifting the throttle, he steers the mower onto the front lawn and cuts lines through the grass.

Midday washes the landscape with a dusty gold hue. Insects sibilate every which way, a crescendo in the slobbering heat. I wander to a lumber pile and pry an axe from a stump.

An antlion writhes in the burrow at my feet, snatching a bug with its pincers.

I place a log face up on the chopping block and raise the axe over my head. With a strike, I split the wood in half. Godwin doesn't watch. He whips around the yard like a race car driver.

Pain shoots through my foot.

I yelp and collapse onto my backside, examining my left sneaker. The point of a nail protrudes from the vamp. Blood soaks the fabric, blooming from a red dot into a puddle.

The lawn mower goes silent. Boots crunch gravel.

Godwin drops to the ground beside me and reaches for my foot.

"Don't touch it," I beg through clenched teeth. "Nanny! Papa!"

Godwin runs his thumbs from my ankle to toes, perhaps to confirm the nail didn't pierce bone. He shimmies a rag from his pocket and forces it between my teeth. "Bite this."

Without hesitation, he tears the nail from my foot.

I scream as pain sears up my leg.

"You have a tetanus shot, don't you?" Godwin peels off my bloody shoe and inspects the puncture. His calluses grate against my skin.

I spit out the rag. Its taste lingers, a tonic of salt and soot. "You couldn't be gentle?"

"When the pain comes, sugar don't make it better. Sometimes you just need a rope to bite onto and somebody to hold your hand." Godwin recites the words like a proverb. He tucks the nail into his overalls and meets my gaze, his expression all steel.

"You didn't hold my hand," I say.

"Want me to?" Godwin fights a smile. He offers his hand, swearing when I lick my index finger and wipe it across his palm. "Oh, real nice."

Days finish with lightning bugs and box fans and begin with cutting vines and shooing alligators from the backyard. The Okefenokee draws closer each night. I try to ignore it.

As Godwin chops wood into blocks, I hobble onto the front porch and lean against a column. "Nanny, did Papa install a fire hydrant out front?" I raise my arm to block the sun. "Never mind. It's just Godwin."

"Very funny." He splits a log. His shoulders are the color of raw meat. "It's genetic."

"You hear of sunscreen before? What about aloe vera?"

He lowers the axe and pivots toward me. "SPF fifty, baby." He gestures to his chiseled body, his burnt skin glossed with sweat.

"You should get your money back."

Godwin swings the axe. His muscles flex. His cheeks swell with a breath. "It's five dollars," he tells me once lumber sloughs off the chopping block.

"For sunscreen?"

"The show."

"I'd rather watch cotton grow." My face burning, I launch off the column.

Barney Fife, the stray cat, bounds from beneath the fig tree and makes a beeline to Godwin. The animal rubs itself against Godwin's calves, flicking its bushy tail.

Godwin pets the cat with tentative strokes. He flashes a silly grin, beaming in such a way I can't help but smile too. "This's one cool cat."

"You like Barney?"

He scoops the creature into his arms, cradling it against his chest. "I'm usually scared of cats. This one is cool, though. I've watched him play with the neighbor's hound dogs."

A pang of melancholy shoots through me as I watch Godwin tote the animal. For a moment, he looks younger, like the person I knew all those years ago. His eyes shimmer, and part of me—a massive part—wishes they still lit up whenever he glanced my way.

The Green Frog places an order for baked goods and casseroles, so I stay indoors and make biscuits while Nanny frets over whether to send Godwin for extra mayonnaise.

Olan Mills photos smile on the fridge as Nanny and I labor over Pyrex and dough.

Ever since Missouri Jane found what she called "the face of Jesus," a design in the floor tiles, Nanny has tiptoed around the kitchen, careful not to step on the likeness.

Papa returns from lunch. He and his picking group meet twice a month at the café in the basement of Berryville Antique Mall. They play their instruments in exchange for meals.

Music and the work of our hands. That's what defines us, Papa believes.

"Lunch must've been nice," Nanny says when he pecks her cheek. She dusts crumbs from his flannel and scratches a globby stain, jalapeño raspberry jam if I had to guess.

"Ordered that pimento cheese sandwich." Papa chuckles and pats his belly.

Nanny motions to his clothes. "I was looking at your shirt to see if you brought some home with you."

"Why, you hungry?" Papa kisses my forehead, his breath stinking of cheddar. He goes to the hall closet and fetches his tackle box.

"What're you fishing for?" I ask.

Papa shrugs and gives me a wink. "Whatever is stupid enough to bite my hook."

I place a bowl in the sink and turn on the faucet. As I wash my hands, Godwin walks past the kitchen window, dragging a tarp piled with brush.

"Why is he still here?" I ask Papa.

"He's family."

"No, he ain't."

"Susana, mind your grammar." Nanny gives me a disapproving look, then resumes mixing a base of whipped cream, crushed pineapple, and pistachio pudding. She'll take the Watergate salad, known around here as Green Stuff, to Hard-Shell's luncheon.

According to her, a woman isn't truly Southern if she isn't on a church food committee.

Papa nods at the window. "That boy out there—his grandpa worked this land with me, so did his pa. We may not share blood, but we got the same kind of bones holding us together."

"You don't need Godwin's help. You have me."

"This ain't about work, Susana," Papa says with a sigh. "I promised Gus I'd look after his boy. Godwin needs people. All folks do. Nobody should have nobody."

"Take him to breakfast or something. Don't make him clean up our yard." I brace my weight against the kitchen counter. If Nanny and Papa knew what happened—or *almost* happened—a year ago, they wouldn't force me to spend time with Godwin.

He scares me, I think. Or maybe I'm afraid of the propensities I inherited from Mama. Being around him makes the curse feel more alive inside me.

"My mind's made up," Papa says. "Godwin is family. He has our bones."

What Papa calls bones, others would call spirit or grit. We are built from the same material, and that makes us kinfolk. To Papa, the word carries a definition far broader than one in a dictionary. Kin is the history between us. Kin is our sore backs and the dirt beneath our fingernails. Kin is the land we dwell upon. And with that word comes loyalty.

Godwin has a place with us whether I like it or not.

The next day, Godwin and I extend the garden with rows of beans and leafy greens. We kneel and bury seeds. Earthworms wiggle in the cool dirt. I gather them for JC to use as bait.

"Nanny says if you get a bump on your tongue, you told a lie," I say when Godwin sits on his calves and scratches his tongue.

"Susana Prather, you take my breath away." He plunges a spade into the soil and motions to his mouth. "Guess I'll get another, huh?"

I wince from his sharpness.

My chest aching, I place a pinch of ground in my mouth. Its flavor is like the smell of petrichor. Geosmin, the taste of healthy earth.

"You put dirt in your mouth," Godwin says.

"It's how I test the soil. Papa taught me." I lock eyes with him. The annoyance in his gaze morphs into something else. "What?"

"Nothing. I just don't know any girls who stick their tongues in dirt." He motions to my row and seed packets. "Space the collards farther apart."

"Three inches is fine."

"Yeah, well, once the seedlings grow, you'll have to give them more room." Godwin watches me sprinkle the seeds close together. He must sense my defiance.

Rising to his feet, he yanks off his ball cap and slams it on the ground. "You know what your problem is? You can't stand people telling you what to do."

"I can't stand *you* telling me what to do."

"Why? What have I ever done to you, Susana?" he shouts, waving his arms. "I told you to go live your life. Big whoop."

"No, you told me to go live your version of living." I scramble from the earth, brushing rocks and leaves from my knees.

"Fine, you don't agree with me. You wanna work this dirt until you're buried in it. I don't care what you do," Godwin yells. His chest rises and falls beneath a ratty T-shirt cut to shreds. "I've seen what's out there is all."

A barred owl hoots from somewhere in the Okefenokee.

Godwin curses and shakes his head at the sky. "When I was in elementary school, I went on a field trip to the zoo. I remember the tigers, how they paced their cage. They weren't aggressive, just restless, like they needed to step outside for some air. That's how I feel, like I can't breathe this air anymore, and if I don't find a way out, God knows what'll happen."

"Is that why you left Berryville?"

He wipes his nose. "I need some water."

"Godwin . . ." I stop him. "I want to know."

"What, so you can psychoanalyze me?" he shouts. "I'm not a good person, Susana, and I can't be different. Me coming back to this god-forsaken town is proof. I can't change. I can't get out. I'm stuck this way, and nobody can do a darn thing about it."

"Did you mean it?" I can't believe I'm asking the question. "What you said last year?"

He shrugs. "Did you?"

We spoke our minds that night, after he took me to a dive on the outskirts of town. I liked the smell of the smoke and how his lingered in my hair from the cigarette he begged off some guy at the bar. I didn't want to wash him off.

Until he said what he said.

Godwin retrieves his ball cap and looks at me with an apology in his blues. "We bring out the worst in each other, don't we?"

Our fight protected me from repeating Mama's mistakes. It proved Godwin and I were headed in opposite directions. We still are.

"I hope you find your way out," I tell him.

"And I hope you get whatever it is you want." Godwin turns and moves toward the house. By the time I walk to the front yard, his truck no longer sits in the driveway.

If the curse didn't exist, I think I'd farm this land, raise a family on it. I would grow old in some old house with a man who loves me. Perhaps I'd go see what made Godwin so desperate for more. Whatever it was, it must've been a wonderful sight.

Everything I have right now, I'd like to keep. Maybe that's what I want—not *more*, just more of the same. I'm still not sure. I haven't thought much about the future.

Doing so has seemed like wishful thinking.

Missouri brings Charlie over for supper. We eat corn on the cob and Boston butt, then linger in the backyard while Papa churns strawberry ice cream.

"Susan had a poster of Chad Michael Murray in the closet," Missouri says with a laugh. She and I swing in the hammock as bullfrogs perform in the wire grass. "Daddy took us to Blockbuster on Fridays. Susan bought the poster and snuck it home without Mama knowing. We giggled about it, felt like we had a boy hiding in the closet."

I rest my temple against her shoulder. "Y'all were close, weren't you?"

"For a while."

"Do you know if Mama sleepwalked?"

Missouri nods and points her toes at the swamp. "Not long after you were born, I saw her sleepwalk outside and had to chase her down."

"She must've been eighteen."

"A lot happened that year." Missouri shoots me a nervous glance. "Why do you ask?"

"Nanny said Mama had trouble sleeping."

"Susana, if you've been sleepwalking—"

"Don't worry about me."

"But I do," Missouri says, her voice cracking. "I should've helped Susan get medical care. Because of her insomnia, she hallucinated and fell asleep at weird times—"

"None of that was your fault."

"After Susan wrecked her car, she worried she'd hurt you." Missouri squeezes my hand. "I should've done more to help her. Maybe if I had, she wouldn't be gone."

"You were seventeen."

"I didn't try hard enough. That's the biggest regret of my life." Missouri wipes her eyes. She gazes at the treetops, the Milky Way visible beyond moss-draped branches. "Your mama deserved better than what this town gave her."

"What do you mean?"

"I shouldn't have said that."

"You don't need to protect me anymore." I finger the name tag pinned to her uniform. "Our family keeps so many secrets. Nanny and Papa rarely talk about Mama—"

"They like to pretend nothing bad happens to us," Missouri scoffs.

I nestle against her as the Okefenokee performs its nighttime symphony, the lullaby accompanied by Papa's banjo and the rumble of the ice cream churn. "Please tell me."

"Susan didn't fit in with kids her own age. She was an introvert, spent more time with horses than people," Missouri says. "I must've been sixteen when I caught her sneaking out to go to a party. Everything changed after that."

"Changed how?"

"Susan acted different, stopped talking to me." Missouri sighs against my hairline. "She became pregnant within the year. People weren't nice about it."

"Do you have any idea who my father might be?" I've asked Nanny and Papa countless times, but they refuse to give an answer.

"There's no point in mentioning rumors," Missouri says. "After you were born, Susan withdrew from everyone. She spent a lot of time near the water. Then, one day, she vanished."

"When did her insomnia start?"

"I'm not sure. I only remember the worst of it." Missouri shudders. "A couple weeks before she disappeared, she began having psychotic episodes. She claimed the house was filled with snakes and ghosts. Papa had to restrain her for her own safety."

My stomach churns. If what Missouri says is true, insomnia and hallucinations mark the beginning of the end.

"I know Susan is gone, but I like to imagine she faked it all, you know? I have this picture in my head of her driving into a clementine sunset. The windows are rolled down. Alan Jackson croons from the speakers. I want to think she's out there chasing a good feeling."

"Maybe she is."

I'd also prefer knowing Mama abandoned me and went searching for a better life. That would mean the curse is escapable.

"Do you believe Mama was cursed?" I ask.

"Aren't we all?" Missouri nudges the ground with her heels, swinging us higher. "Something terrible happened to Susan. That I know for sure. I've felt cursed ever since losing her. Serves me right, I suppose. Maybe all the bad in my life is meant to atone for what I did."

"God doesn't work like that."

"I'll never forget the sight of her sweater in those lily pads," Missouri says with a sob. "If Susan was cursed, then I'm haunted. Ain't nothing in the world can rid me of her ghost."

A tear careens down her face.

"You're not to blame, Missouri." I embrace her as Charlie nets fireflies and Nanny shells pecans on the porch. "If you need forgiveness, you have mine."

She cups my face in her soft hands. "You're the good that's come from all this. Never in my whole life have I loved somebody more than you."

I pray I won't end up as another empty grave.

1854

August Godwin worked hard and spoke tenderly.

He labored in Ruger's fields alongside Suzanna, tilling the dirt with a plow and mule. Suzanna marveled at his diligence. From dawn to dusk, he toiled his way across the land.

The physical strain only added to his contentment. His eyes remained bright and his demeanor carefree. He beamed a sense of security Suzanna hadn't known. She watched him prepare the land for spring planting, enraptured by his peaceful nature.

Nature. Suzanna wondered how a word referring to the outer world could also describe people's inner workings. Perhaps like ecosystems, people were too vast and intricate to fully comprehend.

The other workers thought well of August. They gravitated toward his presence, offering invitations and gifts. Women brought their daughters, who brought jam and bread.

All of Kettle Creek seemed eager for August Godwin to make a home among them.

Suzanna noticed a change within herself, a hope grafting onto her broken spirit. August held her gaze for a second too long. His expression told her she was, in her entirety, miraculous.

Against her better judgment, Suzanna wanted more than food on her plate and a pillow under her head. She dreamed about a kinder life, one with August and a farm of their own.

Whenever he looked at her, she could not fathom being cursed.

They spent their days in tandem, his efforts dovetailing with hers.

Every moment in August's company was soft and irenic. Suzanna had not realized her hunger for such things. All her life, she'd been starving.

August brought her water. He filled her ears with sweet words.

"Miss Yawn, girls like you belong to campfire stories."

Suzanna could no longer deny it. She wanted him.

The Douglases caught wind of August's interest and warned him not to affiliate with the Yawns. At learning of the conversation, Suzanna fell into a rage. Was it not enough that the Douglases murdered her brothers? Must they also ruin her chance at happiness?

Suzanna hated them with her whole being. She despised the curse too, for it swore no good would befall her. Surely, she could decide her own fate.

All creatures were entitled to free will.

Martha Douglas contradicted the thought. Before service one Sunday, she leaned over a church pew and hissed into Suzanna's ear, "You will be the death of him."

Nothing within Suzanna disagreed.

CHAPTER 13

SUSANA PRATHER

AUGUST, PRESENT DAY

I unclip quilts from the clothesline and fold them into a basket.

A train hollers in the distance.

Nature vibrates with creatures. Dragonflies zigzag over the shoreline and land on cypress knees, their gossamer wings like opals.

I wish I knew what they saw last night.

With the basket propped against my hip, I return to the farmhouse. I pass azalea shrubs and the sugarcane grinder Papa left on the patio.

A scorpion crawls across the screen door. I smash it before heading inside.

Nanny flits around the kitchen while dinner simmers on the stove. She spent the afternoon boiling sugarcane into syrup. Its sweet-smoky scent lingers in the house.

The kitchen table has a fourth place setting.

"Are we having company?" I ask.

"I invited Godwin to eat supper with us." Nanny removes biscuits from the oven and arranges them on a plate. "To thank him for all he's done."

Papa enters the front door. Its screen claps shut behind him. "Coon got into the chicken coop," he grumbles once he rounds the corner.

"How many did we lose?" Nanny asks.

"Four hens, one rooster." Papa tosses his hat onto the kitchen counter. He goes to the fridge and pours himself a glass of tea.

A photo album lies on the sideboard, open for all to see. Its plastic sleeves are crammed with pictures of Mama, Ronnie, and Missouri Jane.

"Susana, you get washed up." Nanny ladles pudding and souse into dishes. She waves me away from the scrapbook. "Go on, get."

"I'm fixin' to." I brush my fingertips against the album's pages.

Mama's face. The generational face, one of bloodlines and birthrights and a single name. The woman who cursed me. The woman who birthed me. The woman standing in my shoes.

She is all of us.

I continue to my bedroom and drop the laundry basket onto my mattress. A banana spider draws webs in the corner. Its yellow-black body is the size of my fist.

Climbing heath drapes the windowsill, flowering with magenta bells.

I usually find the plant growing in the airspace between cypress bark.

Gathering books from the desk, I crouch beside my bed and return them to my collection. Over the years, I've purchased hundreds of antique manuscripts from estate sales.

My hand brushes Obediah's Bible. I unlatch the Scriptures and riffle through their browned pages. Obediah's handwriting embellishes the margins with sweeping cursive.

I'm glad Suzanna married him.

Placing the Bible under the dust ruffle, I go to work, detangling my hair, cleaning dirt from my fingernails. I wiggle into a sundress and dab my neck with orange blossom oil.

Godwin rings the doorbell around six o'clock.

Papa greets him with a howdy and a handshake.

I can't recall the last time I saw Godwin so clean. He wears a button-up shirt and a new pair of boots, his hair combed into a semblance of style.

He gives Nanny a plastic cooler. She cracks its lid, exposing frog legs on ice, a hostess gift I reckon is best received by Southerners like us.

Leaving his shoes in the foyer, Godwin pockets his paint-crusted hands and follows Papa to the kitchen. Even his white socks are spotless.

We take our seats around the table. Papa says grace, then passes a bowl of okra to the left. Godwin puts a napkin in his lap, manners not lost on Nanny.

I bet she'll ramble about his politeness for a week.

"Saw you ride at Easy Bend couple years back," Papa tells Godwin. "You still compete?"

Godwin shakes his head. "I gave up the rodeo. Busted my shoulder last summer."

"Bull or saddle bronc?"

"A mean ol' Brahman crossbreed." Godwin flashes a smile and forks souse into his mouth. He meets my gaze. I look down first.

Papa chuckles. "Ain't nobody getting me on those sons of biscuits," he says, his mustache crooking to one side. "You play an instrument?"

"I do fine on the guitar."

"There's a bluegrass night down at Floyd's. You should come. We meet on Thursdays." Papa signals for me to pass the butter dish.

"How's your daddy?" Nanny asks. "Is he getting out any time soon?"

"No idea, ma'am. I haven't spoken to him in weeks." Godwin spoons grits onto his plate. He has a blood blister under his right thumbnail that wasn't there yesterday.

"Busy getting well, I suppose."

"Something like that." Godwin takes a bite of grits, then another. He leans back in his chair and smiles, his face reddening. "Those are fantastic, Mrs. Prather."

"Eat up, then." Nanny heaps another helping onto his plate.

Papa snickers. "If you stick around here long enough, you'll put on a few pounds."

"The boy needs the weight. Look at him. He's withering away." Nanny butters a biscuit and hands it to Godwin. "I trust a good eater."

"That's why she married me," Papa says, patting his belly. "The way to my heart is through my stomach."

"Same here. I've always eaten like a horse." Godwin drinks from his cup. Ice cubes rattle against glass. "Thanks for supper. I haven't had a home-cooked meal in God knows how long. Been living off ramen noodles."

"You're welcome anytime," Nanny says.

"Once I get my stove fixed, y'all should come over, let me cook for you."

"My, a man in the kitchen." Nanny laughs. "Your mama taught you right."

"She didn't do much teaching, wasn't around long enough." Godwin shrugs.

His mama left when he was a junior in high school. She moved to Folkston with her boyfriend; I guess to escape Gus's drinking. That's why Gus got arrested. He drove to the boyfriend's house, drunk as a coot. I'm pretty sure the cops found an open bottle of whiskey in his cupholder.

Papa scoops more okra onto his plate. He glances at me, his reason for insisting Godwin trade work with us etched in the wrinkles around his eyes.

Nanny cuts her supper into bite-sized pieces. "How's your sister?"

"Doing fine. Grace lives in Blackshear with her husband and four kids."

"Been a while since I last saw her."

"She doesn't like Berryville." Godwin's focus lands on me. Suddenly, it's a year ago. Attraction is a table in an old bar and us leaning closer to each other. I see the mess of him. He wishes to know if I mind the clutter.

Forcing away the memory, I spoon blackberry preserves onto my plate.

The conversation shifts to Godwin's education, his double-major in business and entrepreneurship, then to farming. After we empty the daisy-dot dinnerware, Nanny serves peach cobbler. Godwin eats three helpings, so much Nanny gives him leftovers to take home.

He thanks her profusely.

Papa wipes his mouth with a napkin. "I can fix that stove of yours if you want," he tells Godwin. "In exchange, you and Susana could replace the irrigation pipe near the hog pens."

"I have school tomorrow," I say.

"Susana would rather eat dirt than work with me." Godwin accepts a mug from Nanny and stirs cream into his coffee. He fights a smile, his cheeks dimpling.

"That's hardly fair," I scoff.

"Can you really look your grandpa in the eyes and tell him you enjoy my company?"

"I don't mind you all that much."

Godwin rubs his foot against my foot. I step on his toes. He snickers, watching me with a familiar—I can't name it—simmering in his gaze.

He climbed onto the porch a year ago, then changed his mind and walked away. I regretted not going after him. We'd said cruel things. I wanted to apologize, but instead I stood at the window and watched him leave.

Why can't I get him out of my system? I hate this feeling, like I'm being drawn to him, like he's in my blood. We're too different. We've fought too much. We aren't friends.

I've learned change is a road. If people don't walk it together, they drift apart. Godwin and I chose opposite paths, but maybe grit understands grit. Maybe the bones Papa talked about hold Godwin and me together despite our differences.

"How 'bout some picking?" Papa asks.

Godwin swears and lurches from his chair. He apologizes to Nanny, then wags his finger at the window. Outside, dozens of alligators wriggle from the swamp. They crawl toward the house, their scales glinting charcoal green in the porch lights.

My fork clatters onto the floor.

Papa and Godwin abandon the table. They sprint to the backyard and shoo away the gators with rakes and shovels. Their shouts join the reptiles' hissing.

A whippoorwill chants, an omen of death.

"Sweet Jesus . . ." Nanny rises in a stupor. She grasps at the table for support, her skin bleaching of color. "Please don't take her too."

Godwin wrangles a beast into rushes, hollering until it vanishes with a splash. The other creatures gnash their teeth and swish their tails.

They came for me. Nanny knows it.

"Has this happened before?" I ask.

Nanny fingers her cross necklace with a faraway look in her eyes. "Even the swamp believes there's evil in this house. Why else would it send its monsters to us?"

"Are you talking about the curse?"

"I didn't believe Susan. If I had, maybe she would've lived."

"What did Mama tell you?"

"I should've protected her," Nanny gasps. "I was too hard on her."

When I was small, I overheard my grandparents talk about their regrets, how they blamed themselves for what happened to Mama. In many ways, I think they blamed themselves for *me*.

They've never viewed their silence as keeping secrets. My whole life, they've sifted conversation like cornmeal through a sieve, withholding the unwanted bits.

I think there's equal danger in what goes unsaid.

Nanny wipes her eyes and nose with the hem of her apron. "Our sins have consequences, Susana. We lie in the beds we make—"

"Mama didn't die because of you."

"I need to prostrate myself." Nanny shuffles toward the living room, hesitating as she passes the back door. "Sometimes I wonder if all this is God's judgment."

"God doesn't send monsters," I tell her.

"He doesn't need to." Nanny taps her chest. "They're already inside us."

1854

Suzanna denied her affection for August Godwin.

In fear of dooming him, she resolved to keep him at a distance. Love would only bring about his death, she thought, as it had others'. She couldn't bear to have more blood on her hands.

With the onset of crisper weather, Suzanna felled trees for Ruger's outbuilding. It required sixty-one logs, each thirty to forty feet high, ten to fourteen inches wide.

Day after day, Suzanna trekked into the forest with other workers. They felled and debarked pines, laboring until dusk, then roped the logs to wagons and dragged them to Ruger's property.

August joined the effort, stripping lumber with a drawknife. He shared his plans to settle his land and talked of the cabin he'd build for him and his future bride. He said the process would take nearly a year, after which he'd like to marry.

He watched Suzanna, utterly rapt.

She distracted from her pain with the chop of an axe blade. She believed cosseting hope, both August's and her own, would worsen the heartache. He could not marry her without cursing himself. For that reason, Suzanna behaved coolly to prevent an attachment. If she couldn't love him, she'd protect him so he could find happiness elsewhere.

Despite her discourtesy, August persisted. He warmed her food over the fire and offered bandages for her wounds. He was so kind that Suzanna couldn't help but imagine herself as his wife. A home with him would be a comforting place. Of that, she was certain.

But life would not allow her such a good thing. She was destined for misery.

Everyone in Kettle Creek believed so.

As time passed, Suzanna's feelings toward August dimmed with practicality. She convinced herself they were an impossible match, for he was blithe and optimistic while she possessed nary an affable quality. They seemed in constant disagreement with each other.

They argued over which tree to fell and how long to rest.

Suzanna became annoyed with August's cheerfulness. He smiled too often, she thought, which seemed unfitting for such a violent place. He sang and whistled as he worked. He never met a stranger, nor wavered in goodwill. After the losses she'd endured, Suzanna considered anything other than solemnity an offense.

Eventually, Suzanna realized she was at fault for their conflict. August did not oppose her. On the contrary, he navigated her ill moods without a temper. This infuriated Suzanna. She needed a reason to spurn his interest, so she sought to anger him into a quarrel.

She refused to follow his instructions and disregarded his gestures, the toadflax he placed next to her waterskin, the striped candy he tucked into her coat pocket.

Regardless of Suzanna's endeavor—and to her surprise—she and August made an effective team. Their movements were so in harmony, Suzanna wondered if they were extensions of each other. She relaxed into their rhythm. She left her rifle at home.

She no longer felt unsafe.

Thus, she discovered two of the same could not attract each other. Such was proven by nature. Its forces reached for their opposites. Indeed, Suzanna realized her draw to August was caused by their differences. If her instincts proved true, one day their chemistry would lead to alchemy, and their opposing elements would alloy into a new form.

Suzanna worried that day would damage August beyond repair.

When an encounter with poison sumac caused workers' forearms to bubble and ooze, Ruger halted the felling. While those afflicted recovered, August and Obediah stacked logs on risers.

Suzanna noticed cows huddled in the pasture under smoky clouds. "Y'all better cover that timber. Storm's coming," she told August and Obediah.

August dozed in a patch of clovers with his hat tilted over his eyes. "I'll get around to it."

"They won't dry proper." Suzanna rose from a stump and marched to the lumber. As drizzle strengthened into a cloudburst, she unrolled Ruger's canvas and heaved it onto the pile, battling her skirt as she scrambled over logs.

Thunder pealed in the distance, followed by rain crashing from the heavens.

August jerked awake.

"Suzanna, let me help you." He climbed the stack and grabbed a fistful of canvas. He pulled it one way, Suzanna the opposite, their efforts a tug-of-war in the downpour.

"You should've listened!" Suzanna yelled. She wanted to quell whatever he felt for her. "Now the wood's damp because of your laziness."

Shouting into the storm, they unfurled the fabric over logs and staked it to the ground. Frustration gushed from Suzanna, words sharp and bleeding. She continued to scold August until they stood across from each other like gunmen in a duel.

August threw his hat to the mud and looked at Suzanna with pain etched across his face. "What've I done to earn your contempt?"

Suzanna went silent. She loathed herself for speaking cruelly. Pushing him away had not protected him, only created a rift. "You shouldn't be so nice to me."

"Whyever not?"

"I don't know how to receive it."

August leaned over her, blocking the rain from her face. "You just open your hands."

Tears warmed Suzanna's eyes, unleashed by a feeling like healing. As the storm lashed down, she gazed a question at August. *Do you feel anything for me?*

He released a desperate breath. *I feel everything for you.*

Their relationship evolved, and with time came the learning of each other. They bickered during the day, but night found them the same, laughing in the warmth of firelight with a gleam in their eyes that said, *I'll do it again if it means being close to you.*

Suzanna couldn't name the emotions wilding inside her chest. What she felt for August was both strange and familiar, as if God had written on the pages of her soul *him, it'll forever be him.* The sensation pinned itself to her, closer than a brooch.

They were not alike, nor were they dissimilar. Some would later argue their spirits were so in tune, their conflict was but a stumble before they fell into a waltz.

Suzanna wanted redemption from the past. If she ignored the

voices calling her cursed, perhaps she'd quiet the fear within herself that believed them.

But then Mrs. Yawn suffered a miscarriage early in her pregnancy. The loss reminded of other losses, unburying them one by one, cracking open their coffins to examine their bones.

John fell off a horse and broke his arm.

As the voices grew louder, Suzanna listened. She determined they were right. Not only was her family cursed, but she'd curse August if she allowed him to love her.

Suzanna grieved in ways she didn't understand.

The oaks turned amber in mid-October. Autumn perfumed the breeze with a tart scent like that of an unripe watermelon rind, the season bringing shorter days and blacker nights.

August called on the Yawn family.

He emerged from the cabin while Suzanna hauled a bucket of milk from the cow pen. Without noticing her, he walked toward the lake and vanished into a thicket.

Suzanna rushed to the kitchen, where her mama hovered over a table, cleaning six bullheads. "What was August Godwin doing here?"

"He brought us a mess of catfish." Mrs. Yawn scraped the creatures' scales with the back of her knife, then sliced their bellies and used her fingers to work out the guts.

"Did he say why?" Suzanna poured the milk into a churn.

"Being neighborly, I reckon."

Vicy Ann sat upon a wooden horse while Louisa flipped through a speller. Neither girl added to Mrs. Yawn's response.

Suzanna hurried out the back door and ran to the lake, following a footpath worn into pine needles. She found August standing knee-deep in water, untying a rowboat from a cypress tree. "You didn't wait around for me."

He turned, his eyes like springtime.

Before meeting him, Suzanna had imagined herself as a tangle of thorns too overgrown for gentle things. August rooted a new feeling within her. From it bloomed a loveliness that lifted her chin and pinkened her cheeks.

August removed his hat and climbed onto solid ground. "Forgive me. I lost my nerve."

"What took you so long to come?"

He brushed his fingertips against her hand. "I wasn't sure if you wanted to see me."

"That's my fault." Suzanna held her tongue, afraid she'd say too much. Her voice waned to the nocturne of crickets in the composting swamp grass.

"I started work on my house. Chopped the first tree this morning." August lowered his gaze and pocketed his fists. "I intend to farm my land, make a living off it."

Suzanna felt the need to remember, to make note of his smallest detail, for in her soul she knew she'd one day tell their story.

"I came here to ask something of you," he whispered.

"What is it you want?" Suzanna looked at August, his face an open book. Even in silence, he conveyed a thousand words. His mouth spoke one.

A thousand words, and he chose *you*.

It was a tale as old as time. Girl met boy. Boy saw a home within girl, and he resolved to give anything to belong there, with her, to build somewhere the two of them could find peace.

"Why me? You know what they say," Suzanna gasped.

"I'm not here to choose you," August said. "I'm here asking you to choose me."

He beheld her with a sort of finality, as though he'd wandered the wilderness year after year in search of himself. Instead, he found her. *Her.* And he realized she was both an end and beginning, a terminus, a dawn. Unknowingly, he had been looking for her all along.

Suzanna backed away from him. "It's not that simple."

"It can be." August followed her. "If you don't care for me, I'll leave, and we can lay this matter to rest. But if you do care, please don't push me away."

"I couldn't bear to hurt you."

"Only you decide what you do to me."

Suzanna burst into tears. "You don't understand. Everyone I love suffers . . ."

"I'm not afraid of you." August cupped her face in his work-worn hands. "You decide the life you want, Suzanna. Don't live like you're cursed."

The Okefenokee filled their silence, pulsing as though it possessed a heart. Warblers sung in treetops while egrets fished among lily pads.

August returned the hat to his head and tipped its brim. "I'll call on you again."

With that, he boarded his rowboat and paddled across the lake.

CHAPTER 14

SUSANA PRATHER

AUGUST, PRESENT DAY

JC places his cafeteria tray on the table.

He slides into the space of bench next to me and offers an ice cream cup. "Got you the last one. Almost wrestled a linebacker for it."

I swallow a bite of grilled cheese. "Shouldn't you give it to Cleo?"

"Nah, she's on another diet." JC rolls his eyes and spoons pasta salad into his mouth. He must plan to work a shift after school. He wears his uniform, a blue Columbia button-up with the Okefenokee Swamp Park logo sewn to the pocket.

The first day of classes taints the atmosphere with sweaty enthusiasm. Students pack the cafeteria, a sea of camo and cheetah prints. Their voices reverberate in the rafters, where fans swirl the sticky heat. Even the blades appear to struggle, beating in slow motion as if the air is cane syrup.

I peel open JC's ice cream cup and a wooden spoon and sigh once the vanilla meets my tongue. Its aroma is heaven compared to the cafeteria's summertime fumes.

The stench of grease and body odor will linger until October at the earliest.

Berryville High is half the size of Pierce County High, with fifteen hundred students. An accomplishment for the district, Principal Chancey told the newspaper.

A couple of years ago, the rural school had an enrollment of eight hundred.

Teachers complain about underfunding, their classrooms divided between trailers and a brick structure built in the 1960s. I doubt money is the issue. The school has a football stadium worth more than downtown and large enough to house twelve thousand people.

Around here, folks think of football as they do church, a ritual in need of regular attendance and complete devotion. Friday nights, everyone crams into bleachers to watch Holler Sloan carry the team to victory. Nanny and Papa go to the games, really because there's not much else to do. Their dates consist of high school sports and Dairy Queen.

Stokes plops down across from us, bringing a Sonic cup and the smell of weed. "First day, and Principal Chancey already hates my guts." He rubs his bloodshot eyes and sags forward. His shoulder bones jut from his back. "I wanna drop out."

"The hell you will," JC says between chews. "You'll graduate and go to Tech like we talked about. You ain't working for Willy your whole life."

"Look here, I'm an entrepreneur." Stokes fishes a wallet from his pocket and exposes wads of cash. "I won't be working at the repair shop much longer."

"Where'd you get the money?" I ask.

"Odd jobs, you know." Stokes returns the billfold to his shorts.

He's lost more weight, his body all angles. He wears unwashed clothes stained with motor oil and neglect.

"These jobs . . ." I struggle to find the right words. "Are they legal?"

"Yeah, of course." Stokes doesn't meet my gaze. Instead, he munches ice from his Styrofoam cup.

"Whatever you're doing, I want in on it," JC says with a huff. "No matter how much I work, I never have more than fifty bucks to my name."

"You're welcome to cut grass with me. I'll put you in charge of the string trimmer."

JC lowers his ball cap when his dad—Berryville High's PE teacher—ambles past us.

"Are you taking gym this semester?" Stokes asks.

JC shakes his head. "I got excused because I'm on the school's fishing team. Not sure why. I mean, fishing isn't the pinnacle of athleticism."

I lift his brim. "So you're hiding because . . ."

"Dad wants me to sign up for football tryouts." JC props his elbows on the table, resting his forearm against mine. "I can't play this year, not if I want to keep my work schedule."

Cleo peels JC and me apart and squeezes into the gap between us. "Move your tush."

I scoot to make room for her.

"Wanna come over after school, JC?" She caps a bottle of green liquid.

"Sorry. Can't. I'm guiding boat tours." He wrinkles his nose at her juice. Twice a year, she insists on doing cleanses to prepare for pageant season.

"Fine." Cleo glares at me as if I'm to blame for JC's schedule. She wraps her arm around his shoulders and kisses his cheek. "Come over afterward."

I lick the bottom of my ice cream cup.

"Oh, Susana, I almost forgot." Cleo smacks a brochure next to my tray. "I signed up you and Daisy for the Berryville Family Reunion Pageant."

Stokes cackles.

"That's your thing, Cleo. I'm not a pageant girl."

"Come on. It'll be fun, give us something to bond over." Cleo prods my thigh with her manicured fingernails. "You owe me for spending all your time with the boys."

Not wanting to argue, I shove the pageant brochure into my pocket.

Daisy sits beside Stokes, her tray piled with fries. "New year, same table. Y'all really like to shake things up." She waves to her boyfriend, who mingles with the baseball team. "Holler!"

"Together again, huh?" JC smirks. "You two give me whiplash."

Holler meanders to our table. "What's up, guys?" He gives high fives before dropping into the spot next to Daisy. "Mind if I sit here?"

"*The* Holler Sloan wants to sit with us?" Stokes fakes a gasp. "Don't you have other friends? You know, those people you hang out with more than us?"

"Sure, but I have one girlfriend." Holler gives Daisy a hard kiss, smushing her body against his. He steals a fry off her plate, and she punches his bicep.

"You up for that camping trip?" JC asks.

Holler grimaces. "I gotta pass, man. The swamp and I don't get on."

He's terrified of reptiles, insects, anything that goes bump in the night. Once a month, he tolerates a fishing trip to spend time with JC and Stokes, but camping?

I bet he'd rather eat raw chicken livers.

Daisy swings her legs across Holler's lap. She leans in for another kiss, and he obliges. Nobody on staff will say a word about their PDA. At this school, Holler could get away with murder.

"Cheer practice starts today, right?" Holler asks between pecks. "I won't be able to focus with you on the sidelines. Gah, you're the prettiest girl in school."

His compliment paints a grin across Daisy's face. She doesn't consider herself smart or funny, but she knows she's beautiful. If her looks aren't enough, nothing ever can be.

Daisy told me as much. She said if she's anything like her mama, she'll lose her figure by thirty, break her heart by forty. She's accepted the timeline like a terminal diagnosis.

She hopes to get married before she fattens and Holler finds someone else.

"How's your lunch, Daisy?" Cleo veers her focus to the tray of junk food.

"Really?" JC scoffs.

"What?" Cleo bats her eyelashes as if she doesn't understand his frustration.

"Holler complimented his girlfriend. What, you saw that as competition? Honestly, Cleo, the world doesn't revolve around you." JC rolls his eyes and leaves the table.

Cleo turns beet red. She apologizes to Daisy, then follows JC across the cafeteria.

"Just break up already," Stokes mutters once they're out of earshot.

Daisy huffs and returns her attention to Holler. "Would you come to church with me on Wednesday? I want to introduce you to my friends."

"We've talked about this. I'm not a churchgoing kind of guy," Holler says. "Besides, there aren't many people like me at United Methodist."

The congregation is notoriously white.

"Oh yeah, no worries." Daisy leans against his shoulder and

gnaws a fry. Until their next breakup, she'll do her best to keep him happy.

She doesn't come from money like Cleo. Her family lives two miles from town, in an old millhouse. Her daddy can't keep a job, and her mama teaches preschool at the Methodist church.

Here, everyone knows Daisy for who she is under stadium lights. Nobody associates her with her parents' affairs or cares that she works part-time at the drive-in. I suppose Daisy views Holler as her ticket to a better life. With him, the stadium lights never go off.

Stokes prods my leg with his foot. "You're quiet."

"I got a lot on my mind is all."

He leans over the table and touches my ear. "Is this mud?" He shows me his index finger, now smeared with ash-gray dirt.

A shadowy feeling darts through me. I rub goose bumps from my arms and muster a half smile. "Must be from gardening."

Last night ripples in my thoughts, muddling the cafeteria with memories of constellations and moss-draped trees. I lowered beneath an obsidian surface. Moonlight trickled from above, illuminating scales and teeth and plants knotted into pillars.

August Godwin asked Suzanna Yawn to marry him.

I clutch my head until the images fade. I assumed coming to school would put me at ease, but it only proved I don't belong, not at Berryville High or with those I call my friends. I barely fit in before the sleepwalking. Now I'm a stranger in a body people recognize.

"You okay, Susana?" Daisy asks.

"Maybe I should visit the nurse." I grab my tray and rise from the table as Stokes, Daisy, and Holler swap bewildered looks. I won't go to the nurse. He'd recognize my symptoms.

I doubt I'll be able to hide my sleep deprivation much longer.

Shivering, I carry my tray across the cafeteria. People stare at me—I get the sense they're staring. What do they whisper about whenever I leave a room?

I don't belong here. I want to go home. Although the swamp might take me in the end, it understands the curse. Nothing else does.

My eyelids heavier than they were yesterday, I shuffle toward a garbage can.

I'm not afraid of sleepwalking anymore. I've grown used to it, or maybe I'm too exhausted to fight it. At this point, I like the idea of peace, even if it means I lose my mind.

There's no breaking the hex. I can't decipher it, see the truth of what I am and say otherwise. All that's left to do is wait.

"I am not cursed," I whisper as I have countless times, the words lingering in my mouth like pecan bitters. They're without nourishment.

Why didn't Suzanna marry August?

My head aches with flashbacks and theories. I can't shake the feeling Godwin is in my life for a reason. We're all connected somehow, the swamp included.

Everything is a puzzle, and I don't have all the pieces.

1854

The decision was Suzanna's wormwood.

To love August meant his demise, while to lose him surely meant her own. She wanted to believe herself capable of free will, but the curse felt too close, stitched into her bones. She was certain wedding August would fulfill Martha's prophecy and guide him to an early death.

Still, the words *perhaps not* echoed within the labyrinth of her mind. If August and Obediah were correct, if the curse was mere superstition, did not Suzanna owe it to herself to open her hands to happiness? Choosing otherwise would undoubtedly beget a curse of its own.

For weeks, Suzanna ruminated on her conversation with August, imagining every possible scenario. He'd stated his choice, aware of the risks associated with marrying a Yawn.

Suzanna yearned to disregard her worries.

With cotton sold at auction and logs stacked to dry, the din of harvest season quieted into autumn.

Mr. Yawn needed to remain at home to care for his ailing wife. Her night terrors had worsened, making her lucid moments few and far between. Nothing allayed her madness except for visits to the cemetery, where she wept over her children's graves.

Suzanna worked her daddy's shifts in Ruger's fields. She ambled behind the plow, horse reins clamped between her teeth, and tilled the dirt into soft rows. She preferred the harsh work over watching her mama languish. She trudged and shoved, plodding through manure. The clip-clop of hooves kept time.

Her shoes, once belonging to a dead brother, dissolved. Their soles folded, and their seams unraveled until they were strips of leather bound to her ankles by frayed laces.

Blisters marred her heels and bubbled her toes. Suzanna pressed onward, limping as pain seared her feet. The suffering matched other sufferings.

Obediah entertained the dayworkers with his tall tales. He gathered them near the cow pen and boasted about killing wild boars, showing off his collection of ivory tusks.

He noticed Suzanna hobbling from the field. "What's the matter with you?"

Suzanna rolled her eyes at his hubris. "Go back to your storytelling, Obediah."

"I'll fetch a doctor."

"You'll do nothing of the sort." She moved toward the barn.

Obediah shook his head. "Stubbornness ain't a virtue, you know?"

"Yeah, well, neither is bragging." Suzanna entered the barn and collapsed onto a crate, peeling off her shoes.

Blood dripped from her raw flesh.

The sight was so grisly, Suzanna looked away. She couldn't afford new boots, nor to give herself time to heal. The best she could do was bandage the wounds and return to work.

A silhouette spilled across the floorboards. Suzanna glanced over her shoulder, expecting to see Obediah. Instead, August stood on the barn's threshold. His eyes softened for her, opened almost, as if they were doors welcoming her to come inside and get warm.

"Did Obediah tell you?" Suzanna's voice cracked. She slumped against her thighs, suddenly exhausted.

"He might well have done." August snatched a bucket from a hook and knelt in front of Suzanna. He cradled her battered feet in his hands, careful not to brush the damaged skin.

She relaxed at his touch.

It promised she was safe.

"Pass me that canteen, would you?" August motioned to a water-skin abandoned on a stool. He removed his coat and rolled his sleeves.

Suzanna gave him the vessel. "I don't need any fuss."

Her muscles ached, the soreness reaching inside her chest. She'd given all her energy to preserving herself. She'd buried her emotions deeper with the hope they wouldn't show themselves. But they remained present. She had only made them silent.

In August's company, they began to whisper again.

August emptied the canteen into the bucket. He drew a handkerchief from his pocket and baptized it. Lifting the hem of Suzanna's skirt, he reached for her ankle.

She recoiled. "What're you doing?"

"Washing the dung off your feet." He pressed the rag to her soles, bathing her injuries with gentle strokes. "Don't want those blisters of yours getting infected."

"You aren't supposed to wash me." Suzanna panicked. If people learned of August's gesture, rumors would spread like wildfire. They'd accuse him of indecent behavior.

At Hard-Shell Baptist, men and women were separated before feet-washing occurred.

"Who's gonna find out?" August finished cleaning the grime from her soles. "I understand you aren't used to people wanting to help, but not everybody is out to hurt you, Suzanna. You don't have to spend your whole life fighting."

He gazed at her as though she was more than curses and war.

Suzanna wanted to believe him. She watched his fingers roam her skin, a feeling like music—the squealing timbre of a fiddle—swelling within her.

August seemed a miracle. He'd endured hardships without losing his soft heart. To Suzanna, he was both home and everywhere she'd never been.

He was the *more* she wanted.

Rising from the dirt, August disappeared into a horse stall and returned with a bottle of moonshine. He crouched at Suzanna's feet. "May I?"

She nodded.

"This'll burn," he said, pouring the alcohol over her wounds.

A fierce sting lapped up Suzanna's legs. Gasping, she braced herself until the pain subsided. "I'm grateful I met you," she whispered.

August turned scarlet. The color welled up his neck, across his cheeks, intensifying the blue of his eyes. "Shoot. I ain't got a wisecrack for that one."

"I was mean to you." Suzanna couldn't fathom why he wished to marry her. She'd yet to show contrition for how she'd treated him.

"You didn't encourage my ego, that's for darn sure," August said with a laugh. "Have you given my offer any more thought?"

"Why do you want me?"

He tapped his chest. "There's something in you that's also in me."

"I'll give you trouble."

"Well, if you're the worst that happens, I'll count myself lucky." August smiled, his voice quieting to an earnest whisper. "I think we suit each other, don't you?"

Suzanna couldn't deny they were each other's counterpart. They both worked hard and loved the land. They wanted to pioneer new beginnings, raise a home from the ground up.

Despite their differences, they shared a common core, one forged from pain and loss.

"Have you dug a well?" Suzanna asked.

"Not yet."

"I'll help you pick a spot."

August's smile widened into a grin. "Is that an answer?"

"I know the land is all."

"There ain't nobody like you, Suzanna Yawn."

Each time he looked at her, with eyes beaming enough hope for them both, she forgot her pain a little more. She released her grip on what Martha had said.

Her entire being ached to defy her curses and receive him, to choose the life she wanted for herself. Together they were fire. Surely love would not leave her burning.

She blinked to subdue her emotions. "I fear you'd regret me."

"When will you realize you're not a mistake to make?" August removed his shoes and placed them near Suzanna's feet. "You'll take my boots. Not a word about it."

"I ain't letting you walk around barefoot."

"I'll keep my socks, then." He stood and turned to leave.

"August—" Suzanna rose from the crate. "I think we do. Suit each other."

Beaming, he left the barn, wearing old wool socks in place of shoes.

It all seemed too wonderful to be true.

Suzanna felt a sharp pang of suspicion. Even if August was sincere, nothing guaranteed he wouldn't be ripped from her fingertips.

The scales must be balanced, Suzanna thought. Misfortune would offset joy as it had time and time again. August couldn't rescue her from the past.

Nobody could save—

CHAPTER 15

SUSANA PRATHER

AUGUST, PRESENT DAY

I lurch awake, spewing a mouthful of water.

The world comes into focus, all mud and freezing wet. I lie in darkness. Swamp glistens near my feet. A crescent moon and the Little Dipper gleam silver beyond cypress trees. A warm night, but I shiver. My teeth chatter as crickets orchestrate in the weeds.

Coughs.

I turn my head toward the sound. A feeling like fear washes through me. Godwin sprawls on the ground, sopping wet. His Adam's apple bobs as he swears and gasps for breath.

"What're you doing?" I dig my heels into peat and scramble away from him.

"Saving your skin." He props on his elbows and looks at me with eyes wide.

His wristwatch glows blue. Half past midnight.

"I'm fine." I climb from the bank, a groggy sensation nagging my head. I spin to get my bearings. Laundry hangs from the clothesline. Barney Fife paces near the chicken coop.

A headlamp rests near the water, beaming at rushes.

"You about drowned," Godwin says with a scoff. He rises and points at a rowboat abandoned in the wire grass. "If I hadn't seen you zombie walk into the swamp—"

"You're frogging?" I motion to the gig washed ashore.

"Did you hear me? I dove in there after you." Godwin utters profanities and stretches his arms behind his neck. I've never seen him in a fright.

"Don't mention this to my grandparents." I hug my chest to lessen my exposure. My pajamas hug my body like papier-mâché.

"Susana," Godwin calls as I move across the yard. "You owe me an explanation."

"I do not."

He blocks my path. His fingers cup my shoulders and hold me still. "Tell me what's going on, or I swear I'm walking right up to that house."

I can count on one hand the moments I've felt time stand still. One: Floyd's Gas Mart at midnight when I locked up with JC. We blasted music and danced under fluorescent lights, then loitered in an empty parking lot, watching the lumber mill across the street.

Two: That summer rain when I was eleven. I sat on the front porch while Papa dozed in the swing. Wind chimes sung with the storm, and I realized nowhere could fit me as well as here.

And now, in the darkness with Godwin, as fireflies wink around us and my breaths count the seconds. I stop breathing. I go still. Time vanishes into the ether. There is only us. His hands on my arms, a familiar emotion in my chest. Familiar like the volumes stacked under my bed.

As if he's a book I've read before.

"Tomorrow," I say with a nod.

"Tomorrow, what?"

"I'll explain, cross my heart." I'll tell him about the curse, how for the past month I've sleepwalked into the swamp. No lie could rationalize what he has witnessed.

Godwin backs toward his rowboat. "You scared me is all."

Welcome to the club.

CHAPTER 16

SUSANA PRATHER

AUGUST, PRESENT DAY

Our fallout happened a year ago last June.

I ran into Godwin at a concert in Waycross. He'd recently graduated and was planning to move across the country for college. I'm not sure why I lingered around him that night. I knew he and Betty were still dating, but when he talked to me, I remembered how we used to be all those years ago, before I pushed him away.

He told me his daddy had been arrested for battery and driving under the influence. Maybe it was sympathy that persuaded me to accept a ride home.

Or maybe it was my curse.

Instead of driving to Kettle Creek, Godwin took me to a dive on the outskirts of town, a place known for serving underage customers. I told him I didn't want to go inside. I was afraid my grandparents would find out and think I was becoming like Mama.

Really, I worried going into such a place would make the curse stronger. I feared myself and what I might do. Godwin was too beautiful for my own good.

He shone a light on feelings I didn't know I carried.

Somehow, I ended up on a stool at the bar, eating boiled peanuts while Godwin played a game of pool. Following in his daddy's footsteps, he pawned cigarettes off strangers. He ordered whiskey on the rocks but waited for the ice to melt before drinking.

He took awkward puffs from a cigarette, then passed it to a stranger with a beer belly.

I asked why he'd brought me to the tavern. He just looked at me with sad eyes and a fake smile and ordered another round. I realized I was caught in the cross fire of his grief.

Like it or not, he had a lot of Gus Godwin in him.

Eventually we sat at a table and talked about his mama leaving. The more he drank, the closer he leaned. I should've walked out on him, but I liked the way he looked at my mouth.

His hand skimmed my knee.

Part of me considered doing something wrong, making one mistake. I knew Godwin wasn't right for me, and we wouldn't end up together. Still, I tilted forward, breathing his smoke, wondering what it'd be like to kiss the whiskey from his lips.

Mama had fallen into a similar trap. Either because of the curse or her own propensities, she'd ended up pregnant. I decided I couldn't afford to take risks.

Godwin touched my thigh, and I flew into a rage. I accused him of cheating on Betty, said he was acting like his daddy. He claimed I'd distanced myself from him out of fear.

We dissolved into a fight. Godwin swore the curse had become my entire personality. He brought up Mama, said I was terrified of living my own life. He told everyone in the bar he no longer recognized me as his old friend; I'd become too cold and cautious.

I yelled at him for drinking. I listed all the reasons why he shouldn't smoke. When I blamed him for making a move on me, he asked why I'd leaned in to kiss him. I couldn't answer.

He told me I had no idea what I wanted. I said I wanted to get away from him.

The next thing I knew, I stood alone in the parking lot with JC on the phone. Crying, I begged him to pick me up. He said he was on his way.

I regret the choices I made that night. Right or wrong, if I'd done what I wanted, I would've left with more than Godwin's smoke on my clothes.

Everything he said was true. I just didn't want to believe it.

I hope he'll believe me now.

School drags on in a blur of lectures and number-two pencils. After sixth period, JC and Stokes rush to the fishing hole near Shiloh Cemetery, and I drive to Godwin's house.

His Chevy sits out front along with a dumpster full of junk. The neighbor's bloodhound lies in the yard, barking when I climb from my car.

Godwin steers a tractor across the western field. He notices me and stops the machine. Removing his headphones, he drops from the cab.

My stomach churns as he approaches. All day I've thought about what I'll say to him.

I'm still at a loss.

The sun beats down, and insects create white noise. I stare at the antlion burrows near my feet until Godwin reaches me. He wears sweat and exhaustion. His burns have faded into a golden tan, all except for a strip of pink across his cheekbones.

"Want to come inside?" he asks.

Glancing around to make sure we're alone, I nod and follow Godwin to the farmhouse. We pass the dumpster, which contains trash, a plaid recliner, and cases of beer.

The items must belong to Gus.

"Why'd you throw out your dad's stuff?" I ask as Godwin and I climb the porch steps. The floorboards, unstained pine by the look of them, creak under our weight.

Godwin must've replaced the rotten planks and pressure-washed the others.

"Dad won't have use for beer after rehab," Godwin says. "I don't want it around me. Better to get rid of the temptation, you know?"

He doesn't want to end up like Gus.

I should've realized it earlier. Godwin left Kettle Creek because he feared becoming his father. Returning must've stolen his control, made the fate seem unescapable. Maybe he and I aren't so different. We're both desperate to escape our parents' shadows.

"Won't your daddy miss his other belongings?"

"He ain't coming back here, Susana. He'll get out of rehab and involve himself in another mess. I know better than to think he'll change." Godwin opens the screen door and signals for me to enter. He doesn't smile, but his cheeks dimple.

I cross the threshold and leave my shoes near the door, beside Godwin's dirty Nikes. My hot skin is greeted by coolness from a new AC unit. "Will you sell the land?"

"Grace doesn't want it," he says with a shrug. "Even if Dad got his act together, I doubt he could manage the farm. Place was a disaster when I showed up."

It isn't anymore. The house is spick-and-span, unrecognizable from how I remember. Instead of papered, the walls are painted white and decorated with national park posters and rodeo buckles. The furniture has been replaced, maybe to banish the smell of cigarette smoke.

"You could rent it out, go back to school. You don't have to stay here." I meander into the living room. The only items out of place are a guitar abandoned on the couch and Darn Tough socks, the same ones Papa uses, wadded in a corner.

Jack London and John Muir books stack on the coffee table.

"Make yourself at home. I'll be right back." Godwin tosses his ball cap onto a chair, then goes down the hallway to his bedroom. He leaves the door ajar, mess visible through its crack.

At least he's not a total clean freak.

Pine-Sol and turpentine prickling my nose, I wander to the adjoining kitchen, outdated except for a new refrigerator.

On the tile countertop sits a French press and half-eaten bag of pork rinds. An ironing board leans against the wall, draped with one of Godwin's button-up shirts.

I peer into a closet full of gear. From what I can tell, the contents are organized by sport. Rods with tackle. Bedrolls with tents. A miscellaneous bin of spurs and ski pants.

As Godwin bumps around his bedroom, I retrace my steps and examine the framed rodeo buckles. Bronc Riding Champion. Bull Riding Champion. All-Around Youth. A photograph shows Godwin and his daddy posed in front of a bucking chute.

Godwin's graduation photo hangs near the fireplace. He, Betty, and a handful of their classmates at Berryville High's stadium grin, all dressed in caps and gowns.

Footsteps creak the floorboards.

I spin around.

Godwin stands behind me wearing a clean T-shirt. "Dad wasn't always a drunk," he says and motions to the rodeo picture. "He drank, but he wasn't a drunk."

My gaze must linger on the graduation photo a beat too long.

"It's not because of what you think."

"You and Betty?" I force out her name.

Godwin nods. "Everyone thought we broke up because I wanted to leave town and Betty didn't. The truth is, she arranged to go with me, even bought a suitcase from the Waycross mall."

"What happened?"

"A couple days before we planned to leave, my meemaw sat me down and asked if Betty was worth a front porch. I think it was her way of asking if Betty chose to stay in Berryville, if I'd stay with her, if she'd be enough for me."

My heart skips. "You said no."

"I hadn't found somebody worth staying for yet." Godwin pockets his hands and goes to the sofa. Placing his guitar on the floor, he occupies a cushion. "About last night."

"Right." I blink away the image of Betty and lower into an armchair.

"You ain't a mermaid, are you?" Godwin rubs his mouth, perhaps to hide a grin.

I can't help but laugh. "No, I sleepwalk."

"That's some deep sleep. When I pulled you from the water, I thought you were dead."

I flash back to last night, us in the dark, his hands on me like they belonged there. "The sleepwalking began on my eighteenth birthday."

For the next hour, I tell Godwin about the curse, how the swamp gives me dreams of the past. I share what I know about Suzanna Yawn and the other women in my bloodline.

"You don't have to believe me," I say. "You've made it clear you think my family's stories are malarkey. I don't blame you."

Godwin sinks into the couch's pillows and crosses his arms.

"Everything you said last year was true. My whole life, I've been terrified of the curse, and I pushed you away because of it. I'm sorry for hurting you."

"Not all of it was true," he whispers.

"I suspect I have a couple months until I go insane. That is, unless I break the curse."

"How do we break it, then?"

"You believe me?"

"Got no reason not to," Godwin says, leaning against his thighs. His expression tells me he feels cursed too, and he's sorry for that night at the bar.

A sharp emotion cuts through my chest. For a moment, we're kids again, jumping hay bales and riding horses in the pasture. I'm not afraid of letting him get close.

"I want to help you." He nods, and I get the sense my honesty restitched the bond between us, or at least began the mend. "What else have you learned?"

"Not much. History books are slim pickings. Papa has the best genealogy records around, and his collection is mostly folklore and secondhand accounts."

"This side of the Altamaha River used to be considered wild country. No farms or towns until settlers moved down here in the 1800s," Godwin says. "I figure the people in these parts didn't have much use for history books."

"Plus, censuses were lost when the courthouse burned."

Godwin picks at his bottom lip. "I ain't a superstitious person. I think life has a knack for kicking everybody in the shin. Good, bad—it's all part of being here."

"But you believe me?"

"I saw a spook light once. Must've been nine or ten. Spotted it near those train tracks by the lumber mill." His focus goes to the wall, to the picture of him and his daddy. "The older I get, the less everything makes sense. If you say you're cursed, who am I to tell you otherwise?"

He believes my story because in many ways he sees it as his own.

Godwin rises, and I do the same. "I've missed talking like this."

"Like what?" I follow him out the screen door, onto the front porch. Cool air flees my clothes, replaced with sweltering humidity.

"I've missed you being open with me." Godwin braces his weight against the railing and points at the western rim of his property. "See that field over yonder? I'm going to fence it, buy some cattle. Dad wanted to cultivate the land, but I can't do it on my own. Full-grown cows sell for over three grand apiece. I'll run this place like a business, make it profitable."

"You feel cursed too, don't you?"

"Everyone has their curses, Susana, except not all of us get the chance to break them."

I fill the space beside Godwin and sit on the top rail. "After you left Berryville, what made you realize you never wanted to come back?"

"Other than my parents?" He looks at me, squinting against the sun. "I hiked to a glacial lake in Wyoming. The basin was surrounded by snowcapped mountains and fir trees. Staring at it, I realized I needed to start fresh, live someplace where my name didn't mean anything."

"I've never seen more than an inch of snow."

Godwin smiles. "I'll take you out there someday."

We behold his land in the gold of afternoon. I savor the quiet, a feeling like peace washing over me. I'm not alone in this anymore. The curse isn't my secret. It's ours.

Ours. The word brings tears to my eyes.

I think Godwin and I will become friends again. Maybe we never stopped—we only stopped talking—and this is Godwin's way of proving it.

He nudges my leg. "How's your foot?"

"Better." I examine the scab from the nail puncture. The wound healed after a week of doctoring it with antiseptic and bandages.

August Godwin helped Suzanna Yawn.

The connection blazes through my mind like a flare. I don't think meeting Godwin was a coincidence, neither was him dragging me from the swamp.

His ancestor loved my ancestor. If history repeats itself, maybe we will too.

Dispelling the thought, I sweep a ladybug off the railing and place it on Godwin's knuckles. He rotates his hand, letting the bug trail his palm's creases.

He leans against me. His shoulder presses into my side.

"I should go. Nanny will be getting supper ready." I hop off the rail, warming from Godwin's proximity. I don't know how to do this, navigate my feelings in a healthy way. I've always thought of love as being what got Mama into trouble.

Godwin escorts me to my car. "I won't say a word about your sleepwalking."

"Thanks for believing me." I open the driver's-side door and slide behind the wheel.

Godwin shuts the door and pats the car's roof.

He watches from the driveway as I reverse onto the road.

1854

You will be the death of him.

Suzanna recited Martha's prophecy until it strangled every hope, poisoned every thought. She had the sins of her forefathers in her blood, hence her family's misfortune. She was destined for misery. Cursed was the ground beneath her feet.

Cursed was anyone she loved.

The words possessed Suzanna, growing in power. She fought her anguish in the fields, where she knelt in dirt and buried seeds. Her mind was made.

She would refuse August to protect him from tragedy.

One afternoon, while Suzanna planted, August deserted his task and approached her. "Felled the last tree for my cabin," he said. "I'll start building once the logs dry."

"Pleased to hear it." Suzanna rose and wiped her hands on her dress.

If souls were breakable things, in that moment, hers shattered.

August stood at arm's length, cradling his hat against his chest. He removed a bundle of irises from his waistcoat pocket and offered it to her. "Suzanna, I'd like to ask your daddy for his blessing. I want to marry you if you'll have me."

"You don't want the likes of me as your bride, August."

"I ain't just be wanting a wife. You and me—we'd be partners."

"The Bible says something about couples being equally yoked. I pull too hard, I think." Suzanna left the irises in his hand. She lowered to her knees and resumed work.

A tear cut down her cheek.

"The Bible also says something about iron sharpening iron," August said, his voice cracking. "When I'm with you, I could cut through stone."

"You'll love another girl and make her happy—"

"I love you." August crouched in front of Suzanna and gathered her hands into his. "I know why you're doing this. I understand you're scared."

"Hate me if you need to," she breathed. "I have to save you."

"Don't let them win, Suzanna. You ain't cursed. Stop living as if you are." August clutched her hands to his chest. "Let me be your home. Marry me. Choose me."

"I can't," Suzanna wept.

August placed the bouquet next to her.

The lavender-blue flowers wilted, their petals flapping in a lazy breeze. Suzanna later gathered them and doctored their stems. By then, they were past the point of saving.

"Good day to you, Miss Yawn." August returned the hat to his head and withdrew, his absence so acute, Suzanna collapsed onto her elbows and sobbed.

The choice only furthered her suffering.

CHAPTER 17

SUSANA PRATHER

AUGUST, PRESENT DAY

Cleo drops her sandals beside the front door. "Hi, Agnes."

Nanny steps from the kitchen with a half-peeled potato in her hands. She glances from me to Cleo to Daisy. "What brings y'all over?"

"Studying," Daisy says, still giggling from the conversation we had on the drive here. She waves her phone at Cleo. "Should I message him back?"

"We'll be in my room." I lead the girls past the den.

Missouri Jane sits in front of the TV, shelling last year's pecans. She straddles a bench Papa made, with boxes on either side, one for whole nuts, another for cracked.

The garden's most recent harvest surrounds her. Blueberries, watermelons, and sweet corn fill baskets and plastic bags, all packaged and ready for delivery.

"You'll lose brain cells watching that show," Nanny tells Missouri. "Flip the channel to something more wholesome, why don't you?"

"To what, *Love Boat* or *Fantasy Island*?" Missouri snickers.

We all know Nanny watches reruns when she thinks no one's home, same as we know she sips Jim Beam whenever she has a sore throat. Of course, she won't admit either.

She maintains that alcohol is from the devil and television is for loafers.

"Lawdy mercy, Susana. You look terrible," Missouri says with a gasp. She gawks at me as if I have a second head. "Mama and Daddy have been working you too hard."

"What're you going on about?" Nanny carries a basket of laundry from the kitchen. She places it on the sofa, then fetches her ironing board from the hall closet.

She irons everything from bedsheets to Papa's wool socks.

"Don't you see the bags under Susana's eyes? She's worn slap out." Missouri shatters a pecan and picks its bitters. "Susana, honey, you need to go rest."

"I had a long day is all."

The curse must be eating away at me quicker than I thought. I've been exhausted for so long I barely recognize my fatigue anymore.

"Daisy, your mama sells makeup, doesn't she?" I whisper as the three of us continue to my bedroom. If I want to keep my secret, I need more than Missouri's expired concealer.

"Yeah, she does. Want me to place an order for you?"

"I'll take anything that'll hide my dark circles."

Daisy's mama goes live on Facebook once a week to peddle her cosmetics and other wares. Last Tuesday she did a demonstration with a product guaranteed to reduce body fat. All five of her viewers watched as she coated her gut with an "herbal wonder salve" and plastic wrap.

"Mom will know what you need," Daisy says. "I'll bring the stuff to school tomorrow."

Godwin emerges from my bedroom, wearing brown overalls and a ball cap.

I freeze at the sight of him. "Godwin."

"Godwin's here!" Nanny shouts.

He cracks a smile and rattles his toolbelt. "I finished those repairs for you."

"What repairs?"

Daisy blocks his path. "How often do you creep around Susana's bedroom?"

"Nice to see you too."

"You better not have read her journal or anything."

"I can't read cursive." Godwin winks at Daisy as he slides past us. His attention shifts to me. "You have quite the book collection."

"My sister is doing great by the way. Super happy without you."

Cleo yanks Daisy's arm. "Oh my gosh, chill."

"No more late-night swims, all right?" Godwin whispers to me. He brushes his hand against mine, gliding his fingers across the base of my thumb.

Before I can respond, he vanishes down the hall.

I follow Cleo and Daisy into my room.

Propped against the wall are two panels built from wooden slats.

"Did you ask Godwin to do that?" Cleo points at metal pieces drilled around the door and window. "What exactly did he repair?"

My heart racing, I go to my desk, where Godwin left a bag from the hardware store. It contains time locks and words scribbled onto notebook paper.

Game on!

CHAPTER 18

SUSANA PRATHER

The curse is no match for Godwin's barricade.

Each night, I secure the panels over my door and window and set the time locks for five-thirty. The panels do their job, keep me put. They snap open while the world is still dark, and the swamp thrums in wait for sunrise.

Nature scrapes its tendrils against wood as I dip in and out of sleep, growing its vines over my windowpane. It hisses beneath the house and through air vents.

I pin a cushion over my ears.

Papa often says, "If it ain't broke, don't fix it." I suppose I hold the same belief when it comes to the barricade. As days move slowly like molasses, and my sleepwalking becomes a thing of the past, I feel less urgency.

The panels are a makeshift solution—a glorified Band-Aid—but they give me back a sense of security. I know they won't delay my kismet forever. The threat still looms, staring at me from picture frames, listing what'll happen if I don't break the curse.

Days turn to weeks. I don't sleepwalk or dream about Suzanna Yawn. The longer I go without mishap, the less motivated I am to delve into my family's history.

I fall asleep while staring at the time locks, my miniature wardens counting down to my release. Sometimes I awake when their gears click and their shanks pop from their locking bars, and I pat myself down to confirm I didn't enter the swamp.

The barricade gives me hope that I'll be able to live with my curse.

Great-Grandpa Clyde locked Susan in her bedroom. He must've known about the sleepwalking and its consequences. Because of him, Susan lived longer than any other firstborn daughter in my bloodline. She had Clyde, and I have Godwin.

He texts every morning to check on me. He scours the Berryville Library for history books and prints articles off the internet, highlighting information on local folklore.

We're a team. At least, Godwin says as much whenever we swap nebulous theories between chores. He wants to break my curse. That alone floods me with gratefulness and relief.

I feel like I have a chance again.

One afternoon, he shows me a carboard box from his attic. It contains photo albums and bric-a-brac, some nearly a hundred years old. We examine the items and diagram his ancestry from him to Gus to Augustus to Augie. The path stops there, several generations before the original August Godwin. His family didn't preserve their records as well as mine.

Despite the barricade, I grow more tired by the day. The makeup I purchased from Daisy's mama hides my dark circles and pallid complexion, but it doesn't lift my sagging eyelids.

If Godwin notices my exhaustion, he doesn't mention it. His

interest in the curse lessens with time, maybe because we're both frustrated by our lack of progress.

Or maybe he thinks I'll be able to evade my fate with the locks alone.

The curse has possessed my thoughts for years. I don't want it to consume any more of me. I know what's coming, but right now I want to be here, with Godwin, as Susana Prather, not the women in my bloodline.

We sit on Nanny and Papa's front porch most evenings. Godwin pets Barney with careful strokes while dipping pork rinds into peanut butter. I say his tastebuds are broken, and he tells me I look pretty in the orange light.

I don't want to confuse my feelings from the dreams with reality. Godwin isn't August. I'm not Suzanna. We aren't in love and torn apart by the curse.

Godwin doesn't love me.

The flashback has replayed within my mind. Before the hex, Suzanna chose not to marry August because she feared Martha's statements would come true. What if she was so convinced of being cursed, she somehow cursed herself?

I've thought about it all so much, I've given myself headaches.

People can't have free will *and* curses. I mean, how can anyone make independent decisions with the past whispering in their ears?

I can't decide how much of me is me and how much was passed down from other people. What if I have no control over myself? What if Pastor Walker was right about generational sins?

Nanny and Missouri Jane blame themselves for what happened to Mama. They're convinced God is punishing them as atonement. I don't believe that. I don't think the curse is God's wrath, or that He judges us for the sins of our forefathers.

None of this makes a lick of sense. If the curse isn't punishment, why does it exist? If I don't have free will, how do I break the cycle?

I can't shake the feeling I'll soon follow in Mama's footsteps.

Suzanna's hex mentions *the truth of what you are*. Perhaps the remedy for the curse lies with my family's secrets. My whole life, Nanny and Papa have swept Mama under the rug of everything to forget. They won't breathe a word about my daddy.

The photos watch from my bedroom's walls as I drowse. To anyone else, they look like portraits of me styled after different eras. I glance from picture to picture until they flicker like a thaumatrope, the similar faces blurring into Suzanna Yawn.

A shiver crawls up my back like spiders.

The curse follows a pattern. After the sleepwalking takes its course, insomnia will set in, followed by imaginings. Confinement might delay my insanity, but for how long?

Even Susan Minchew lost her mind in the end.

CHAPTER 19

SUSANA PRATHER

Godwin sprays me with the garden hose.

"Oh, you're gonna get it." I scurry around Papa's truck and hurl a soapy sponge at Godwin. He ducks, laughing, and sprays me again.

"Come on," he taunts. "Give it to me good."

I charge at him and play tug of war with the hose. He pulls me into a headlock, aiming the spout at my face. I squeal as the icy water blasts my chin and soaks my dress.

"Stop fooling around!" Nanny shouts while potting azaleas in hanging planters.

"Truce?" Godwin murmurs. I nod, but he doesn't loosen his grip. Standing behind me, he wraps his arms around my waist and grins against my temple.

I smile too.

We fill the dying days of summer with each other. I go to school and make deliveries. Godwin works his farm and helps Papa with chores. Then we all converge—Nanny, Papa, Godwin, and me—for evenings of card playing and string picking.

On Friday nights, we go to the football game at Berryville High. Papa buys us nachos and sodas. Nanny waves her foam finger, cheering for Holler.

Godwin shouts and laughs and makes me laugh too.

He tries to grow a mustache. It's so blond it's just about invisible. Still, Papa tells him it's coming in nicely because I reckon that's what all guys tell each other.

I should worry more about the curse, but it's easier to pretend my life is car washes and football games and rides on Godwin's tractor. He fits with my family like he did when we were kids. We plant broccoli and carrots in the garden. We talk about our mamas, the struggles of growing up in a town where gossip is bandied about.

Being around Godwin rewinds the clock to an innocent epoch before the curse got in the way of us. I confide in him, maybe because he already knows the worst of my secrets.

He accepts my vulnerability with soft smiles and nods.

The more I tell him, the less I can ignore my feelings. They bubble up inside me, heating my cheeks whenever he glances my way. I can't let this happen.

I must keep my heart in check.

Nanny and Papa invite Godwin over for supper. As we wait for him to arrive, I pace the living room, my stomach in knots. I sit on the sofa's armrest and rearrange my hair. I try to play it cool, look pretty, but the moment Godwin waltzes through the front door, I grin like an idiot.

We gather around the kitchen table for okra and fried chicken. Godwin jokes with my grandparents, looks to me for a quip, but all I do is smile because I'm glad he's here.

Papa shrugs as if to say, *She's an introvert. She doesn't talk much.*

Godwin snickers. With him, I never shut up.

He tells us about his new plan to lease his land to a cattle farmer. Doing so would give him the freedom to leave Berryville and reenroll in school.

At hearing the news, I lose my appetite. My face feels wobbly with emotion as though my features are distorted and melting with it.

Our lives don't align—I know that. Godwin won't stick around, and I won't leave. We're better off staying friends. I just wish my heart agreed.

When another heat wave strikes, Godwin coaxes Nanny and Papa into a pool day. We dig sunscreen and floaties from the shed and pile into the pickup. Godwin sits beside me in the truck bed, wearing board shorts and a T-shirt, with his hat on backward.

I'll call him a friend, but I want him closer.

As we pass through Berryville, Papa stops at Penny Pinchers. Godwin and I go inside to buy drinks and ice. He dances down aisles and tosses junk food into my arms.

"For Nanny," Godwin says, and I cackle. Meandering back to the pickup, he uncaps a soda bottle with his teeth and hands it to me. "You're funny, Susana Prather."

"I didn't do anything."

"When I say *you're funny*, what I mean is *I like it*." Godwin hitches a shoulder, his eyes roving around the parking lot. He looks at me and blushes.

I realize *I like it* means *I like you.*

You're funny might be my favorite two words.

"I think you're funny too." I take a swig of orange Fanta, but I can't stop smiling, so the beverage escapes my mouth and stains my shirt.

"Got a hole in your lip, huh? Want me to check it out for you?"

I nudge him, and he nudges back.

Missouri Jane and Charlie meet us at the recreation center. We rush to the pool, hopping across the searing concrete, and mark our territory by hurling towels onto strappy chaise lounges.

One of JC's younger brothers perches on the lifeguard tower. He blows his whistle at Charlie, who has done a running leap into the deep end.

A third of Berryville showed up in search of relief from the heat. Mrs. Shealy tans near the pavilion. Principal Chancey serves half-melted Popsicles to his grandkids.

Papa marches to the pool, wiggling off his shirt in the process. He signals to Godwin before cannonballing into the water. His splash drenches Lucinda, who bobs in an innertube.

"What was that?" I ask Godwin.

"Huh? I didn't see nothing." He tosses his ball cap onto a towel and steps toward me.

"Don't even think about—" I sprint to the deep end.

Godwin follows and sweeps me over his shoulder. With a holler, he crashes into the pool, triggering another shrill blast from the lifeguard's whistle.

"Y'all are too close," I say once I come up for air. I splash Papa and shove Godwin underwater. "If y'all keep hanging out, I'll have to post your bail."

Godwin high-fives Papa, and I get a lump in my throat. Because I see the good that's woven into my life. Because Godwin has found good here, with me.

For hours we risk sunburns. We dive for rings with Charlie and eat tomato sandwiches. Missouri spritzes Godwin with bronzer, and we all tan while Nanny reads her magazines.

Godwin rolls onto his side, lowering his aviators. "I should've apologized before I left town. It's a crying shame I didn't knock on your door."

"You've knocked plenty since then."

"Yeah, well, I regret not parting on better terms."

"Why didn't you take me straight home that night?"

He shrugs. "I don't have a clear-cut answer."

"Tell me anyway."

"After my dad got arrested, I was a mess, you know? Betty and I were on the fritz, and I was days away from road-tripping out west. I went to the concert to blow off steam, but when I saw you, I just . . . wanted my old friend back."

"We hadn't talked in years."

"I told you I didn't have a clear-cut answer," Godwin says. "Truth is, I still had a crush on you. Believe me, I wasn't planning to cheat on Betty—"

"What, then?"

"Honest, Susana, I don't know. I figure you've always felt like home to me." Godwin twists onto his back. "Maybe I thought if I spent time with you, I wouldn't feel so lost."

"You're one of us, Godwin. You have a home," I whisper.

"A darn good one." Godwin nods, and something about his expression says he doesn't take any of this for granted. "I still have it, I think."

"Have what?"

"A crush on you."

My heart skips.

"Is that okay?" He studies me with a chary gleam in his eyes, and I don't know how to let him down. A couple of weeks ago, we couldn't stand to be near each other. He might think he likes me, but I blame our feelings on vicinity and a shared secret.

Missouri and Nanny interrupt with their bickering.

I relax into my chair, behold the crowded pool, and count my blessings, one of which lies next to me with a sullen look on his face.

Godwin and I will only repeat our history, damaging each other in the process. He'll try to get closer to me. I'll push him away. At least now, he'll understand why.

Over the next week, I attempt to keep Godwin at arm's length. I spend afternoons at the library, researching on my own. I go fishing with JC and help Cleo pick out a dress for the upcoming Berryville Family Reunion Pageant.

No matter what I do, I find my way back to Godwin. I run into him at the Green Frog, and we talk for hours. I end up in his driveway, and he invites me inside for coffee.

I get the eerie feeling I don't have control over what happens to me. If love doomed Mama, it'll doom me too. Nanny said I inherited her propensities.

My panic magnifying into fear, I study my notes on the other firstborn daughters and sneak Nanny's scrapbooks off their shelf. I need to learn my family's secrets, pinpoint the *truth* of what I am so I can say otherwise.

Suzanna's hex was meant for the townsfolk of Kettle Creek. How did it backfire on her? Why has history repeated itself all these years?

I whisper over and over that I'm not cursed.

After so many nights without sleepwalking, I become restless. I toss and turn in my bed, listening as creatures rattle the wooden panels and let out embittered wails.

The temptation to remove the barricade gnaws at my mind. It's an itch I can't scratch, an incessant craving. I must know more about Suzanna, and the swamp holds the answers.

Until the time locks click open, I wait like a monster in a cage.

I can't help but wonder if I'm starting to go insane.

CHAPTER 20

SUSANA PRATHER

SEPTEMBER, PRESENT DAY

The shaft of a shovel protrudes from the burial ground.

It's been here my whole life, this marker of a robbery gone wrong. I drift past it and head to the oldest part of the Hard-Shell Baptist cemetery.

Gopher tortoise holes mar the sand. Papa told me they range from six to eight feet deep, an unsettling fact to learn in a graveyard.

With a handful of crayons and printer paper, I wander among tombstones in search of Suzanna. She rests in peace alongside Obediah and their sons. Her headstone appears to be white marble. It's weathered and blackened with age, overgrown with ash-gray lichen.

Suzanna Yawn Owens. 1837–1867. Faithful to her trust even unto death.

A lump hardens in my throat as I kneel on the grave and do a rubbing. The entire Yawn family occupies the plot, all dead for almost two hundred years.

My nose stings as if I have a reason to grieve them.

Wind sweeps across the cemetery, blasting me with sand. I shield my eyes and tuck the rubbing into my pocket. I'll add it to my notebook once I get home.

The earth trembles.

Ants pour from their hills in waves of legs and exoskeletons.

"Leave me alone!" I rise and kick the bugs from my shoes. Nature doesn't like that I've avoided the swamp for so long.

My heart pounding, I step toward the church.

Keziah Douglas stands on the opposite side of the graveyard, accompanied by her oxygen tank. She places bouquets of white daisies on her husband's and son's graves.

Mr. Douglas died in a mill accident when a blade spun off its gear and decapitated him. Brady Douglas fell dead while shopping at Penny Pinchers.

I'm not the only person in Kettle Creek with the word *cursed* associated with my name.

Something about our last interaction nags at me, so I approach Keziah, weaving around tortoise holes. My car is the only vehicle in the parking lot. Keziah must've walked here.

She lives down the road in an old millhouse.

The widow studies the tombstones, unmoved by the blustery weather. She wears a steely expression and a floral-print dress outdated by several decades.

"I'm sorry to disturb you—"

Keziah snaps her head to look at me. Her eyes are red-rimmed, her jaw slack. She emanates an air of authority so strong it's as if she put it on with her morning perfume.

"You knew my mama, didn't you?" I tug my shirt to peel it from my perspiring chest. September refuses to loosen its grip on summer, bathing the landscape with a dripping heat.

As if to spite me, Keziah fans herself with an offering envelope.

"Last time we spoke, you mentioned something about me cursing the town. What'd you mean by that?" I steady my voice. I don't want to give the woman a slab of gossip to barter at her next luncheon. She already has enough ammunition to use against me.

"Your birthday was several months ago, correct? You don't have much time left," Keziah says in a clipped tone, her words punctuated with a scoff. "At least the curse ends with you."

She wags an arthritic finger at my belly.

I go cold and numb. The breath drains from my lungs. If I die, will the past die with me? I don't have a daughter to inherit the curse.

But neither did Great-Aunt Susie.

Keziah smacks a mosquito from her arm. "Susan Prather was a liar and a flirt and blamed everybody but herself. I pray you only got her looks."

"What did Mama do?"

"Figures your family didn't tell you," Keziah sneers. "All their secrets . . . they think nobody knows what happened. We ain't fools."

"Tell me *what*?"

"You didn't choose your blood." Keziah tilts close to me, reeking of decay. Maybe I imagine it, but an emotion akin to pity crosses her face. "All you can do is minimize your wake."

Her meaning knifes through me. She wants me to die quietly, avoid causing any more pain. To her, there's no breaking the curse, only preventing it from claiming another generation.

Staving off a panic attack, I back away from her and rush to the parking lot.

1854

Suzanna's affection for August did not abandon her.

No matter how often she rejected it, the feeling returned like water drawn back from a shore, rushing to kiss it again and again. Love was not back and forth, Suzanna decided. It knew its own mind, and Suzanna knew hers, but she couldn't shake her fear.

The turmoil was all in her head. She reminded herself of this and listed every reason for deserting her belief in the curse. Eventually she conjured enough resolve to spurn her previous decision. She wanted to marry August.

She prayed he'd forgive her folly.

Willard Ruger threw a party to celebrate the season's end. Neighbors and farmhands arrived at his home as evening chilled the air. They flocked across the porch into rooms illuminated with firelight.

Such festivities overwhelmed the senses. Folks danced in the drawing room, whisking the fog of pipe tobacco smoke and lantern vapor. Fiddlers from Old Nine stroked melodies from their strings while Ruger's youngest daughter, Alice, accompanied on the piano.

She'd been blind since birth and dedicated her days to memorizing the ivories.

Elizabeth Ruger had begged for the amusement, claiming she was deprived of socialization. Her father had obliged by allowing her to organize the affair.

She'd endeavored to host a proper gathering like those mentioned on the society page of the *New York Herald*. She'd ordered a new striped dress and converted the parlor into a refreshment room, offering a modest spread of tea, coffee, and biscuits.

The party was the closest thing to high society she'd ever know.

Suzanna observed the excitement from a spot of wall near the staircase while her daddy and brother communed in the Rugers' dining room.

Mrs. Yawn and Louisa had stayed at home to care for Vicy Ann. Earlier that day, the child fell ill with a temperature and stomach pain.

The family worried she'd contracted slow fever.

Suzanna wouldn't have come to the party if she didn't hope to see August, nor would she have borrowed a dress from Elizabeth, a silk gown dyed periwinkle blue. The garment was old and tight, exposing her shoulders and trimmed with lace.

Its color was far too cheery to befit her.

Regardless, Suzanna had accepted the dress and a hoopskirt. She'd plaited and pinned her hair, the efforts a prayer that when she confronted August and told him she'd changed her mind, he would say he wanted her still.

Without and *him* could not exist together, Suzanna decided. She refused to allow Martha's words to further deter her from happiness. She was not her blood, nor its curses.

She needed to live as though free of them.

August understood the risks of marrying a Yawn. He knew of Suzanna's misfortune and still wished to love her. If by some chance Suzanna was wrong about the curse, if it was indeed more than superstition, did not August's consent absolve her conscience?

The days following his proposal had tormented Suzanna. Cursed or not, she realized her agony would continue if she forsook August. He was her chance at starting anew.

Suzanna placed her lemonade on a table and watched the front door. She waited for August to appear on the threshold, nearly all of Kettle Creek present except for him.

Ruger's gathering was a testament to the Okefenokee. People of every color fellowshipped under one roof, brought together by the swamp's promise of refuge.

Nature was haven. People were not.

The Douglases leered at Suzanna from across the way. They whispered into each other's ears and nodded in her direction with eyes full of venom.

Despite her indignancy at being the subject of their conversation, Suzanna focused on the door. Her heart grew more anxious by the second.

Elizabeth breezed down the corridor, breathless from dancing. "August isn't out back," she told Suzanna. "I'll search the parlor."

Suzanna had confided her feelings to Elizabeth, prompting her insistence on lending a dress and scouting the party. Elizabeth must've realized Suzanna coupling with August would put an end to Obediah's attachment, leaving him free to love another.

Hands combed around Suzanna's waist.

"Now, if you ain't the prettiest girl." Obediah's voice. He rested his cheek against her temple and pulled her close. His wool coat was drenched with scents of hay and pinewood.

"Obediah." Suzanna relaxed against him. "Have you seen August?"

"What is this you're wearing?" He toyed with the lace trim of her sleeve and sniffed her neck. "You smell like Elizabeth Ruger."

"Behave yourself." Suzanna batted his hands, surprised he still looked chastened by his recent loss in a wrestling match. "Do you know if August is coming?"

"He decided to ride up to Atlanta."

Suzanna froze. "Why?"

"To poach a couple farmhands from his cousin. Didn't he tell you?"

The journey alone would take sixteen days, add a week or two for August to make hires.

"I reckon he'll live with his cousin's family while those logs of his dry."

Which meant August would remain in Atlanta for the better part of a year. Without knowing of Suzanna's changed feelings, he might return with a wife.

Suzanna gripped Obediah's lapel. "When does he plan to leave?"

"I said goodbye to him before I came here."

The words barely from Obediah's mouth, Suzanna lurched into motion. She fled the Rugers' home and sprinted toward the road.

Obediah chased her. "Suzanna!"

She lifted her skirt and ran faster, past oaks bent into violent angles. If she lost August now, she'd never forgive herself.

"He's gone!" Obediah yelled. "Suzanna!"

The night air was a saccharine paste in her lungs. She gasped and sobbed, all of creation joining her lament. The dew cried with her, and cicadas screamed. Howls echoed from the swamp, the sounds so monstrous, Obediah slowed his stride.

"August!" Suzanna tripped on her petticoat and hit the ground.

Curses. Memories belonging to her and to silent mouths. Weeds swallowing headstones. A church bell ringing for the graves. Mama weeping at midnight.

Brothers dangling from ropes.

Suzanna groaned into the earth. She had found the home she'd always wanted. His doors had opened for her, but she'd refused to step inside them. She couldn't accept that she was worthy of such a kind place. If curses existed, they didn't only surround her . . .

They *were* her.

"No, no." Suzanna shook her head to keep the notion from papering the walls of her mind. She was to blame for August leaving. The discrepancy between her words and feelings rather than the supernatural had taken him. She'd allowed fear to push him away.

Obediah dropped to his knees beside Suzanna. He scooped her from the dirt and into his lap, whispering consolations as she buried her face in the crease of his neck.

"I'm cursed," she said.

"No, you ain't."

"How do you know?"

Obediah cupped her face in his work-worn hands. "Because cursed people curse other people. I count my blessings every time I look at you."

The curse was more than bad luck, Suzanna realized. For so long, she'd viewed it as a divine force orchestrating misfortune when really, it existed within her. The curse was a pattern she could not disrupt, a lie she willingly swallowed. She'd built herself on it, functioned out of it.

She'd given it power over her.

If only she hadn't accepted Martha's words so readily, she might've been capable of receiving August at the start. The gulf between her belief in the curse and her desire to live beyond it had prevented her from deciding her own fate.

Suzanna wondered if the curse was rooted so deep within her she'd never fully cut it out. It would grow and climb like kudzu until it suffocated her and everyone she loved.

"You can't give up, you hear me?" Obediah rested his forehead against Suzanna's brow, his face hazing into shadows and stubble. "The world is a wicked place, but you exist in it, and since God made you, I must believe He made other things good too."

Fighting the weight of silk and crinoline, Suzanna rose to her knees and gazed down the road. She beheld the dark, filled her lungs with its miasma.

August was gone, and with him went Suzanna's hope. Her pain would lessen over time, but she knew no matter how much she healed, her scar would forever be eager to bleed for him.

"You love August, don't you?" Obediah asked.

She nodded.

"I'll go after him."

"No, Obediah—" Suzanna grabbed his sleeve to keep him from leaving.

"Look, I know you won't choose me. That don't make a difference. I love you, and I always will. Some men look at women, and it's all or nothing. I'm not like that. Because you—*you* are everything to me regardless of what happens next. I'll find August, and I'll bring him back to you." Obediah climbed from the road, and Suzanna rose with him.

His gaze told her all he wanted was for her to find happiness.

Much of him was a tall tale, but one myth was true to its size. He loved her, and she belonged to him in a way no other person would.

Obediah leaned forward. "May I kiss you? Just once."

Their story began in childhood, two youngins racing across fields with daisy chains around their necks. They grew up like that, bound to nature, bound to each other, the swamp their home, woven into their muscles and bones. Fate would soon write them apart, but here, in the quiet, they had their together. *Happily ever after* could just as easily occur in a moment.

Suzanna glided her thumb along Obediah's cheek. She anchored her index finger behind his ear and rose onto her toes, drawing his mouth to hers.

A kiss to count for a lifetime.

They collided in a blaze. Obediah embraced her, kissing fiercely.

Their love was the wilderness. It could never be fully explored.

CHAPTER 21

SUSANA PRATHER

SEPTEMBER, PRESENT DAY

I awake to sunlight ribboning through lace curtains.

The panels lie neglected on my bedroom floor, damp with footprints. I didn't put them up last night. I chose to fall asleep with my window raised and a stool nearby.

Water drips from my pajamas. I savor the feeling of it, a drug-like sensation lingering in my body. The sleepwalking did something to me. It satisfied a hunger, scratched an itch.

I sit up in bed and wipe the swamp from my eyes. A sweet taste, like honey and rainwater, fills my mouth. I'm warm and floaty, my fear numbed to a euphoric buzz.

After battling the curse for months, I'm grateful for relief.

Nobody needs to know about my sleepwalking, not even Godwin. I understand removing the barricade is dangerous, and I shouldn't like the way the dream made me feel.

I'm too exhausted to care.

In last night's flashback, Suzanna changed her mind about the curse. She realized her own belief rather than enchantment had led to losing August.

There's something unnatural about what's happening to me. I wish breaking my curse was as simple as choosing not to believe lies, but the sleepwalking and this feeling say otherwise. Perhaps Suzanna wasn't cursed; she only did the cursing.

Same as before, I strip my sheets and change my clothes. I erase all evidence of the night, and what I can't wash or dry, I hide under makeup.

This can be my secret.

After school, I stop at Floyd's Gas Mart to purchase bait for Papa. Mark Shealy loiters at the counter while Floyd Sloan bags minnows.

Mark steps aside when I approach the register. "I'm telling you, Floyd. Weird stuff be happening out in the Okefenokee. Gators are moving into new territory by the droves."

I place a container of night crawlers on the counter.

Floyd winks at me and scans the bait. "That'll be four dollars, Susana." He accepts my money, tucking the bills in his cash drawer. "Your pa coming to pick with me tomorrow?"

"He wouldn't miss bluegrass night."

"Glad to hear it." Floyd chuckles. He's related to Holler somehow, either a great-uncle or distant cousin. A poster of Holler's football headshot decorates the store window.

"Those gators know something we don't," Mark says. "It ain't the right time of year for them to move about. Gives me the willies, to be honest with you."

"What's causing it, do you think?" I ask him.

"No telling. Critters sense bad things before we do."

"Explains why my hound dog won't go within ten feet of you, you coot." Floyd nudges the container of worms toward me. "You take care now, Susana."

The alligators must sense the curse's progression.

I leave the gas station and drive toward Kettle Creek. I roll down my window, sucking the viscous breeze into my lungs. It reminds me of petrichor, the smell after a rainstorm. A beautiful word that says, "You had a terrible time of it. Take a breath. The air is sweeter now."

Today, I just want to feel good.

Godwin doesn't hear me pull up to his barn. Wearing a felt hat he shaped himself, he unlatches the corral's gate and deepens his voice as he calls in the horses.

They gallop from the pasture and cluster around a trough.

I whistle at Godwin. He looks at me, and his mouth stretches into a smile like sunshine. A gnawed toothpick juts from its corner, pinned between his teeth.

My vision gets hot and blurry. I'm not sure how to explain my decision to sleepwalk. I could say I'm facing the curse, but that would mean I can look it in the eyes.

No, this choice doesn't feel brave, only hopeless, maybe even selfish. I'm tired of resisting and not getting anywhere. I don't have any more fight left.

I won't tell Godwin. I don't want him to realize he'll lose me.

After we fix an irrigation pipe near the hog pens, we drive separately to meet Nanny and Papa at the Green Frog. I stop at JC's house on the way.

He asked to borrow a couple of books for a school project.

Eventually I end up in a corner booth at the Green Frog, across from a mural of the Okefenokee. Nanny and Papa order sweet tea and pulled pork and quiz Godwin about combines.

Missouri Jane waits on us, forcing Papa to eat a side salad. The small plate of iceberg lettuce and croutons hardly compensates for the biscuits she brings moments later.

I observe the interaction like someone at a drive-in movie. My family seems far away, divided from me. I feel as though I'm out of my skin. Maybe I'm still high from sleepwalking. Maybe dissociating is another symptom of sleep deprivation.

Once we finish eating, we meander outside with our leftovers in Styrofoam boxes. I catch a glimpse of the pond, its lily pads, and I get a familiar craving.

Tonight, I'll sleepwalk again.

Godwin and I move toward our vehicles. I give a performance, faking small talk so he won't sense my secrets. If he believes I have the curse under control, he'll act normal.

I need some normal right now.

"Let's race," Godwin says casually.

"You're on." I run to my Cadillac while he sprints to his truck. I crash behind the wheel, key the ignition, and back from my parking spot.

Godwin reverses toward the highway. He does a three-point turn, blocking my path. I whip around him onto the road and speed toward Kettle Creek.

We cut across town in a whirlwind of squealing tires. I take back-roads to Jacksonville Highway. Once I reach the dirt road to Kettle Creek, I slam the accelerator, grinning as dirt plumes behind me and hair slaps my face.

A bittersweet feeling tightens my chest. I'm acutely aware I'll never repeat this moment.

Godwin almost drives into a fence, and I nearly kill three rabbits when joggling over a cattle guard. We brake in Nanny and Papa's driveway.

I stumble from my car, laughing at the foolishness of it all. "What took you so long?"

"Yeah, yeah, rub it in." Godwin steps from his truck. He grins and eases back the brim of his hat. "We should hang out sometime, just the two of us."

"And do what?"

"Three words. You. Me."

"What's the third word?"

"I forgot. The first two were enough." His cheeks dimple, and I fight a smile.

"Sweet talker, huh?"

"No, ma'am. I just call it as I see it." Godwin holds my gaze, his message loud and clear. He wants to go on a date with me.

"You should come to Floyd's tomorrow night." I'm terrible at showing my feelings. No matter what I do, my emotions get lost in the maze of me and never find their way out, so they wander the same halls, circle back to the same rooms.

Godwin nods, settling into a comfortable sort of quiet. After a while, he points at the house. "I left something for you on the porch."

He returns to his truck and waves as he retreats up the drive.

Suzanna lost August because of her belief in the curse. Maybe I should let Godwin take me to supper. I could wear my favorite dress and curl my hair and not think about the past.

I don't want to repeat Suzanna's mistake.

A box of old books waits on the porch with a note taped to its lid. *For S, from G.*

My heart does things an organ shouldn't do.

I rummage through the assortment—a family Bible, classic novels, an almanac printed in 1871. They must've come from Godwin's house. All of them are filled with handwritten notes and underlines.

Smiling so big my cheeks hurt, I hoist the box onto my hip and drift into the house. I place the books on the kitchen table and sort them into stacks.

My hand stalls over a battered copy of John Muir's *Wilderness*

Essays. I lift its cover and there, written on the title page in neat print, are Godwin's words.

> A hundred years from now, I hope this book ends up in a collection like yours, and someone knows how much it meant to me. Until then, I give it to you, so you can see what changed my thinking for the better. I like that we have nature in common.
>
> —Godwin

Reflexively, I flip through a tattered Bible and pause at a list of names scribbled on a back page. The roster begins with Richard Godwin, born 1811, died 1850.

August Godwin was his son.

My stomach drops at the sight of the name inked beside August. *Suzanna Godwin.*

"You home, Susana?" Nanny opens the screen door and bustles into the kitchen with her leftovers in one hand and Penny Pinchers bags in the other. "What're you, a stunt driver?"

"Godwin wanted to race." I shut the Bible and repack the books into their box, trying not to appear shaken by the mention of Suzanna.

"Where'd you get those?" Nanny motions to the books.

"Godwin left them for me."

"Be careful with him. Y'all seem close."

"We're friends."

"Too close." She places the bags on the counter and her leftovers in the fridge.

"You and Papa insisted he come around. I'm nice to him. Isn't that what you wanted?"

"I see how y'all look at each other," Nanny says. "Don't forget what happened to your mama. You have it in your blood."

"What, the need to get pregnant?" I ball my fists to keep them from shaking. Anger pulses through me, so intense floaters dot my vision. "I spoke with Keziah Douglas."

Nanny gapes at me.

"What did Mama do?"

"Don't you pay that old bat any mind," Nanny snaps. "She has it out for us."

"Why? What aren't you telling me?"

"I better go feed the chickens."

"Nanny—"

"I don't want to rehash the past," she yells. "I don't want to relive it either." Her expression hardens, and her eyes go blank as if she's gazing into a memory.

Before I can respond, she vanishes out the back door.

A creepy-crawly feeling slithers up my spine. I brace my weight against the table, lightheaded at the thought of what Nanny and Papa might be hiding.

Keziah said my family had secrets.

1855

Vicy Ann died the first of January.

Her body was laid to rest behind closed doors until the burying ground thawed. Fever took her, then continued its pilgrimage to the Douglas homestead, where it stole breath from two youngins under the age of twelve.

The Yawns had warred against the illness. They'd concocted elixirs of bearded lichen to fight Vicy Ann's disease. They'd boiled yellow bonnet lilies into tea, praying the concoction would help the child breathe. For a while, she appeared on the mend.

But then came the frost, winter's bite too severe for the infirm.

Mrs. Yawn had called for the preacher and a Muscogee woman living in Old Nine. When the spiritual failed to help, she resorted to old wives' tales and placed a knife under Vicy Ann's mattress, hoping to cut her pain. Eventually the girl succumbed to her afflictions.

John stopped the clock at time of death to spurn bad luck. Mr. Yawn turned a portrait of Vicy Ann to the wall so no other family member would die.

One by one the Yawns laid hands on the deceased, believing the gesture would mitigate their souls. Suzanna placed a bundle of Vicy Ann's hair on the mantel, for legend claimed if they knew where her spirit dwelled, they'd never be haunted.

Suzanna cleaned the house as her parents mourned. She hung wax myrtle in the kitchen and washed Vicy Ann's blankets with sweet pepperbush and lye.

The loss was emptiness. An empty space of bed, an empty seat at the table.

Suzanna felt too hollow to grieve her sister, as if other losses had cut all emotion from her body. She'd poured out her tears for her murdered brothers and August Godwin. Now, in the wake of Vicy Ann's death, Suzanna bore immense guilt for not saving more of herself for her sister.

A spell of good weather allowed a funeral.

Mr. Yawn carried Vicy Ann from the bedroom and placed her on the table. Suzanna washed the girl, then clothed her ashen body in her Sunday best.

The family gathered with an assemblage in the church cemetery. Townsfolk paid their respects, swapping furtive glances as Mrs. Yawn wailed over her fourth child given to the grave.

Elizabeth Ruger commented on how Vicy Ann looked becoming in her pinewood coffin, with a bouquet of rose pogonias nestled between her hands.

As though beauty in death was a great achievement.

The burial ended with figures in black dispersing like a murder of crows. Suzanna walked behind her family's wagon, calloused to her mama's weeping. She beheld the landscape as it conflated saw palmettos with slash pines and cinnamon ferns.

Even nature had the decency to quiet itself in solidarity.

Life had become a penumbra, Suzanna thought. She was on the dark side of the moon, or perhaps she'd died, and this was hell.

Ibises peered down from their rookery without a sound.

No amount of hair on the mantel could prevent Suzanna's private haunting. She was petrified of the dark things that slept within her, afeared of her own loneliness. Obediah had gone after August months prior. Without them, she felt untethered, loose to float into madness and sorrow and whatever else.

Tragedy must've befallen them, for Suzanna had yet to receive word.

Being alone withheld Suzanna from rest. She could not lie in the bed that had cradled her sister's corpse, nor could she shut her eyes without dreaming of August.

Her intuition said to lament them both.

Mrs. Yawn confined herself to the cabin, debilitated by sorrow. Night after night, she rose in terror and sprinted outside with Suzanna on her heels.

The woman died in mid-February.

What led to her demise, no person could be sure. The Yawns reported she'd awoken at dawn, lucid and eager for work. She'd poled a boat across the lake in search of pink lichen.

John later discovered cured meat absent from the cupboard.

Although folks dubbed Mrs. Yawn's death an accident, Suzanna knew her mama had gone looking for an end. The woman had guzzled moonshine and discarded its bottle on a carpet of sphagnum moss. Then she'd waded into the ebony water, where chatoyant eyes blinked among pipewort and cypress knees.

She must've tucked meat into her corset to lure beasts from their hibernation.

Reptiles tore her limb from limb and scattered her pieces among lilies.

Mr. Yawn blamed insanity for his wife's passing, in part to prevent criticism. If people learned the truth, they'd call Mrs. Yawn a coward.

Her decision was calculated. All creatures, big and small, had their limits.

Mrs. Yawn had chosen death over burying another child.

Suzanna understood, which frightened her. She berated herself for not feeling more, but her relatives were like soldiers cut down in war.

Cry for each loss, and the fighting wouldn't get done.

Louisa and John sobbed inconsolably, sick with despair, while Suzanna felt only relief. She was liberated from her mama's night terrors. Perhaps now she'd find peace.

Once a search party gathered Mrs. Yawn's fragments, the family buried them in a bucolic plot next to Vicy Ann and the boys. Four living bodies convened around five tombstones.

Suzanna counted three more people to lose.

Nights were quiet after the funeral. Suzanna dozed in a rocking chair near the hearth with the rifle clutched to her chest. She despised herself for relishing the serenity, for missing August and Obediah as much as her own flesh and blood. Her ache for them seemed untoward. Nevertheless, she nodded off to their memory in the tranquility death had given.

As months passed without news of the boys' whereabouts, Suzanna took over her mama's duties. She tended her siblings and the homestead while her daddy worked Ruger's land. At dusk each day, she ventured to the Okefenokee's banks to watch mallards feast on weeds. The visit became routine, a reprieve from domestic chores.

Suzanna knelt on peat, lured by the swamp, whether it be magic or wilderness or the temptation to follow in her mama's footsteps.

Talk of the curse resurrected in Kettle Creek. The Douglases blamed the Yawns for the deaths of their children. Martha Douglas paraded through town, swearing up and down the Yawns were jinxes. She claimed anyone who associated with them would receive bad luck.

Adding to her theatrics, she prophesied further calamity.

Sure enough, on the fifth day of April, Mr. Yawn was attacked by wild hogs and left in a wretched state. His leg was so gnawed, a doctor from Old Nine amputated the appendage.

With Mr. Yawn unable to earn a wage, Suzanna charged John with housework and labored in Ruger's fields. Her daddy would either die from infection or live as a cripple.

Suzanna needed to provide for her family and keep her siblings alive until John was old enough to find work. The burden overwhelmed her, the tasks unnumberable. Eventually she grew so worried out, she collapsed from exhaustion on a walk to town.

Perhaps August and Obediah would return.

Suzanna clung to the hope with a white-knuckle grip. She imagined a day when August would greet her with open arms, and she'd feel safe again.

The hope dimmed when a dove flew over the Yawn's cabin. John said it was a sign, an omen signaling the approach of sad news. Suzanna's thoughts went to August and Obediah. What if August had found a bride in Atlanta, or worse, he and Obediah had met their deaths?

Without a reason to celebrate, Suzanna forgot her eighteenth birthday. She could nary recall the month, to say nothing of the day.

On that chilly morning, she lowered a bonnet over her plaited tresses and knotted its ribbon under her chin. She attended a church service unaccompanied.

The curse began as a seed, a seemingly innocent thing, which then sprouted and grafted. It grew with time, sinking its roots deeper, winding boughs around its hosts.

Suzanna addressed the congregation. "You are what you say I

am. May the curse of my mama's spirit and mine be placed among the people of this here land. Your kin shall walk in your footsteps. Generation after generation. Your voice will decide their days. Your deeds will stain their hands. Until you see the truth of what you are."

The curse never held power on its own. Like a parasite, it required a source. People fed it eagerly, nourishing it with their aligned thinking.

"Your kin will be what you say I am. Until they scrape and crawl from your silence and lies and say otherwise. With my blood I make what only my bones can break."

The curse was an idea, a whisper in the backs of heads. It infected family trees with propaganda and superstition and watched chaos ensue.

"I don't yearn for this life anymore. I'd rather join my dead than spend another moment with you. Let me reunite with them in peace."

All people were the same, the cursed and cursers. They issued their hexes and sustained those given to them. Repeating, repeating. They wished to blame everything but themselves.

In response to Suzanna, lightning veined the sky, and thunder clapped like a gavel approving her judgment. Even the earth quivered in agreement.

Suzanna lumbered toward the Okefenokee. She'd reached her limits.

She had nothing left to give.

Gasping, Suzanna crashed through blackberry bushes and wrestled her skirt from thorns. She reached the shore, where earth vanished beneath still water. If she hesitated, she'd lose her nerve, so she continued onward and followed a trail to the lake.

The waterway expanded into a deep lagoon.

Suzanna froze, a tear slipping down her cheek. Death would resolve her agony, but what if August returned in search of her? He and Obediah would find a tombstone instead.

How cruel it would be to subject them, along with her surviving family members, to the loss. Suzanna didn't want to cause pain, but she herself was lost and losing. From her well of grief, she couldn't see the sun.

August Godwin would not return. Suzanna released all hope.

Possessed by nature or her own despair, she took a step.

CHAPTER 22

SUSANA PRATHER

OCTOBER, PRESENT DAY

I go with Papa and his banjo to Floyd's Gas Mart.

A bell chimes when we enter the convenience store. JC waves from the register, dressed in his Okefenokee Swamp Park uniform.

"Does Floyd know you're wearing that?" Papa asks.

"I didn't have time to change," JC admits. "Tomorrow I'll wear my gas station T-shirt to the park, you know, to even the score. Consider it cross promotion."

Papa chuckles. "Boys out back?"

"Same place." JC throws bottle caps at my head as I pass the counter. I snatch a bag of peanuts from a shelf and hurl it at him. He ducks, laughing.

Papa and I move across the store to a hallway lined with bathrooms and storage closets. We exit through an emergency door onto a patio decorated with string lights. Musicians form a circle, seated on crates and lawn chairs.

"Seab, Susana, y'all come join us," Floyd yells.

Godwin looks up from his guitar, a grin reaching across his face.

The other musicians include men from church and a Burrell who chain-smokes Marlboros and talks exclusively about NASCAR. They remove their instruments from cases, everything from mandolins to fiddles.

Resisting the urge to run to Godwin, I saunter to the chair beside him. I sit and hug my cardigan around me, sipping the coffee I bought from the Green Frog.

The night is cooler than I anticipated even with Floyd's usual oil barrel bonfire.

"You better keep up now, kid. Us here are pros," Mark Shealy tells Godwin.

"I'll do my best, but don't expect much." Godwin toys with his guitar's tuning pegs. He wears jeans and a Carhartt jacket. His hair is wild and damp as if he showered and dried it with a towel before racing over here.

"Seab, you start us off," Floyd says.

"Let me get my tuning right." Papa adjusts his banjo's pegs. He plucks a couple notes, and the other musicians join in, improvising a rendition of "Blackberry Blossom."

The melody sweeps across the patio, building into a sound I consider one of the best in the world. Godwin strums and picks along. He's better than I expect. His fingers dance across the guitar's neck and strings, though not as fast as Papa.

Nobody here rivals Seaborn Prather.

I savor my coffee and bounce my heels as Mark Shealy guides the performance into another song. I bet the workers over at the lumber mill can hear the ensemble.

As Floyd plucks a ditty from his bass, Godwin leans close to me. He wedges a pick between his teeth and whispers from the corner of his mouth, "Did you like the books?"

I nod. "Where'd you find them?"

"The cellar."

"You shouldn't let me keep the Bible. It lists your ancestors."

"Really? I didn't look."

"It says August Godwin married Suzanna Yawn."

Godwin raises his eyebrows. "You're kidding. That can't be right."

"Quit your flirting, boy, and ask the girl to dance," Mark shouts across the circle.

"Yeah, it'll give you an excuse to hold her hand," Floyd says with a laugh.

Papa huffs. "In case y'all forgot, that girl's granddaddy is sitting right here."

I choke on my coffee.

Godwin turns redder than a radish. He tousles his messy hair and studies the square toes of his boots. "Nah, I got two left feet. Besides, Susana ain't one for corny gestures."

"Who says?" I pivot toward Godwin, resting my knees against his thigh.

His mouth crooks with a smile. "You wanna dance?"

"Do you want to?"

Godwin signals to Papa. "Mind if I dance with her, sir?"

"Be my guest. Her nanny ain't around to stop you."

"Well, all right then." Godwin looks at me with certainty, as if he's sure about us, he's sure about me. He places his guitar on the pavement and offers his hand.

My heart racing, I tuck my coffee into a cupholder. "This'll be embarrassing."

"I'll make sure of it," Godwin says with a wink.

Before I can persuade myself otherwise, I take his hand, curling my fingers around his knuckles. He pulls me from my chair and into his arms.

The men cheer as we spin around the circle in a clumsy swing. Godwin twirls me, blurring the patio into streaks of bonfire and string lights.

"Watch those hands, boy!" Papa yells.

"Yessir." Godwin raises his palms to the base of my rib cage. He snickers, blushing when I pull him closer. His touch lingers like the warmth of coffee in my throat.

"Dad called from rehab earlier today. He's not coming home for a long while," Godwin says once the music relaxes.

"What does that mean for you?"

"I'm not sure yet." Godwin spins me again, and I collide with his chest, laughing. "We don't have to do what people expect us to do or what we said we'd do."

"Have you changed your mind about leaving?"

"I don't know my own mind well enough to change it." He rocks me side to side and presses his mouth to my ear. "I'm learning what I want."

A breath catches in my throat.

He gives me goose bumps.

I like the way he treats my grandparents, how he works hard and understands Kettle Creek. I like his ambition, responsibility, and sense of duty. I like it when he deepens his voice to call in his horses and when he blushes for no reason.

He looks at me as if I'm someplace beautiful.

I like that too.

Godwin ends our dance after the next song. "I should go. I have to be up early."

"Me too." I step back and rub my arms. I feel cold without him. "Would you give me a ride? Papa likes to hang around for a while."

"Yeah, of course." He goes to his guitar and packs it in a case.

"Godwin's gonna drive me home," I tell Papa.

"Ain't that sweet." Mark puckers his lips and makes kissy faces.

Papa stops playing his banjo. If looks could kill, his would bury Mark alive. "Golly, it's a wonder you haven't been punched."

"Good night, y'all," Godwin says with a wave.

"See you at home, Papa." I throw my coffee cup into a trash can and follow Godwin to his Chevy Silverado. He places his guitar case in the truck bed, then clears the passenger seat, tossing a pair of wire cutters into the back.

I climb inside, my sinuses prickling with the faint smell of cigarettes. The interior is as I remember. A layer of dirt coats the dashboard.

Gus Godwin's ratty bandana hangs from the rearview mirror.

"The guys aren't always like that," I say when Godwin cranks the ignition.

"Really?"

"No, they are . . . but usually Papa calls Mark 'an ornery son of a gun,' and they eat boiled peanuts and talk about George Strait."

"Hey, the night isn't over." Godwin cracks a smile. He drives onto Swamp Road, our voices replaced with the rattle of air in vents and the crunch of gravel under tires.

The landscape scrolls past, from pine forests to farmland.

"What kind of music do you like?" Godwin asks.

"All kinds. I don't know." I laugh, maybe because his question strikes me as rudimentary, like something a person would ask on a first date.

"Why're you laughing?"

I nudge him. "Why're we awkward?"

"I'm not awkward." Godwin nudges me back, and I laugh harder. He rubs his mouth to loosen the grin from his face.

"Okay, okay." I prop my elbow on the windowsill. Outside, fields lift into a navy sky dotted with constellations. "Have you been to LA?"

"Yeah, once," Godwin says.

"Are the stars pretty?"

"The stars?"

"Isn't it the city of stars?"

Godwin looks at me with his mouth agape. "Susana, you can't be serious. That's it. I'm taking you away from this town." He pretends to jerk the wheel, and I grab his arm.

His gaze lowers to my hand on his body. The humor drains from his expression, replaced with something bated. I recognize the gleam in his eyes.

Last time he stared at me this way, I almost kissed him.

My cheeks burning, I remove my hand and sink into my seat, jittery with emotions I can't name. They energize me like caffeine on an empty stomach.

We enter Kettle Creek and pass a chimney, the remnants of an old homestead. The rubble used to be Willard Ruger's house from my dreams.

Papa told me the place burned down in 1860 while Alice Ruger played her piano. She was blind and didn't notice the fire lapping up the parlor curtains. By the time she smelled smoke, it was too late. She perished in the flames.

According to local folklore, late at night when cicadas weary of their calls, one can still hear the melody from Alice's piano and her spirit wailing for salvation.

I suppose we're all ghost stories in the end.

"Papa found a skunk in the chicken coop earlier. He shot it dead with an air rifle," I say to lessen the tension between Godwin and me.

He snorts with laughter. "What is this conversation?"

"I don't know, but it's nice, right?"

"Yeah." Godwin holds my gaze a second too long, as if he's waiting for me to say what I'm thinking, what we're both feeling.

I shouldn't keep my sleepwalking a secret from him. If he learns I haven't been honest, he'll repeat what he said at the bar and claim nothing has changed.

Maybe he'll be right.

"Last year, after I left you at the bar, what happened?" I pivot toward Godwin, a pang of guilt tightening my chest.

Godwin snickers. "Bill Owens and I found bicycles and jousted with pool sticks."

"After our fight?"

"I was all riled up."

"Did you win?"

"My shoulder was sore the next day." He shrugs, oblivious to the fact I hoped for a different answer. I thought he might tell me he'd spent the night brooding.

I want him to say what I want to say, but I want him to say it first.

Godwin turns into Nanny and Papa's driveway. He parks near the carport, then hurries around the truck to open my door for me.

I let him walk me to the house. Nanny must've gone to bed. The porch lights are off.

Once we reach the screen door, Godwin tells me good night and extends his arms. I loop mine around his waist, colliding with him. I can't explain why, but three words swell to my tongue. I swallow them down. It wouldn't make sense to say *I miss you*.

Unless *I miss you* means *you are missing from me*.

"See you tomorrow." Godwin releases me from the hug.

I straighten my skirt and rearrange my hair, grateful for the darkness. I don't want Godwin to realize what his touch does to me.

He ambles toward his truck and stops midstride. "Let's go back."

"What?" I tense when he spins around. His face beams a question, and my knees buckle in response. We might've rebuilt our friendship, but I'm still afraid of the same things.

"I don't need sleep," he says. "You want to?"

"No, I have school tomorrow."

"Come on, Susana."

My heart goes haywire. I don't trust myself to be alone with Godwin.

"Next time. Good night." I rush inside and latch the door. I stand frozen in the foyer, half relieved, half angry at myself.

There's no *together* in the end. Until the curse takes me, Godwin and I will part ways like this, giving our final words through doorways before we shut the doors.

I wander back a step to accept the space I must create. It's safer not to pretend he and I will fall in love in the end. At least when I die, he'll only grieve me as a friend.

The thought nauseates me.

Godwin's truck rumbles awake, but it doesn't leave. Headlights cut through curtains and paint swirling shadows across the floor.

I hurry to the dining room and peer out the window. Godwin's truck hasn't moved.

He's waiting for me to change my mind.

Unable to breathe, I lower to the rug and hug my knees. I want to throw caution to the wind and race out the door, into his arms. I want to do what I almost did a year ago.

My phone vibrates against my hip. Godwin's name appears on the screen, above a text message containing a playlist titled *Who Needs Sleep*.

I tell him to go without me.

Eventually he leaves, but I remain pinned to the floor by heavy emotions. My skin tingling, I imagine what would've happened if I'd changed my mind.

I would've kissed him.

That's why I didn't go.

1855

The swamp did not take Suzanna.

Try as she might to give herself to the depths, the Okefenokee returned her. Its spirit possessed her, or so the people of Kettle Creek believed. They no longer referred to her as a Yawn. In conversations, she was known only as "the witch."

Her outburst at the church prompted the title, as did reports from trappers who claimed all living creatures were enraptured by her; she lived and breathed with a heartbeat that pulsed within the earth. Her disappearance only encouraged such tales.

Suzanna withdrew to an island deep within the swamp. There she built a commissary with help from her brother. Willard Ruger funded the project, believing the investment would provide needed material to those who dwelled in the wilderness. Suzanna ran the store. As compensation, Ruger cared for her family, ensuring their bellies never went empty.

Alone and unbothered, Suzanna lived in peace at the water's edge. Beasts kept her company, reptiles during the day, bobcats at night. She broke ground behind her home and planted vegetables. She hunted and skinned hogs, bears, and snakes.

Trappers visited the commissary for provisions. They brought their pelts and coins to trade. No one dared to lift a finger against Suzanna. They feared her, the girl homesteading land few had treaded upon. They boated their sick to her doorstep for herbal remedies.

She'd learned to create medicine from a Muscogee living near Blackjack Prairie.

Without news from August and Obediah, Suzanna accepted her

solitude. Living apart from civilization eased her soul. Where the ground trembled, nothing mattered besides survival.

She did survive. At first, doing so exhausted her, but moment by moment, breath by breath, she rediscovered her will to live. It burned in sunsets and jobs well done. It found a home beside crackling fires, with the savory taste of catfish stew.

Autumn grayed into winter, and days grew cold. One morning Suzanna noticed ice webbing from the shoreline. To her, the frost seemed an omen biding its time.

When the swamp iced over, if it ever did, an end would draw near.

The augury haunted her thoughts. Unable to rest, she spent nights huddled in firelight, restocking the commissary's shelves. Lanterns warred against the dark, and from the Okefenokee cried all sorts of living things, as if they, too, were distressed by the sun's early descent.

One evening in December, as Suzanna prepared for closing, two men visited the store. They roped their boat to the dock, then climbed groaning steps to the commissary's porch.

"Fresh out of supper if that's what you're here for," Suzanna called from behind the counter. She penciled numbers into a ledger as the patrons moved about.

Floorboards creaked under their boots.

Suzanna glanced up, and her lungs emptied. August Godwin stood an arm's length away, unchanged except for a couple of inches added to his hair and tan where paleness used to be.

"G'evening." August placed a beaver fur on the counter. "I'd like to barter this here pelt for matches and cornmeal if you're so inclined."

Obediah watched from across the room. He locked eyes with Suzanna and he tipped his hat. Then, without a word, he slipped outside, closing the door behind him.

He'd fulfilled his promise and brought August home to her.

Suzanna drew a breath and held it captive. She fumbled with the ledger, knocking it off the counter. "I can give you a box and two pounds."

"Fine by me," August said with a nod.

"How long're you back for?" Suzanna gathered the items, unable to pry her gaze from him. She could hardly believe he was real and not a figment of her imagination.

"I ain't going nowhere."

Suzanna gave him the matches and cornmeal, then mounted his pelt on a rack with other animal skins. "Did you hire those farmhands?"

"Not yet. I figure I'll find help around here when the time comes." He leaned against the counter, beholding Suzanna as if she were a world wonder. "I'm sorry it took me so long."

"I didn't think I'd see you again."

"Obediah found me months ago. We planned to ride straight here, but then my cousin got into trouble, and his wife had a baby." August bowed his head. "I wrote to you—"

"I didn't get any letters."

He snapped to attention. His eyes widened, and Suzanna got the sense his letters contained more than his whereabouts. Perhaps Obediah had told him of her feelings.

"Have your cousin's matters been settled?" Suzanna inched around the counter until she and August stood face-to-face, nothing between them.

"In a manner of speaking." August reached for Suzanna's hand but hesitated. His fingers brushed the trim of her sleeve. "I heard about your mama and sister. You have my condolences."

Tears warming her eyes, she gestured to the commissary, its shelves and barrels, the rafters weighted with antlers. "I built this place with my brother."

August clenched his jaw. He seemed to understand the hell Suzanna had endured. That, or he blamed himself for their separation. "May I come around tomorrow?"

"Please."

He slid the cornmeal and matches into his pack and headed to the door. Before crossing the threshold, he turned. "Suzanna, there's nobody else."

She winced as though someone had yanked a knife from her chest. It'd been there all year, carving into her heart. She'd grown accustomed to the pain, but now it was gone.

"August, I was a fool—"

"What's a year if I have you now?" he said while his eyes said *I love you.*

Thus began the happiest time Suzanna Yawn would know. She fell into love and never crawled out. Grief wounded her, but so did her affection, and from it she never recovered.

August and Obediah visited the commissary day after day. They brought pelts to trade and sat with Suzanna on the porch, where they shared tales of yesteryear.

They divulged the troubles that had prevented their return.

August's cousin had been caught stealing livestock from a neighbor. In accordance with the law, he'd been sentenced to death and hanged in a public execution.

His wife gave birth to a son not long after.

August and Obediah had stayed with the widow to assist her with the farm. As luck would have it, the barn caught fire, killing the hogs and all but two horses. The widow believed her husband's errors had cursed their land. She packed her wagon and, with August and Obediah as escorts, moved south to live with her family.

She renamed her son August in hopes the child would not follow in his daddy's footsteps.

"Return tomorrow and shoot the buck that's been feeding on my field," Suzanna instructed once August and Obediah finished telling their story. They agreed but did not arrive the next day. Instead, they came two mornings after, outfitted for a week of trapping.

They waltzed into the commissary with rifles and bedrolls.

Suzanna shook her head. "You needn't go today. Won't have luck killing him."

"Now's a fine time to hunt," August said.

"You can go, but you won't get him today."

August stepped outside. Immediately one of the hammers popped from his gun. He picked up the piece and tried to click it into place without success.

Obediah wagged his finger at Suzanna. "This is your doing, ain't it?"

August propped the rifle against his shoulder. "One barrel will shoot."

They departed for their hunt and returned empty-handed. Suzanna laughed at the sight of them while gutting fish on the porch steps.

"I don't think you had a deer here," Obediah said.

"He's out there, but you came on the wrong day." Suzanna wiped her knife on her skirt. "Come back next Tuesday, and you'll get him."

Out of curiosity, the boys followed her instructions. They arrived Tuesday morning and ventured into the field behind the commissary. Not even fifteen minutes had passed when a buck appeared in the wire grass. August shot the animal with his one-barrel rifle.

He and Obediah carried it to Suzanna, who bled it a safe distance from gators.

"You got a bit of miracle in you," August told Suzanna.

"Monsters more likely." She carved the antlers from the buck's skull, then doused their base with salt. Once dry, she mounted the rack above the commissary's door.

"How'd you know about the buck?" August asked.

"Nature has patterns," Suzanna told him. "If you pay attention, it'll tell you things."

"Folks in town say you're of the supernatural kind."

"Do you believe them?"

August chuckled. "Suzanna Yawn, there ain't nothing ordinary about you."

Months passed without talk of marriage. August and Obediah called on Suzanna, trading their trappings for hot dinners and a roof over their heads.

Eventually they would return to Kettle Creek for spring planting.

Suzanna grew tired of waiting for August to propose. After so many days apart, she wanted him and a fresh start, to leave the swamp as a Godwin, not a Yawn.

Her feelings bewitched her unabashedly. She refused to let the curse or even the thought of it prevent her from wedding August. Too much of her life had been governed by fear.

She was determined not to give the curse any more power.

Then again, perhaps August had decided against marrying her. She'd become a pariah, the so-called witch. People looked at her and saw disaster.

Her past was unescapable, her history already written.

Suzanna couldn't bring herself to broach the topic, worried August would confirm he'd realized her damage and changed his mind. So often hope dwelled in the not knowing.

On a warm afternoon in late March, August visited the commissary alone. He found Suzanna crouched on the dock, her lissome form bent over rotten planks.

She abandoned her task and rose to greet him.

"I finished building my house," he told her. "*Our* house."

Lilies unfolded along the shoreline, feathering into pink-white blossoms.

"Your daddy gave me his blessing, Suzanna." August removed

his hat and lowered it to his side. "I've never loved you more than I do now, and tomorrow I'll say the same. Please marry me. Please be mine—"

"I'm yours, I'm yours." Suzanna rushed forward and drew his mouth to hers. With tears spilling down her cheeks, she gripped his collar and pulled him closer.

His kiss felt like healing, so she kissed him again.

Sunlight blazed through treetops, and the swamp buzzed awake as though it were spring; the hard winter was over. Flowers blossomed while reptiles peered from the black water.

August cupped Suzanna's face in his calloused hands. "I believe in love at first sight and second and third. I believe in loving you until I go blind and even then, *even then*."

His touch was the opposite of punishment. In it, Suzanna rested.

Cypresses groaned and swayed their moss. Greenery sprouted from mud, vining across the dock as August and Suzanna kissed. They drifted into a delicate and haunted love—

CHAPTER 23

SUSANA PRATHER

OCTOBER, PRESENT DAY

I wake up with JC's hand on my breast.

He drags me from the Okefenokee, screaming for help. We collapse onto peat. It gives under our weight like the rubber mulch on the elementary school playground.

We lie wet and dripping and gasp at the darkness. JC does so with panic while I breathe with disappointment. I didn't want to come up for air and leave the dream the swamp gave me.

Sinking my fingers into dirt, I crawl up the embankment and rise onto hesitant feet.

The night is still young, clocking around eleven if I had to guess. Stars glow faint and shy, dotting the blue-gray sky with needlepoint constellations.

JC coughs and wrings his ball cap. "Susana, are you all right? What were you doing?"

A vinegar taste burns my mouth. I swallow to make room for words, but the sourness only sours my stomach. JC won't forget tonight. He'll ask questions.

To answer them, I must explain my curse.

Godwin squeezes from a cluster of saw palmettos. He takes one look at my wet clothes, and panic ripples across his face. "Susana likes to go for night swims is all."

"In the swamp?" JC gawks at me as if I sprouted a third arm.

"What're you doing here?" Godwin shines his flashlight at JC, who blenches and squints.

"Mr. Prather said I could go night fishing. What're *you* doing here?"

"I saw your headlamp from my barn and came over to make sure nobody was breaking into the house." Godwin veers his attention to me. "Did the panels stop working?"

"I chose not to use them." Before Godwin can respond, I confront JC and fake a smile. "Go on home. I'll see you at school tomorrow."

"You expect me to believe you went for a swim?" JC stands and points at the swamp. "Ain't nobody swims out there, Susana."

"Why didn't you use the panels?" Godwin asks me.

"Let's talk about this later." I stride toward the farmhouse, my teeth chattering from the cold and thoughts of Godwin and JC learning my secrets.

A dull pain abides within my body. I rub my shoulders and neck, roll my head side to side. The flashback took a toll, maybe because I was pulled from it prematurely.

Godwin follows at my heels. "How long has this been going on?"

"I'll tell you tomorrow."

"Susana—" He blocks my path. "When'd you start sleepwalking again?"

JC huffs. "You were sleepwalking? Do your grandparents know?"

"I don't want to worry them."

With a scoff, JC makes a beeline to the house.

"No, please!" I run after him and clamp my fingers onto his bicep.

"You're keeping secrets. Why?" JC spins around, his bottom lip quivering. He studies my face, perhaps to winnow the truth from my expression. "Susana, it's me."

My chest aches from his desperation. I have every reason to trust him. Before Godwin, before my life stretched to accommodate more friends, I had JC.

He traded his secrets for mine, and we shared their weight.

"Were you planning to tell me?" Godwin shouts.

I signal for him to lower his voice.

"Cut the crap, Susana." He crosses our divide and leans so close to me his breath warms my skin. "After everything we've been through, why didn't you tell me?"

"I don't know."

"How'd you expect this to pan out, huh?" Godwin presses a fist to his mouth. He takes a deep breath, then motions to my bedroom window. "I made those panels to keep you safe."

"I'm sorry. I couldn't resist it anymore." My voice cracks. I reach for Godwin, but he steps back. "Sleepwalking feels good—"

"It'll kill you, Susana!"

"Yes, well, it's gonna kill me regardless."

Godwin flinches, his expression tight with the realization I've given up on breaking the curse. "You're selfish, you know that?"

"It's my life, Godwin."

"What, you planned to die and never tell me goodbye?" He shakes his head. "You haven't changed. I was an idiot for thinking otherwise."

JC swears. "Are you dying, Susana?"

"Godwin, please listen—"

"How can I trust you? You've never been honest with me."

"You don't know that."

"Our whole relationship, we've gone around in circles. I've tried to get close to you, and you've pushed me away for whatever reason." Godwin shrugs. "I can't compete with the curse, Susana. It beats me every time and honestly, I'm tired of picking a fight with it."

"I'm not pushing you away!"

"Then what is it you want? What're we doing?" Godwin stares at me. After a while, he clicks off his flashlight. "Until you can answer those questions, I'm out."

"What's going on?" JC watches Godwin retrace his steps and disappear into the gloom.

A tear running down my cheek, I reach for JC's hand. "I'll tell you."

"Tell me what?"

CHAPTER 24
SUSANA PRATHER

OCTOBER, PRESENT DAY

Cheerleaders bounce down the hallway in a procession of pom-poms.

Holler jogs ahead of the pack, giving high fives to students and faculty and commanding everyone to place their barbecue orders for the Berryville Family Reunion. Every year the marching band and football team sell plates as a fundraiser.

I remove textbooks from my locker.

After two o'clock, Berryville High reeks of pencils, feet, and tater tots. I breathe through my mouth and slam the locker door. JC stands on the other side.

I jump, spilling my books onto the deteriorating linoleum.

"Sorry. I didn't mean to scare you." JC gathers the texts and hands them to me along with a plastic shopping bag from Penny Pinchers. "Take this."

"What is it?"

JC rummages through the bag and removes a bundle of sage.

"Put that away before someone sees."

As students chant the school's fight song, JC grabs my arm and pulls me into the empty band room. He unfolds a piece of paper. "Look, I stayed up all night reading articles on the internet. A priest in Arkansas posted this prayer, said it'd get rid of curses."

"What else do you have?" I peer into the bag. It holds sage, sea salt, olive oil, and a wooden cross. "Are we hunting vampires or baking a pizza?"

"Sure, laugh it up. I just want to help."

"Thank you." I squeeze his hand.

Last night, when I told him about my situation, he thought I was kidding. His disbelief led to confusion to shock to him realizing why I'd passed out in his truck.

"Are you gonna stop sleepwalking?" JC shuffles his Timberlands against the floor. He shoots me a tentative look, his question tainted with another.

He wants to know if I plan to resist my fate.

"I can't break the curse." I clench my fists, digging my fingernails into my palms until they leave crescent shapes. "I'm really tired, JC."

My nose stings, and my eyes water. I cannot bring myself to put the truth into words, that I'd rather go gently into death than continue hoping for a miracle. Exhaustion has gnawed me to pieces. Searching for answers has taxed my emotions.

"I'll help you," JC says with a nod. "We'll figure out a way to break it."

"Godwin and I tried everything."

"Please don't give up."

"I've made my peace. I always knew this was a possibility, you know? None of the other women in my bloodline managed to break the curse."

JC grips the sides of my arms. "I'm not letting you go this easily."

The expression on his face takes me back to the county line incident, when I promised he wouldn't lose me. I suppose I must fight the curse, if not for myself, then for him.

"I'm running out of time."

"But we still have time." JC places his backpack on a piano and unzips its main compartment. "I wrote down some of what you told me. Suzanna's curse was meant for the townsfolk, right? We need to pinpoint why and how it backfired on her."

I peer over his shoulder as he flips through one of his notebooks.

"That whole curse-of-mama's-spirit thing explains the sleep-walking. You said Suzanna's mother had night terrors and went insane, correct?" JC reaches a page covered in scribbles.

Loose sheets of paper tumble onto the piano, some historical accounts printed off the internet, others hand-drawn family trees.

I thumb through the documents. "You've been busy."

"Like I said, I'm not letting you go." JC turns his notebook to show me a diagram similar to the one I made. "We should look for repetition in your family history."

"It's called insanity and death."

"The pattern is more complicated than that. I mean, look at us."

"What do you mean?"

"We're both kin to Suzanna and Obediah." JC turns his face, maybe to conceal his expression. "You said we're basically their clones."

"Yeah, and Godwin is a spitting image of August."

"See, I think we should consider every detail of your life." JC taps a highlighted section of his notes. "Have you tried saying you're not cursed?"

I laugh.

"Just checking. Some of the curse's phrasing is obscure."

With a sigh, I lower into a plastic chair. "I don't understand what Suzanna meant by blood and bones and 'the truth of what you are.'"

JC continues to study his notes.

"Nanny and Papa are keeping secrets from me," I tell him.

He snaps to attention. "How do you figure?"

"They won't explain Keziah Douglas's grudge against our family." I stand and pace the room. "They all blame themselves for what happened to Mama, but they won't tell me why."

A bell signals the next period.

"Do me a favor, all right?" JC slides the Penny Pinchers bag's handles onto my wrist. "At least read the Bible or something before you go to bed."

I leave the band room, joining students in a migration down the hallway.

JC treads on my heels and clings to my purse strap. "One more thing. What's the deal with Godwin? Are y'all together?"

"No."

"But you want to be."

"No."

"He wants to be."

"I don't know."

"Liar. Godwin obviously doesn't know you as well as I do," JC says as we near our English class. He smiles and leans to my ear. "You lift your eyebrows when you lie."

He jogs ahead, then spins and walks backward.

All the emotions from last night sweep through me. I stop in my tracks, hyperventilating as pain settles in my chest. "I ruin everything when it comes to him, always have."

I lost Godwin on purpose when we were fifteen and he wanted more of me. I leaned in to kiss him that night at the bar, then got mad when he leaned in too. For years, I've drawn him into a war between myself and the curse, yanked him along as I decided what had power over me.

He made the right choice by walking away.

I'm a sinking ship. I'll only drag him down.

"There're bad things inside me, JC." I dry my tears and force away the thought of Godwin. For now, I'll fold down the page of this chapter and move on with the story. Perhaps one day we'll turn back and pick up where we left off.

No, I must release Godwin from my turmoil. I can't hold on to the possibility of us.

Maybe is worse than *no* because *maybe* leaves room for *yes*.

"Hey, I didn't mean to kick a beehive." JC rushes back to me and pulls me into an embrace. "I'd rather not talk about Godwin anyway. I get jealous."

"Of him?" The bell rings a second time and I release JC. We saunter into the doorway of our classroom. Mrs. Capers stands at the whiteboard, listing examples of oral tradition.

JC gazes at me with that familiar softness. "Yes, Susana. Of him."

Pictures reel through my mind, flickering into something like a memory. I stand across from Obediah and August. They love me, and I love them, but I end up being their downfall.

My heart drums, echoing in my ears. What if the past has bled into the present? What if my life is nothing more than Suzanna's story reimagined?

I need the water's relief.

1856

Martha Douglas flew into a rage.

At hearing of August and Suzanna's engagement, she rose from her rocker and shattered a teacup against the wall, or so claimed the gossip circulating Kettle Creek. August's property bordered the Douglas homestead. If the wedding occurred, Suzanna would emerge from the Okefenokee and take residence nearby as Martha's neighbor.

The thought of a Muscogee living so close boiled Martha's blood. She called on August in the guise of friendly concern, gifting him a sweet potato pie and a warning.

She begged him to avoid the Yawns, for their nearness brought misfortune. She vowed Suzanna would curse him and everyone in her vicinity.

August stuck his finger in the pie's center. He tasted its filling, then said with a grin, "Ma'am, I reckon you curse me with a mighty good stomachache."

News of the tête-à-tête burned through town, sparked by Obediah and a copious amount of whiskey. From the settlement, it traveled across Ruger's fields, past the oaks bent into tortured angles, to the swamp's labyrinth of channels.

Suzanna caught wind of what had occurred. Whether gleaned from nature or the trappers frequenting her commissary, she learned of Martha's bearing and sought an end to the slander.

Her rifle loaded on her person, Suzanna departed the wilderness, rowing her boat toward Kettle Creek. She reached the shore of Ruger's land and walked the mile to Martha's homestead.

Douglases paused their work. They gaped at Suzanna, their eyes glazed with terror, as though she were the Grim Reaper come to claim their souls.

Suzanna went to the cabin and drummed her fist against its door.

Martha answered, then recoiled. She reached for the flintlock pistol strapped to her hip but stalled at the sight of Suzanna's rifle. "Why're you here?"

"Word travels fast." Suzanna aimed her weapon at Martha's face, steeling herself to pull the trigger if the woman aggressed. "From this day on, you will not interfere. You hear me?"

"You will be the death of him," Martha said.

Suzanna was unmoved. "I ain't got nothing more to say to you."

"Look at what you have become," Martha screeched. "The devil walks with you."

"I will marry August Godwin." Suzanna advanced, drawing back her rifle's hammer. She was hell-bent on disproving Martha and every voice calling her doomed.

The woman gave a nod, a sign of surrender.

Appeased, Suzanna turned and retraced her steps.

Martha followed. "Release me from your curse, I beg you!"

Suzanna paused, a feeling of satisfaction warming her body. Revenge did not require violence. Indeed, a mere word could set it into motion.

"Undo your hex," Martha gasped. "If you wish to punish me, do your worst, but please spare my children and their children."

Suzanna thought of her brothers dangling from Hangman's Oak, the years of torment she'd endured. Through clenched teeth, she whispered, "When you resurrect the dead."

Martha Douglas turned white as a sheet.

August and Suzanna were married a week later at Hard-Shell Baptist. Their wedding was performed in secret to avoid unwanted guests. In attendance were Suzanna's family, Obediah Owens, and the Rugers, who filled pews in the quiet of night.

Elizabeth lent Suzanna a yellow gown for a wedding dress. She fashioned a veil from tulle, insistent all women should feel bridal for their nuptials.

Bells chiming at witching hour, August and Suzanna fled the church and went to the land they'd call home. There, bound in blankets, they dozed under a full moon.

"I like this story," Suzanna whispered against August's chest.

Everything that had happened before seemed just that. *Before.* So far removed, this was their beginning, the first page and opening line.

August lifted her chin and kissed her lightly. "Darlin', we might be a story now, but one day, you and me, we'll be folklore."

They would go down in history as a tall tale.

Unfortunately, lore could never be more than a whisper, a noise in the dark most people would hear, disbelieve, and forsake.

CHAPTER 25

SUSANA PRATHER

History forgot August and Suzanna.

Except for their names in Godwin's Bible, I can't find re-cord of their marriage. According to censuses and ancestry books, Suzanna was a Yawn, then an Owens.

Papa tells me he once heard a relative mention Suzanna's first husband. Rumors suggested he'd died not long after the wedding.

I guess Suzanna was the death of August.

The flashback leaves me in a euphoric stupor more potent than the other dreams. I go to school. The day passes in a blur of classes and JC quizzing me about my sleepwalking. If he knew how it felt, he'd understand why I choose not to stop.

Somehow I end up with Missouri Jane in Nanny and Papa's front yard. We roll nut gatherers beneath pecan trees. The wire cages trap nuts, collecting them by the dozen.

I blink my surroundings into focus.

Nanny kneels in flower beds and yanks wild onions from the dirt. She must hear the squeak of the nut gatherers. Each time Missouri and I pause, she tells us to stop dillydallying.

My eyes play tricks on me.

Rubbing them, I sink to the ground and then empty my roller's contents into a plastic bag. Blood smears my right foot, oozing from my big toe. I must've stubbed it.

We cut our feet on the ground that holds us up.

I think there's a metaphor about family in there.

"Are you okay, Susana?" Missouri prods me with her roller.

"Sorry, yeah, I'm just out of it." I take deep breaths until I feel sober-minded. The aftereffects of sleepwalking have never lasted this long.

Godwin stops by around five o'clock to help Papa remove a stump. He works near the carport, swinging an axe onto a wedge. His muscles flex with each blow.

He won't even glance in my direction.

"Nice view, huh?" Missouri sits next to me with a cup of lemonade.

"The weather's good." I lie on the grass and rub the heat from my face. I should've told Godwin about my decision to sleepwalk again. I should've done a lot of things. He has every reason to distance himself from me, and maybe it's for the best.

"That's not what I meant, and you know it." Missouri drips condensation from her glass onto my neck. I flinch at the cold and throw pecans into her lap.

"He's angry with me," I tell her.

"What'd you do?"

"Nothing. That's the problem."

"Oh." Missouri reclines onto her elbows. She takes lazy sips of lemonade, watching Godwin toil away. "I like him for you."

"It can't happen."

"Why not?"

"Love's what got Mama into trouble."

"Honey, I don't think love had much to do with it," Missouri says.

"I'm afraid I'll hurt him. I already have."

Godwin dries his sweat with the neckline of his T-shirt.

My stomach in knots, I roll to face Missouri. "I think it's safer for me to not go there, you know? If I don't open myself up to anything, I can't lose."

"True, when you invite someone into your heart, you create a space only they can fill. You do so aware that person will eventually cease to exist to you or in life and you'll be left empty. Love isn't love unless there's an impending 'I miss you.'"

"I don't love him."

Missouri thumbs my nose. "Could've fooled me."

With a final chop, Godwin drops the axe and kneels to gather the wood. He looks at me for a split second. His expression is stone, but his eyes are sad.

"What if I'm not good enough?" I whisper to Missouri.

"By no means am I an expert, but I don't think relationships are about finding someone who is the same level of good enough. I think you look for someone who sees your good, who celebrates everything you are, and you do the same for them."

"Is that how you feel about Randall?"

She nods. "We get each other. We're both the black sheep of our families."

Godwin hauls the wood to a pile, his attention flickering to me every so often. Attraction burns softly, I think. Maybe we don't always see the flames, but we notice the smoke.

Usually from a distance.

I groan and cover my eyes. "I can't explain it."

"Listen here." Missouri peels away my hands. She gazes at me gently as if I'm taking my first steps and need someone to hold my arm. "There are good-looking people, and there are people you see who see you, and you understand each other. You look at them, and they're home. You know they're beautiful because they've been beautiful to you."

"When'd you become a poet?" I laugh.

"Don't tell anyone, but I've been taking writing courses at the community college."

"Missouri!" I sit up with a gasp.

"It ain't worth any fuss." Missouri yanks me into a hug, rocking side to side until our giggles wane. She motions to Godwin. "Remember. You can regret doing nothing too."

He goes to his truck and wiggles off his shirt, replacing it with a plaid button-up.

I'm worried he already regrets me.

After supper, I make a delivery to the Green Frog. Keziah Douglas dines at a table, sawing a catfish fillet with a butter knife. She glowers as I carry a box of eggs to the bar.

With banana pudding, Lucinda bribes me into small talk. I scarf down a polite amount, then make a Southern goodbye to the restaurant's exit.

Keziah stirs cream into pitch-black coffee.

I'm not sure what comes over me, but I steer a course to her table. "What did Mama do to you? My grandparents won't tell me."

"Susan cursed my family," Keziah says, matter-of-fact. She adjusts her oxygen tube, her veiny hands shaking as she lifts a mug to her lips.

"Why?"

"It was her revenge, I'm certain. Everyone knew she was lying, but she wouldn't let it go. She wanted me to pay. I didn't believe her, so she made sure nobody would believe me."

"Lying about what?"

Keziah considers my face with something like pain on hers. "Your nose—you didn't get it from Susan. And your eyes are lighter than hers."

She wears Martha's hummingbird brooch.

"You don't curse me, do you?" Keziah whispers.

"I hardly know you."

"Say I'm not cursed." When I don't respond, Keziah slams her mug onto the table. "You're just like her, aren't you? You'll curse everyone in this town."

The feeling of déjà vu washes through me. For a moment, I'm back in a dream, standing across from Keziah's ancestor. We've had this conversation before.

I will myself backward, but I remain glued to the floor with my knees locked. There's something important here, maybe a conclusion to draw or a parallel to notice.

"Why do you hate me?" I can't think straight. My mind is a merry-go-round spinning me from Suzanna to Mama to a gut feeling.

Cursed people curse other people. I'm cursed like Mama and the women before her. Suzanna cursed August. I don't want to curse Godwin.

What if cursing is inevitable? What if destruction is the only legacy I can leave?

"Tell me!" I shout, drawing attention from patrons. "What did Mama do?"

Keziah regards me with venom in her gaze. She signals for me to lean close, then cups her mouth and says with absolute conviction, "My family is dead because of Susan Prather."

1861

The happy years were few and far between.

Following their union, August and Suzanna cleared land for

planting. They inhabited the cabin August had built, spending their days in the fields, their nights with each other.

Suzanna abandoned the swamp and committed herself to farming. Her brother ran the commissary in her stead. Over time, with August to love her, she grew less fearful of the curse. It seemed to have forgotten her, or perhaps it was sated when she took the name Godwin.

Despite her newfound peace, Suzanna refused to venture into town. The Douglases had suffered misfortune and believed their hardships the result of Suzanna's hex.

August slept with a revolver under his pillow.

Two years into marriage, Suzanna buried her firstborn, then her second. She wished for more children and received miscarriages. Before long, five wooden crosses sat under a hickory.

Suzanna worried the curse had remembered.

A wildfire swept across the county, burning the Douglas homestead before reaching Godwin land. It swallowed August and Suzanna's cabin and killed their livestock.

Great with child, the couple took up residence in the commissary, intending to run the store until they could rebuild their home.

August claimed tribulations were inevitable and denied belief in the curse. His lack of consternation did not ease Suzanna's concern. Night after night, she paced the commissary, rubbing her swollen belly and muttering prayers to the dark.

Not two weeks later, a rattlesnake sprang from knapweed and bit August. His leg distended and blackened. Suzanna wanted to amputate, but August told her it was too late.

The poison was already in his bloodstream.

August grabbed a shovel and went behind the commissary to a patch of solid ground. He dug a hole six feet deep as necrosis swallowed his foot.

Suzanna wailed at him to stop.

Digging his own grave was bad luck.

August knew if he died, Suzanna would attempt to bury him. He didn't want her to endanger their baby. She was full term, expecting to go into labor at any moment.

He dug his own grave and waited for the venom to stop his heart. By some miracle, he did not die. The grave remained unoccupied.

Suzanna gave birth to a daughter who lived all of three days. They laid the babe to rest on their fifth wedding anniversary.

Trappers brought news of war and secession, drawing August into lengthy conversations. Suzanna wondered if the fighting would reach the Okefenokee.

Already she sensed violence in the air.

No good would befall her and August. Of this, Suzanna was certain. She held the curse liable for their miseries and blamed herself for August's pain.

Her grief unbearable, Suzanna isolated in the wilderness. She retreated into the depths of her own mind, withdrawing to a place so far removed, not even August could reach her.

In this solitude, she dissolved into madness, consumed with superstition. Martha's prophecy tormented her. If true, August would die because of the curse.

The thought of losing him made Suzanna ill with terror. She wept hysterically and screamed into the swamp. Her love for him was the only part of herself she still recognized.

One hot summer night, August found her at Hangman's Oak, crouched in a puddle of skirt. She gazed up at the vacant boughs as though in a trance.

"Come home, Suzanna."

"Our home is ash because of me," she whispered. Around her, fireflies blinked over wire grass, swirling at the sound of her voice.

"I am your home." August dropped to his knees and forced Suzanna to look at him. "Why do you behave as though I'm already lost to you?"

Suzanna drew a sharp breath. She touched his face, the creases around his eyes, the blond hair growing from his cheeks.

"This obsession of yours must stop. We ain't cursed." August had wearied of her silence. He'd endeavored to lift her spirits and regain her closeness, yet she refused to confide in him.

"Everything has been taken from us. Our children are dead—"

"You're not to blame, Suzanna."

"I've brought hell upon us. You should resent me." She rose and staggered from the oak. Its branches snapped and writhed, reaching toward a leaden sky.

August jolted to his feet, glancing from the tree to Suzanna. "Awful things happen to everybody. Our troubles ain't divine punishments."

Wind came from nowhere and danced with the grass.

Bats swarmed from the oak, squealing as they soared into the gloom.

"The curse is inside your head, don't you see?" August gathered Suzanna in his arms, cradling her against his chest. "Let go of the superstition. Come home."

August reminded her of their blissful days when they'd lived in harmony, content with their work and each other. He remembered their blessings.

She ruminated on their losses, so possessed by them she had no memory of joy.

"You stink of liquor." Suzanna broke from August's embrace, overwhelmed with dread. He'd taken to the bottle after the death of their sixth child, whiskey in the evening, moonshine at night. He wasn't a drunk, but Suzanna believed his taste for spirits would incite God's wrath.

She lowered to her knees, then her elbows. She clawed at the dirt, panting as her mind raced to a possible future in which August was dead and she was alone.

"Why do you shut me out? I'm your husband!" August yelled.

Hangman's Oak crackled like bones popping into place.

"Talk to me." August waited, but Suzanna only whimpered into the earth. He dried his eyes and straightened his coat. "I reckon I am lost to you."

He entered a stretch of prairie, fading to mist and shadows.

Suzanna wept for him.

Not a month later, August went to Fort Pulaski as a bugler, claiming the time apart would do him and Suzanna well. He saw no reason to stay at the commissary.

Suzanna remained married to the swamp and her own desolation.

CHAPTER 26

SUSANA PRATHER

OCTOBER, PRESENT DAY

Papa watches TV in the living room.

He reclines in his lounge chair with a plate of peach cobbler.

A black-and-white cowboy film plays on the television. John Wayne delivers an iconic line, and Papa's mustache twitches, followed by a gravelly laugh.

I toss my keys onto a side table, barely able to will my legs into motion. My eyes are dry, and I hurt all over, either from poor sleep or the three-hour FFA meeting I had to attend.

Papa glances at me as he drinks from a kitsch mug. He must sense my fatigue because he smiles and pats his knee. "Hey there, sugar lump. How was your day?"

"Uneventful." I collapse onto his lap as I have my whole life. He braces me against his shoulder, and I swipe my finger across his plate. Nanny would smack my hand. Not Papa.

He passes me his fork.

My eyelids drooping, I shovel buttery peaches into my mouth while John Wayne shoots at a band of outlaws. Papa half watches me, half watches the TV. He slugs the rest of his coffee, then props his socked feet on the ottoman and cracks his toes.

"I ran into Keziah Douglas at the Green Frog yesterday," I say.

Papa finishes off the cobbler. "Is that so?"

"She told me her family is dead because of Mama." I lock eyes with Papa, and words get lodged in my throat like ice cubes swallowed sideways.

He veers his attention to the TV. "Pain needs someone to blame, Susana."

"Why does she think Mama cursed her?"

"There ain't nothing supernatural about what happened." Papa's heart pounds against my shoulder. "The curse makes an easy scapegoat is all."

I sit up and pivot to face him. "What about the stories? My whole life, I've been told Mama lost her mind and was taken by the swamp—"

"Your nanny says that, not me." Papa sets his jaw. He massages his neck, which is red with rosacea, then emits a drawn-out sigh. "Mental illness runs in my family."

"Do you worry about me?" I'm not sure I want to know the answer. His mama, sister, and daughter went insane and died grisly deaths. Deep down, he must believe I'm fated for the same.

"Blood gets diluted over time," he says.

I tense with adrenaline and desperation and something hungry. I should wash off my makeup and show him what the curse is doing to me. If he realized I'm running out of time, maybe he'd stop talking in riddles and finally tell me the truth.

"Does my daddy know I exist?" I ask.

Papa ups the TV's volume to end our conversation.

"What aren't you telling me?" I fight the urge to shake him. Carrying the hex—knowing it's in my blood—makes me want to scream.

It's been three months since my eighteenth birthday.

Suzannah Owens lost her mind at month four.

Susie Prather died in a car wreck at month three.

Mama vanished into the swamp at month five.

"Talk keeps the past alive." Papa nudges me off his lap and rises from the chair. He gathers the dishes, then lumbers to the kitchen, leaving me with John Wayne and a warm seat.

Nanny and Papa's secrets will be what kill me.

Shaking, I drift to my room and lock its door. I sink onto my bed, rock back and forth, and scream into a pillow to ease my frustration.

The past lives on even after mouths go silent.

It's a beep inside this house like a failing smoke detector. No matter how much I search, I can't find it.

A beep inside this house. A beep inside me.

My skin numbs with a velvety sensation, beginning at my face and inching down my torso. I need to sleep, but I also need the water to give me relief.

I lie on my side, pressing my cheek against a lattice quilt.

Suzanna Yawn Godwin Owens watches from her picture frame. After last night, I think I understand why the curse backfired on her. She hexed the people of Kettle Creek in an act of revenge. They'd allowed superstition to drive them to hatred and murder.

Not only did they believe lies about themselves, but they planted lies in others.

Though Suzanna intended to teach them a lesson, she was convinced the past had doomed her, and thus the curse affected her. She'd accepted Martha's lies. She must've given the curse power to take hold of her. Like Godwin said, believe something long enough and it's bound to come true.

"I'm not cursed," I whisper, but the words are only syllables against fabric. I don't know the truth of what I am or how to say otherwise. "Please let me go."

Shimmers flicker near the window like hatches drifting up from stagnant water and sparking in the sunlight. They have gossamer wings, or maybe they don't.

I rise onto my elbow.

The creatures flutter to the ceiling and multiply into a swarm, blinking from gold to orange to black. Their wings expand into jagged spans.

Dust rains from their vibrating bodies.

Careful not to disturb them, I lower my feet to the floor and stand, the creatures whirring in response. They soar around me, organized like swallows or minnows.

An onyx coil twitches in the room's corner. Hissing, it straightens into a serpent and slithers under my dresser, whipping toward me with fangs bared.

I don't have time to squeal. I stumble backward and trip, hitting the rug with a bruising *thud*. I grab a muck boot from under my bed and hurl it at the snake.

The shoe bounces to a stop near the wall.

All the creatures have vanished.

1862

Obediah Owens made a name for himself.

Since childhood, he had aspired to become someone of importance. He wanted to tell a story about a kid born into poverty who grew into a man of means. That was the American dream, he thought. That he could go from a litter of youngins raised within a shack a stone's throw from a sawmill to becoming a person history would remember.

The narrative obsessed him. He lived each day for the chapter it would add to his tall tale. Over the years he built a reputation for his swamping and brawling. The folks of Kettle Creek revered him, spoke his name around campfires.

He acquired his wealth as a farmer. By age twenty-two, he was well-fixed, owning more cattle than anyone in town. At age twenty-four, he became the county's first justice of the peace.

In other parts of the nation, the title would give him authority to perform marriages and handle minor civil matters. Here, it appointed him the law.

Obediah lived alone on four hundred acres that bordered the Okefenokee. He kept his boat in a run and cut logs to use as a foot-path over the swamp.

He did not marry despite Elizabeth Ruger's interest.

A woman had already bewitched him, body and soul. He was cursed with a love for her that would not die. No matter how often he visited her and went hunting with her husband, he could not belong to her any less.

To ease his restlessness, Obediah spent much of his time on horse-back. He patrolled Trail Ridge and stagecoach roads, traveled from Waresboro to the St. Mary's River to the Florida state line. With need for a postal worker, he tasked himself with retrieving letters from Trader's Hill for the settlers of Kettle Creek.

Folks regarded Obediah as their sheriff and newsman, especially after he noticed seagulls flying west. The birds so far inland could only mean one thing: a storm was coming.

Obediah spread the ominous news, and his instincts proved correct.

A hurricane swept the coast and flooded the swamp.

One might gauge Obediah's popularity by the well incident. He talked of an abandoned well near Spanish Creek, said it had the best sweet water around. His praise resulted in hundreds of settlers driving their buggies to sample the water.

If not farming or policing, Obediah could be found with his cane pole, fishing near the Yawn homestead. He called on Mr. Yawn, John, and Louisa at least once a month.

Such was the story he lived until war broke out.

The legend of Obediah Owens took a turn on April 12, 1861, when shots were fired on Fort Sumter. Obediah soon became a private in the 24th Battalion, Georgia Cavalry.

His myth was greater than a list of roles. To understand him, one needed to consider the woman he'd always love, for she was both his commentary and footnotes.

Everything he was somehow connected to her.

Obediah did not stay gone for long periods of time, maintaining that his responsibilities in Kettle Creek required his utmost attention. Something did lure his loyalty, but it wasn't his cattle or letters or law. He wanted to remain close to Suzanna.

He burned for her. His spirit was bound to hers. He sensed her in the wire grass and channels and dead of night. Such were delusions, he reminded himself.

What a terrible sin to love another man's wife.

August Godwin was shot November 7, 1862. He returned home with a bullet in his stomach, another lodged beneath his collarbone.

Soldiers rode into town with August laid up in a wagon. They boated him to the commissary and left him to expire. Suzanna called for doctors, created salves from lichens.

The swamp iced over the morning August died.

Folks were distressed by the phenomenon, for the water had never frozen in whole. They said the witch was responsible. She must've hexed the land with her devilish magic.

Upon learning of August's death, Obediah made a foray into the Okefenokee. He rode his old mare between slash pines, the dainty *click-clack* of hooves accompanied by gnats fizzing in his ears. Out here, insects buzzed around his head regardless of the season.

He practiced his condolences to the forest, its cold and heedless distances calming him. He was ashamed of his mixed feelings. He'd lost a dear friend, someone he considered a brother, yet his thoughts went to Suzanna and her lack of a husband.

Obediah resolved to wait a suitable amount of time, after which he'd propose marriage. Barring a miracle, she'd refuse him, but he needed to inquire for the sake of his own sanity.

The mare startled at something and balked, crunching a sheet of ice. She was not easily ruffled, so Obediah dismounted and examined the ground.

Frost glazed the chalky sand and crystallized a nearby blackberry bush.

His senses heightened, Obediah led the horse to frozen water and tethered her to a tupelo. He stepped onto the channel's glossy surface. It supported his weight. He took another step, both surprised and made uneasy by the ice's thickness.

Never had he encountered such an anomaly.

Across the waterway, Obediah found an alligator trail broken into brush. Scat—the twisted links of a small predator—stippled the path.

The works of a bobcat, Obediah guessed.

He moved with the flying scud of the sky toward the commissary. Nature kept silent as if to honor the dead. Not a creature stirred, not even the ibises in their rookery.

Obediah grew unsettled as he approached the stilted building. He climbed onto the porch and opened the door, hinges creaking, floorboards groaning under his feet.

Darkness lightened only by a single lantern swallowed him.

Sheets draped the storeroom, perhaps to ward off haints and bad luck. The air reeked of sweat and tears, the musty smell Obediah recognized as grief.

"Hello? Anyone here?" Obediah passed shelves of kerosene and turpentine and rounded a corner, entering the room Suzanna and August shared.

Suzanna perched on a stool with her ink-blue skirt puddled around her and a rifle strapped to her back. Her hair was braided into a halo, now frizzed and unkempt.

"I came as soon as I could," Obediah said.

August lay across the bed. He appeared a shell of the person Obediah remembered. His skin was like the moon, almost silver in the dimness.

Suzanna watched her late husband with a faraway look in her eyes. "He'd gotten a taste for liquor. I warned him not to drink, figured if he acted right, God wouldn't take him."

"God didn't fire those bullets, Suzanna."

"I knew he would die. Martha told me the curse would bring about his death. I didn't believe her, or perhaps I did and chose to marry him anyway." Suzanna abandoned her stool and knelt beside August. She took one of his stiff hands, pressing it to her lips.

Obediah tensed with a possessive feeling. He withheld his rehearsed speech in fear Suzanna would intuit his motives. Betraying his love too early might discourage her from receiving him, and he couldn't bear dashing his own hopes.

"He died a hero," Obediah said.

"Did he? Looks to me like he just died." Suzanna twisted her wedding band. "There ain't no winners in war, Obediah. Good and bad get lost over time until all that remains is the fighting. I don't see any good in dead left to bury."

"You need help?" Obediah resented himself for asking the question. He didn't want to bury August. Doing so while coveting the man's widow seemed immoral.

"August did the digging. All I gotta do is toss dirt on him."

"Where's the grave?"

"Out back, next to the cinnamon ferns. I promised August I'd be buried with him." Suzanna lifted a candle off the side table and cradled it against her bosom. She floated across the room as if underwater, the firelight dancing across her steely expression.

"I'll make a headstone for him."

Obediah skimmed his fingers across Suzanna's back. He loved her so much he didn't mind if she loved him less. His excess would overflow, overspill into her cracks and grooves, any void spaces, until they were both complete.

August was dead after all. He would not wish for Suzanna to remain alone in the swamp. Obediah had been his closest friend. Surely, if August could've picked another man to love his wife, he would've chosen Obediah to take his place.

"Let me care for you," Obediah whispered. Six years prior, he'd put aside his feelings and returned August to Suzanna. Was it not fitting that he might stand a chance with her now?

Suzanna drifted to the room's threshold. She appeared a shell too, hollow of herself. "There's no saving me, Obediah. I'm cursed. I *am* the curse."

"You've been out here too long." Obediah would ferry her to his farm where she could heal in the quiet and sun, away from Kettle Creek and the swamp's haunted shallows.

He would love her back to herself.

"August went to war because of me," Suzanna gasped. "I pushed him away, and he died. I fulfilled the prophecy, don't you see?"

Obediah looked from the corpse swaddled in blankets to the widow observing from the doorway. "Why don't you spend the night with your family? I'll watch over August."

Wind slammed against the commissary, rattling its shutters.

From somewhere in the Okefenokee, gators bellowed.

"I don't want you staying here alone," Obediah said, shivering from a chill like a premonition. Although he didn't believe the rumors about Suzanna, there was no denying that she'd changed. The inexplicable—a dark shade of magic—stalked her.

He would not allow the supernatural to deter his affection. Suzanna had been his soul mate since childhood, the only girl he dreamed of marrying.

She was his North Star, always guiding him home to wild places.

A creature swooped from the rafters, bigger than a crow.

"What in tarnation!" Obediah tripped on his own feet.

The bat flew circles around the room. One, two, three. It let out a screech, then dropped onto August's body, puncturing his chest with talons.

Obediah grabbed a straw broom from the floor and swung it at the animal. "Git!"

"Don't bother him. That ain't no bat." Suzanna lolled against the doorframe, dribbling candlewax onto the floor. "He's the ol' devil here to taunt me."

The creature hissed at Obediah.

"Leave me to bury my dead. I have no need for company." Suzanna extinguished her flame and sank into darkness, floorboards creaking and groaning like the wind-beaten walls.

"Wait, Suzanna, come back!" Obediah dropped the broom and clutched his holster. He waited for Suzanna to return, sensing her presence like his own goose bumps. After a while, he ventured into the storeroom and searched its maze of covered furniture.

Suzanna was nowhere to be found.

Years later, around bonfires in war camps, Obediah spoke of the strangeness that had occurred. His story ended with him rushing across the frozen swamp, through mist thicker than smoke. He swore he spotted Suzanna among the cypresses.

She walked over ice, and even her footsteps were as noiseless as a dream.

CHAPTER 27

SUSANA PRATHER

OCTOBER, PRESENT DAY

Godwin works in the garden, harvesting the last of the summer squash.

I rush across the backyard and step over rows of carrots to reach him. I straighten my skirt, peel the hair from my forehead. "I know where August was buried."

Godwin looks up, his irises devastatingly blue above sunburnt cheeks. "I'm out, remember? You and JC can play Nancy Drew with the whole curse thing."

I squeeze my eyes shut to block out the world and last night. My face feels wobbly with emotions, some left over from the dream. I'm losing my mind—I must reckon with that. Soon, the imaginings will become so frequent, I won't be able to distinguish reality.

Until yesterday, the oddities were tangible. I could touch the plants growing from my vents and hack the vines off my windowsill.

Other people witnessed the swamp's behavior, the gators circling JC's boat, those crawling toward the farmhouse. It was all real until it wasn't.

"Listen, Godwin, I should've been honest with you, and I wasn't, and I'm sorry."

He sighs.

"I need you to do me a favor. Just one. Then, I'll leave you alone."

"We better come to an understanding," he says, placing yellow squash in a bucket. "My whole life, I've dealt with inconsistent—heck, roller-coaster—relationships. Mom ran off with some guy. Dad was drunk, not drunk; in my life, then out. I can't open myself up to someone who might treat me the way they did."

"Okay."

"Some guys like hot-and-cold," he continues. "I'm a long-haul, build-something-solid, go-down-with-the-ship kind of guy. That's why I dated Betty for so long. We weren't right for each other, but I trusted her, and I committed, you know?"

"I hear you."

Godwin sits back on his heels and wipes his palms on his shirt. "Whatever this is between us, Susana, I need to be able to trust it, and I can't right now."

A pit forms in my stomach. I want to take Missouri's advice and tell Godwin I love him and have loved him since we were kids, but I was too afraid to admit it because I didn't know what to do with my feelings. He deserves to hear the truth before I die.

"I'll help you, but after that, I'm stepping back for a while," Godwin says. "You're a great girl, and I'm glad we're friends again. I just can't fall back into my old habits, you know?"

"Fair enough." I swallow hard, my vision blurring with tears. I won't tell him about the imaginings. He warned me not to sleepwalk, and I did it anyway.

If I'd made different choices, maybe I'd still feel clearheaded.

Maybe I'd be closer to Godwin.

I don't want to lose him.

"All right, so what's this about graves?" Godwin twists his ball cap backward. Tufts of copper-golden hair spill over the strap.

"I think August was buried near the commissary. He dug his own grave after a rattlesnake bit him." I crouch in the dirt to ground myself, but I can't shake the foreign sensation crawling under my skin. It feels unhinged and intrusive, as if it belongs to someone else.

"Granddaddy was hard-core," Godwin says with a laugh.

"You're kin to August's cousin, actually." He tilts his head, and I tell him I'll explain later. "Anyway, Suzanna mentioned breaking the curse with her bones—"

"No."

"What do you mean *no?*"

"I'm not digging her up."

"I don't want you to dig her up. I want you to help me dig up August."

Godwin laughs and scrambles from the earth, propping the bucket of squash against his chest. "Sure, yeah, because that makes sense."

"Listen, Suzanna promised August she'd be buried with him. That didn't happen, maybe because Obediah wanted her buried with him."

"And you think her ghost is angry or something?"

"I don't know. Suzanna blamed herself for August's death. Maybe she had a guilty conscience. Maybe fulfilling her promise to him will break the curse."

"How?"

"Because of what Suzanna said." I unfold a piece of notebook paper from my pocket and read it aloud. "'With my blood I make what only my bones can break. I don't yearn for this life no more. About everything I love rests underground. I'd rather join the dead than spend another moment with you lot. Let me join them in peace.'"

"Suzanna said that before August died. I don't see how grave robbery makes sense."

"Wouldn't you want to be buried with your wife?"

Godwin huffs. "I'll be dead. My body could be used as fertilizer for all I care."

"Look, I get that it's a long shot, but I don't know what else to do." I take a deep breath to steady my voice. I'd rather keep my panic and desperation under wraps. "Suzanna loved August. Burying him with her might break the curse. *Might* is enough for me to go on."

"I need a drink." Godwin shoves past me and makes a beeline for the farmhouse. He deposits the produce on the back porch, then goes around to the driveway.

"Godwin, I'm slap out of ideas!" I shout as I follow him to his truck.

He reaches into the bed and takes a Gatorade from a cooler. Empty beer bottles form a pile beside the ice chest, mixed with pine straw and mulch. Gus must've left them.

I force my gaze away from the longnecks. "What's the harm?"

"For one, being traumatized by digging up a corpse." Godwin uncaps the Gatorade and guzzles it. Once emptied, he chunks the container into the truck bed's corner.

"August has been dead for over a hundred fifty years. He couldn't be more than bones." I'd dig up a whole cemetery if doing so would save me from becoming another cardigan among lily pads, another picture on the wall, another madwoman lost to her family's gloomy history.

Stuff is mounting up, the sense of threat. I have days or weeks until my life becomes a nightmare I can't wake from. That alone scares me more than anything.

"How will we find the grave?" Godwin asks.

"In my dream, Obediah said he'd create a headstone. Suzanna told him the grave was behind the commissary, near the cinnamon ferns."

"Will we get in trouble?"

"Only if we get caught."

"Have you double-checked the Godwin family plot at Hard-Shell?"

"August isn't there, I'm telling you."

Wind harasses the pines and rattles pecans off their trees.

Godwin scans the yard as if he senses something unnatural going on. His focus goes to the feeder hanging beside Nanny's pruned azaleas.

A lone hummingbird bobs to plastic yellow flowers for nectar. Year after year, the bird chooses not to migrate with the others. It stays put, a side effect of living in Berryville.

This town makes homebodies of us all.

Whatever Godwin feels, I feel it too, a shift in the atmosphere. The curse is subverting the natural order somehow, twisting the energies of this place into a vortex where the pressure drops. I should've recognized the signs. Nature has been crying out to me since my eighteenth birthday, trying to get my attention. Perhaps the curse affects more than me.

"You think I'm related to August's cousin?"

I nod. "The cousin was hanged for stealing livestock. His wife named their son August Godwin, hoping the kid wouldn't grow up to be like his daddy."

Godwin's reservation crumbles. He suddenly looks ten years older, exhausted, and overwhelmed, like he needs to sit in the cane rocker on the porch and let everything sift.

"You have company." He nods at the truck rolling down the driveaway. It jounces over a pothole, slinging gravel, and slows to a stop.

JC climbs from the driver's seat. His smile deflates at the sight of Godwin. "Don't mean to interrupt. I've been thinking on the curse, and I got some ideas."

"Susana wants to dig up a grave," Godwin tells him.

"Which one?" JC approaches us and pockets his hands. "I'm thinking we get Suzanna's bones, and Susana tells them she's not cursed."

"Knock yourselves out," Godwin says, patting JC's shoulder.

"Let's go tonight." I seize Godwin's arm to keep him from leaving. "I want to move August's body from the commissary to the Hard-Shell cemetery. JC, may we use your boat?"

"Yeah, sure. Text me the details. I'll meet you wherever." JC glances from me to Godwin. Maybe I imagine it, but something like annoyance tenses his face.

Godwin sighs. "What, y'all plan to manhandle two corpses?"

"I'll do anything to help Susana," JC says.

A smile tugs at the corner of Godwin's mouth. He nods and licks his molars, his jaw extending to one side. "I hear you loud and clear, pal."

Godwin looks at JC as though he's got him sussed.

"Cool, well, I'll see you tonight." JC squirms, visibly unnerved by Godwin's response. He gives me a brief hug, then backtracks to his truck.

He stares from the rearview mirror as he drives to the road.

"That boy wants to kiss you," Godwin says.

I flinch at his statement and whirl to face him. "How can you tell?"

Godwin leans so close his words heat my skin. "Isn't it obvious?" His gaze falls to my lips, and the air between us seems alive with electricity.

We're hitting the brakes, choosing space. We won't do anything stupid.

"I'll knock on your window around nine." Godwin removes his ball cap and ruffles his hair. "If this plan of yours works, it'll be worth me having nightmares."

His attention dips to my mouth a final time.

Every inch of me burns with blush and something I'm afraid to name. I don't want to hurt Godwin or trigger the propensities Mama gave me, but I'll regret doing nothing.

The thought of repeating Suzanna's mistakes nauseates me.

Godwin wipes his forehead with the bottom of his T-shirt, exposing his chiseled abdomen. He must be the fire Nanny warned me not to play with.

"Thanks, I'll text you after . . ." I trail off into the sight of Godwin's muddy hands and dimpled cheeks, his musky scent of soil and sweat.

He wears dirt well.

Godwin flashes a smile. He touches my waist lightly, the warmth of his fingers another dose of déjà vu. "I'm glad we came to an understanding."

How we look at each other, I doubt it'll be long until our brakes give out.

CHAPTER 28

SUSANA PRATHER

JC steers his boat into the Okefenokee's federal area.

Here, the dark is darkest, the stars the only light. Bullfrogs gurgle and croak among cypress knees, and the terrain projects a frequency I feel more than hear.

I straighten on my bench seat and place my sneakers on a spade borrowed from Nanny's garden shed. Days ago, I used it to unearth an irrigation pipe.

Tonight, I'll use it to exhume a corpse.

Godwin pivots on the bench in front of me, wearing brown overalls and steel-toed boots. His expression asks if I'm sure about this. I'm not, but I have no other ideas.

JC aims his flashlight ahead and guides us through a patch of sundews. The carnivorous plants reach from black water. Their spikey heads resemble viruses under a microscope.

"Suzanna said *her* bones will break the curse. Why're we going after August?" JC keeps his voice at a reverent murmur as if the swamp might overhear.

I lean back to discern his words from the motor and the water licking and lapping the hull. "I realize this sounds ridiculous, and I wish I had a better answer for you, but I think uniting Suzanna and August might break the curse. She promised him they'd be buried together."

Aloud, the theory seems like the longest shot in the history of shots. Really, it's my last shot.

"I nominate Owens here to carry the body," Godwin says.

JC scoffs. "He's your relative. Y'all share the same name for cripes' sake."

"We're loosely related." Even in the darkness, Godwin is as white as a ghost. "I'll dig the hole, and you two can feel around for bones. I've touched enough coffins."

"What do you mean?" I ask.

Godwin hitches his shoulders and arches his back, perhaps from a shiver. "When I was a kid, Mom had my grandma exhumed from her grave and reburied in a different plot. I think it had something to do with my jerk of a step-grandfather. Anyway, I remember standing in the cemetery and watching a bulldozer lift Grandma from the ground. Mom forced me to touch her casket, said it was the last time I'd be that close to her."

"Man, that's Deep South for you," JC says with a laugh. "I don't think a person is truly Southern unless they've had a ghoulish experience. When I was a kid, I hung out at Uncle Bill's funeral home. My friends and I played in the coffin showroom and raided the crematorium bin, you know, where the unburnt pieces were kept. I still have a knee implant—"

Godwin swears and plugs his ears.

"Your boy got a weak stomach, huh?" JC whispers to me.

I smack his leg and point to the left. "We're getting close. The commissary is on the edge of that island, where the channel widens into flat prairie."

The flashbacks drew a map in my mind.

JC directs us to what remains of a dock, now rotten planks sloughing from peat into a carpet of lily pads. He ropes his boat to a post slick with algae and signals for us to deboard.

I take the lead, slinging my leg over the gunwale and dropping into half a foot of water. I slosh to the embankment as an owl bellows from the treetops.

On stable ground, I power up my flashlight.

The commissary is nothing more than decomposed rubble enveloped in cobwebs and foliage. A barrel stands among the debris, held together by rusted hoops. Eventually nature will take a final gulp, and the commissary will disappear, taking its history with it.

My sinuses prickle, not from the cool air or smell of decay.

So much happened here, and nobody knows it besides me. I suppose I'm realizing the significance of everything. Suzanna had August and Obediah, and I have Godwin and JC.

I wipe my nose before the boys can notice my emotion. "August is over this way."

With Godwin and JC at my heels, I trek around the ruins to where my dream showed August digging. There, camouflaged by ferns and thorns, is a headstone made of white marble. It's so weathered its inscription is unreadable.

I lower to my knees and motion for JC to hand me a shovel.

Godwin clicks on his headlamp and goes to work, clearing vines, uprooting plants. Once we expose the ground, we cut into the dirt with our tools.

Foot by foot, hour by hour, we dig a hole.

"Do you reckon we're four feet down?" JC inspects the walls of earth around us. He plucks a worm from the disturbed soil and places it within his hat, a makeshift bait container.

Slippery critters writhe inside the ball cap, knotting themselves into a wad.

"Let's see." Godwin shimmies the boot off his left foot. He uses it as a ruler, measuring from the floor to the crevice's rim. "Four and a half."

JC rolls his eyes. "Your shoe is not a foot long."

"Sure is," Godwin says. "Big as those subs from Floyd's."

"You're fibbing. Ain't no way." Godwin tosses the shoe, and JC catches it. He turns it over in his hands and whistles. "Where do you buy your boots?"

"Jot Em Down in Blackshear." Godwin accepts the boot and laces it onto his foot.

"Nice, I go there sometimes." JC locks eyes with me and shrugs. "What?"

"We're digging up a grave."

"Yeah, I see that."

"And y'all are gabbing about footwear." I stomp my spade into the earth, ignoring my achy muscles and the dread gnawing at my stomach. With a grunt, I shovel dirt from the pit.

The ground crackles, the sound of splintering wood.

Godwin cries out and goes down in a dusty plume. He sinks two feet, landing on his backside. His headlamp darts side to side, its beams falling onto material that must've been pine, now damp and coal black. A skull fills the circle of light.

Yellowed and cracked with teeth missing.

Godwin takes one look at the skeleton below him, pressed against his skin, and emits a cross between a shout and a scream. He claws at the dirt and flails his limbs.

I reach for him. I no longer feel inside myself.

Swearing with each breath, Godwin clasps my hand and lets me pull him from the bones. He scrambles up the wall, out of the grave.

His fear is radioactive. It absorbs my fear and magnifies JC's fear until everything is fear.

JC shines his flashlight into the putrid coffin. "Now what?"

"Fetch me a tarp." I swallow bile, unable to stop trembling.

We excavate the grave and clear away the decomposed wood. Piece by piece, we gather August's bones and wrap them in tarp and twine. They weigh about as much as a watermelon.

What a morose irony that no matter how much a person loves, how big their life, they'll end up as this—lighter than stone, fragments mixed with other dead things.

Godwin doesn't say a word on the ride to the boat ramp.

"I'm sorry." I rub circles on his back as cypress groves reel past. I shouldn't have pushed him to help. I was selfish and desperate, and I knew he'd come along if I asked.

He glances at me with soft eyes and nods.

JC docks the boat onto his truck trailer, then drives us to Hard-Shell Baptist. We trek across the cemetery to Suzanna's gravesite, carrying August and our shovels.

The church doesn't have cameras. No one should be out and about at this hour.

Exhausted from digging up August, I knife my shovel through the sand near Suzanna's headstone. I blister my blisters and give sore to my soreness. In a way, the pain feels appropriate, maybe even cathartic, as if suffering is part of the rite.

I touch the dirt to remind myself from where I came and to which I'll return.

Years ago, I asked JC if he'd get matching bracelets with me to commemorate an experience. He said no. Because the item could one day remind him "I lost you." Because having something is something to lose. But to me, having something means "I had you."

If only for a moment.

Perhaps that's why headstones exist, to not only mark a grave but to signify *being had*. I think at the end of life all that matters is how well a person loved and who loved them back.

Godwin and JC labor alongside me, this time in silence.

We reach Suzanna as sunrise lightens the sky from navy to dusty blue. Her coffin is sturdier than August's box, likely made from oak or ash instead of pine.

"I'll wait in the truck." Godwin lifts himself from the grave, his face so filthy his eyes glow neon white. He hightails it across the cemetery.

JC wedges the blade of his shovel beneath the coffin's lid. When I nod, he forces his weight against the shaft, and the casket pops open.

Its hasps crumble from rust. Its wood bends like rubber.

Suzanna's remains lie within, nothing more than bone fragments wrapped in fibers. Her skull is cracked and held together by teeth.

A rifle sits at her side, rusted and rotten.

"I'm not cursed," I tell the bones.

To complete the transaction, I lower August into the coffin. JC shuts the lid and boosts me from the hollow. I crawl onto sand and grass and dry-heave.

"We better hurry. The sun will be up soon." JC backfills the grave and smooths its surface. He sighs as if to say *it is finished*, then escorts me to the parking lot.

I'm not sure what I expect to happen, but I expect more than nothing.

Nothing happens.

Godwin is asleep when JC and I reach the truck. He sprawls across the back seat, twitching with REM, his breaths heavy and uneven.

After everything I've put him through, he deserves to be free of my curse. I must respect his want for space and let him go. So far, all I've done is risk his well-being.

Keziah Douglas said I'd curse everyone in this town.

I don't want to curse Godwin more than I already have.

JC drives me home and leans over the center console to hug me goodbye. I fold into him, still tasting the grave and the bitter acidity of nausea.

"See you at school," JC whispers as Godwin snores quietly.

I leave him and Godwin at the mailbox and run down the driveaway. I climb through my bedroom window, change into PJs, and slip under quilts without so much as brushing my teeth.

1863

Martha Douglas took an axe to Hangman's Oak.

She boated into the swamp at daybreak, as first light warmed the horizon, and blazed a trail across flat prairie. She'd traveled the route twice in her fifty years, once to witness the lynching of Muscogee raiders, another to see the Yawn boys dangling from their nooses.

Delirious with grief, she waded through grass, clutching her axe and a handkerchief belonging to her firstborn. The war had taken her sons from Kettle Creek.

All four of them had perished in the fighting.

Martha blamed Suzanna's hex for the tragedy. Ever since the encounter at the church, the Douglases had suffered bad luck, losing their home to fire, their kinfolk to violence and disease.

The curse was retribution, Martha decided, if not conjured by witchery, then allowed by God as punishment for her wrongdoings. She'd hatched the plan, given the order.

Blood stained her hands.

Martha had considered killing Suzanna in hopes of breaking the curse, but she feared spilling more blood would only worsen her fate. Guilt tormented her, plaguing her sleep with nightmares of bloody fingers and the Yawn boys snapping to stops on their ropes.

Her feelings toward Suzanna had shifted from hatred to anger to something desperate and vulnerable. She'd asked for Suzanna to reverse the spell, and the girl had refused.

Unless Suzanna said otherwise, the Douglases were cursed.

This enraged Martha. All she'd wanted was justice for the 1838 massacre. Someone had to pay for the crimes.

She was paying now.

Hangman's Oak stood in solemn remembrance. It branched into gnarled limbs ribboned with ropes, the frayed pieces swaying like bunting.

The tree was a monument to the past, Martha thought. It remembered her evils.

With a scream, the woman swung her axe into the old trunk. She hacked at bark and wood, chipping away piece by piece. She needed to acquit her conscience, reduce history to a forgettable stump. Perhaps doing so would liberate the next generation from her misfortune.

Hours later, the oak fell to its death, shuddering as it greeted the dirt. Martha collapsed with it. She wept into her bloodied hands as birds and bats soared from the tree's boughs.

The Okefenokee still remembered.

History would not so easily forget.

Martha realized the curse was rooted too deeply, impossible to cut out. It would pass down her bloodline, generation after generation.

Her kin would follow in her footsteps.

CHAPTER 29

SUSANA PRATHER

OCTOBER, PRESENT DAY

The curse didn't break.

I cry into a swamp-drenched pillow. My muscles cramp and spasm, weak from grave digging. All that effort for nothing.

Darkness swirls across my room as the wallpaper's floral design coils and blooms. Over my desk, a glowing orb appears, what people around here call a spook light.

It's not real. The snake wasn't real.

Lowering my dripping legs to the floor, I drift toward the spectral shape. I reach, and my hand passes through it. Another imagining.

A genealogy book rests on the desktop, flipped open to my family tree. The curse passed from Suzanna to Suzannah to Susan to Susie. From there, it rerouted to Papa and trickled down his line to Mama and me. Who'll inherit it next? Missouri's future daughter, or maybe Charlie's?

I need to break the cycle. If I can't outlive the curse, perhaps I can make sure it dies with me. There must be commonalities among the other women in my bloodline.

Acting differently from them might disrupt the pattern.

Shaking, I curl into a ball on the floor and wait for sunrise. The flashback replays through my head, showing Martha at Hangman's Oak. I don't understand why I dreamed about her.

Daylight forces the shadows from my thoughts. I rise from a puddle and blink until the world is lucid and I feel less dizzy. From now on, I must use the barricade at night.

I can't sleepwalk anymore. I need to postpone my insanity for as long as possible.

At school, I pal around with JC and Stokes to distract myself. I relax until JC looks at me, and I remember the skeleton and how it felt in my hands.

The gravity of what we did weighs heavier.

JC pulls me aside before English class and asks if I sleepwalked. I tell him my long-shot idea was as long as I thought. His expression melting, he promises not to give up.

I lock myself in the bathroom when I get home. I scrub my hands, cleaning under my fingernails to erase the lingering bits of grave. Once bedtime rolls around, I secure the wooden panels over my door and window and pray for more time.

The sleepwalking pauses, but I don't think my curse loses momentum.

Godwin visits the house to work on the pump. He waves at me but doesn't say a word, and I honor our agreement and keep my distance.

Nanny and Papa whisper more than usual. I hear them speak in low tones whenever I leave a room. They won't admit it, but I'm sure they know more than they're saying.

Even Missouri has a gleam of secrecy in her eyes.

Maybe they're conspiring against me, or maybe I'm imagining

their furtive glances. I can't decide what's real and what's a side effect of the curse.

Everything bleeds like watercolor, muddying into one shade.

I latch the time locks onto the panels and pace my room, barefoot, dressed in a hand-me-down nightgown. Wind pounds the house as if to protest my restraint.

The wallpaper comes alive, its design sprouting leaves and thorns. I climb into bed and watch the illustrated foliage spread across the ceiling.

My eyelids dip.

Godwin, Godwin, Godwin.

We lie on a shady embankment, swaddled in a blanket of glossy-black greens. In the silence of us, a pause from stolen kisses, breaks a whisper. *You make sense to me.*

I look for him in places he shouldn't be. A dark shade of magic. Love and loving, then waking up. All a dream, an impossibility. I won't make folklore out of us.

> But I wish to lie in the reeds with him
> And build a cavern of quilts
> In firelight
> To escape our darks.

> And beneath our canopy of cotton and threads,
> We'll whisper folktales
> As whippoorwills perform our song
> To the equinox moon.

> I wish to collide with him
> As the water greets the shore,
> To melt into each other
> Dissolving into unstable ground.

CHAPTER 30

SUSANA PRATHER

OCTOBER, PRESENT DAY

The imaginings aren't the worst of my problems.

Without sleepwalking, I wake up with stomach cramps and hurry to remove the panels and reach the bathroom. I wish the toilet an aggressive good morning.

Makeup can't hide what the curse is doing to me. My body grows weaker, and my face sinks into itself, becoming all edges and purplish hollows.

I medicate with naps and caffeine, but as days pass and I continue to spend my first waking moments coughing up bile, my fatigue intensifies until even standing is a challenge.

The urge to sleepwalk nags at me. I want to dream again, to feel its relief. The want becomes a craving I feed by sitting near the water.

Somehow the Okefenokee pacifies my curse, or at least slows its progress. I find if I drink my morning coffee on the small dock Papa built, I'm clearheaded throughout the day.

Nanny and Papa take interest in my new habit. They ask questions, but I don't trust them enough to give real answers. They won't reveal their secrets. Why should I?

JC and I meet after school to brainstorm ways to break the curse. I do it to give him peace of mind. He thinks we'll find a solution, and I want him to think that for as long as possible.

He's not ready to admit I'm a lost cause.

Godwin stops visiting the house altogether, which makes our agreement harder to keep. I thought he'd come around for dinner or ask me if the grave-digging worked.

I expected him to step back, not sprint in the opposite direction.

Missing him feels a lot like guilt.

While making deliveries, I drive past the Hard-Shell cemetery and spot Keziah among the headstones. She stands near Suzanna's grave, inspecting the fresh mound of soil.

She gazes at my car as if she knows what I did.

I don't care what Keziah suspects. I needed to do something, and I didn't have any other ideas. The plan should've worked. I reunited Suzanna with her dead. I spoke to her bones.

One night, a voice wakes me at witching hour. I lurch from my pillow and confront the darkness. No one waits in its shadows. The gloom is blameless and behaved.

I sense a presence, though, like a stale breath on my skin.

Books tumble off my desk and spill pages across the creaky floorboards. *Suzanna to Suzannah to Susan to Susie, rerouted to Mama and me.* A tree reaches from the ground, a wrist with a hand, all connected by tendons and joints.

I pin a pillow over my head to dull the imagining.

Berryville sheds the rest of its summer weight, slims with cooler weather and barren fields. The chamber of commerce hosts its annual scarecrow contest, so local businesses clutter downtown with hand-made figures. I help Missouri construct one for the restaurant.

We spray-paint a hay bale and PVC pipes green and fashion them into a frog.

Autumn is an eerie blur of imaginings and not-imaginings, stepping on pecans and remembering I can't walk barefoot in the front yard. The waiting is what I hate the most. I watch the clock, mindful of each second. My heart is in a constant race.

Eventually my clock will stop.

I do my best to settle into the rhythm. I go to familiar places and do familiar things, watch movies at the drive-in, bake apple pies with Nanny, but it all strikes me as odd, like I wandered into an alternate dimension that only resembles my world.

Piano music drifts from the ruins of Willard Ruger's house.

I can't help but wonder if Alice's spirit plays the song.

I'm not sure who's thinking for me anymore, the curse or myself. All I know is I can't look Nanny and Papa in the eyes, and they don't appear to mind.

All of us seem to have things we'd rather keep buried.

CHAPTER 31

SUSANA PRATHER

OCTOBER, PRESENT DAY

Holler Sloan hosts a pasture party on Halloween to celebrate an undefeated season.

All semester, football has been the main topic of conversation. Friday nights practically shut down the town.

Holler and the team invite everyone from school to join them after the game. They frequent a field near Shiloh Cemetery, one tucked behind pine forests, accessible by a single dirt road. Their party just so happens to take place during Berryville's Fall Festival.

According to Holler, police will be too busy monitoring carnival games and hayrides to bust teenagers for having a good time.

Cleo and Daisy ask me to go with them. I agree because we're childhood friends, and I want one last high school experience before the swamp takes me.

I leave Nanny and Papa at the stadium with the understanding

I'll hang out with friends and return home by midnight. All true, but when I climb into my car, I feel like a liar.

We reach the party around ten o'clock. Already the crowd is tipsy on victory and beer. Students blast music, toss objects into bonfires, and play games on foldout tables.

Cue instant regret.

"You don't want to stay for long, right?" I follow Cleo and Daisy between Chevys and Fords, entering a swarm of denim, flannel, and backward ball caps.

"Not for long." Cleo adjusts her crop top and untucks the hair from behind her ears.

Daisy runs ahead, tugging at the back of her minidress. She insisted we all get ready together and smothered my bathroom counter in makeup and curling irons.

I must've looked terrible because she sat me down on the toilet, under Nanny's knee-highs, and spent thirty minutes painting my face.

Thanks to her, I no longer resemble a corpse.

My ears ring with country music, and my sinuses prickle with dew and the fizzy musk of alcohol. I shouldn't be here. I don't like hanging out with my friends.

That's not true.

I like *some* of my friends.

There should be a word for people you've known forever, who you spend time with out of habit because there's no one else to take their place. Cleo, Daisy, and I might not come out and say it, but we understand what we are to each other. We all seem okay with the arrangement.

JC waves from a bonfire and hurries to greet us. He's dressed as Forrest Gump, wearing a gingham button-up, khakis, and a red ball cap.

Cleo freezes midstride. "I didn't know you were coming."

"Yeah, well, I can't stay long." JC gives Cleo an obligatory peck.

He pulls me into a hug, then gestures to his costume. "Great idea. I had everything in my closet."

"Wait, you knew he'd be here?" Cleo glares at me.

"He needed help with his costume."

"Figures." She marches toward a keg. I follow and tell her not to worry, but she whirls on me, trembling with anger. "You always come first!"

"This isn't a competition."

"It sure feels like it." Cleo looks over my shoulder at JC, her cheeks mantling with emotion. "I'm obviously the loser."

"You win everything, Cleo."

"But not him." She laughs as if she can't believe her own boyfriend doesn't want her. She's hometown royalty, a pageant queen, a Shealy. Most guys would bend over backward to ask her on a date, and she ended up loving the one who couldn't care less.

"I'll never be first place to him," Cleo says with a nod. She motions to a cluster of girls, a few I recognize from the Miss Berryville Teen pageant. "I better go say hi."

"Sure, I'll find you later."

JC leans against a car, scrolling on his phone. He looks up when I approach him. A grin sweeps across his face, and I feel a sharp pang of remorse.

"Cleo's mad at you."

"How come?" He pockets his phone and scoots to make space for me.

I lean against the hood, its metal cold through my jeans. "Do I have to say it?"

Whatever this is—whatever we are—needs to stop. I've allowed JC to love me all these years, okay with being his first place. I figured if he didn't bring up feelings, we didn't need to talk about them. He deserves more. So does Cleo. I won't stand in their way any longer.

JC shoots me a nervous glance, his throat bobbing with a swallow.

"Sometimes the people you love don't love you back, so you take what you can get."

Maybe I'm not ready for this conversation.

"Either break up or start treating Cleo like your girlfriend." I launch from the car and distance myself from JC. The party spins around me, a slow-motion revolve of headlights and bonfires. I draw the smoky night air into my lungs, but I can't catch my breath.

"Susana!" JC chases me. "Sometimes I think about you. That's the long and short of the sentence. And to be honest, it's a lie. Because *some* of the time isn't *every* time."

My heart drops.

"*Every time* I think about you"—he gasps as if the words have been caged all these years, eating him up—"I get that you don't love me back—"

"I can't do this right now." I move as fast as my tired legs will carry me and enter the crowd. History repeated itself. Obediah loved Suzanna, and she loved August.

Daisy's voice drifts from a truck bed.

She and Holler make out in the back of an F-150, wrapped more in each other than their shabby blanket. Except it's not Holler. The guy has lighter skin and longer hair.

I jerk my gaze away from them.

When we were kids, Daisy discovered her parents' affairs. She cried on my shoulder, unable to fathom why people would cheat on each other.

An uneasy feeling crawls through me. I guess we're all on a merry-go-round spinning in the direction our families choose, and none of us can get off, not even if we jump.

The thought sends panic rushing through my body. I continue walking, but my head whirls from JC's confession to Daisy kissing someone who is not her boyfriend.

Stokes loiters near the keg, exhausting his red Solo cup. He waves me over. "Susana Prather, what're you doing here? This ain't your scene."

"Cleo and Daisy wanted me to come." I motion to the empty space around me.

"They ditched you, huh?" Stokes cracks a smile and flips the curls from his forehead. "You know, there ain't a rule that says you got to be friends with someone because y'all used to be friends. You're allowed to walk away from the people who treat you like crap."

I brush my index finger against his bruised cheekbone.

"Yeah, I should practice what I preach." Stokes empties his cup with a final gulp. He sniffles and massages his eyes. They're bloodshot and glassy, their pupils dilated.

"Will you remember our conversation tomorrow?"

"Guess we'll find out," he says with a shrug.

"Stokes—"

"Dad hasn't hit me in a while."

"He should never hit you."

"Look, I don't know how to walk away. He's the only family I have."

"We can figure out something."

"I'm just like him." Stokes bows his head. His bottom lip quivers. "I've tried not to be, you know? I thought I could prove everyone wrong—"

"Susana!" Cleo signals from the pageant posse.

I grip Stokes's bicep and force him to meet my gaze. "Stay here, all right?"

He leans against a truck, and I rush to Cleo's side.

"Is it true JC spent the night at your house a week ago?" Cleo swaps glances with the other girls. They study me with arms crossed and brows raised.

Who told them JC came to my house? Do they know about the grave robbery too?

"He went frogging," I say.

"All night?"

Before I can defend myself, a football player shouts from the fire-pit. He pushes Stokes, who, within seconds of my leaving, managed to cross the party and stir up trouble. "Hands off, Burrell!"

"Go on. Say it to my face!" Stokes yells, slurring his words.

"Man, you're high as a kite."

"I overheard you and your trolls." Stokes throws a punch.

The football player dodges it and shoves his fist against Stokes's belly.

"Hey, cut it out!" I run to Stokes and loop my arm around his narrow waist. He lets me usher him away from the crowd, through rows of parked cars.

"I'm tired of people talking crap," he mumbles, his head lolling side to side.

"You need food."

"Do you think I'm a bad person, Susana?"

"No, of course not. I think you're hurting."

"Bad people hurt too—" Stokes trips on his shoelaces and crumples to his knees. He tries to stand but loses his balance and falls over. "I can't do this anymore. I can't. It's too much."

"Let's go find JC and see if you can stay at his place."

"Doctors said I was born with meth in my system." Stokes emits a caustic laugh. It wanes to a sob. "I came into the world like this. My life was always going to be this."

He beats his fists against the ground.

"Listen to me." I cup his sunken face in my hands. What I say next isn't only for him but for me too. "You're not your parents."

Stokes grabs my waist and wrenches me against him. His mouth latches onto mine, sucking my lips. I shove him with every ounce of my strength.

I scramble away, and the world goes hazy. I touch where Stokes kissed me. I thought it'd feel different. I didn't expect my first to come from him.

A silver-dollar moon reflects in windshields.

"I'm sorry, Susana. I'm so sorry." Stokes curses and reaches for me with tears pouring down his cheeks. "Please forgive me. I'm sorry."

"It's fine." I stand and dust off my jeans as Stokes weeps into his hands. I know he's intoxicated and high and lonely. I forgive him, but I can't stay here.

Cleo and Daisy will find another ride home.

Next thing I know, I'm at my car, and I'm crying hard. I brace myself against the hood and gasp for breath. Stokes shouldn't have kissed me, but it was only a kiss. I don't understand how something so small could trigger this reaction.

Shaking, I unlock my car and collapse into the driver's seat. I fumble with my keys, start the ignition. His mouth tasted like smoke and cough syrup.

I sob against the steering wheel as the engine purrs to life.

Pictures reel through my mind. Godwin and me splashing in the pool. JC sprawled on the floor of Hard-Shell Baptist, smiling from his bundle of quilts. Mama in scrapbooks. Mama on my bedroom wall. Mama buried under shushes and upped TV volumes.

My eyes sting with tears, blurring the darkness. I flip on the headlights and shift the vehicle into Reverse. I whip it around, then soar up the dirt road.

The speedometer grazes sixty.

Stokes took the kiss from me, took my control.

I've been out of control my whole life.

Emotions claw through me, muddled into feelings I can't process. They're raw and exposed, and I'm violated and vulnerable, and nothing makes sense. I can't outrun myself, but I drive faster. Hair flaps around my face, and the night zooms past.

I watch the speedometer climb to eighty.

CHAPTER 32

SUSANA PRATHER

OCTOBER, PRESENT DAY

Nanny and Papa left the porch lights on.

They glow from the farmhouse, beacons among pecan trees and Spanish moss. I ease my foot onto the Cadillac's brake as I near the lopsided mailbox.

My body doesn't want to go home.

As if possessed, I gear the car into Reverse and slam the accelerator. Tires spin dust before shooting me backward. I roll the way I came, flying past the oaks.

I entered the world like this. My life was always going to be this.

My face a phantom in the rearview mirror, I reach Godwin's house and swing into the driveway. I park beside his truck and stagger from behind the wheel.

Godwin must've heard my car. He stands behind the screen door, watching as I march up the porch steps. Without a word, he nudges open the panel and steps aside.

He wears joggers and an oversized T-shirt. His hair is mussed, his eyes somnolent.

I cross the threshold, and the screen claps shut.

Godwin studies me, his expression asking what I need from him. I step forward, and he moves closer. My chaos settles into him and his house and butterflies in my stomach.

I want it to feel right. I need control.

Before I can stop myself, I rise onto my tiptoes and kiss him lightly. Our lips brush for a moment, then I sink to my heels. "I want you. I've always wanted you."

Godwin pulls my face to his. He collides with me, kissing deeply. I clutch his shirt and anchor myself to him. At first, the contact is foreign and jarring, a dance I don't know.

My skin burns with his fingerprints. I savor his lips as shock waves pulse through me and our bodies find their unison.

His kiss is a current sweeping me away. I am against him and part of him and tumbling in a river of limbs and skin until we're pressed to a wall and he's washing over me with hands in my hair. I can't breathe or see or think anything other than *him, him, him.*

The monsters inside me get their way.

I am not Mama, but I feel like Mama right now. I want to kiss Godwin because I love him, not because of the curses in my blood. I'm making this choice.

Nanny spoke of love and lust as though they are wildfires. One spark can burn everything in a hundred-mile radius, leave a person empty and destitute.

I saw a wildfire once. I must've been nine years old. Flames gobbled up the land until all that remained were chimneys and stumps. I guess I thought love worked in a similar fashion; it had the ability to reduce me to nothing more than bricks and ash. I kept my distance from it as one does with flames. Strange how the space didn't rescue me, only made me feel cold.

Nanny was wrong. I'm not ruined or empty. What I feel reminds me of summertime and peach cobbler and woodburning stoves. I am warm and safe, gasping not from a lack of fresh air but from holding my breath for so many years.

Godwin fills my lungs again. If what I feel for him could burn . . .

Let me go up in smoke.

CHAPTER 33

SUSANA PRATHER

OCTOBER, PRESENT DAY

I'm too happy for my own skin. I need more room.

Careful not to make a sound, I ease open the front door and tiptoe across the foyer. I inch past the living room. Papa forgot to turn off the television.

Andy Griffith is frozen on its screen.

"Where were you?" Nanny's voice.

I jolt and clutch my chest.

Nanny waits at the kitchen table with her usual mug of chamomile tea. She wears her yellow bathrobe and a scowl. The microwave's clock reads 1:26.

"Sorry. I lost track of time," I say and step toward my bedroom.

"Daisy phoned to make sure you got home okay. That was over an hour ago." Nanny slams her mug onto the table. "You were with Godwin, weren't you?"

I'm up a creek without a paddle.

Nanny rises from her chair and shakes her head. She examines me, perhaps to gauge the damage done. "What am I supposed to do with you, Susana?"

"Nothing. You can trust me."

"I've seen too many girls throw away their futures. Too darn many." Nanny overlaps the panels of her bathrobe. "You'd understand if—"

"If I knew the truth? Tell me, then."

A shadow falls over Nanny's face. Whatever openness had been there shuts like a door.

"My whole life, I've carried this pressure, like I can't mess up, I can't fall in love or feel anything really without the threat of becoming *her*. Do you realize what that does to me?"

Tears drip from my cheeks and splatter on linoleum.

"What're you hiding from me, Nanny?"

"It's late. We aren't thinking right," she says, dropping her gaze to the floor. "I don't want you hanging around Godwin, and that's that."

"I'm sick and tired of the secrecy in this family!" I shout as Nanny turns to leave. "You won't tell me what happened to Mama. You won't talk about my daddy—"

"Lower your voice."

"You treat me like who I am is out of my control. Blood holds all kinds of curses, right? I got monsters and demons and whatever else you think Mama had."

"Don't turn the tables on me. You're the one in trouble."

"Why? Because I love a boy? That ain't fair, Nanny, and you know it."

"Mind your grammar," she says through clenched teeth.

"You'll lose me too. Is that what you want?" I regret the words the moment they leave my mouth. Nanny bursts into tears, and my heart sinks.

I'm dying. She will lose me.

Papa charges from the hallway, wearing long johns and his favorite wool socks. His silver hair sticks up like a rooster's comb. "Quit your fussing, both of you."

Nanny dries her eyes with her sleeves.

"What's all the racket about?"

"Nanny doesn't want me to see Godwin."

Papa scratches his head. "Susana got two eyes, don't she?"

"She was out with that boy doing God knows what," Nanny whispers as if the news is too shocking to deliver at normal volume. She eyes my belly and for a split second, I imagine Mama telling her parents she's pregnant with me. They shake their heads in response. *If only she'd stayed away from boys. If only she'd had better sense.*

That darn curse is to blame.

"I'm going to bed," I say before Papa can react.

Movement catches my attention.

The back door appears to flutter and crawl. Hundreds of moths blanket the screen, batting their wings. They sibilate and reach their legs through mesh as if trying to reach me.

Dust rubs off their flailing bodies, smearing the door ashy yellow.

I ignore them and continue to my room. Once locked inside, I retrieve the wooden panels tucked behind my dresser. They're heavier than usual, or maybe I'm weaker.

Groaning, I drag one to my window. I can't lift it high enough. My arms give out, and the panel slams the floor. I hunch against my thighs and cry because the curse is winning, and there's nothing I can do to stop it. I'm too frail, too exhausted.

Something breaks within me.

The night replays through my mind in excruciating detail.

What happened with Godwin was my choice. I shouldn't feel guilty or afraid, like I sealed my fate. I love him, so why do I suddenly feel ashamed?

Nanny won't ruin this for me. A couple of minutes ago, I was on cloud nine, practically floating with how much I liked kissing Godwin. I'm sure I want him.

I won't end up like Mama.

Freezing cold, I hug my chest. The room is too big, and I'm too small. Mama smiles from her photo under streaky highlights and a side bang.

Stokes didn't mean any harm. It was nothing.

A tap echoes from the window, followed by an eerie whoosh. The lace curtains swish, and the Okefenokee glimmers beyond.

> Don't think of it as self-sabotage.
> It'll give me relief from the nausea and
> > stomachaches.
> I don't need the panels.

> I'll die with or without them.
> But sleepwalking will give me a nice feeling.
> Relief.

I go to the window and raise its pane, allowing a damp breeze to sweep inside. A train bellows in the distance. Insects drone louder and louder. Peaceful water, restful black.

> Shakespeare wrote his Ophelia into the lilies.
> Her family was the death of her too.

The curtains blow inward, flapping carelessly while nature reaches for me. Honeysuckle vines curl over the windowsill and vein down the wall to the floor.

A sharp wind barreling into my chest, I tilt back my head and take a breath.

1865

Obediah would gladly take whatever love Suzanna chose to give.

He understood she'd already known the love of her life. Her heart would forever belong to August Godwin, her soul mate, whom she'd buried too early. Obediah accepted such. He would not endeavor to replace August, only to cherish Suzanna for what she meant to him. He was so in love with her, even a portion of her seemed better than naught.

Indeed, there were soul mates, pairs like doves, and there were those committed to a creature who'd never love back. The outliers, Obediah called them. Halves without a whole.

His mind had been made for quite some time. He would ask Suzanna to marry him and move from the commissary to his farm, where she could start anew.

All through the war, Obediah rehearsed his proposal. He spent lonely nights in battlefield camps thinking of Suzanna. She could ruin his life, and he'd let her. He'd hand over the hammer because crumpling for her sounded nicer than standing tall without her.

At least the pain would make her part of his history.

Eventually the fighting ended, and Obediah returned to Kettle Creek. Three years had passed since August's death. Suzanna remained at the commissary.

Mr. Yawn had since expired, leaving John and Louisa to work the homestead.

Obediah wasted no time and boated into the Okefenokee, still wearing his threadbare uniform and an unkempt beard. He rowed as fast as his arms would allow.

The swamp donned its afternoon best, a golden fashion for the late hour.

Autumn crisped, and Obediah marveled at how much time had passed. The landscape had changed, and it'd done so day by day. Change was often a slow progression.

He worried Suzanna had done the same.

The incident with the bat, along with town gossip, had nagged at him. Witch or not, Suzanna was the only woman he dreamed of marrying. He wouldn't let talk of curses dissuade him. Besides, the rumors would add to his fable. *Famed swamper and his sorceress wife.* Of course, his feelings weren't rooted in the possible narrative. He reminded himself of that.

Obediah stiffened once the commissary appeared. It looked all but abandoned, its roof blanketed in pine needles, its porch swallowed by plants.

A wisp of smoke curled from the chimney.

"Suzanna!" Obediah tethered his boat to the dock and took nervous steps toward the building. He'd waited three long years for this moment. Everything he wished to tell Suzanna raced through his mind, jumbling into mawkish nonsense.

My dreams won't let me let you go.

My spirit wasn't running. I think it was searching for you.

His face burned with embarrassment. He wouldn't admit the cloying thoughts. He was Obediah Owens, the man known for wrestling bears and gators.

It was all true. If not for Suzanna, Obediah might've vanished into the Okefenokee and never returned. She brought him back to Kettle Creek time and time again. He belonged in the wilderness, but in many ways, she was his freedom.

She made him feel at home in even the wildest of places.

The commissary's door swung open. Suzanna emerged with her rifle pressed against her shoulder. One look at Obediah, and she bolted from the porch. She dropped her weapon and flung her arms around him, squeezing tight as he swept her into an embrace.

"War's over, Suzanna. I'm back for good." Obediah couldn't bring himself to let her go. He carried her a few steps, surprised by her lightness.

"Let me get a proper look at you." Suzanna drew back, still propped in his arms, and examined his face. "My, you've gotten old on me."

"I ain't done nothing of the sort," Obediah said, cracking a smile. He believed the war had aged him a decade. All trace of youth had fled his features, exchanged for creases and scruff.

The past three years had taken a toll on Suzanna too. She was haggard, her figure scrawny from poor eating. She wore a forest-green dress Obediah hadn't seen before.

He lowered her to the ground and cradled her face in his palms. To him, she appeared herself. The fog in her eyes had faded, replaced with startling clarity.

"I've missed you." Obediah realized love and people were living documents, ever revising into deeper stories. His whole life had been leading him to this chapter.

"Come inside. I'll put the kettle on." Suzanna laced her fingers with his and led him to the commissary, retrieving her rifle along the way.

Obediah paused on the threshold.

"After what you've been through, coming here must feel strange." Suzanna propped her gun against the wall and sauntered to the stove. "I reckon some places feel different because we're different in them, don't you?"

"It ain't that." Obediah stepped inside and removed his hat. "What I'm fixing to say I've thought about an awful lot. I would've said it years ago, but the timing wasn't right."

Suzanna poured water into the kettle and set it to boil.

"You must know . . . I only think of you. Whether I sleep or wake, it makes no difference. It is you who fills my every thought. I would be remiss if I didn't state my feelings. I love you, Suzanna. I know it like I know my own name."

She whipped her attention to him. "You love me?"

"Desperately," Obediah sighed. He knelt in front of her and took her hand, kissing her wrist, then her knuckles. "Please be my wife. Marry me."

His words were too casual to belong to someone who felt so deeply.

"After all these years?" Suzanna lowered to the floor, spilling tears when Obediah gave a nod. "I do fine on my own. I don't need another husband."

"You're my dearest friend," he said. "I'm not August. I don't expect you to care about me the same way, but love can be friendship. Love can be us."

"I don't want to curse you."

"My clover runs too deep, remember?" Obediah dried her tears with his thumb. "A lifetime ago, I asked what it was you wanted, and you said food on your plate and a pillow under your head. I promised I'd dream for the both of us. I admit the only dream I could muster, try as I might, was you and me. Nothing else seemed bigger."

Suzanna rested her temple against his shoulder.

"Be at peace with me," Obediah whispered. "Leave this godforsaken place."

"I expect Mama's smiling in her grave right about now." Suzanna toyed with one of his brass buttons. "Love can be friendship, I think."

Not long after, Suzanna packed a carpetbag and left the commissary. She and Obediah were married at his farm, by the local preacher. They fell into a gentle affection and with time, it grew into something like love. Obediah dared not wish for more. He was grateful to have Suzanna in his home, to care for her family as his own.

They lived quietly, removed from town. Suzanna tended the garden and the livestock. She regained her strength, the youth returning to her cheeks. Obediah watched her heal, in the process healing himself. War faded into the recesses of his mind until it was but an ugly scar.

A year into their union, Suzanna gave birth to healthy twin sons. She and Obediah named the boys Seaborn and Berrien. Such joy was foreign to Obediah. He relished each second, awestruck by Suzanna. She was a fine mother, tender and vigilant.

Obediah memorized the verses of her lullabies as she rocked the babes to sleep.

> *Your daddy is a good man, a great man.*
> *He goes to the forest, works as hard as he can.*
> *And in the forest, he stretches his back.*
> *Before he begins swinging his axe.*

> *With that axe he chops, chops, chops.*
> *And turns a tree to a pile of logs.*
> *And with those logs he builds a house.*
> *To keep you warmer than a little field mouse.*

When sleep wouldn't draw near, Obediah whispered the words. He wondered how long their spell of peace would last. Perhaps the good years were reparation for their suffering.

Suzanna became wary as time went on. She feared the curse would return as it had two years into her marriage to August. She filled the cabin with talismans and refused to leave her children, not even to fetch water from the well.

Obediah noticed her declining health. She moved with labored steps, weakening until she could no longer carry their sons. She claimed the curse had returned to steal her away.

Her obsession worsened until she denied sleep and spent nights hunched over the bassinet. Obediah begged her not to worry, but she grew paranoid and bitter.

She ruminated on her losses, terrified of losing more.

The Okefenokee seemed to notice her shift of mood. It struck Obediah as hostile, like a battalion preparing to attack. Something about its ebb and flow unnerved him.

He discovered roots sprouting beneath the bed, reaching for Suzanna.

Banishing thoughts of witches and curses, Obediah persuaded Suzanna to sit with him on their cabin's porch. She lowered into a rocking chair, wincing as her spine met the backrest.

The babes napped in a basket at Obediah's feet, cooing softly.

"Promise me—" Suzanna coughed and relaxed into the chair. Her face was sunken, her limbs frail. "When I'm gone, you take another wife. Our boys need a mama."

"You ain't dying, Suzanna."

"Not even the great Obediah Owens can keep death away." Suzanna released a jagged breath. "Don't you worry none. When I die, I'm coming back to see you."

"When you die, you're taking me with you. That's an order."

Suzanna rose from her rocking chair and lowered onto Obediah's knee. She nestled in his arms, lighter than bird bones. "Elizabeth Ruger has adored you since we were children."

"You're the only wife I want." Obediah held Suzanna, afraid to loosen his grip. He bolstered her head against his shoulder and kissed her temple.

"Tell me, is it true you killed that bear?"

"With a wooden club. I ripped a stump from the ground and beat the critter dead."

A sigh breezed from Suzanna's lips. "Was it all true?"

Since adolescence, Suzanna had questioned his stories, believing he'd lost himself in the myth that was Obediah Owens. She'd asked for his genuine accounts, and he'd maintained his mystery because he liked the tall tales, perhaps more than he liked himself. Even so, he hadn't lied once, not about wrestling gators, nor loving the girl he now called his bride.

"Was it all true?" Obediah repeated. "Every last bit."

Not two weeks later, Suzanna went up and died in Ruger's field. Nobody understood her presence there or what incited her death.

Willard found her lying among cotton as though she'd merely drifted off to sleep.

Obediah was riding back from Trader's Hill when Suzanna expired. As he passed through Kettle Creek, the moon shone bright as day, painting the pine forests silver.

Shy of two miles from his homestead, his mare froze and bowed her head. Obediah looked forward. There, standing in the road, was Suzanna.

He slumped in his saddle and wept. He knew she was gone and the woman before him was her ghost here to bid one last goodbye.

The specter did not utter a word.

Obediah rode toward her. "Good evening." He tipped his hat, then continued down the road. When he looked back, Suzanna was gone.

He buried her the next day in the Hard-Shell cemetery.

Despite her wishes, Obediah did not remarry. He raised his sons with help from Louisa and took them fishing in the swamp. He swore if they listened, they'd hear Suzanna's spirit alive in the channels and prairies. Often, he felt her presence among the cypresses.

He found solace in knowing death had not completely robbed him of her.

Deep within the dirt, a coffin vaulted Suzanna's remains. It contained her bones, a coin stitched into her corset, and the rifle she always carried. It did not hold a curse.

The curse lived on, eager and waiting.

Biding its time until the next Suzanna rose to take her place.

CHAPTER 34

SUSANA PRATHER

NOVEMBER, PRESENT DAY

The swamp is preparing to take me.

Weak from the night, I sit in a puddle of blankets on the narrow dock extending from my grandparents' backyard. I soothe myself with coffee from a daisy-dot mug and let the morning light soak into my skin and draw the world into focus.

Fog sweeps over the water, and the grass shimmers with frost. An alligator suns on a log while egrets fellowship in a tupelo, the creatures still as if waiting to thaw.

This is all I have left, a few more dawns to relish the sun and my lucid thoughts.

Holding back tears, I lean against the dock's weathered planks. A splinter pierces my palm. I pluck it free, releasing a single drop of blood.

The blood disperses into the water like smoke.

I gulp coffee from the bottom of my mug. It's thick with honey and oozes down my throat, leaving a bitter aftertaste. I brewed it extra dark for extra caffeine.

My eyelids still weigh heavy.

Last night feels like a week ago, or like it didn't even happen. I was at a party, and Stokes kissed me, and I panicked. Maybe it shouldn't have bothered me, but I snapped and drove to Godwin's house. I kissed him. We kissed a lot. Then I went home, and Nanny freaked out.

The curse reared its head after that. I couldn't resist it, nor did I want to, nor could I resist Godwin. I wanted him and still do. Everything feels upside down like the trees reflected in the water. I feel good and guilty and in love and terrified.

I think I'm at my breaking point.

The Okefenokee sprawls before me, a mirror framed by aquatic plants and cypresses. Its surface ripples a painting of muddy greens. I don't understand how I can feel both afraid of the swamp and drawn to it. At this point, why should I fight the lure?

Truth is a drumbeat: I was born this way. I was always going to end up here.

My nostrils prickling with the earthy musk of tannin, I comb my fingertips through the water. It'll take me like it took Mama. I'll wade into the depths, my eyes glittering madness, and end up as pale hands tangled in lilies. Someone will find my pieces or clothes and pencil my name into the ledger of firstborn daughters lost to the curse.

"Leave me alone," I tell my intrusive thoughts.

They continue to whisper, reminding me cursed people curse other people and I'll leave hexes in my wake. I spiral into the ideas as the sun climbs higher. I am the reflection of the women before me. I was doomed from the moment I took my first breath.

My story has already been written, so I give in and let go.

Nanny and Papa call for me when I enter the house. They eat breakfast in the kitchen. Papa hunches over a bowl of cereal with a Band-Aid decorating his sun-spotted hand. He motions for me to sit next to him, but I grab my keys from the table and leave.

This is what cursed Prather girls do.

I go to Godwin's house and find him in the barn feeding horses and hauling around tack. He notices me and drops a hay bale, grinning so big his face is all stars and dimples.

My heart beats in the tips of my toes.

"So much for space, huh?" Godwin looks at me, into me, as if every moment is last night, or it could be if we continue to stare like this.

"You don't have to come any closer." I lean against a stall door.

Godwin pets a horse's velveteen nose, then moves toward me. His expression is lightning in my bloodstream. "Yeah, no, that ain't gonna work."

He rests his forearm above my head, the barn shrinking to the walls of his chest and shoulders. I brush my lips against his mouth, and we stay like this, not quite kissing, breathing each other's air. I could slice the tension with Nanny's cake knife.

Godwin runs his calloused hands along the sides of my neck and through my hair. "I want you too," he whispers into the space between our skin.

Words so simple they sound like poetry.

I pull him closer, fitting with his grooves. He sweeps me up into his arms and presses me against the stall door. We kiss, and I'm a wildfire, but I always have been, and if I'm destined to burn, I want to go out like this, as flames, not embers.

Nuzzling my neck, Godwin fixes me to his frame. I could pick his hands out of a lineup. I fade into the feeling of them, quiet my thoughts in the darkness behind my eyelids.

The person I've become feels like a stranger in my own body. She goes against the grain of what I know, yet I don't stop her from taking over.

Maybe I never knew myself to begin with.

Godwin smiles against my neck. "We should've done this ages ago."

If someone asked me about him, I don't think I'd be able to talk without glowing. I kiss him across the barn and into a hay bale.

We spend the next few days slowing time with each other. I play hooky from school. Godwin and I row his boat into the Okefenokee, intending to fish but kissing instead. We take his truck to the Berryville Drive-In and get stuck on back roads.

A week into our relationship, I develop insomnia. I use the barricades at night as a precaution. Not sleeping is somehow more frightening than sleepwalking.

The insomnia is a telltale sign of what's coming. I distract myself with Godwin.

He must sense my oblivion because he also behaves as if he's on fire. We act young and reckless and move too fast. I can't stop myself.

Nanny corners me one evening and says I look ill. She asks if there's anything I want to tell her. I ask her the same. After a lengthy deadlock, we part ways.

I sneak out my window and go to Godwin's house.

He thinks we're in love. He says as much while boiling water for ramen and recounting our relationship timeline. I do love him, but I also think our romance helps me reclaim control of my life. Being here, doing what we do, feels like rebellion.

I insist we get stuck on more back roads and pay to not watch movies at the drive-in. I slip away to his house night after night. Eventually I stop going home except to swap clothes, and I do that when Nanny and Papa aren't around.

I have nothing to lose.

Godwin and I take his tractor for a slow drive across his land.

He must hear my stomach growl because he drapes his arm over my shoulders and offers me a pack of crackers. That's what I love about him. Even in silence, I never go unheard.

He asks me to make peace with my grandparents.

I tell him I already know what they'll say.

My whole life, people have spoken of love as though it's finite. I grew up thinking I needed to ration myself because if I handed my heart to another person, I'd never get it back.

Nowadays I don't think love is so limited. I don't believe I should regret giving a boy part of me I wanted him to have. Even if I love and lose, I still loved.

That's a piece of me I'll always keep.

Maybe I'm delusional and impulsive, and this is proof of the curse inside me. I don't care anymore. Nanny and Papa can believe whatever they want. I'm on this train barreling toward a cliff. I can't jump off, but I decide how I spend my final moments. If I can't sleep or leave town, I'll stay with Godwin, and we'll make out in truck beds and pretend we're free.

Sunday morning, I go home to swap clothes. The carport is empty, so I assume my grandparents are at church. But when I step into the living room, I'm confronted with solemn expressions and crossed arms and eyes that call me a failure.

I've waltzed into an intervention.

Nanny and Papa regard me with disappointment. I could've broken the pattern if I'd resisted more, if I'd stayed away from Godwin, if I'd had less of Mama in my blood. When I quit trying to choose different, I became a lost cause.

At least, that's what their faces tell me.

"Principal Chancey said you've been skipping school." Nanny's voice is firm. Her stare roams my body, avoiding my gaze. "Why're you doing this, Susana? What'd we do wrong?"

I don't say a word.

"Running around with that boy . . . it isn't like you." Nanny sniffles and dries her eyes. "I don't understand. We raised you right. You know better."

"This isn't about either of you."

"What, then?" Papa asks. His expression breaks my heart.

"I don't want to talk about it."

"Tough luck, we're talking," Papa snaps, which is so out of character for him, I flinch. "Look, I get you're mad, but try to understand where we're coming from."

You're just like her, aren't you?

I stumble back a step as Keziah's voice rings through my head. Nanny and Papa act concerned, but they're liars. They won't tell me the truth.

You'll curse everyone in this town.

"Stop!" I scream at the voice. I hurry to my bedroom, leaving my grandparents wide-eyed, and collapse on the mattress. I can't sleep, but I don't feel awake. The world is spinning, and the quilts below me reek of the swamp and everything I cannot escape.

CHAPTER 35

SUSANA PRATHER

NOVEMBER, PRESENT DAY

Lightning veins the sky, and dust plumes around my car.

I don't bother to crank up the windows. Instead, I slam the accelerator and veer into Godwin's driveway. I desert my vehicle next to his truck and climb onto the porch.

As wind chimes sing for the storm, I rush inside.

The door claps shut, and everything goes silent.

"Godwin, you home?" I cross the foyer and rove down a hallway. The house smells different, stale, not of fresh paint and laundry detergent.

Floorboards creak to my right.

Godwin appears in the kitchen's entry, wearing jeans and a wrinkly button-up. He flushes at the sight of me. "Hey, I thought you had to run errands."

"Nanny and Papa were at the house—" I step toward him, and he steps back. Something about his expression deflates the air from my lungs. "What's going on?"

"The rehab people called about Dad." Godwin reverses into the kitchen, fidgeting with his bracelets. "They, um, said he chugged a whole thing of mouthwash."

A knot tightening my stomach, I scan the kitchen. Liquor bottles line the counter. The air carries a sweet aroma reminiscent of black licorice.

"I was cleaning out the pantry." Godwin wags his finger at the cupboard and stack of dry goods on the floor. "I dropped a bottle of whiskey, and it shattered."

Sweat glistens on his brow.

"The nurse said Dad needs to stay at the center. I knew that was a possibility—heck, I expected it—but hearing it made the whole thing real, you know? Dad isn't coming back," Godwin sputters. His eyes are glossy and bloodshot. "Whatever. I figured I'd be stuck with this place for a while. It just feels set in stone now, like I don't have a choice."

I can't believe I need to ask. "Have you been drinking?"

"Noofcoursenot." Godwin's response slurs into a single word. He drops his gaze, and suddenly it's the night we got together. I'm at the party. Stokes kisses me before I kiss Godwin. Then, it's a year before that. I'm at the bar, yelling at Godwin while he drunkenly yells at me.

My knees weaken at the memories.

"You told me you'd stopped drinking, that you didn't want to end up like your daddy." I remember the beer bottles in his truck bed. "How long has this been going on?"

"It's not what you think." Godwin stumbles to the table.

"Are you *drunk*?" I grasp a fistful of his shirt and yank him closer. His breath reeks of alcohol, so pungent it could remove paint. "You lied to me!"

He pries my fingers from his clothes. "Stop looking at me like that."

I turn on my heels, aching with so many different pains, I can't tell one from the other.

"Susana, I messed up." Godwin chases me into the living room. "I didn't plan for this to happen. A month or so ago, I was struggling, and I saw the bottles. People drink all the time, and they're fine. I'm not an alcoholic. I'll stop. I can stop."

He folds into me, becoming small like a child, as if my arms might protect him.

"Why didn't you tell me?" I can't break my curse, neither can he break his. We're both morphing into our parents, or maybe we already have.

"Because I didn't want you to think I'm out of control. I don't usually overserve myself, but I was upset, you know? The stuff with Dad is a lot to handle."

His secrecy nauseates me.

Unwrapping him from my body, I storm to the kitchen and snatch bottles from the counter. One by one, I pour their contents down the sink.

I dump the empty containers into a trash can, then brace my weight against the table.

Godwin clutches his mouth and slides down the doorframe. "I'm not my dad," he gasps. Tears stream his splotchy cheeks, dripping onto the floorboards between his boots.

He wanted space, but I kissed him anyway. I've used our relationship as ammunition against my lack of control. Would I have driven to his house that night if Stokes hadn't kissed me? Would I have done any of this if I wasn't cursed?

I tug my neckline, but I can't ease the pressure under my sternum.

Nanny warned me, but I climbed over the rails of her advice and jumped. This is the pattern, the unbreakable pattern. I am Mama, and Godwin is Gus.

Sick bubbles up my throat and burns my mouth.

I fooled around with Godwin. I'm not sure if what we did was wrong. All I know is I'm like *her*, the comprehensive *her*, centuries of secrets buried and shushed. Even if choices weren't mistakes, if they were treated like shame, then shame they became.

Thunder rattles the house, rippling old coffee in a cowboy mug.

Godwin rises from his crouch. "Susana, look at me, please. Are you ignoring me now?" When I don't respond, he swears and kicks a chair, splintering wood. "I shouldn't have moved back here. I should've let this house rot."

Something inside me snaps.

"Go on, then. We both know you'll skip town eventually. Here, I'll help you pack." I march to the living room and grab books, his Carhartt jacket, the photo of him and his daddy.

"Hey, stop that." Godwin scoops his belongings from my hands and drops them onto the sofa. He grips my shoulders, holding me still.

"You won't stay in Kettle Creek, and I won't leave!" My voice breaks, melting into sobs. "We both know how this will end."

"How can you say that?" Godwin follows me to the foyer and bumps into a side table.

Trembling, I shove open the screen door and stagger onto the porch. Drizzle paints dots on the front steps. Gales bend trees and swing wind chimes.

"I mess things up. I'm sorry." Godwin hurries outside, wiping snot from his nose. "I left town because I didn't want to end up like Dad, and look at what happened."

My skin numbs until I no longer feel the breeze or the skirt billowing around my legs.

"I didn't want to drop out of college." Godwin hunches over and hugs his stomach. He cries harder, and I sense these tears aren't shed for me. He's mourning the loss of his dreams. He's angry at his parents and life, maybe even himself. "I hurt Betty, and I hurt you. I'm sorry."

I go to my car and slide behind the steering wheel. Godwin begs me to stay. He jiggles the door handle, apologizes over and over, but I key the ignition and reverse from the driveway.

Godwin sprints to his house, and I speed home.

This is my fault. We cursed ones rub off on everything and everyone.

I burst inside and Papa lurches from his recliner. He's been cracking pecans in the living room as rain pelts the roof and *Magnum, P.I.* plays on the TV.

I slam the front door, panting at the sight of Godwin's truck pursuing me down the drive.

Papa abandons his nutcracker and watches me tear off my wet cardigan.

"Susana!" Godwin's voice.

Papa moves to the door and peers through its screen. His eyes ask if he needs to get his gun.

I touch his arm to assure him I'm okay. After a couple of minutes, I relent to Godwin's yelling and step onto the porch. "Go home, Godwin!"

He waits in the yard, drenched head to toe. "I'm not leaving."

"Why?"

"Because you're worth the dang front porch!" Godwin shrugs and gazes at me with soft eyes. "Look, I want to be wherever you are. I don't think I had a home until I entered your house. I didn't have a reason to stay until *you*."

My heart in pieces, I enter the cloudburst and slosh across the lawn. I halt at arm's length, heaving as pain and rain soak every bit of me. "I can't love you and watch you leave. I am too in love with you to lose you and be okay. I won't be okay. I won't."

Godwin shields his eyes from the torrent. Water drips from his nose, rolls off his bottom lip, and plasters clothes to his body. "Then I won't go anywhere."

"But you will. You'll get bored of this town and me and decide to move on—"

"Aren't you listening?" Godwin cups my face as a deluge of rain washes the landscape misty blue. He combs his fingers through my hair, resting his forehead against mine.

"You left Betty. She loved you, and you left her. I'll be another Betty."

"I can't believe what I'm hearing."

"This isn't working." I sink away from him.

"We're not breaking up."

"Please go before we make this any worse."

He lowers to the mud and sits with his legs crossed. "I am not leaving you."

"That night I showed up at your house, I was upset. I'd gone to a party, and Stokes had kissed me. He was drunk. He didn't mean anything by it. But I lost my head."

"What're you saying?"

"Don't get me wrong. I wanted to kiss you. How we started, though—I should've acted differently. We went too fast."

Godwin scrambles from the earth. "You said you wanted me," he says, clenching his jaw. Still, the muscles around his mouth twitch. "I thought you'd made up your mind."

"I do want you."

"But you think being with me was a mistake." He steps forward, jabbing his thumb against his chest. "*I'm a mistake.*"

"You said we bring out the worst in each other." I motion to our soaked, distressed bodies and the pouring rain. "Look at us, Godwin."

He shakes his head. "Is this about the booze in my house?"

"It's about us becoming our parents." I tense once the words leave my mouth. They're cruel, but I feel cruel; my pain is cruel.

Godwin huffs as if I punched him.

"We aren't right for each other." I'm not sure I believe it, but I don't feel right, I haven't done right.

"Please don't push me away, not again."

"Go home, Godwin." I drift toward the farmhouse with hot tears streaming my cheeks.

"Better you leave than me, right?" Godwin treads at my heels and grabs my arm. "I don't understand, Susana. What's happening?"

"I'm not myself anymore," I sob. "Everything I did . . . I wasn't myself."

Standing behind me, he loops his arms around my waist and rests his chin in the crease of my neck. "I've made mistakes, but you're not one of them. You hear me?"

"The curse didn't break. I'm losing my mind, Godwin."

"What?"

"Didn't you notice? I can't sleep. That's why I haven't needed the barricades."

A look of realization washes across his face. He creates distance between us, the desperation in his eyes replaced with anger. "You know why our relationship goes around in circles, Susana? Because you can't get past your darn fear. It has such a hold on you."

"The curse is real."

"I'm not saying it isn't. I just think you give it too much power. You decide the life you want, not your mama or anything else."

"Yeah, well, my sleepwalking disagrees." I hug my chest, shivering as water continues to pound my scalp and shoulders.

Papa emerges from the farmhouse. "Godwin." His voice is firm and loving. "You run on home, son. Y'all can talk again once y'all cool off."

"I'm not my dad." Godwin stretches his arms behind his neck. He shudders and rubs his face, then looks at me blankly as if he somehow erased his hurt. "All right, well, if you can't watch me leave, now's when you should look away."

I don't.

He climbs into his truck and drives to the road.

Papa joins me in the rain, says everything will be okay.

Everything won't include Godwin and me.

I ruined us too well.

EARLY 2000s

Keziah Douglas sat on her porch steps as police lights blinked red-blue in her driveway.

She pinned one of her late husband's cigarettes between her fingers and took slow pulls. No one would judge her for smoking after hearing such news, and if they did, to hell with 'em.

Her son Brady had made a run to the grocery store in desperate want of ice cream. He'd been under a great deal of stress as of late, what with his father's sudden passing and the Prather girl stirring up trouble with talk of assault.

According to the officers now milling about a squad car, unwrapping their fast-food burgers on its hood, Brady had dropped dead in the frozen-food aisle. Why they had stayed after delivering the news, Keziah didn't know. She would phone Sheriff Cleveland in the morning and file a formal complaint.

Keziah crumpled a tear-soaked tissue in her fist. She'd cried for days after losing her husband. She'd likely cry a great deal more, but for now, her eyes were empty.

She finished the cigarette, lit another, and rose onto achy legs—her joints weren't what they used to be—then started down the stone walkway toward the dizzying lights.

Perhaps the officers thought her stoicism unusual. She'd watched episodes of *Dateline* in which people became suspects because of their strange reactions to bad news. Faking anything didn't suit her. She'd garnered a reputation for being cutthroat honest, and she wasn't about to change herself to suit the law's opinion. Besides, what she felt wasn't only grief but rage, the kind she assumed drove people to murder.

Well, she'd tell them what was unusual: eating on her property while she grieved her husband and son, both gone within a scant two weeks' time. They had no business.

The officers' careless conversation reached her ears as she approached.

"I'm telling you, I ain't never seen anything like it. Kids don't just drop dead."

"This family got all kinds of bad luck. You hear about Mr. Douglas?"

"Mm-hmm, blade at the sawmill chopped his head clean off."

She paused and took a long, stabilizing drag. Mr. Douglas had kicked the smoking habit when Brady was in elementary school. He'd stashed the remainder of his final pack in his sock drawer under cufflinks gifted to him by a high school sweetheart. Keziah had never minded that he kept both. The past deserved remembering, she always said. Nowadays, she wasn't so sure.

The smell of her microwave dinner hung in the late-autumn air, drifting from the millhouse's screen door. She'd never liked beef stroganoff. Then again, she'd never cared for cigarettes. She assumed she'd inherit other traits, perhaps his love for bow hunting or taste for boiled peanuts.

All losses came with their own hauntings, Keziah thought. Grief was not a ghost, rather the dissolve of one person into everything gone from them. Now Keziah saw her husband and son reflected in her new self, which was both a comfort and a fear.

"People say the Prather girl put a curse on 'em."

Keziah blew smoke. She expected all of Berryville to blame the curse. Once folks learned of Brady's sudden death, they'd point fingers at the Prathers, mention old feuds and witches.

She'd heard stories about the Prather family and the hex placed on the Douglases long before she married into the family. A folktale, she'd thought and given her worries to other matters. But when the grisly accident at the lumber mill took her husband, the stories resurfaced.

Now she wasn't sure whether to accuse the supernatural or accept the tragedies as punishment. Her son had done wrong.

The child growing in Susan Prather's belly was proof. Brady had admitted it might be his.

"Come on. You don't believe all that curse mumbo jumbo."

"How else do you explain two dead men in two weeks?"

"Susan Prather ain't a witch."

"You're just saying that 'cause you're sweet on her."

Susan Prather must've claimed assault to salvage her reputation, Keziah told herself. The girl was a known flirt, a promiscuous one at that. If the child belonged to Brady, then who could prove the whole ordeal wasn't consensual, as he claimed? No one would believe a nice boy like Brady had . . .

Keziah couldn't bring herself to think the word. She smoked the cigarette to a stub, then fired up another and kept walking.

Those who believed Susan Prather's accusations would go so far as to claim she had jinxed Brady in revenge.

"Susan's sweet on everybody."

"Runs in the family, I guess. Her mama was a fun time back in my day."

"You better not talk like that around Cleveland."

"Lighten up. We ain't hurting anybody."

After bathing her lungs in smoke, Keziah flicked ash from the cigarette.

If they'd been cursed for their sins, she worried she'd inherit their punishment. Perhaps it was the hexed Douglas name that had prompted their deaths in the first place.

Keziah banished the notion. All of it was a coincidence: the mill accident, the grocery store. God hadn't struck down Brady, nor had Suzanna Yawn's hex. Even if Susan wanted revenge, she couldn't have incited Brady's demise with a few witchy words.

She needed to believe her son's account of what had occurred between him and Susan. Keziah didn't want the public to think of her the same way they did the Prathers. That was the real damage, more than rumors of assault and teen pregnancy. If people believed her family was truly cursed, she wouldn't outlive the gossip.

Keziah decided: The baby wasn't her grandchild. She'd deny all relation to the child. She'd tell everyone Susan had been spotted with multiple boys over the past year. Any of them could be the father. She'd distance herself from the Prathers, and maybe the bad luck would spare her.

"I think there's something to all this curse talk."

"That so? Then I reckon I'll see you boys back here in another two weeks."

"Nah, if that Douglas lady dies, we won't have a reason to come back."

Keziah spun on her heels and backtracked to the house. She'd hear no more. She gasped for breath. Her lungs were rocks inside her chest.

Leaning against the porch's column, she stubbed out the remainder of her cigarette and hacked into the crease of her elbow while doubt gnawed at her certainty.

CHAPTER 36

SUSANA PRATHER

NOVEMBER, PRESENT DAY

I whip my Cadillac into the church's lot and park under an oak.

Keziah stands in the Hard-Shell cemetery as she does most afternoons. If she hears me coming, she doesn't bother to glance my way. She props baby's breath against her husband's and son's headstones, accompanied by her oxygen tank.

Last night's dream has repeated in my thoughts, making my return to school unbearable. I should've used the panels. I didn't expect a pause from my insomnia.

I never would've guessed what I now know.

"You think I'm your granddaughter, don't you?" I say once I reach the gravesite. A chill snakes through my body. "That's why you've always given me special attention."

Keziah shoots me a bewildered look, seemingly taken aback. She backfills a gopher tortoise hole with the heel of her loafer.

"But you'd never claim me as your kin, because doing so would mean accepting what your son did." I fight back tears. "Is it true? Is Brady Douglas my dad?"

"The curse won't end," Keziah whispers, shaking her head. "All these years, I've tried to figure out what did it—if my son brought judgment upon the family, or if Susan bewitched us."

My heart feels like broken glass in my chest.

"I'm cursed too," she murmurs. "Suzanna Yawn hexed the Douglases centuries ago. I'm all that's left of them. Makes sense I'd inherit their bad luck."

"Mama accused your son of raping her, didn't she?"

The question turns my stomach.

"He wouldn't have done it." Keziah locks eyes with me, her fear unmistakable. She's afraid of the curse and furious, either at my family or life in general. "You have Douglas blood in you; I see it. You're not only Susan."

There's something conflicted in her voice, like she wants to love me but can't because of history. If I am her biological granddaughter, I'm the only family she has.

I stagger back a step. "No wonder my grandparents didn't tell me."

Nanny and Papa must've kept the secret as a kindness. They wished to spare me from knowing how I came to be, or more likely they didn't believe Mama either and regarded me as a great unknown, a result of someone's cursed propensities.

"Please." Keziah yanks her tank into motion. She crushes an anthill, leaving a swarm of homeless, confused insects. "The feud between our families—we can put a stop to it."

"Whatever you're looking for, Keziah, I don't have the power to give it to you." I turn and move toward the parking lot, unable to catch my breath.

"You can release me from the curse," Keziah yells. "Just say it!"

I keep walking. I can't walk fast enough. How do I contend with all this? If it's true—*it is true*—then I'm here because a boy hurt Mama. Nobody believed her, not even her own family. I remember Nanny saying as much, which explains why she feels so much guilt.

"Agnes and Seaborn Prather aren't high and mighty. They've been lying for nearly thirty-five years. Haven't you heard the rumors?" Keziah flinches when I whirl around.

"At least they didn't abandon me!" I shout. "You chose not to be my grandma. Whatever happened with your son wasn't my fault. You could've accepted me, realized I was a chance for you to redeem the past. I don't owe you anything."

"Ask them about Susie."

"My great-aunt? What about her?"

"It's all in the blood, ain't it? Your mama had to get it from somewhere."

"Get what?"

Keziah holds my gaze. "Everyone thought it was strange when Susie Prather disappeared for months, then returned with Agnes, Seaborn, and a newborn baby. She claimed the child belonged to Agnes and Seaborn, but folks weren't convinced."

Fat tears release down my face.

"Suspicions grew when Missouri Jane was born less than a year later," Keziah says, hitching her shoulder. "Don't you see the pattern, Susana? Like mother like daughter. Surely, it's not hard to imagine why people didn't believe your mama."

I open my mouth to call Keziah a liar, but then I see it: the curse is genetic. Suzanna Yawn mentioned blood and bones. It passed down Seaborn Owens's line, first to his daughter Suzannah, then to her daughter Susan, and so on. Susie died before she could bear children, so the curse skipped to Papa and manifested in Mama.

But if the curse is in the female line, Papa couldn't have passed down the gene.

My body lurches into a run. I get in my car and drive home while my mind races from Brady to Mama to Susie.

"No, no!" I beat my palms against the wheel and scream at the windshield. Next thing I know, I'm standing in Nanny and Papa's house with Missouri Jane in my face.

She asks what's the matter and guides me to the living room where my grandparents—or *not* grandparents—read sections of the newspaper. The clock vibrates the house.

Suzanna animates in her oval portrait. She cocks her head and watches me, wearing an ink-blue gown and a halo of braids.

> The similarities between the women before me:
> People buried their secrets under silence.
> The truth has been here all along
> Alive within this house.

My chest heaving, I confront Nanny and Papa. "No wonder I didn't find answers. They're with you. They've always been with you."

If my family had been honest from the start, perhaps the curse would've broken a long time ago; the swamp wouldn't have taken Mama. They've kept so many secrets.

The clock echoes louder and louder, and I float away until I'm standing across from time running out. Faces turn in their picture frames. Immediately, I'm back in July, blowing out birthday candles and wishing for cooler weather.

I clutch my head, the room spinning into a noisy blur. A melody thrums from nowhere, a cello or fiddle, the weeping notes of an organ. "Help me, please. I don't have much time. The swamp is gonna take me like it took Mama."

Papa gathers my body in his arms and lowers onto the couch. He squeezes tight, restraining me. "Ain't nothing gonna take you, sugar lump."

Dirt is other things.
Living things alive no more.
Their grave we disturb.
We wear on our shoes
Billions of dead tracked around by those still here.

We rub our status in their faces.
Life
Alive
Beating
Breathing

Body to bones
To dust
To matter
For worms and roots
And ground beneath shoes.

The humble reality is
We support the world
Whether we try to or not.

No matter what we wear down
Or who we screw over,
We'll inevitably hold up
What lives on
After us.

I scream and claw at the sofa's floral upholstery as thoughts ricochet through my mind. "I've tried everything. I can't break it. Don't let the swamp take me—"

"The swamp won't take you," Papa says.

"You don't understand. I'm exactly like her." I wheeze. "You can save me. Please. I'm going insane. I've ruined everything."

Nanny and Missouri stand frozen, gaping at me with tears in their eyes.

"Admit it. Brady Douglas is my daddy, and you didn't believe Mama when she told you what happened. You kept it a secret, like you kept Susie's pregnancy a secret. That's why me being with Godwin scared you so much, right? Like mother like daughter like daughter."

"What's she talking about?" Missouri asks Nanny and Papa.

I believed myself intertwined with them, my spirit, their spirit, my blood, their blood. "You're not my grandparents, are you?"

CHAPTER 37

SUSANA PRATHER

NOVEMBER, PRESENT DAY

S ay it isn't true!" Missouri yells. "Is Susan not my sister? Is she not *your daughter*?"

Nanny turns red and fumbles for words. Her attention darts from me to Papa to the scrapbooks lined up on a shelf. "You know people 'round here. They say all kinds of nonsense."

But she and Papa say nothing at all.

"What're you hiding from me?" I lurch from Papa's arms, scrambling across the living room like a wild animal. I reach for a scrapbook. I whip it open, page after page, then release it to the floor and grab another.

Nanny yells at me to stop. Papa clamps a hand onto my shoulder. They should've told me about Susie and Mama and Brady. I'll prove what Keziah said.

The truth is here—I hear it whispering.

A clock ticking.

A whippoorwill screaming.

A beep inside this house.

I snatch the oldest scrapbook from the collection and sidestep Papa. Nanny shouting at me, I sprint down the hall to my bedroom. There's no use confronting them anymore.

My family will only lie to me.

Gasping, I lock the door and drop to my knees. I leaf through the scrapbook, its paper brown with decades, as Nanny and Papa jiggle the doorknob and beg me to come to my senses.

I feel around the sheet protectors, reach into the sleeves. I give the scrapbook a shake to loosen anything Nanny might've tucked between the pages.

A baby picture of Mama peels from its glue.

"Susana, honey, open the door," Missouri says from the corridor, her voice shaky as if she knows the curse has taken hold of me. "Whatever's going on—let us help you."

They didn't help Mama.

I flip the scrapbook upside down and shake harder. An envelope flutters to the rug. Maybe it contains a birth certificate or letter, anything that'll prove Mama is Susie's daughter.

"Unlock this door right now!" Papa rams himself against the panel.

With trembling hands, I guide notebook paper from the envelope. My heart drops at the sight of Mama's handwriting. The pages are covered in glitter gel pen cursive.

One glance at the opening line, and the oxygen evaporates from my lungs.

Papa kicks open the door, flanked by Nanny and Missouri. They gawk at me, Nanny gazing in horror at the letter in my hands.

"What is this?" I gasp.

Dear Mama and Daddy,

I'm sorry for leaving you, but I gotta do what is best for Susana. The car accident made it clear I'm a danger to her and everybody else. Please take care of my baby.

She isn't to blame for what happened.

Although you won't understand my decision, I ask you to forgive it, same as I forgive you for not believing me. The hallucinations and insomnia are more than I can handle. Either I do this myself, or I wait for the curse to do it for me.

I won't risk hurting Susana.

Maybe ending my time on earth will save her from the hell I've endured. At the least, it'll give me back some degree of freedom.

You won't find me. Sparing you from that is my parting gift.

Tell Ronnie and Missouri Jane that I love them and I'm sorry for not being strong enough. I wish I could've been the one to break the curse.

> Love always,
> Susan

CHAPTER 38

SUSANA PRATHER

NOVEMBER, PRESENT DAY

Nanny dries her eyes with the sleeve of her cardigan.

"I thought it'd be better if nobody found out," she tells me. "Saying the swamp took Susan was easier. I figured the story would encourage you to stay on the straight and narrow."

She reduced Mama to a cautionary tall tale.

"Did you know?" I wave the letter at Missouri.

"Know what?" She accepts the paper from me and skims its contents while Papa weeps quietly in the doorway. Her gaze snaps to mine, then glosses with tears. "No, she didn't. It wasn't like that. The imaginings had gotten so bad. She wasn't in her right mind."

Nanny lowers onto my bed and buries her face in her wrinkled hands.

"Mama, tell Susana what happened," Missouri pleads. "Tell her Susan didn't choose to die. The swamp took her because of the curse."

"I lied to protect you," Nanny sobs. "I'm sorry. I wanted to keep your hope alive. Nobody found her body, so there was a chance, at least in my mind, that she'd left town instead."

My knees give out. I brace myself against the dresser.

"Susan ended her own life," Nanny says in a measured tone. "Blaming the swamp meant I didn't have to acknowledge that my daughter chose to die."

"That whole story about the swamp taking her . . . you intended to scare me. You thought if I believed it, I wouldn't end up like her, right?"

Nanny shakes her head. "I didn't want you to feel responsible."

"*You* didn't want to feel responsible!"

Missouri swears under her breath. "All that crap you said to Susan about getting pregnant. We should've been there for her. She was hurting, and we didn't see it, or we chose to ignore it. No matter what happened, she's gone, and I blame us."

A sharp ache spreads through my chest.

Mama believed so much in the curse, she was convinced, like I am, that it'd result in her death. She chose to die, hoping she'd protect me from herself. I don't agree with her decision, but I empathize, and I think I understand enough to forgive.

The realization strikes me like a ton of bricks.

All this time, I knew the likelihood Mama was alive was close to none. Still, part of me hoped she'd return and say her death was a big misunderstanding.

She won't come back.

I take the letter from Missouri and tuck it into its envelope. Then, I gather the scrapbook, allowing my emotions to process in the weepy silence.

Although the swamp didn't take Mama, the curse is still a threat to me. Every firstborn daughter in my bloodline met a tragic end. I assumed they'd suffered mental illness, but perhaps unshakable belief was what drove them all to madness.

"Tell me. Is Brady Douglas my daddy?"

Nanny and Papa nod. Missouri clutches her mouth, visibly shocked.

"And Mama——" I choke on the words. "Is she your daughter?"

"Susan is our daughter. She just didn't come from us," Nanny says.

A tear drips from my chin and splotches my skirt. I hunch over, shuddering as pain cuts through me. I feel as though my world has been flipped upside down and inside out.

"My sister got pregnant at sixteen years old," Papa says. "At the time, she was finishing high school and working as a waitress. She had a good set of pipes on her, wanted to become a singer. I figured she'd become famous like Dolly Parton.

"When she told Agnes and me, we offered to raise the baby as our own. Susie lived with us in North Carolina until she gave birth. Then, we adopted your mama and moved back to Berryville. We introduced the baby as our biological child. Doing so made sense at the time."

"Susie had a bright future ahead of her. Nobody wanted a scandal," Nanny says.

"You're not my grandparents."

Papa draws me into his arms. "You and me"—he looks me in the eyes and taps his chest—"we got the same kind of bones. Blood gets diluted over time, but not bones. The same material holding you up holds me together too."

"I really like being your granddaughter." I break down and cry.

He kisses my knuckles, itching my skin with his mustache. I assumed I'd be angry at him for lying, but all I feel is crippling disappointment. "You are mine. I am yours."

Nanny and Missouri join us, rubbing circles on my back.

"You belong with me. I am your people."

Kin is the history between us. Kin are our sore backs and the dirt beneath our fingernails. Kin is the land we dwell upon. I did come from Seaborn and Agnes. I carry their spirits with me.

We stay up all night, talking about Susie and Mama. Once dawn pinkens the horizon and Papa falls asleep in the armchair, Nanny and I slip outside. We eat biscuits and fig preserves on the front porch as dew melts and robins peck for worms.

Nanny rocks the rocker. I swing the swing, wrapped in the thickest quilt I can find. My body is weak and cold, so tired I can hardly walk more than a few steps.

"I've been hard on you." Nanny props her bare feet against the porch railing, flexing her toes at an old cobweb. "All these years, I've been so afraid of losing you."

"I understand, Nanny."

"Your papa told me about the curse before we got married. I thought it was hooey." Nanny plants her feet on the floor, stilling the rocker. "After what happened with Susan, I figured the curse wasn't a spell but the consequence of my sins, like Susan had died because I'd been a bad mother. I just . . . didn't deserve to keep her."

I lean forward and grab her hand. "You don't need to carry the guilt any longer."

A tear spills down Nanny's cheek. "I'm sorry for making you feel like you don't have a choice. Everything I said, I spoke out of fear."

She and Papa have spent my entire life protecting me from the past. Their secrets, although painful, were intended as a kindness. They did what they thought was right.

Missouri Jane emerges from the house, dressed in jeans and a denim jacket. She loops a wool scarf around her neck and motions for me to follow her. "Let's take a walk."

I climb from the swing and will my legs into motion. Missouri must notice my weakness because she offers her arm. I brace myself against her, wobbling down the porch steps.

The curse gnaws at me despite the new information. Every bit of my strength goes to keeping myself lucid. I'm dying. I'll die soon. All I want is to leave my family on good terms.

If belief is the root of all this, how do I unbelieve?

Surely, the curse isn't only in my head. The pile of brush—vines I hacked from my windowsill and left for Papa to burn—is proof something bigger than me is at work.

Missouri leads me across the yard, through a pecan grove. "Your great-grandma planted these trees. They used to be so heavy with nuts, their branches would snap off."

"Why'd they stop producing so much?"

"Daddy says when she died, they knew it." Missouri goes to a bench nestled between azaleas. Over a century ago, Seaborn Owens planted the bushes near Skull Lake. His daughter Suzannah uprooted and moved them here.

Every spring, they flourish into cathedrals of magenta blossoms.

I collapse onto the bench. Missouri sits next to me, propping my body against her side. We gaze out at a barren field. Come mid-March, it'll be plowed and planted with cotton.

Missouri rests her cheek against my hairline. "It all makes sense now, why Mama and Daddy stopped talking about Susan. Mama felt guilty, and Daddy . . . well, after losing three women to the curse, he must've wondered if his blood was poisoned or something."

"Maybe it is." I close my eyes, letting the sun blaze red through my lids and into my brain. "The folks at Hard-Shell say we must atone for sins, even old ones."

"Remember what you told me?" Missouri brushes the hair from my forehead. "God doesn't curse people. We do. With how we speak, the choices we make."

"I've messed up," I say, my voice cracking. "What if the curse won't leave me because I acted like Mama and Susie? I'm just like them—"

"You're not." Missouri waits until I reopen my eyes. When I do, she pivots on the bench to face me. "I'm sorry for what people have said to you. There is God, and there's what people say about God. I'm learning the two aren't always the same."

"I can't make sense of what's happening to me," I whisper. "The curse is real. If it's not punishment, why does it exist? Why have so many women suffered?"

I want to tell her about my sleepwalking, but the words evade me.

"Think of it like this. When you're born, you get a handful of cards. Some of those cards your mama and daddy gave you. Some you simply have. Ain't fair, just is. And over the course of your life, people hand you cards, you give cards, and eventually you pass cards to your own youngins. But are games about the cards? No. They're about how you play them."

Her analogy makes my head swim.

"You have no control over what's handed to you, Susana, but you decide how you live."

"Cursed people curse other people."

"But free people *free* other people. No one's free until they let go of the lies they carry," Missouri says with a nod. "I reckon we all have curses, you know, heavy things passed down to us. I think it's something we choose every day."

"Not being cursed?"

"Not living in our curses. To me, a curse is a lie you believe about yourself. It has power over you, and you build yourself on it, function out of it."

"This is bigger than a lie."

"I'm only telling you what I know to be true." Missouri studies me. "The past is dead and gone. It doesn't hold us captive unless we let it. Don't let it."

My throat tightens. "It's not that easy. I was born this way."

"What we don't change, we choose." She continues to stare at me, and I get the sense she understands what I'm feeling. For years, I've blamed my shortcomings on the curse and used superstition and fear to avoid confronting difficult topics. It was easier to say "I can't help but be this way," instead of "I'm choosing this."

Maybe I've given the curse too much power.

"You've helped me realize a lot," Missouri whispers. "I've been choosing the wrong things for years because I didn't think I deserved better. I need to make changes."

We drift into silence, watching a white-tailed deer graze in the field.

"Have you talked to Godwin?" Missouri asks.

Rain drizzles from the clear blue sky, like a summer storm.

Months ago, Godwin told me he loved summer storms and how they came from nowhere, all at once a downpour, all at once over. I summer-stormed into love with him.

"He doesn't want anything to do with me, and I don't blame him. All the stuff I told myself I wouldn't do I did. Maybe this is better, you know? I've made too many errors for us to continue. Besides, I've never understood the right way of loving somebody."

"Nothing you did with that boy doomed your relationship." Missouri sandwiches my hand between hers. "As with lies, you decide the role love plays in your life. How you open yourself up to it, that's your choice. And when you and the person you love make mistakes—which you will—give yourselves grace to grow from them."

I rest my temple against her shoulder.

"Your mistakes are yours, not your mama's."

All this time, I think the fear of becoming someone else has prevented me from becoming myself. I am not the women before me, but I am affected by them. I carry their lives with me. Perhaps to find peace, I must reconcile that I am myself even with their inheritance.

I choose whether to live with their curses.

Suzanna Yawn functioned out of the lies Martha fed her. Maybe to break the curse, I must let go of the lies I believe. The past can't dictate my decisions anymore.

Free people free other people.

I know where to start.

Leaving Missouri, I drive to Godwin's house and knock on the front door. He doesn't answer. I go around back and squint against a burst of sun.

His tractor cruises across the pasture.

"Godwin!" I hobble toward him and wave my arms.

The machine stops. Its hatch swings open, and Godwin appears. He drops from the cab and throws his ball cap onto dirt. He strides toward me, each step faster than the previous.

"Why're you here, Susana?"

"You shouldn't have to carry what I said!" I stumble forward, sinking into dirt. "You're free of it. I take it all back. You're not your daddy. You decide where you go from here."

Godwin halts at a safe distance.

"I don't curse you," I gasp, my eyes burning with tears. "I'm sorry for hurting you and ruining us. You have every reason to hate me."

"Yeah." Godwin licks his molars, his jaw extending to one side. He flushes and studies the horizon as if he can't bear to look at me.

"I'm learning what it means to love someone," I say. "I can't promise I won't make mistakes or that we won't fight. I just know I love you, and I'm willing to put in the work. See, I'm not scared anymore. I know what I want."

Godwin meets my gaze, and his blue eyes soften with tears.

"Please forgive me." I wait for him to respond. When he doesn't, I nod and backtrack across the pasture, crying so hard I can't walk a straight line.

"Susana!" Godwin runs after me. I turn around, and he sweeps me into a hug.

We are not our parents. We are *us*, not *them*.

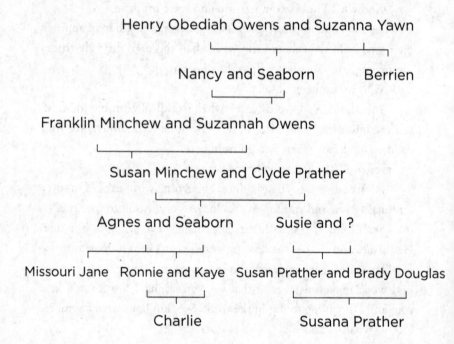

CHAPTER 39

SUSANA PRATHER

NOVEMBER, PRESENT DAY

The swamp freezes over the morning of the Berryville Family Reunion.

I stand at my bedroom window, as I have most nights since the sleepwalking ended, and watch the landscape harden with an icy shell. The trees glimmer, their glass branches frosted with crystallized moss. Ice stretches from the shore, across the water, merging into a blank sheet.

Nature quiets with the phenomenon, maybe frozen too, and sits in wait for dawn.

A chilling sense of dread sweeps through me. This hasn't occurred since 1862, when August Godwin died. I understand what it means. My insomniac body shuffles away from the window, through a curtain of willow limbs. The curse has come to a head. Time is out. I've held on to reality as long as possible. I've chosen not to function out of my curses.

None of it was enough.

Garlands dangle from the ceiling and brush over my shoulders. I elbow a path to the door, my entire bedroom a garden of willows and wildflowers. A swallowtail butterfly lands on my arm. It can't be real, so I let it flex its brown wings as I drift to the kitchen.

My grandparents—I'll always call them my grandparents—waste no time in getting ready for the festival. They rush from the kitchen to the dining room, carrying boxes and coolers.

Over the years, they've become famous for their canned vegetables and fried apple pies. No matter where their booth is located, people manage to sniff them out.

I make a beeline to the coffeepot and pour its contents into a mug.

"You're up early." Nanny eyes my work jeans and sweater, what I wore yesterday. I didn't bother to change into pajamas. What's the point if I don't sleep?

"Gotta prep for the pageant." I still my hands long enough to sip the dark roast.

Nanny and Papa haven't asked about the curse since our big talk. I suppose they are wishful that confessing the truth about Susie and Mama has placated whatever caused my episodes.

I haven't talked about the curse either. For days, I've dealt with imaginings and soldiered on despite my intense exhaustion. I've spent most afternoons with Godwin, passing the seconds on his front porch and telling him I love him in case my world ends today or tomorrow.

My gut says it'll end today.

"Swamp froze over, did you see?" Papa opens the freezer and removes a pound cake. He balances it on his left arm, using his right to reach behind my birthday cake leftovers and retrieve a German chocolate. He carries the baked goods to the table.

I almost respond with, "You see it too?" I guzzle my coffee instead and pray the caffeine will steady my mind. Regardless of what happens, I can't afford to have an episode onstage.

Cleo entered Daisy and me into the reunion's pageant. At the beginning of the school year, I promised Cleo I'd compete, I think to make up for spending time with JC.

I'd forgotten about the event until a few days ago, when Nanny reminded me and drove us into town to rent a gown from a costume shop. Unlike Miss Berryville Teen, the reunion's pageant requires all contestants to wear antebellum fashion to honor town history.

I selected a navy dress. Out of the options, it had the least frills.

Not knowing what else to do, I get ready. I lace myself into a corset and petticoats, slide the rented gown over my head. Before she goes to her evening shift at the Green Frog, Missouri comes to the house to do my hair and makeup. She coaches me on what to say, how to walk.

"Pretty as a picture," Missouri says as she fastens a cameo choker around my neck. She pivots me to a mirror as vines worm up the bathroom walls and flower into magenta heath.

My heart skips.

The girl staring back at me looks identical to Suzanna. Her dark hair braided into a bun, she wears a gown with off-the-shoulder sleeves, tapered at her waist before blooming into a hoop skirt. I glimpse the frozen swamp beyond the window and suppose it's fitting I confront the curse matching the woman who gave it to me.

Balling my hands into fists, I leave the bathroom in what feels like a death march. Lily pads carpet the floor. Pictures move as I walk past their frames. I've done all I can. The curse hasn't released me. I choose not to live in it, but it lives in me.

Soon, I'll have to face it for the last time.

JC waits in the living room, peering out the window at the frosted landscape. He must sense my gaze on him. He glances over his shoulder, and his expression softens. "I came to look at the swamp. Bet it'll make the news."

Fireflies dance across the space in a glowing swarm. They sweep around my legs, illuminating the hem of my dress with buzzy light.

They must be imaginings, same as the vines curling from the ceiling, budding into blooms and chinaberries with waxy golden casings.

It's nearly impossible to discern what's real and what's a hallucination.

"Ain't never seen anything like it." JC smiles at me, and I get the sense he's talking about more than ice. "Ran into Mark Shealy at Floyd's. He said the freeze is a sign of the times."

"Or the lack of it." I keep my voice low and drag my satin skirt toward him. Missouri rushes past us, balancing pies on her forearms. She follows Nanny and Papa onto the porch.

"So, um—" JC locks eyes with me, then glances away. "I haven't seen you in a while."

We haven't talked since the pasture party.

"Stokes told me what happened. Are you okay?"

"The simple answer is no."

"Is that why you haven't been at school much?" JC studies his boots, maybe worried his confession at the party ruined our relationship. "If you're planning to leave the friend group, I'd understand. We've all been hanging on by a thread—"

"No, of course not."

"You have every reason to want out."

I squeeze his hand. "About Stokes. I know he's sorry, and I forgive him. I just don't want to be around him. Thinking about what happened gives me a weird feeling."

JC nods.

"We should talk about what you said."

"Right now?"

"I don't want you waiting around for me. Obediah spent most of his life hoping Suzanna would one day love him back. That's no way to live—"

"They got married."

"Yes, but Suzanna didn't love Obediah, not the way he loved her."

I cup the side of JC's face. "You deserve to end up with someone who's your first choice and who chooses you first. Don't settle for second best just because it's there."

"I guess I always thought you and me would end up together."

"We've been on different paths since day one. I'm glad we got to walk side by side for a while," I tell him. "You're my friend. That won't change."

"I don't like this talk." JC lowers the brim of his ball cap. He wrinkles his nose, and I smile. "Cleo and I need to have a chat, huh?"

"I think so."

JC hugs me goodbye and says he'll see me at the pageant. With peace between us, I feel less afraid of the day. Oak trees border an endless dirt road.

> The lie is the curse, fear is the catalyst.
> Thunder a gavel approving the sentence.
> I am floating, sinking, the house teeming with
> creation,
> Until I stand outside, and reality is real again.

Papa signals for everyone to load themselves into his truck. Nanny and Missouri haul cakes from the kitchen, arguing about how to best transport them without smearing their frosting.

Godwin climbs from his truck. He whistles at the sight of me, grinning from ear to ear.

"We're on our way out," Nanny tells him.

"I won't keep you." He motions to my dress. "Hey, you look—"

"Ridiculous, I know." I ease down the porch steps, careful not to trip on my skirt.

"That wasn't the word I had in mind." Godwin approaches with a soft gleam in his blues. He gives me a side hug, perhaps to avoid Nanny's disapproval.

"Will I see you at the fairground?" I ask.

"I wouldn't miss that pageant for a million dollars." Godwin winks, and for a moment, all I feel is relief. We're brand new, a clean slate. Our relationship isn't fated to repeat history. Even if this is my last day, I hope our decision to try again has somehow redeemed the past.

Papa leans from his truck's window. "All right, son, that's enough sweet talk."

Godwin escorts me to the vehicle. He opens the truck's door and helps me crawl inside, stuffing my skirt into the footwell. "I'm gonna make a sign: Susana is prettier than Cleo."

"Don't you dare." I laugh and nudge his arm. Like an anchor, he's kept me from slipping too far. I might've already succumbed to the curse if not for him.

"Fine. How about: I love you?" He sneaks a kiss. I bask in the warmth, let the world blur into one shade of loving him. Curse aside, if I had a future, I'd choose Godwin and farming and living as myself, not the women before me. I've decided the role I want love to play in my life.

I know how I want to open myself up to it.

Nanny climbs in behind me and shuts the door. She props her elbows on the windowsill, staring at Godwin with eyes narrowed. "Behave yourself."

"Yes, ma'am. Of course, ma'am." He tips his ball cap, then meanders to his car, sneaking glances until Papa keys the ignition and drives to the road.

My happiness from him wears off the closer I get to town.

We reach the fairground and unload the merchandise. Nanny and Papa set up their booth next to the funnel cake truck, and I go to Stage Three to check in for the pageant.

A woman with a clipboard hands me a numbered armband.

I head backstage into a frenzy of hair spray and lipstick. Girls crowd the space, all wearing antebellum dresses. I remind myself this isn't a dream or imagining.

Daisy storms from a back door with her mascara smeared. She wears a pink gown decorated with fabric flowers and her blonde hair curled into ringlets. "Susana—" She touches her corseted waist and bursts into tears. "I think Holler just broke up with me for real this time."

"I'm sorry, Daisy."

She tilts her face to the rafters and dabs her eyes. "I can't ruin my makeup."

"Let me help." I beg a tissue off a pageant mom and wipe Daisy's marks.

Her bottom lip quivers. "I'm a toxic person, Susana. That's why boys don't stick around. My parents are the same way. They've cheated on each other so many times I've lost count."

Clipboard lady appears in the chaos. "Places, girls!"

"That's our cue." Daisy sniffles and forces a smile. "How do I look?"

Every girl wants to be beautiful, but if *beautiful* becomes the most interesting thing about a person, they'll always feel consumable. Daisy sees herself like that, like she's on offer, and if she doesn't give, people won't love her. I think she confuses being desired with being loved.

"You look perfect," I say.

"At least I have that, right? Let's get this over with." Daisy rushes to join the lineup of contestants, and I glance around for Cleo.

She and her mama huddle near a vanity, quarreling at low volume. Mrs. Shealy says Cleo should've worn a bigger dress; she's popping out of the one she bought. The woman leaves in a huff, and Cleo peers into a mirror, fussing with her hair. She examines her waist and sucks it in.

"Cleo."

My friend whirls around. She looks over my gown and opens her mouth, perhaps to criticize its color. She must change her mind. "I'm glad you're here."

"This should be a hoot and a half."

"You'll do great." Cleo approaches, fluffing her yellow skirt. I'm not sure why, but I throw my arms around her neck and pull her close. She tenses before relaxing into a hug.

We played dress-up as little girls. Cleo snuck Daisy and me into her mama's closet and handed us garments to try on. We've grown past those days and each other, but I think history makes our relationship sacred.

A voice booms from speakers, welcoming audiences to the Berryville Family Reunion Pageant. Cleo and I hurry to the contestant lineup as music begins to play. In single file, we parade onto the stage to our duct-tape markers.

The MC reads names from a podium.

I squint at spotlights, hoping my skirt won't reveal my dirty sneakers. I didn't see the point of buying high heels. Missouri offered to lend me a pair, but I figured I'd trip in them.

Crowds watch from lawn chairs and a makeshift grandstand. A Ferris wheel rotates behind them, surrounded by carnival games and food stalls. The air smells only of corn dogs.

Godwin stands near stage right with a handmade sign: That's my girl. He waves it above his head and whistles when the MC reads my name. JC and Stokes flank him.

They all clap and cheer.

What happens next is a thing of nightmares. The day goes dark, the sky replacing its blue with black. Church bells toll in the distance, and the temperature drops.

At first, I assume the shift is an imagining, a delusion of residual bad belief and exhaustion, but the audience grows unsettled, looking from the sky to each other.

I lock eyes with Godwin. He must realize what's happening because he lowers his sign and jumps a barricade. His face tight with fear, he charges toward me.

A numb kind of acceptance settles my nerves. I shiver as frigid air cuts through my clothes and neon lights ignite carnival rides.

My breaths quicken, the realization like a punch to my chest. I should've warned Godwin before the pageant. I should've said my goodbyes just in case.

Stars dot the horizon as if the time is night, not two in the afternoon.

The music sizzles into static, then cuts off. People murmur as the MC declares technical difficulties and promises the pageant will resume shortly.

Wind tears bunting from the stage. It steals a girl's parasol and carries it out of view.

A security guard blocks Godwin and threatens to remove him from the fairground.

"Ladies and . . ." The MC goes silent. His face loses all expression, relaxing into a blank stare. He turns on his heels and deserts the stage.

People swap confused glances. Then, one by one, they fall into a trance.

They rise from their seats and follow the MC to the fairground's exit.

Cleo sinks her fingernails into my bicep. "What's happening?" She gasps when the clipboard lady shuffles past us in a zombie march to the steps.

The woman lumbers as if she's sleepwalking.

Daisy screams. The other girls do too. They gaze in horror as dozens of people stumble across the fairground, multiplying into hundreds.

The curse should've only affected me. Where is it taking them?

Godwin climbs onto the stage. "Is this . . . ?" I nod, and he swears.

His attention veers to the exodus of people drifting toward the parking lot.

Pageant girls stop wailing. Their heads loll to one side. They lurch into motion, departing the stage as a horde of debutantes.

"We need to leave." I pry Cleo's hand from my arm.

"And go where?" Godwin follows me down the stairs, between rows of abandoned chairs. JC and Stokes join us, both pale and wide-eyed.

"I think I know where they're going," I say and motion to the sleepwalkers.

Daisy lowers herself from the stage, crying as she jogs toward us. She trips on her dress and slams against Stokes. "Is this the rapture?"

"Jesus ain't come back just yet," JC says. He embraces Cleo, who has sprinted from the chaos. She clings to him as if he might protect her.

Holler appears in the mayhem. He runs toward us, then stops dead in his tracks. With eyelids drooping, he joins the procession of sleepwalkers.

Daisy screams into her hands. "Holler!"

"They're headed to the swamp," I tell Godwin. "We must get there before them."

"And do what? We should leave town while we still can."

"Not an option."

"Why not?"

Stokes wobbles into a sleepwalk. He forsakes our group, swallowed by the crowd.

"Because we're next!" I yell. "Unless we stop this."

"How do you propose we do that?" Godwin asks.

"I have no idea, but staying here won't do us a lick of good."

My mind racing, I grab Daisy with one hand and Godwin with the other and drag them toward the fairground's exit. JC and Cleo trail close behind, matching our pace.

The festival echoes with circus music and the grind of feet against gravel. People, many of whom I recognize, swarm us. Mark Shealy and Lucinda. Floyd, still holding a cup of boiled peanuts. Principal Chancey with a blue ribbon pinned to his flannel.

JC tugs my skirt. "This is the curse's doing, ain't it?"

"What curse?" Cleo asks.

I ignore the questions and speak to Godwin instead. "Will you drive?"

He nods and digs keys from his jeans.

Daisy freezes the second we enter the parking lot. Her arms fall limply to her sides, and her body resumes motion, now at a drowsy pace. She's gone too.

"No, no we can't leave her!" Cleo screams and reaches for Daisy. She looks at me with a mixture of bewilderment and grief. "Why is this happening?"

Nanny and Papa emerge from the gloom, lost in sleep.

Tears blur the parking lot into shadows.

Godwin loops his arm around my waist and guides me to his truck. He unlocks the passenger side door, forcing me inside. JC and Cleo pile into the vehicle. Godwin slides behind the steering wheel, keys the ignition, and reverses from the parking spot.

We speed to the road, weaving around sleepwalkers. Church bells ring louder. I recognize them as belonging to Hard-Shell Baptist. I shouldn't be able to hear the grim dongs from town.

Headlights illuminate the backs of those teetering along the highway. When I glance in the rearview mirror, I gasp. Uncle Ronnie, Aunt Kaye, and Charlie shamble on the roadside.

"I don't know what to do," I blurt, my body convulsing with sobs. I touch Godwin's shoulder, and he nods as if he hears the thoughts reverberating through my mind.

He'll fall asleep soon. We won't be able to drive much longer.

"You need to continue without us." Godwin laces his fingers with mine. "Take my truck, okay? You can end this, Susana. You can save us." His voice cracks, and doubt shines through.

He doesn't think we'll escape tonight. He doesn't believe I'll break the curse.

Pain slices through me, so violent it sends bile gurgling up my throat. I sag against my thighs and puke onto the carpet.

CHAPTER 40
SUSANA PRATHER

NOVEMBER, PRESENT DAY

Godwin brakes at the Green Frog Restaurant.

He whips into the parking lot and ejects from his truck, signaling for me to take his place behind the steering wheel. JC and Cleo exit the vehicle, both too stunned to speak.

"I don't know what to do," I say over and over. "I don't know what the curse will do to us. I've tried everything. The curse won't break. It'll pass on . . ."

A man steps onto the restaurant's porch with a to-go box tucked under his arm. He wobbles down the steps, chuckling as he moves to his car.

Godwin looks from the man to me.

"Curse hasn't reached this far yet," I say.

With Godwin in the lead, we break into a sprint and burst through the restaurant's front doors. JC slides across the foyer, knocking over a gumball machine.

Patrons are scattered throughout the dining area like normal. Silverware clatters, set to a track of sizzling grease and the tangy croon of bluegrass music.

Missouri approaches us with a pitcher of sweet tea. "What're y'all doing here?"

"You need to leave." I snatch the pitcher from her hand and place it on a table.

"Weather's looking bad. Got dark real fast. Is a storm coming?"

There's no use explaining. Missouri can't run from this. Soon, she'll fall asleep and begin her slow trod to the swamp with the rest of Berryville.

I wrap my arms around her. "I did my best. It wasn't enough."

Her hands drop and swish limply at her sides.

"I'm sorry, Missouri." I cry harder because I know when I pull back, I'll see she's gone.

"You gotta go, Susana." Godwin pries me from Missouri. He supports my weight as she ambles to the exit in an enchanted daze.

Staff marches from the kitchen and out the front door. Customers follow, abandoning their plates. Napkins tumble from laps. A fried chicken leg bounces on the floor.

JC shakes Cleo, but her eyes are vacant. He shouts for her to wake up, but she swivels away from us and joins the procession.

"Look at me." Godwin cups my face. "You need to leave us here, all right?"

"If I leave you, I may never get you back. What if all this is a reset? Maybe we're in a time loop, and we're all doomed to repeat the cycle. Maybe Susie and Mama never died. Maybe I am *them* two curses later."

"Doesn't matter. If the curse repeats itself, I gotta believe other things do too." Godwin releases me with a nod. "You will get me back."

JC sags into sleep and meanders to the door.

"Drive fast. No cops are gonna stop you." Godwin hands me his keys and drags me to the parking lot. He scoops my skirt as I climb into his truck, then stuffs the fabric into my lap.

I crank the ignition and look at Godwin one last time. He gives me a brief kiss, then shuts the door. His silhouette reflects in the rearview mirror until I drive out of view.

Townsfolk prowl the roadside like the undead. They depart Berryville's city limits, heading toward the Okefenokee. About two miles from the Green Frog, the sleepwalking horde veers from the highway, into a patch of trees near an old boat ramp.

Mustering what remains of my resolve, I park Godwin's truck and follow the sleepwalkers. Branches and thorns claw at my dress as I elbow a path through foliage.

The thicket spits me onto a frozen embankment. From its sandy shore extends a boardwalk slick with algae and lichens.

Within seconds, the swamp melts, returning to its normal state. Ice crackles and dissolves. Fireflies blink above lily pads while alligator eyes glint within shadows.

"What do you want from me?" I demand of the wilderness.

People stagger from vegetation, sloshing through black water. They wade from their ankles to knees to chests. Then, one by one, they vanish beneath ripples.

"I tried to break the curse!" I shout at the moss-draped cypresses.

Holler enters the swamp, easing himself below its ebony surface. Water rises from his mouth, over his eyes. He sinks without a sound.

Cicadas scream for him.

I lift my skirt and stride down the boardwalk, the swamp vibrating as though awakened by my presence. "Why put the town to sleep? If I'm the one you want, take me."

A barred owl peers from its hollow.

You are what you say I am. May the curse of my mama's spirit and mine be placed among the people of this here land. Your kin shall walk in your footsteps. Generation after generation. Your voice will decide their days. Your deeds will stain their hands. Until you see the truth of what you are. They will be what you say I am. Until they scrape and crawl from your silence and lies and say otherwise. With my blood I make what only my bones can break.

Moonlight spills between clouds and brightens the wetland.

"You don't want me," I say with a huff. "Suzanna cursed the whole town."

All this time, the dots were there, eager for me to connect them. The townsfolk called Suzanna cursed, so cursed they became. Everyone in Kettle Creek and Berryville were doomed to repeat history, and they have for almost two hundred years.

I lower to the boardwalk. Unless I break the curse, the clock will restart, and this will happen all over again.

Suzanna's face gazes up from the black water. She is every woman before me. She has walked in my shoes. My life has been a mirror of hers. Until now.

"Tell me what to do!" I scream.

Godwin stumbles onto the shoreline. His face is blank with sleep. He steps from sand to peat to water, submerging himself with everyone else.

"He's not his dad," I yell.

Stokes wades into the swamp. Cleo and Daisy appear moments later, hauling their antebellum gowns into the depths.

"They're not their parents. They don't have to repeat history."

Nanny and Papa sleepwalk from shadows. Missouri trails at their heels, flanked by Ronnie, Kaye, and Charlie.

People continue to emerge from the woods and splash into the Okefenokee. Their scalps carve through knapweed before sinking.

"The past doesn't control me. I decide my future. I am not what you say. I am not cursed. I *break* curses, and I'm breaking theirs. Let them go!"

Keziah Douglas appears in a gust of fog.

I stagger back a step. "You."

CHAPTER 41

SUSANA PRATHER

NOVEMBER, PRESENT DAY

Keziah fingers the hummingbird brooch pinned to her lapel.

She rushes down the boardwalk with fire in her eyes. "Are you doing this?"

"No, I'm not a witch." I flinch when JC barges from the shoreline. He squelches into the swamp with ungraceful steps, his red ball cap vanishing into mire.

Keziah rolls her oxygen tank. Its wheels get stuck between wooden slats. With a groan, she yanks it into motion, nearly stumbling into quag.

"Why aren't you asleep?"

She wags her arthritic finger at the walkers. "Make it stop!"

A branch snaps off a tree. I duck, shielding my head as the swamp rumbles and ripples. Alligators circle the boardwalk. Their scales knife through water like obsidian blades.

Keziah watches the horde submerge one by one, head after head. Her leathery face tautens with panic. "They'll die! Please set them free!"

"I don't know how."

The fog clears like smoke blown away with the wind. Down the boardwalk, where swamp lifts into wire grass, appears the flat prairie from my dreams. A rotten stump, maybe three feet in height, stands where Hangman's Oak used to be.

"That's impossible." I force the cool, damp air into my lungs and blink as if the scene might correct itself. The location doesn't make sense. We're nowhere close to the prairie.

Even from a distance, I notice the roots stretching from the stump, all black with decay and half-buried in peat. Martha tried to cut down the curse, but the Okefenokee remembered.

"You can put a stop to this," Keziah shouts, tugging at her tubes. "If you wish to punish me, do your worst, but please spare everyone else."

"I don't want to punish you," I yell. Nature thunders in response. Wind rips through the swamp, peeling Keziah's graying hair from its clip.

She hugs her belly and weeps. Tears paint lines down her wrinkled cheeks and drip onto the boardwalk. "I deserve the curse. You're my granddaughter, and I abandoned you."

My heart feels as though it might crack open my chest.

"You look so much like Susan," Keziah sobs. "I should've believed her. I couldn't accept what Brady did. Blaming the hex was easier than acknowledging my family's mistakes."

For eighteen years, Keziah has believed the past condemned her. She's held on to the lie and given it power, like Martha Douglas.

"I'm cursed. Everybody knows it." Keziah claws at her neckline as breaths rasp in her throat. "I'm sorry for how I've treated you. Please forgive me."

I close the gap between Keziah and me and touch her rawboned frame. "Whatever people have said, you don't have to carry it anymore. I don't curse you."

The woman crumples to the platform and sobs louder.

"I don't curse you, Keziah. You're free."

My body shudders with compounded grief. I scan the shoreline, the last townspeople dipping into water, and let myself feel every emotion—fatigue and frustration, visceral anger.

I've spent my whole life in agreement with the curse and everything said about me. Not anymore. I might've lived cursed, but I won't die cursed.

"We're all trying to break something. I understand that now. Sometimes we succeed, but we must know what needs to be broken, and every day we must choose to rebel against the parts of us that still like being cursed. The sleepwalking ends with me. It all ends with me."

Keziah stops crying.

I kneel beside her and grip her arm so tight her skin turns blue. "I am not my curses, and neither are you. We don't have to agree with them any longer."

Sunshine trickles from treetops, ribboning between tufts of Spanish moss.

"We decide the life we want, Keziah. We get the choice. From now on, we don't have to repeat the past. We can fix this," I say as light blazes through the gloom.

Buried things are dangerous things.
Secrets and silence give the curse power.

Maybe if the women in my bloodline had talked about the sleepwalking and what they experienced, the curse would've broken a long time ago. They all believed they were cursed and doomed, thus fulfilling the prophecy.

The earth shakes, launching egrets from their perch.

Keziah pulls me closer. She removes her oxygen tube as if she knows we're dying and wants to taste the sour air one last time. "You're free too."

Water blasts upward, splintering the boardwalk. I stand and make a run for the shore, but the Okefenokee devours me in a single gulp. I reach my hands at the sky and hold my breath as the wetland swallows everything in reach.

I'm not cursed. The swamp can't take me or anyone else.

My dress ballooning, I float upward, away from the boardwalk. Gators soar like airplanes in a lily pad sky. They flick their tails and swarm around me.

I'm not cursed.

Free people free other people.

The sleepwalkers levitate in the gloom, suspended among fish and reptiles. I reach for Godwin. His hand brushes mine, then slips away.

CHAPTER 42

SUSANA PRATHER

JANUARY, PRESENT DAY

There's a peach stand on Jacksonville Highway with PECHES written across its side in sloppy paint. I used to consider the roadside stall an eyesore. I took offense because it set a poor example for my hometown. Now I find the ramshackle shack and its homemade sign an aesthetic.

I think if you look for it, you'll find beauty in uncomfortable things, the inconveniences, the uglies. You won't cover your mouth when the air fills with dust. You'll savor the earth, taste the smut. You'll stop looking for perfect and instead relish simply existing.

Being here. That's a beautiful, often uncomfortable, sometimes ugly thing.

Maybe the world is full of PECH stands, and we drive by without stopping.

I veer my Cadillac onto Swamp Road and head into Kettle

Creek. JC passes me in his truck, honking hello. He must've swung by the house to go fishing with Papa. Now that he and Cleo aren't together, he spends all his free time with a rod and reel.

"Fish might snap a line, but they'll never break your heart," he tells anyone who'll listen.

The breakup wasn't as grisly as Stokes predicted. JC claims it was mutual, and by how Cleo has behaved, I'm inclined to believe him. She's decided to leave town after graduation. To do what, I don't think anyone, not even Cleo, knows for sure. She applied to a small university in Tennessee, said she wanted to find herself apart from Berryville.

In a couple of months, JC will head out of state for an ivy league. I made him pinky promise not to change too much, and he swore nothing could take the country out of him. He'll bring his rod and ratty ball cap and scare the intellectuals with *ain't* and *cain't* and *bless your heart*.

Stokes will miss JC more than anyone, I bet. He moved in with JC's family to get space from Willy and seems to be doing better. He and I made amends over Christmas break and have planned a summer road trip with JC and Godwin.

Our group looks different nowadays. Cleo got custody of Daisy in the breakup, and Holler made new friends, so I don't see them often. Last I heard, Daisy is hoping to apply to a cosmetology school in Atlanta and has sworn off boys for the time being.

I pull into my grandparents' driveway and park beside the carport. Barney Fife lounges beneath the fig tree, wearing the paracord collar Godwin made for him.

Papa waves at me from the riding lawn mower. He doesn't recall the Berryville Family Reunion. I've asked him and Nanny about it. They remember loading baked goods into the truck and driving into town. From what I can tell, the dip in the swamp wiped everyone's memories.

After the curse broke, I woke up in my bed, drenched with water.

I suspect people across the county experienced the same. I spotted a ton of laundry on clotheslines.

Keziah seems to be the only person who remembers. I ran into her at the Green Frog not long ago. She waved me over to her booth, and we spent hours talking and eating banana pudding. Something about her is different, more at peace. Eventually I'll want to revisit the topic of Brady and Mama, but for now, I'm okay with letting the past rest.

Nanny steps onto the front porch with the landline wedged between her ear and shoulder. "Missouri Jane got to Charleston and is fixin' to see her new apartment!"

She accepted an internship with a coastal newspaper.

"Yes, well, I told you it'd be small. What'd you expect at that price?" Nanny says into the phone. "Pour baking soda on it. That'll get the stain right out."

I smile and fetch my work gloves from the shed.

At first, when the curse broke, I wasn't sure anything had changed. My insomnia and imaginings stopped, but the rest of my life appeared the same. I just felt lighter, more myself, like a weight had been lifted.

"Give me a hand, would you?" Nanny asks when I return. She and I labor in flower beds while Papa mows. She shovels earth into a wheelbarrow and exchanges it between plots.

"Why do you move around the dirt?"

"Helps the plants grow better." Nanny mixes ground with a gardening fork. "You don't have to change all the dirt, but a little change— the addition of something new—does wonders. Even plants can't reach their full potential in familiar ground. Same goes for people, I suppose. We all need to change our dirt from time to time. Speaking of, we've never had that talk."

"About changing dirt?"

"About you not staying in Kettle Creek your whole life."

"I grow well here. This ground suits me."

"You don't have to change all your dirt. Just find something new to add to the pot." Nanny packs soil around a pansy. "I don't want to hold you so tight you miss out on living."

"Why can't *this* be my living?"

Nanny motions to Papa. "Berryville wasn't always my home. Seaborn was traveling with the railroad when I met him. I was eighteen, living in North Carolina. We married four months after our first date. I tell you that because . . . you'll always have a home here. This land belongs to you, and you belong to it. It's in your blood. But until you change your dirt, you won't know where you best grow. I give my blessing, Susana. I won't hold too tight."

Papa cuts off the lawn mower. "What're y'all gabbing about?"

"Nunya business."

Papa calls us his pretty ladies and chuckles when Nanny rolls her eyes. His voice is a bass and banjo. His laugh is a fiddle. Everything about him is music, and I love the melody he makes.

My body aches at the thought of leaving. If I think too much about it, I'll break down, so I clear my throat and nod at Papa. "How'd you know he was the one?"

Nanny watches my grandfather, beaming a love I can only hope to feel someday. "I know his spirit, and he knows mine. I'd be lost without that man."

For as long as I can remember, she's reached for his hand at mealtimes before he bows his head to say grace. She's complained about his mustache but still leaned in for kisses. I've watched them live in tandem, both themselves and yet so equally one.

I know the life I want when I look at them.

The curse doesn't hold me captive. I am not condemned by the past. This is a fresh start, my own slate. I decide where I go from here, and I know where to begin.

Leaving my grandparents in the yard, I run up the road, past oak trees and winter fields. My sneakers pound the orange dirt, stirring dust.

Godwin slows his truck alongside me. He rolls down the window and props his elbow on the sill. "Howdy. You need a ride?"

Over a century ago, a boy met a girl on this same dirt road. He looked at her the way Godwin looks at me and offered a ride. Our story isn't their story. This feels like a do-over, a chance to redeem the past and reach a different, if not happier, ending.

Tears warming my eyes, I climb into Godwin's truck. The landscape reels into golden hour, and wind tosses my hair into a frenzy. I stretch my arm out the window and into the breeze.

The swamp did not take me, nor will it take anyone else again.

AUTHOR'S CLOSING NOTE

F*ree people free other people.*

If nobody has told you before, I want to say it now. You decide the life you want. The past doesn't define you, nor does your bloodline. You don't have to carry around your curses.

The lies spoken over you, the lies you've accepted as truth.

You can lay them down and live beyond them.

As I conducted research for this book, I was shocked to learn the key to breaking generational cycles, according to many mental health professionals, is simple. Talk about the past.

When people tell their stories, and when descendants understand their family's experiences, new lines of communication open, and healing begins.

According to therapists, ways to break generational cycles include:

- Having conversations with our parents about their backgrounds and how they coped
- Noticing embedded patterns, attitudes, or narratives from our families that we continue to portray

- Talking about those areas with a trusted friend, family member, or therapist
- Considering healthier ways of coping and communicating
- Cultivating empathy and compassion for our families and their struggles
- Creating a new narrative that we want our children to embody and believe about their family, themselves, and the world

We don't have control over what's handed to us in life, but we determine our response. We choose whether to function out of our curses or to live freely. I don't believe the choice is a one-time decision. I think it's something we must decide every day and actively pursue.

This book portrays various forms of generational trauma such as abuse (physical, emotional, and sexual), sexual impropriety, financial/social scandals, abandonment, unexpressed grief, wartime shell shock, and neglect. I'm listing these because until I started my research, I didn't fully realize how my own family trauma had affected me.

Like the curse in Susana's story, trauma often goes unnoticed. It can influence our way of thinking, become an unconscious driver in our lives. Sometimes the trauma we carry doesn't come from us. According to studies done on mice, specifically one completed in 2013, emotional trauma can transmit across generations, influencing behavior, fears, and so on.

Known as *epigenetics*, the events in someone's life can alter how their DNA is expressed, and that change can pass down bloodlines.

Elizabeth Dixon, a clinical social worker, wrote a fantastic article about generational cycles.[1] In it, she talks about how we inherit emotional trauma from our mothers and grandmothers. She says, "When your mother was in your grandmother's womb, she carried, at that

---

1. Elizabeth Dixon, "Breaking the Chains of Generational Trauma," Psychology Today, July 3, 2021, https://www.psychologytoday.com/us/blog/the-flourishing-family/202107/breaking-the-chains-generational-trauma.

time, the egg that eventually became *you*. This means that a part of you, your mother, and your grandmother all shared the same biological environment. In a sense, you were exposed to the emotions and experiences of your grandmother even before you were conceived."

Writing this book shook me. I faced countless moments in which I had to dissect my history and examine my own thinking. Doing so led me on a journey to grace and forgiveness—grace for the messy parts of me, forgiveness of the past, and compassion for my family tree.

I encourage you to do your own research.

Dig up your curses and other buried things, look at them, and make peace.

At this point, I bet you're curious to know which parts of the book were inspired by real people and events.

Susana Godwin was my great-great-great-great-grandmother. Her gravestone says she died in 1897 at 104 years old. However, there are discrepancies between other records. She was Creek and settled in the Okefenokee Swamp of South Georgia, where she ran a commissary. She married Richard Godwin and had ten children, two of which were Seaborn and Berrien.

People referred to Susana as a witch due to events documented in Robert Latimer Hurst's *This Magic Wilderness*. She refused to ride in wagons, instead walking behind them. She was close friends and neighbors with legendary swamper Obediah Barber.

Known as the Southeast's Paul Bunyan, Obediah was the first white man to settle on the southeastern rim of the Okefenokee. He became a source of legend, folklore, and music and was fondly nicknamed "King of the Okefenokee."

There are countless tall tales about Obediah, one of which focuses on him clubbing a bear to death with a tree stump. My favorite story involves him, Susana, and a bat the size of a crow.

Documented in *This Magic Wilderness*, the night Susana's son

Seaborn Godwin died, the water in the creek froze over, preventing horses from crossing. Obediah visited Susana to pay his respects. At the time, she was living alone on an island.

When Obediah arrived, a bat as big as a crow flew around the room and landed on Seaborn's body. Obediah grabbed a straw broom and swatted at the creature. Susana stopped him, saying, "Don't bother 'im. That ain't no bat—hit's the ol' devil."

I incorporated other tall tales into the novel, such as the story involving the buck and Suzanna's ghostly goodbye.

My ancestor Susana Godwin visited Obediah Barber regularly. Folktales claim she told him, "Obediah, when I die, I'm a-comin' back 'n' meet ya." The sequence of events mentioned in my book align with the narrative preserved in Southern lore.

The folktales surrounding Hangman's Oak near Trader's Hill also played a central role in creating this story. According to the tales, an elderly Native American named Suanee was carried to the oak for execution. He cursed the town, saying, "May the curse of my father's spirit and mine be placed among the people as long as there is a Trader's Hill."

After the hanging, a bright light burst from the oak, followed by a low moan. Lore claims on certain nights, the light can still be seen, and one can hear the moan on the wind. I think it's true—a person isn't truly Southern unless they've had a ghoulish experience.

Most of this book was founded on actual history, superstition, and Southern culture. I incorporated my own experiences of rural living along with those of my family.

As a child, I frequented cemeteries and made rubbings of headstones. My dad has always been enthralled by genealogy, hence all the available material for this story.

What Godwin said about watching a bulldozer lift his grandma from her grave . . .

Yep, true story.

My ancestors farmed near Waycross and Blackshear, Georgia. To this day, my family owns land there. My great-grandparents Agnes and Claude Godwin, who partly inspired Nanny and Papa, raised hogs. Agnes worked at the local Green Frog Restaurant.

I take a lot of pride in my heritage. I come from people with grit who worked the land.

With so much of this book founded on truth, I could spend pages examining it piece by piece. Instead, I want to end this author note by talking about what sparked the initial concept.

My grandma was raised near the Okefenokee. Her whole life, people in town said she was adopted. Her parents denied the claims, but she grew up with the voices nagging at her. It wasn't until her mother lay dying that my grandma learned the truth. She was adopted.

Her birth mother was her father's sister Leona.

Leona had become pregnant when she was a teenager. Afraid of scandal, her family sent her to Savannah to have the baby in secret. Her brother and sister-in-law adopted the child—my grandma—and claimed she was their own.

By the time my grandma learned the truth, it was too late for reconciliation.

Leona had dementia.

My grandma tried to learn about her biological father, but her family refused to talk about the past, and eventually the secret died with them. My grandma has spent her life carrying the weight of an unspoken history, and I've seen how that has affected her.

I wrote this book as someone who's witnessed, in more ways than one, how silence and secrecy impact a family. I wrote this book as a declaration: I will not continue the cycle. I am not defined by my generational curses and trauma, not the pain, addiction, neglect, abandonment, and so on. I forgive the past, but I will not live there.

I choose freedom and so can you.

ACKNOWLEDGMENTS

This story would've never reached the page if not for support from my brilliant editor, Kimberly Carlton, and the TNZ Fiction team. Thanks to them, I began the journey to dissecting my family history, in many ways finding myself and healing in the process.

I also want to thank my line editor, Erin Healy; my literary agent, Tessa Hall; and everyone else who's played a role in bringing this book to readers.

Unlike other projects, writing *Curses and Other Buried Things* required double the allotted time and took me on an emotional roller coaster. I must recognize the people who counseled and encouraged me during the process.

Mom, for listening to my story ideas and receiving my revelations with a soft heart. I love that this book grew our relationship and debunked lies we both carried. Thanks for believing in me, for being a shoulder to cry on, and for letting me write this novel at your dining room table.

My family, for supporting me as I pursued my author dreams. I don't know what the future holds, but I'm grateful for every second I spent writing and suffering forward. I am a better person because of the past five years. Wherever I go from here, know nothing is wasted.

Stephanie Kehr, for walking alongside me through some of the lowest and hardest seasons of my life. Your friendship, wisdom, and faith have changed me for the better.

Candace Dorsey, for calling out my curses and speaking truth over me. Thank you for reminding me who I am. You're one of the reasons I walk freer.

Collin Church, for reading my late-night poetry and beating my imposter syndrome with a metaphorical stick. Finish writing that book! The world is waiting.

Hiking on Purpose, for being my uncommon community. Words cannot express how grateful I am to have so many amazing women in my corner.

Elizabeth and Lucy Maxon, for meeting needs I didn't realize I had. You've been extravagant with your love and helped me navigate the emotions tied to this book.

The Jackson Family, for proving kinship extends beyond family ties.

My Instagram community, for reminding me words change lives. I want to specifically thank the girls of Literature Approved. Meeting you made a tremendous impact on me.

My prayer warriors. Every victory in my life belongs to you also.

Mrs. Capers, for being one of the first voices to tell me to write. I will forever acknowledge the role you've played in my life. I carry your legacy with me.

Jesus, for wanting me when I lived in my curses and loving me into freedom.

Writing has been a faith journey more than anything else. Through it, I've learned the miracle isn't the end goal. It's every day, every hardship, every breakthrough, the intimacy gained from walking forward, trusting God is good and He has a plan.

As I write this, I realize the miracle I've prayed for has come into fruition.

Lastly, I want to thank *you* for reading this book. May you leave these pages freer than you came. The past is written. Your story is still being told.

You decide where you go from here.

DISCUSSION QUESTIONS

1. Susana wasn't the only character struggling to break a curse. What curses were at work in the other characters' lives?

2. Near the end of the book, Susana learned the lie was the curse, fear was the catalyst. What role did fear and lies play in Suzanna's and Susana's lives?

3. Do you think Susana could've broken the curse sooner? How?

4. Keziah Douglas told Susana, "You're free too." Could she have broken Susana's curse? What does "free people free other people" mean to you?

5. Were Nanny and Papa responsible for the curse? Why or why not?

6. Think about your own life. What lies do you believe about yourself and/or others? Could those lies be viewed as curses?

7. What role did family play in Susana's story? How has your family influenced you?
8. The book highlights that curses are also negative things we say to others. What are examples of curses we might give?
9. Considering how Susana found freedom, how can we break curses in our everyday lives?

ABOUT THE AUTHOR

Caroline George is the multi-award-winning author of *Dearest Josephine*, *The Summer We Forgot*, and other YA novels. She graduated from Belmont University with a degree in publishing and public relations and now dedicates her time to storytelling in its many forms.

From a small town in Georgia, Caroline now resides in an even smaller town in Wyoming, where she works for a ranch. When she's not glued to her laptop or filming cowboys, she can be found hiking, sipping a lavender latte, or practicing her horsemanship.

Instagram: @authorcarolinegeorge
Twitter: @CarolineGeorge_
TikTok: @authorcarolinegeorge

.